MONSTERS IN THE MIST

BOOK TWO OF THE TALES OF THE TERRITORIES

PETER WACHT

KESTREL MEDIA GROUP LLC

Monsters in the Mist
By Peter Wacht

Book 2 of The Tales of the Territories

This book is a work of fiction. Names, characters, places, and incidents are the product of the author's imagination or are used fictitiously. Any resemblance to actual events, locales, or persons, living or dead, is coincidental.

Copyright 2023 © by Peter Wacht

Cover design by Ebooklaunch.com

All rights reserved. In accordance with the U.S. Copyright Act of 1976, the scanning, uploading, and electronic sharing of any part of this book without the permission of the publisher constitute unlawful piracy and theft of the author's intellectual property.

Published in the United States by Kestrel Media Group LLC.

ISBN: 978-1-950236-34-3

eBook ISBN: 978-1-950236-35-0

Library of Congress Control Number: 2023903641

❦ Created with Vellum

ALSO BY PETER WACHT
THE REALMS OF THE TALENT AND THE CURSE

THE TALES OF CALEDONIA
Blood on the White Sand (short story)*

The Diamond Thief (short story)*

The Protector

The Protector's Quest

The Protector's Vengeance

The Protector's Sacrifice

The Protector's Reckoning

The Protector's Resolve

The Protector's Victory

THE TALES OF THE TERRITORIES
Stalking the Blood Ruby (short story)*

A Fate Worse Than Death (short story)*

Death on the Burnt Ocean

Monsters in the Mist

The Dance of the Daggers (Forthcoming 2023)

Bloody Hunt for Freedom (Forthcoming 2024)

THE SYLVAN CHRONICLES
(Complete 9-Book Series available at Amazon)

The Legend of the Kestrel

The Call of the Sylvana

The Raptor of the Highlands

The Makings of a Warrior

The Lord of the Highlands

The Lost Kestrel Found

The Claiming of the Highlands

The Fight Against the Dark

The Defender of the Light

THE RISE OF THE SYLVAN WARRIORS

Through the Knife's Edge (short story)*

* Free short stories can be downloaded from my author website at PeterWachtBooks.com.

YOUR FREE SHORT STORY IS WAITING

THE DIAMOND THIEF

This short story is a prelude to the events in my series *The Tales of Caledonia* and is free to readers who receive my newsletter.

Join Peter's newsletter and get your FREE short story.
PeterWachtBooks.com

SETTING THE STAGE

The Tales of the Territories continue the adventures of Bryen Keldragan and Aislinn Winborne as they travel across the Burnt Ocean to the Territories, what will eventually become the Kingdoms of *The Sylvan Chronicles*.

The events occur more than one thousand years before the happenings in *The Sylvan Chronicles* and take place in the lands far to the west of Caledonia that have been opened for colonization thanks to territorial grants sold by the deceased King Corinthus Beleron. There they take on new challenges, make new friends and enemies, and continue to battle those who have turned to the Curse.

In the Territories, sometimes called New Caledonia, as in the other realms, the ability to use the Talent sets apart the person gifted with this unique skill. But being able to use the Talent is only part of the dynamic. For if a Magus chooses to follow a darker path, the Talent becomes the Curse.

Both *The Sylvan Chronicles* and *The Tales of Caledonia* are a part of the larger world known as *The Realms of the Talent and the Curse.*

1

A FORTUITOUS MEETING

The small fire crackled softly, the ragged flames doing just enough to warm him on a chilly night. He had selected this spot with care, having used several similar locations much like this one during his travels through the Highlands. A small notch in the mountain gave him a vista of the peaks to the east. It guaranteed him a beautiful view when the sun rose in the morning.

Just as important, the boulders and trees at his back helped to shield his fire from any prying eyes.

Although apparently not as well as he would have liked this evening.

He remained sitting -- calm, confident -- despite the movement he detected in the darkness just beyond the flames.

They were trying to be quiet. They probably believed that they were doing a good job of sneaking up on him.

Unfortunately for them, they weren't as skilled at skulking through the night as they thought they were.

Rusty most likely. Probably a bit complacent as well.

He could use that against them when the opportunity presented itself.

He didn't know who they were, but he could guess.

He had to give them credit though. They were taking their time and demonstrating a surprising caution for just a single target.

Probably because they didn't know what to make of him. Hence their unease.

Good. He could use that as well when the time came.

The hardest part now was the waiting, and that's what began to gnaw at him. He took a few deep breaths to keep himself still and focused.

He wasn't going anywhere, so there was no point in feeling anxious. To calm his nerves, he worked out in his mind how he believed the next few minutes were going to play out.

He was prepared for what he anticipated would happen. He had placed his sword against the cracked stump so that the hilt rested right next to his hand.

And a small part of him was actually looking forward to the encounter.

It had been an uneventful journey through the Highlands since he had exited the portal right in front of the Crag, having no cause to even think of using his steel.

Until now, of course.

He had made it with little trouble into the northwest of the Territory. Probably no more than ten leagues away from the Northern Steppes now. Once he reached the grassland, it would be just a few more days across that broad expanse before he came upon the Northern Peaks. From there, just a few days more to Shadow's Reach.

He hoped that Aislinn, Bryen, Declan, and the rest of the Blood Company were doing well aboard the *Freedom*. That it wouldn't take them too long to complete the passage across the Burnt Ocean and join him. Having been in the Highlands for only a short time, there was already a great deal that he needed to relay to them.

Although he missed his friends, he had been enjoying his travels through the snow-capped spires. He stopped in every village he came across, almost every single one of them centered around a broch that had been built within the past year or was well on its way to being completed.

After talking with so many of the Highlanders struggling to make their way in this rugged land, he could understand the need for such fortifications. Why the towers were so essential to their survival.

He hadn't yet come up against the many perils threatening the people living among these peaks. Although he had a feeling that was about to change.

Only a few more minutes passed before a stout fellow with a large axe in his hand and the hilt of a sword peeking above his shoulder ambled out of the darkness, seemingly without a care in the world. The visitor stopped on the other side of the fire, giving him a cocky grin.

"Hello there, friend," the newcomer said in a way that suggested that he was fighting to restrain a cackle.

"That remains to be seen," came the reply, the old man's grey eyes flashing in the dim glow of the flames.

"Remains to be seen?" asked the visitor, clearly confused. "What do you mean by that?"

Studying the visitor with a keen eye, he took a moment before responding. Clearly, the axe-wielding fellow had put a great deal of work into finding him. The location he had selected for his campsite was well off the beaten trail and well hidden unless someone had come this way before. Or unless you knew exactly what you were looking for.

His visitor was a soldier.

Or rather the visitor had been a soldier.

Or probably the visitor still was.

Depending on the need.

He was certain of it. He could tell by the man's bearing even though the fellow was trying to hide it.

Regardless, at that moment the man was more than just a soldier. The whip coiled on his belt gave him away.

"I mean I don't know yet if you're my friend. That still needs to be determined. Of course, I won't be holding my breath for the answer."

He watched the man on the other side of the fire nod. The soldier gave him a half smile and then a wink, as if they both already knew how the game they were engaged in was going to end, yet both still felt the need to play it.

The soldier lifted his weapon and rested the haft of his axe against his shoulder, his smile shifting into a smirk.

He knew what his visitor was thinking. The sometime soldier wasn't quite sure what to make of him. Few people traveled in the Highlands by themselves anymore.

That suggested to the soldier that he wasn't aware of the dangers haunting these peaks or he simply didn't care.

The first possibility didn't bother the soldier. Many people having just arrived in the Highlands learned of the perils hidden within these mountains too late to help themselves.

The second possibility obviously did. And with good reason.

He should have been frightened by the soldier's appearance. Or at least nervous.

He wasn't.

He was irritated.

That made the soldier uncomfortable. That and the fact that his annoyance at the soldier for interrupting the quiet of the evening radiated from him, almost as if it were a physical thing.

"You know, it's not safe to be out here on your own."

"That's what I've been told," he replied in a disinterested tone.

The soldier with the axe waited for him to say more. When he didn't reply, the soldier scrunched up his face, not realizing that with his drawn features and his unkempt whiskers he made himself look like a ferret when doing so.

The old man enjoyed his visitor's growing discomfort. That clearly annoyed the soldier.

Good. Something else that he could use against him when the time was right.

He also could tell that the soldier was losing patience. The soldier had come up here for a reason and time was a wasting. The fellow wanted to get this done so that he could enjoy the fire for the night and then move on. So best for the soldier to just push ahead despite his feeling that there was something not quite right about him.

"Looks like you could use some company," said the soldier as he gripped the hilt of his axe tightly, finding some comfort in the steel as he took a step closer to the flames. "You look a bit lonely."

"I prefer to be on my own," he replied quietly.

The soldier stopped for just a second, then shrugged, ignoring the comment that had been infused with the hint of an order. In an attempt to demonstrate that he was in charge, the soldier sat down on a rock across the fire from him.

"What are you doing out here in the Highlands all on your own, friend?"

"Just passing through ... friend." He said the last as if it left a bitter taste in his mouth.

The soldier ignored him, intent on his task and looking forward to the fun he believed that he was going to have when this was over. "Shadow's Reach, I take it?"

"Thinking about it."

"What would you do in Shadow's Reach?"

"I have a few things in mind."

"Shadow's Reach is still a long way off," said the ferret-faced fellow, dropping the blade of his axe to the ground, then leaning forward, elbows pressed to his knees as his fingers reached for the warmth of the fire.

"I've been enjoying the hike. I'm not in a rush."

"Have you now?"

"I have."

"You're not the easiest person to talk with, friend."

"I'm not your friend, friend." He stared hard at the much too confident soldier sitting across from him. His eyes cold. He was less than impressed by what he saw. Less a soldier now and more a thug.

He was getting tired of this conversation. He was getting tired of his unwanted guest. He hoped that his visitor would move things along at a faster pace.

"No reason to get angry, friend." The soldier emphasized the last word, wanting to make sure the old man understood that he was losing patience as well. "I'm just trying to have a conversation with you. I'm trying to help you actually. I wouldn't want you to lose your way in these mountains."

"You're trying to buy time so that the men with you get to their assigned positions in the wood behind you."

"You don't say," the soldier replied, grinning.

Clearly, the soldier didn't care about his revelation. Actually, the soldier seemed pleased that the cat was out of the bag.

"I do. The problem, though, is that you wanted your men to surround the campsite. They've realized that they can't because we're on a ledge. If I were you I'd be a little concerned because it took them a bit longer than it should have to figure that out and then reorganize themselves. Definitely not a good sign. Doesn't say much for their grasp of tactics or their decision making. Although it seems that they've finally worked things out and now believe that I won't be able to make a break for it."

"You're quite sure of yourself." With the light of the fire, the soldier took a closer look at the old man. He was glad that finally he could drop the pretense. After a time it became exhausting. "You look familiar, friend."

"I've been told that before."

"Very familiar, friend." For some strange reason, the soldier believed that he knew this old man, or at least he had seen him before, but for the life of him he couldn't recall when or where.

"I have a fairly common face."

The soldier grunted. "Where have you served?"

He smiled thinly then. Finally, they were getting to the meat of it. The fellow across from him must have concluded that his men had been given plenty of time to find their places.

Even so, the visitor with the axe waited a little longer. Probably still worried that he was going to try to escape.

His visitor had nothing to fear. He wasn't going anywhere. He was invested now. Besides, he already knew how this was going to end.

"Caledonia."

"That's not a very helpful response, friend," the soldier said through gritted teeth, struggling to reign in his rising anger. Talking with this old man was like talking to the child of the woman he had taken up with. Getting a useful response for the simplest of questions was like pulling teeth. The doomed old man's arrogance was both impressive and aggravating.

"I'm not here to help you ... friend. Now are we going to get to the reason you're really here? I've had a long day and I'd like to get some sleep."

The soldier snorted in laughter. Arrogant indeed. It wouldn't take him long to whip that trait out of the old man. And he'd enjoy doing it. "You know how to use that, friend?" He pointed to the sword leaning against the cracked stump.

"I wouldn't have it with me otherwise."

"It looks like it's a nice blade. Well made."

"It is. It's served me well over the years."

"You're not going to need it where you're going, friend.

You'll be trading it in for a pickaxe or shovel. So I think I'll take it for my own."

"You can try," he replied. His smile became more menacing as he sensed that the next stage of the combat was about to begin. Finally they were getting to the heart of the engagement rather than dancing around the edges. This entire exchange had grown more than tiresome.

"I'll do more than try, old man. I'll carry it with pride."

"You can dream, but I can guarantee you that you'll never touch the hilt of this blade."

"Promises, promises."

"I keep my promises, friend," he said, biting off the last word. "You'll find that out soon enough."

"As do I, friend." The soldier pushed himself up from his seat, having enjoyed the warmth for a time, now feeling the need to end this little charade. "Are you ready to go? Clearly you know what's going on. There's no need for you to make this any more difficult than you already have."

"And where is it that you think I'm going?"

"To the mines, of course." The man motioned for him to come around the fire. "Come on, friend. As I said, no reason to make this difficult. Hand over the sword and then we can enjoy a quiet night before moving on tomorrow morning."

"And if I don't want to work in the mines?" he asked.

"You don't have a choice, friend. You're surrounded. You're outnumbered. Just count yourself lucky that we didn't treat you the way we've treated some of the others who've proven obstinate."

"You don't want to hurt me too badly because you get paid more if you deliver healthy prisoners who can work."

"Now we're understanding one another," the soldier said with a bright smile as he hefted his axe. "That wasn't so difficult after all, now was it?"

"So that's the way of it. Into the mines. I get worked to death. You take the golds for me."

"It is, indeed. Sorry, friend, but that's the way of the world here in New Caledonia. The strong survive. The weak don't. And as I said, I'll take your sword as well. You're not going to need it where you're going and I've got a use for it."

The slaver whistled sharply, three men stepping out of the darkness. All three held their whips loosely in their hands, swords sheathed across their backs.

It was exactly as he thought. They wanted him as healthy and whole as possible. It would be easier for him to recover from a slash from a whip than one inflicted by a sword.

"You sure you want to do this. I'll give you one chance for you and your men to leave here unharmed."

The soldier turned slaver stared at him, and then he and his men broke out into a loud laughter that echoed off the surrounding peaks.

"You really are annoying," the slaver said, "but you're funny as well. We'll have a good time getting to know one another as we head to the mine."

The leader of the slavers nodded. His men stepped around the fire in response. They pulled the grips on their whips back toward their shoulders, allowing the steel tips to trail along the ground.

They were experienced in their work. They knew how to use their weapons.

He believed that the one coming at him from his left would aim for his left leg. The two coming at him from his right would aim for his right leg and his right arm, assuming by where his sword was placed that he was right handed.

Easy. No fuss. A quick capture.

He could see it in their eyes. These slavers had done it before many times. They assumed that they would do it many more times in the future in just the same manner.

One old man, even an old man with a sword, would offer them little in the way of a challenge.

That was their mistake. The slavers were ready for what they assumed would be a simple takedown.

And he had to admit that it did prove to be a simple takedown. Just not for them.

He moved faster than the shadows playing across the fire, the three slavers barely seeing him pull his sword from its sheath. The slaver to his left didn't know what had happened until he looked down and saw the steel sticking out of his gut.

The man whimpered softly in pain, an acknowledgment of his own end clear as his eyes glazed over. The dying slaver dropped to the ground with a heavy sigh when he pulled the blade free.

The eyes of the two slavers coming at him from the other direction widened in shock. They had never seen anyone move so rapidly or with such lethality.

The two slavers pulled back their whips, preparing to send the spiked tips streaking through the air.

They were too slow. Much, much too slow.

He glided around the fire as if he were a part of the gloom, slashing with an economical motion across the throat of the closest slaver.

The man released his whip, his hands pawing frantically at the blood gushing from his throat. He dropped to his knees, sagging, unable to stop the flow of red as his life poured out onto the rocky ground.

With the last slaver distracted by his dying friend, the old man cut down with his steel, slicing through the whip that was streaking toward his neck, the sharp tip whistling off into the darkness. Reversing his motion, he brought his steel up in an arc that sliced from groin to gut.

Satisfied with the efficiency of his work, he stepped back and returned to where he had been sitting, staring across the fire at the man with the axe who had felt the need to converse with him instead of just sending all of his men at him at once.

The slaver was overconfident, and he had paid for his arrogance in his men's blood.

"You should have accepted my offer when you could have," the slaver hissed through clenched teeth, still trying to come to grips with the slaughter he had just witnessed.

It was at that moment that the third slaver, hands pressing futilely to the horrific wound across his midsection, ribs and organs exposed, dropped face first into the fire, sending up a shower of sparks.

Obviously, the leader of this band of slavers was not happy, his right eye twitching. A nervous tic, probably brought on by stress or anger or a combination of both.

The old man smiled as he reached that conclusion. The slaver hadn't expected this to happen. His men were all experienced in their work.

Yet, he had made the three who came for him look like fools. That meant the lead slaver looked like a fool as well, and the man with the axe couldn't have that.

"Are you lucky or good?" the soldier turned slaver asked, playing for time as he tried to work out a new strategy as quickly as he could.

"Probably a little of both," he admitted.

The slaver nodded. He had decided what he was going to do next. The old man had killed three of his friends in just a few seconds. The old man would have a harder time against his entire gang.

"Let's see how you do against the rest of my men."

Once again, the slaver whistled. The rest of his crew walked out from the darkness. Only a few of them still grasped their whips. The rest had opted for their swords.

They didn't want to meet the same fate as their comrades.

Whips were of little use against a man who knew how to use a blade with such practiced efficiency.

"You sure you want to do this?" he asked from across the fire. His tone suggested that he wasn't worried about the number of slavers standing against him. Rather, he sounded more resigned to what was going to be required of him.

"Oh, I do. I really, really do. Forget the mines. I'm just going to cut you into little pieces."

"Mind if we join the fun?"

The leader of the slavers was so startled by this new voice that he jumped an inch off the ground. He turned around swiftly, almost tripping over the rock behind him as he took in the four newcomers who stood at the edge of the shadows.

The petite woman carried a nocked bow. Two of the men held swords. They all radiated a competence that suggested that they knew what they were doing with their weapons.

The last was the largest of the squad, a long, thin scar running across his bald head. He carried what looked like an oversized blacksmith's hammer, a weapon that most men probably couldn't carry, much less swing.

"Who are you?" demanded the slaver.

Several of his men had turned to face these new arrivals. The slavers still held the advantage in numbers. But that didn't make them feel any better.

The slavers' unease was made plain by how they gripped the hilts of their swords nervously and shuffled from side to side. The confidence that they normally enjoyed when taking captives, which had begun to drain away when they observed the old man kill their friends so swiftly, spiraled down even faster upon meeting these four new arrivals.

"Just some concerned Highlanders," the bald man replied pleasantly.

"Concerned Highlanders?" the slaver repeated, still trying to understand what was going on. Who in their right mind would take on a full contingent of slavers? Well, an almost full contingent, he admitted to himself. He didn't want to think about the men who he had lost just moments before, although he was finding it difficult because Rolf, who had collapsed into the fire, was beginning to burn and the stench that he was giving off was horrendous. "You're going to try to help the old man? Are you serious?"

The scarred man chuckled softly. "From what we saw, the old man as you call him doesn't need our help. But we do need some exercise, so we thought that we would join in the fun. Tommie!"

The arrow streaked from the woman's bow, slamming into the chest of the lead slaver. The stout fellow stood there for just a few more heartbeats, not quite comprehending what had happened, before dropping his axe and falling into the fire on his back, joining his already burning comrade.

The shock of that attack set the tone, the fight that followed short and swift. The Highlanders, aided by the old man, made quick work of the slavers.

Forcing them up against the fire, the slavers had nowhere to go. With Tommie staying on the outside and picking her targets, she took down three more men on her own.

After that, it was just a matter of finishing off the rest. All of whom lost interest in the fight before it really even began. All of them desperate to escape.

Yet none of them had the skill or wherewithal to get past the old man with the sword or the scarred fellow with the hammer.

"Thank you for your help, Sergeant Westgard." The old man raised his blade, already wiped clean of blood, to his forehead. He gave the scarred man a nod of respect. "As always, your timing is excellent."

"Thank you, Blademaster," the man with the hammer replied. He raised the head of his weapon to his forehead as well, returning the gesture to his former commander and mentor.

"A pleasure to come across you here. And I see that many of your friends from the Royal Guard are still with you."

"It's that sense of loyalty I instill in others, Blademaster. Once they get to know me, they can't get enough of me."

Tommie snorted in amusement. "It's something all right, though likely not that."

"And just as respectful as I remember them," the Blademaster replied with a grin.

That earned a few quiet laughs from the two Highlanders standing with Tommie.

"We'll check the woods around us, just to make sure," said Martin.

Bertie followed him beyond the fire and in among the trees. Tommie remained where she was, bow on her string. Ready. Just in case.

"So this is what you're doing here in the Highlands, Duff?" asked the Blademaster, having sheathed his sword in the scabbard he held in his hand.

"What do you mean?"

"Helping people in need."

Duff shrugged sheepishly. "Just doing what I can. Slavers. Stalkers. Wraiths. They have no place here."

The Blademaster smiled. "A leopard can't change his spots."

Duff smiled as well, having heard the Blademaster tell him that many times in the past. Hearing one of the slavers groan, he stepped over to the man.

Duff studied the wound across the slaver's chest. It was only a matter of time. He nodded, relaying to the man what he was intending to do. He saw in the slaver's eyes that the fellow understood and appreciated his kindness.

Duff reached down and picked up the man's sword. With a

quick stab, the point of the sword cut into the slaver's throat, speeding the dying man on his way.

Duff's action didn't faze the Blademaster in the least. Especially since he had been the one to teach his former Sergeant that he should never leave a dying man to his misery, even when he deserved it.

"It's been a while, Sergeant."

"It has, Blademaster."

"I take it that these are the slavers that are such a problem in these peaks."

"They are. Or at least these were. And they're not even the worst of the lot."

"I've heard of these men. Of the Stalkers and Wraiths as well."

"It seems like we need to have a conversation, Blademaster, if you're going to be traveling through the Highlands."

"That we do, Sergeant."

2

DISAPPOINTING NEWS

"What was the take, Farkan?"

"Not as good as we would have liked, my Lady," replied the soldier as he paged through the manifest he had acquired from the ship's captain.

Instead of the leather armor so common to the provincial Guards in the Territories, the man wore a pair of loose-fitting trousers and a worn, dirty shirt over his broad shoulders with the sleeves rolled up. He also had a cutlass thrust into his belt along with several daggers.

He was used to the daggers. Instead of the cutlass, he would have preferred the long sword with which he was so familiar. But that weapon wouldn't fit with what he was playing at now.

He could bear it, nonetheless. A job was a job, and this job paid well. He could do without his favored blade for a while longer.

"Explain," the woman demanded sharply. "This ship carried everything we needed. Nothing that we really wanted appears to be in the hold."

"Yes, my Lady, I understand. And my apologies, my Lady."

"I don't need your apologies," the woman hissed sharply. "I want an answer, Farkan."

"Of course, my Lady. I was getting to that." He sighed. This was going to be a difficult conversation. He didn't need this so early in the morning. "When we seized this ship, it had already made several stops. The only thing left in the hold when we got to her was some grain and a few crates and pallets with some pottery and furniture. And the grain was going bad, which explained why whoever ordered it refused to accept it. Weevils." He shrugged his shoulders and gave her a look that said that what was done was done. No sense in getting angry about bad luck.

"Why did it take so long for you to find this ship, Farkan?" asked the woman, her hands clenched into fists.

This was supposed to have been an easy seizure. She had been assured that it would be. Apparently not.

Maybe Farkan was incompetent. Maybe she trusted him too much.

If that proved to be the case, then she would deal with him in a way that would ensure the other captains working for her understood what the cost of failure was.

"The particulars that I gave you were from the best sources that I have," she growled. "They are never wrong. You should have taken the ship before it reached its first port of call."

"Yes, my Lady," agreed Farkan, beginning to feel distinctly uncomfortable. His employer had a very short and sharp temper, and he had no desire to feel the brunt of her anger. Not after the stories he had heard. "We would have, and we were about to do so in fact. We caught up to her three days out from Ballinasloe. However, right before we were about to attack, three cutters came out of the sun. I didn't believe it would be wise to try to take on three ships all at one time. Doing so would have put our larger mission at risk. We withdrew and caught up to her again farther along on her journey."

"You made the decision to withdraw?" demanded the woman. "You didn't withdraw! You ran! I thought you were a man of character, Farkan. A man of courage. Yet you sailed away like a dog with his tail between his legs. A neutered dog, in fact."

The woman's eyes blazed fiercely. She began flexing her fingers and then making and unmaking a fist with her right hand, like she was preparing to strike him. Or reach for the sword at her left hip.

The grizzled veteran began to stammer, his discomfort growing. He knew how good she was with a blade.

"We had no choice, my Lady. I swear. It was three of the Carlomin cutters, the ones with the rams on their prows. If it wasn't them, we would have taken them on. But we couldn't take the risk of one of those ship killers slicing into us. And those cutters were fast. We barely got away. If not for the fog that we found, we wouldn't have. I swear it, my Lady. We wouldn't have withdrawn if we didn't have any other choice."

"The Carlomins," spat out Hakea Roosarian as if the name was a curse.

She stared hard at the soldier, wanting to ensure that he understood that she was less than pleased by his failure. But as she turned her thoughts to her primary rival on the Sea of Mist, she couldn't fault the decision he had made no matter how much she wanted to.

Talia Carlomin and her mother were becoming an increasingly bigger irritant. An irritant that needed to be removed as swiftly as possible. Yet how to do that?

Hakea contemplated that question, lost in thought as she stood atop the floating pier built within the hidden cove, her men continuing to bring out of the hold of the seized ship anything that might be of use to them. Which was very little.

It was going to be slim pickings, which Hakea didn't find surprising. Obviously, the merchant who owned the vessel had instructed his captain to get the most valuable items off first, understanding the risk of sailing along the New Caledonian coast these days.

What the merchant was losing now, other than his ship if she chose to take it – which she would because she needed to get something of value out of this missed opportunity, would have little impact upon him. The merchant still had a dozen vessels sailing back and forth across the Burnt Ocean.

In fact, he'd recoup the loss of the ship in a matter of months. She'd need to try again to gain the leverage she needed on him.

Worse, those two upstart women were enjoying the success that she so richly deserved. The success that she would have been reaping by now if they hadn't refused to bring her into their company as she had proposed.

Talia and Isana Carlomin had stood up to her, the Governor of Fal Carrach, treating her like someone who didn't deserve their respect. Like someone who didn't need to be obeyed.

That was bad enough all on its own. But now they were taking a more aggressive role against the pirates working along the coast. And that meant that they were interfering directly in her business.

Hakea couldn't allow that to continue. Too much was at stake.

She would deal with the two Carlomin women just as she did the father. And soon.

Because not only were their efforts hindering her men working in the Sea of Mist, but also because they were giving the other merchants the idea that they could protect themselves if they worked together. That they didn't need to listen to her entreaties. That they didn't need her.

She had to put a stop to that. Swiftly.

She had come to Fal Carrach to make a name for herself, to make her fortune and to achieve the position in life that she had no chance of achieving in Caledonia. She had had little choice.

Hakea Roosarian was the daughter of one of the lesser lords of Roo's Nest, the youngest brother of Duke Wencilius Roosarian.

She found herself in the Territories because of the mistakes her father had made. Even so, that didn't mean that she couldn't make the most of her circumstances.

Her father and uncle had a falling out, and she really couldn't blame her uncle for what he did as a result. She could place the full weight of blame on her father for that, and she did.

Wittan Roosarian stupidly had tried to remove his brother as Duke of Roo's Nest, thinking that he could steal the seat right out from under him. It didn't work out as he had hoped.

Her father had forgotten one key lesson. Well, many important lessons actually, but in her opinion, this indeed was the most important.

It didn't really matter who ruled in a Duchy so long as you had the Guard behind you. And that's where her father had badly misjudged.

Wittan had thought that he could bring the Guard to his side after just a few conversations and vague promises to its commanding officers that likely would not be kept unless absolutely necessary. The Guard of Roo's Nest had ignored him, hearing the falsehoods in her father's words, and remained loyal to her uncle.

Her father had sealed his fate as soon as that happened.

Hakea had watched when her father was taken to the chopping block. The once proud and very foolish man had been blubbering like a child and pissing his pants when they placed his neck against the wood.

The headsman hadn't wasted any time. With one swing of

that very large axe, Hakea had become the last of her father's line.

She both loved and hated her father for what he had done. She wasn't upset that he had tried to take the throne for himself. She was upset that he had failed.

She meant to take what her father couldn't here in New Caledonia. Once she did, she would rebuild the line.

And even though Uncle Wencilius had killed his own brother, regrettably so he had told her and she had believed him, she was still thankful for what he had given her.

A chance.

He had gifted her a grant to the Territory of Fal Carrach. Probably out of a mixture of regret and guilt, as she had been his favorite niece.

He chose not to kill her for her father's treachery, an act of mercy, but he didn't want her in Caledonia where she could cause trouble. Sending her to New Caledonia was the best solution for everyone.

Yet though she had Fal Carrach, which was more than she could have ever expected to gain in Caledonia, still she wasn't satisfied.

She wanted more. So much more.

And she would do whatever was necessary to get what she wanted.

She was about to rip into Farkan and tell him exactly what he deserved for his failure, desperate to release the anger boiling within her.

Instead, she held her tongue when she saw the handful of men with their hands tied behind their backs who were brought stumbling out of the hatch and made to walk toward the gangplank that led down to the dock.

"Why are they here?" Hakea asked, distracted by the sailors who had survived the assault.

Farkan jumped at the chance to redirect his employer's attention. "They hid during the attack. We didn't find them until we'd come into the cove and were doing a final search for hidden holds."

Hakea nodded, understanding. Most merchants had a storage area or two secreted about their vessels. There were times when they didn't want certain cargo to be found.

"How did you find the holds?"

"It wasn't easy," replied Farkan, hoping that this might be a chance to impress Governor Roosarian and perhaps place himself in a better light. "Whenever we take a ship, I assign a squad of men to work their way through the vessel, knocking on the walls and the decks to see if they can identify any hollow spaces that shouldn't be there. On this ship, there was only one." He motioned toward the sailors who were just now stepping down onto the dock. "They're what we found rather than what we were hoping for."

Hakea nodded. She was surprised and also disappointed. She would have much preferred finding a secret cargo rather than a handful of sailors hiding away like rats.

"You know what to do," she said, her voice cold.

"Yes, my Lady. It will be done as you've ordered."

She allowed her captains the discretion to decide whether to leave alive those captured when a ship was seized, unless she gave express orders that an example needed to be made. Having a few survivors often was useful to her purposes. They helped to spread stories about the pirates ravaging the eastern coast of New Caledonia. Stoking the fear that was already prevalent.

She couldn't do that this time.

These sailors had seen her men at work. They had seen the cove and likely could locate it if they were of such a mind.

Worst of all, they had seen her.

She couldn't permit that.

They needed to die.

3

CREATURES FROM THE DEEP

"Majdi, what do you think you're doing?" demanded Declan.

The largest member of the Blood Company stood with the archers positioned at the stern deck, another row of archers just above them on the helm. Rather than holding a bow with a quiver of arrows across his back, the gladiator hefted a harpoon with several more right next to him stuck point first into the deck.

"I was hoping to do a little fishing," he replied with a straight face, although the comment drew several guffaws of laughter from the men and women standing with him.

Declan stared at Majdi for quite a long time, his grim expression becoming even grimmer, the gladiators around Majdi beginning to get nervous, before he too burst out laughing. That got many of the gladiators around them laughing even more, the humor helping to break the tension that had been building as the three Bakunawa chasing them through the increasingly rougher water drew steadily closer.

"If you catch anything, I get first cut," said Declan.

Majdi grinned at that. "You have a deal."

Declan glanced quickly behind the *Freedom*. He had been tracking the three huge wakes surging toward them for the last hour. They were close now. No more than a few hundred yards behind them. Approaching at a remarkable speed, because the *Freedom* was flying through the water, the hull barely touching the Burnt Ocean as the tempestuous blasts of wind filled her sails and it felt as if she were soaring above the waves.

He thought that he could see the sharp blue of the animals' eyes breaking through the water that surged around the sea dragons as their terrifyingly long bodies slithered through the waves.

At this distance, he couldn't be certain. He was certain that the Bakunawa had just picked up their pace.

It was time. The next battle was about to begin.

The Bakunawa were done hunting. They were ready to feast.

"Archers, prepare to fire!" Declan shouted.

"I can't believe those sea dragons are staying with us." Bryen stood at the helm right next to Captain Gregson, impressed by the Bakunawa's speed and tenacity.

"This is nothing," he replied. "I've heard of those beasts outswimming a typhoon because they had a pod of blue whales in their sights."

"And no blue whales near us to distract these monsters?" Bryen asked.

"Unfortunately not."

"You're not making me feel any better about our chances of escaping."

"I'm not trying to."

But that was the question, wasn't it, thought Captain Gregson. Could they escape the Bakunawa?

When he had first taken the helm of the *Freedom*, he had thought that perhaps they could. This was the fastest ship he had ever been given the privilege of commanding.

Now, he had adjusted his expectations. Their sails were stretched to the breaking point by the gales surging across the Burnt Ocean from east to west, yet even then the sea dragons had no trouble at all staying with them.

The Bakunawa had been pursuing them for several hours now, and they showed no signs of flagging. Worse, the monsters were swimming faster. Narrowing the gap, slowly but steadily.

He could try to evade the beasts, swerving in different directions.

He discarded that idea as soon as it came to him. That would only slow them down.

He wasn't trying to avoid a drift of icebergs. He was trying to elude the fastest predator in the ocean.

The only way to do that was to make sure that the *Freedom's* sails stayed full of the wind, just as they were now. He could try to tack in search of stronger gusts, but he didn't think that he would find much success doing that.

The sails were bursting with air, the masts creaking and cracking as they strained against the powerful rush of wind. Besides, if he shifted off their present course, it would only make it that much easier for the Bakunawa to catch them.

Looking over his shoulder, Gregson cursed quietly. In just the last few seconds, the Bakunawa had swum even closer. They were gaining on the *Freedom* faster than he would have liked.

He was running out of options. At this pace, the monsters would be on them in a matter of minutes.

There was only one choice now. Stay on their current track.

"How long can you keep this up?" asked Bryen, having reached the same conclusion as Captain Gregson.

"We shouldn't have to worry about the wind," replied Gregson, who turned back toward the bow, studying the sails, understanding from his decades on the open ocean that he had little hope of getting even one more knot out of the vessel. Something that he desperately wanted to do despite also understanding that even if they somehow did that, it would do them little good and it would only increase the risk of their losing a mast. "It will stay with us for at least the next few hours. The problem is that we might not have a few more hours left with those beasts in pursuit."

There was little that Gregson could do to stop what was about to happen. The Bakunawa were going to catch them. They had made a good run of it, but it wasn't going to be enough.

Unless ...

"Emelina," Gregson said. "Hard to port, please."

"Hard to port?" his wife replied, seeking confirmation. "Piotr, if we ..."

"I know, Emelina. Hard to port."

Going against her better judgment, Emelina did as her husband ordered, turning the wheel sharply toward the south. She understood his thinking, and although his decision worried her, she didn't disagree with him. At least not enough to argue with him, and she would never do that when they both stood on the helm.

The Bakunawa were about to catch them. There was no denying that reality.

Turning into the fast-approaching storm, the bank of dark clouds blotting out the horizon for as far as they could see, might give them a chance to escape, assuming those animals didn't sink the ship before they reached the tempest.

"You're a brave man," said Bryen, understanding what Captain Gregson had in mind. "Not many others would have made the decision that you just did."

"Not brave," answered Captain Gregson. "Just desperate. I'd

prefer taking my chances against the storm rather than against the Bakunawa. The storm will be much more forgiving than those monsters."

Bryen wasn't in a position to argue with him.

"The question now is, are we going to get into that storm before those beasts attack?" asked Captain Gregson.

Bryen turned back toward the stern. "No, we're not. We're going to have to fight."

The Bakunawa in the center had increased its speed even more, pushing in front of the other two, the animal's powerful tail propelling it through the water and creating a wake at least thirty feet in height. He wasn't too worried about that animal. Not yet. Because he could still see it.

He was more concerned about the other two Bakunawa. Those monsters had disappeared beneath the waves.

That could mean only one thing.

The Bakunawa were about to attack.

"That one had to have struck true," said Jenus. "There is no chance that I miss from this distance."

"I'll give that one to you only because I have no doubt that my last three hit the monster," replied Dorlan. "So I'm still in the lead. Twelve to seven."

"Where did you get that number from?" demanded Jenus. "I haven't missed yet."

Kollea did her best to ignore the good-natured argument taking place between the two gladiators, allowing the noise to wash over her. Instead, she focused on the goal she had set for herself. Trying to hit one of the Bakunawa's glittering eyes that even with the rush of water around the beast's massive head she could see clear as day, the sparkling blue orbs as wide as serving dishes.

"Would you two please shut up!" she shouted, having had enough of their juvenile discussion.

"We're just having a little fun, my love," replied Dorlan in a voice that begged for forgiveness.

"Less fun, more work," she said, loosing another arrow and knowing in an instant that once again she had missed her target, the steel-tipped shaft punching uselessly against the Bakunawa's scales, partially deflected by the spray of water around the beast. "Besides, the only person who's gotten a clean strike is Majdi, and even then that harpoon of his bounced right off the beast's scales like a rock off a stone wall."

Neither of the two gladiators could argue with that. They had both watched in astonishment as Majdi threw the harpoon perfectly, the twenty-foot-long lance flying straight and true, striking right between the sea dragon's eyes. However, instead of punching into the monster's brain, the steel had simply skidded off.

Having seen that, they knew that shooting arrows at the gigantic beast pursuing them clearly was a waste of time. Nevertheless, they needed to release some of their nervous energy and maybe, just maybe, one of them would get in a lucky hit.

Declan understood all of that just as Kollea did. Still, he didn't try to stop the archers. The real fight would begin soon enough.

And who knew? Maybe Kollea or one of the others would get lucky. Although he doubted it.

He didn't trust in luck. If you relied on luck in a fight, you were as good as dead.

"Do you mind if I give it a try?" asked Rafia, the Magus coming to stand right next to Declan.

He nodded to her, giving her a grin. "Be my guest."

Rafia returned the grin with one of her own before turning

her attention toward the Bakunawa that was now no more than forty yards behind the stern of the *Freedom* and closing swiftly.

Reaching for the Talent, Rafia crafted several small balls of white-hot energy, the spheres dancing across her palms. She knew that she needed to do this right. The water splashing up around the beast would, at least to a certain extent, help to protect it from what she was about to try.

She had little hope of destroying the Bakunawa with the Talent, the sea dragon's scales an excellent defense against the energy that she could bring to bear. But perhaps she could make the animal a touch more vulnerable.

With that thought guiding her actions, she threw the spheres of energy dancing above her right hand, targeting the Bakunawa's right eye.

Only seconds later, a string of curses that would have made any sailor proud erupted from her mouth. The instant before the Talent struck, a splash of water got in the way, minimizing the harm that she could cause, the sizzling energy tapping rather than smashing against the side of the beast's head.

The Bakunawa barely registered the attack, continuing its chase, completely unaffected by the strike.

So what to do now? If she did as she had just done, her next attempts would be no better than that of the archers. Despite the monstrous size of the animals, the Bakunawa were difficult enough targets in and of themselves. The fickle ocean only made the task all the more challenging.

"Change the environment if you can," Declan murmured into her ear so that she could hear over the gusts of wind that were trying and failing to keep the ship clear of the Bakunawa.

Rafia wasn't sure what Declan meant at first, her eyebrows knitting together and demonstrating her confusion. Then, as she thought about what he said, she knew exactly what she was going to attempt next. She just needed to time it right if she was to have any chance of success.

With this latest effort, she held the spheres of energy in reserve, instead shooting a stream of energy from her palm directly toward the massive snout of the Bakunawa. Rather than focus on the beast, however, she concentrated the power on the churning sea surging around the monster's head as the sea dragon propelled itself through the ocean.

Rafia smiled. The heat of the Talent boiled the water away into a mist.

That's when she struck with her other hand, throwing the balls of energy right through that hazy vapor.

Her quick thinking was rewarded.

The Talent struck true, each white-hot sphere slamming into the Bakunawa's scales with a fiery intensity that burned through that protection and into the beast's flesh. Two large wounds appeared on its long snout, one just below the nostril on its right side, another just below its left eye.

The Bakunawa reared up in pain, the movement revealing a third of its horribly long body, the sea dragon's scales glittering brightly in the light. Its massive jaws, filled with teeth that were longer than swords, opened as the monstrous animal roared in rage.

The beast was bigger than even Captain Gregson thought possible, the Bakunawa blocking the sun and putting the vessel in shadow even as the *Freedom* sped away. More worrisome, though, was the icy mist that was forming around the sea dragon's gaping maw.

"Watch out!" shouted Declan, the gladiators lining the stern and on the helm ducking for cover, none of them believing that they could escape in time. Still, they had to try as a frozen spittle blasted from the sea dragon's mouth.

Rafia saved them, fashioning a massive shield from the Talent, the spears of ice that erupted from the Bakunawa's gullet shattering against the barrier, breaking into millions of smaller pieces that dropped harmlessly into the ocean.

Thanks to Rafia, no one was harmed and the *Freedom* had gained some distance on the Bakunawa. Although likely not enough.

The sea dragon dove back into the water with a huge splash, its tail working rapidly to get the beast back up to speed.

Two minutes, thought Declan. Maybe three at the most. Probably no more.

Then the Bakunawa would be right behind them again, breathing down their necks. And after seeing what that sea dragon had just expelled, that thought sent a shiver down his spine.

"When the sea dragon closes on us again, tell the gladiators to aim for the creature's wounds. I'll see if I can hurt it some more. Maybe if I give it a few more reminders of the pain that I can cause, it will decide that it should find easier game."

"They know," replied Declan, the soldiers of the Blood Company already back in position, ready for another go at the rapidly approaching sea dragon. "They specialize in taking advantage of their opponent's weaknesses."

Rafia nodded, not surprised. "Obviously we're getting under its skin. That will only work in our favor."

"You mean its scales," corrected Declan.

"A joke at a time like this?" asked Rafia, distracted by Declan's comment for just a moment. She turned toward him with a shrewd eye. "Do you always have to be so precise?"

"I can't afford not to be. A natural requirement of my profession."

"Or perhaps it's just a quirk of your personality that you can't escape," she offered.

"Perhaps," responded Declan, nodding his head as if he were actually considering her suggestion, "and is your irascibility and belief that you are rarely ever wrong a natural requirement of your profession or a quirk of your personality?"

Rafia stared at Declan, not knowing how to react. Few if any but him had the temerity to challenge a Magus in such a way. Then again, he had a good point, even though she had little desire to consider his question with everything else that was going on.

Needing to return her attention toward the Bakunawa that was once again closing the distance between them, she offered Declan a knowing grin. "Clever. Very clever. Don't let it go to your head."

~

"Why aren't we helping Rafia and Declan at the stern?" asked Aislinn, she and Bryen standing near the mizzenmast.

"They don't need our help," replied Bryen. "Rafia has that Bakunawa well in hand for now. Besides, we have our own monsters to deal with."

Aislinn stared at Bryen, sensing that he was using the Talent to extend his senses around them.

No, not around them. Beneath them.

The other two Bakunawa. They had disappeared beneath the waves, which could only mean …

Aislinn, Bryen, and everyone else on board the *Freedom* stumbled, a few reaching for a railing to maintain their balance, when a loud thump sounded off the hull of the vessel on the starboard side, the blow strong enough to send a shudder through the huge ship and knock it to the port side the length of a yardarm.

And then again on the port side, that strike sending the ship back to the starboard side.

The sailors and the soldiers of the Blood Company struggled to keep their feet, a few even falling to the deck before quickly pushing themselves back up, knowing that it was just the start of the next act in a larger play.

"Where are they?" asked Aislinn, understanding now why

Bryen had come here instead of going to assist the gladiators at the back of the ship.

"They're just below us, aren't they?" asked Davin, he and Lycia racing down the deck to stand with Aislinn and Bryen, both understanding the risk as soon as they felt the first thwack on the hull.

"They are," Bryen confirmed. "They've gone deep, but they're about to come back up."

"Are they trying to roll us?" asked Lycia.

The submerged Bakunawa were either testing the strength of the hull or attempting to tip them over. At the speed the vessel was going that latter possibility wouldn't be too difficult to achieve if the sea dragons gave the ship a hard push at just the right time in just the right place.

"Not yet," said Bryen, tracking the massive animals beneath the waves. "They've separated. They're about to come at us from the sides."

"We need to keep these sea dragons off the ship," said Aislinn. "They're so large, if they gain a grip, they could swamp us."

"You take the port side," said Davin to Lycia. "I'll take the starboard."

Lycia nodded, then turned toward the left, Davin moving to the railing on the right side, several squads of gladiators joining the brother and sister.

"What do you suggest?" asked Aislinn.

"Your guess is as good as mine," replied Bryen, watching as a rush of water that dwarfed the already stomach-churning waves they were sailing through burst out of the sea a thousand yards distant and turned toward the *Freedom* on the port side, a wake of a similar size pushing up out of the Burnt Ocean on the other side and curling toward them as well. "Rafia has slowed the Bakunawa chasing us, but she couldn't kill it. These two are going to be just as much of a challenge, if not more so. We're too vulnerable here. One good blow by either of the beasts and we're done for. And if they manage to get on board as you said, well ..."

Aislinn nodded, feeling a bit sick to her stomach. The two sea dragons had increased their speed. Their wakes, twice as tall as the rough chop the *Freedom* cut through, hid their long, sinuous bodies. They were coming right for the center of the ship from both sides. If they struck the *Freedom* at the same time, they would split her in two.

"We can't stop them completely," said Aislinn, acknowledging the hard truth of their situation. "Rafia already demonstrated that."

"No, we can't," agreed Bryen. "But we can slow them down. We might even be able to convince them that we're not worth the risk. If we can keep them from sinking us, we have a chance."

"Then maybe a little fire and ice," suggested Aislinn. "It won't stop them, but it might make them think twice about attacking us."

Bryen smiled. "I like how you're thinking. You can start with the ice. Let's get to it."

Bryen and Aislinn each assumed responsibility for one side of the ship, Aislinn focusing on the port side, Bryen the starboard. They knew what they wanted to do, and they also knew that perfect timing would be essential to any success they achieved.

As the seconds passed, the wake surging toward her growing in size, Aislinn became more anxious. She hated the waiting. She hated even more that Bryen appeared to be even calmer than he usually was.

His composure only made her more jittery, so she forced herself not to look at him. Instead, she kept her gaze fixed on the massive sea creature surging toward her through the waves that now were cresting at thirty feet.

"Aislinn," said Lycia, the Crimson Devil standing right next to the Lady of the Southern Marches.

Her voice revealed her concern. The Bakunawa on their side of the ship had increased its speed, the wake now well above the railing of the ship. The beast was huge, yet still they couldn't get a good look at it because of the water sliding off its body and shielding its advance.

"Bryen," said Davin, trying to get his friend's attention.

The Protector ignored the Crimson Giant, keeping his eyes locked on the Bakunawa streaking toward their side of the *Freedom*.

"Just a few more seconds," said Aislinn, her focus complete, seeing nothing but the swell of water rushing toward them.

"You're not going to have time, Bryen," warned Davin, watching as the Bakunawa swam toward them at an astounding speed.

The monstrous animal had no trouble staying with the ship even though it seemed to Davin as if they were flying just above the waves of the Burnt Ocean. He tried to keep his rising concern out of his voice, but he knew that he had failed miserably.

Bryen didn't say a word in response, not even blinking as he concentrated on the charging monster. His friend's words washed off him just as the seawater washed off the Bakunawa.

"Aislinn," said Lycia, "you really need to …"

"Now!" shouted Bryen, the Bakunawa no more than a few seconds from slamming into both sides of the ship.

At the exact same time, Bryen and Aislinn sent streams of the Talent blasting into the water along both sides of the ship's hull. The energy interacted with the saltwater instantly, the extreme cold creating a thin layer of ice that the Bakunawa plowed right through.

Not a good start, but it was only a start.

The beasts' progress slowed as the two Magii called on

more of the power of the natural world, that thin layer of ice rapidly hardening until it was twenty feet thick and still expanding, forcing the Bakunawa to work even harder to reach their target.

In just a few heartbeats, the massive creatures were struggling to break through the thick and still thickening frozen crust sitting atop the ocean.

Pleased by their success, Bryen and Aislinn used the Talent to add to the barricade of ice, the sea dragons finding it more and more difficult with every twist of their snakelike bodies to advance through the icy sheet.

A few times, as they tried to force their way toward the *Freedom*, the sea dragons reared up, hissing in pain. The sharp curls of the frosted waves sliced off a few of the Bakunawa's scales and then cut into the soft flesh beneath.

As they continued to work to slow the sea dragons, both Bryen and Aislinn watched with interest. Their efforts confirmed that these gargantuan creatures weren't indestructible, and that finding gave them hope.

If the Bakunawa could be harmed, then they could be killed.

They understood that what they had just done wouldn't stop these imposing beasts for long. But they could live with that. After all, the fight was just beginning.

The Bakunawa hissed in anger, whipping their long tails about wildly, desperate to advance, yet the expanding ice floe successfully impeded their charge. Finally, the sea dragons had no choice but to turn away, unable to break through, the *Freedom* speeding by them.

"Nicely done," said Davin, impressed by his friend's and Aislinn's handiwork.

"We're not out of this yet," said Bryen, watching as the two sea dragons slid back beneath the water.

"What are they doing?"

"They're coming up beneath the ice," said Aislinn, who used the Talent to observe as the Bakunawa dove down toward the ocean floor and then corkscrewed back in their direction, their powerful tails giving them more than enough speed to catch up to them.

"Will they be able to break through the ice?" asked Lycia.

"Yes," Bryen confirmed. He had searched beneath the waves as well, and though he and Aislinn had done an excellent job of hindering the sea dragons' approach, the ice cap wasn't thick enough to stop these beasts completely, not at the speed they were surging up from the deep. "They can break through. They're coming too fast for us to stop them."

"Where will they appear?" asked Lycia.

"They'll come up the sides of the hull," Aislinn said, having judged the trajectory of the monsters that were now no more than a few hundred yards from the surface.

"Blood Company to the rails!" Lycia shouted, the gladiators from the Pit responding immediately, shields, spears, and swords at the ready as they braced themselves for the sea dragons' arrival.

The soldiers of the Blood Company had fought a great many different kinds of beasts in the Colosseum. None had the ability to take their breath away as the Bakunawa did.

One of the sea dragons smashed through the ice on the port side, the other doing the same just a few seconds later on the starboard side. The huge animals rising up and out of the water finally gave Bryen and the other gladiators a good look at their attackers. What they observed could only be described as disheartening if not outright terrifying.

These serpent-like dragons appeared to be more snake than anything else except for the large fins on each side of their thick, sinuous bodies, which stretched on for what they judged to be more than five hundred feet. Yet the gladiators could only guess at the Bakunawa's overall size, because they could only see a little more than the first third of the beasts as they twisted their bodies, swaying like cobras as their tails worked feverishly beneath the surface to keep them in place.

Their blue and silver scales, which allowed the beasts to blend in so well with the ocean, glittered in the bright sunlight, reflecting a heat that was absent from the Bakunawa's ice-blue eyes. Sharp, spiky scales that began at the top of their heads and were at least ten feet in length ran down their spines, those scales appearing to be as strong as steel.

The Bakunawa on the port side lunged forward, its jaws scraping against the railing and forcing a handful of gladiators to dive out of the way.

Rather than moving back from the beast, Lycia stepped forward. The Bakunawa snapped at the gladiator. She twisted to the side just in time to avoid the jaws that would have taken her in one bite.

Lycia dodged to the side again as the Bakunawa tracked her movement across the deck, biting down toward her. Multiple times the beast's teeth crunched together, unsatisfied, its snout finally slamming into the deck and cracking several pieces of timber, even leaving a few of its smaller teeth stuck in the wood.

The lack of success and the lost teeth didn't affect the Bakunawa in the least when it pulled back its huge head.

What Aislinn did next, however, had an immediate impact.

Adapting what she had done to slow the sea dragon as it charged the ship, she sent streams of icy cold energy toward the monster's long neck.

The Bakunawa reared back at the touch of the Talent, hissing in pain at the sharp bite of the cold, the scales affected turning a glacial white.

"The patches of white!" shouted Aislinn. "Aim for those!"

Lycia and the gladiators with her didn't hesitate. Daggers, spears, and arrows streaked through the air, all of them targeting the areas that appeared to have frosted over. When the steel struck, the frozen scales shattered, the steel tips of the various weapons digging deeply into the Bakunawa's flesh beneath.

In spite of its multiple wounds, the Bakunawa lunged again, its mouth stretched wide in search of a meal.

The beast was about to snag Nkia right off the deck, its gaping maw closing around her, when Majdi stepped right in front of the Bakunawa, a scutum in hand. And just in time.

The gladiator knew that he couldn't prevent the Bakunawa's attack. The beast was too large and too strong. But he could make the sea dragon regret reaching for any of his friends and especially the woman he had grown fond of.

Right before the Bakunawa's teeth punctured his flesh, Majdi thrust up with his shield, pushing the steel as deep down its gullet as he could. A smart move on his part.

The scutum lodged in the back of the beast's throat. When the creature tried to snap its jaws closed, the sharp steel edges bit into the top and bottom of its jaws.

Despite the immense pressure the Bakunawa could generate, it could do little because of where Majdi placed the shield. As a result, the steel held, only bending slightly, the Bakunawa's attempts to dislodge the scutum actually helping to fix it more firmly in place.

The sea dragon rose up again, hissing in rage, unable to close its jaws.

"Shoot through its jaws!" roared Majdi, seeing the blood begin to trickle down the back of the Bakunawa's throat as the steel edges of the scutum dug more deeply into the soft flesh of the sea dragon's mouth.

The monster began to shake its head wildly in a desperate but clearly useless attempt to remove the shield. The layers of steel bent a little bit more because of the intense pressure, yet still the scutum held.

Lycia and the other gladiators with him didn't need to be told twice. More spears, arrows, and daggers sped through the air. Many smashed uselessly against the beast's nostrils and its large teeth, but just as many streaked through the gap in the creature's jaws and pierced the back of its throat.

Wanting to escape the cause of its terrible pain, the Bakunawa twisted away from the ship, reluctantly dropping back beneath the waves.

Aislinn and the gladiators on her side of the vessel had gained a respite. How long it would last was anyone's guess.

∼

WHILE AISLINN CHALLENGED the Bakunawa on her side of the ship with an icy blast, Bryen chose a different approach. He had observed with a great deal of interest Rafia's success against the sea dragon at the stern, so he played off that theme when the Bakunawa smashed through the ice and pushed itself up on the *Freedom's* starboard side.

The monster's massive tail created a whirlpool beneath the waves to keep the creature on pace with the ship as it glided through the ocean. That action also gave Bryen the target that he was hoping for.

He waited as the Bakunawa surged toward the *Freedom's* starboard side, using the Talent to craft a shimmering shield that blocked the beast's first lunge. The barrier stayed in place to protect against the second, third, and then fourth attack.

With the fifth the massive creature shot an icy blast from the back of its throat, the spears of ice splintering uselessly against the barrier. The Bakunawa reared back, shrieking in rage at its multiple failures, watching hungrily as the prey that it couldn't reach scrambled across the deck of the ship.

"Bryen," said Davin, not understanding why his friend

stood at the railing waiting, not saying anything, not doing anything.

Bryen had let the shield fade away. The Bakunawa began to swim closer to the side of the ship, hissing loudly, beginning to realize that there was nothing in its way that would impede it from sweeping clean the vessel's deck of the tasty morsels scurrying about.

"Bryen!" Davin shouted, trying to get his attention, his friend seemingly lost in his own world.

Davin gripped the haft of his spear nervously, the other members of the Blood Company standing with him all looking at Bryen with worried expressions, waiting for him to do something, to do anything.

They became even more concerned as the Bakunawa pushed itself up even higher and prepared to launch itself across the railing and onto the deck. The swish of its massive tail through the water gave the beast the extra burst of speed that it needed to stay with the vessel and also lift it over the side of the ship, the beast looming over the gladiators.

"Bryen!" shouted Davin, the Bakunawa having reached the apex of its arc, the long neck pulling back, the sea dragon preparing to strike down at them.

Right before the Bakunawa snapped forward, Bryen sent a stream of the Talent into the water right in the path of the beast. The energy blasted into the ocean, the water coming to a boil in a flash.

The sea dragon surged back, the seawater so hot that a cloud of steam rose into the air. That scalding mist blocked their view for a time and prevented the gladiators along the railing from tracking the massive beast.

They did hear an ear-splitting shriek of pain, which made them assume that the Bakunawa had tried to track their ship through the boiling ocean. A desperate move on the part of the beast and probably not the best one. Then an eerie silence descended on that side of the ship.

The gladiators tried and failed to pierce the haze, shields and spears held at the ready. Could the sea dragon not stand the heat? It seemed not. They desperately hoped not.

Several more seconds passed. The gladiators began to wonder if the Bakunawa had dropped beneath the surface of the ocean, seeking to escape the blistering water that continued to bubble and churn next to the ship.

Just when they thought that they might be free of the beast, the furious sea dragon stabbed out of the mist.

The Bakunawa tried to escape the boiling sea without having to dive beneath the surface, swerving toward and then away from the ship. But its scales, strong as they were, could protect it from the intense heat for only so long, several angry red splotches marring its blue and white hide.

Bryen was quick to make use of that knowledge. Even when the creature was blocked from view by the steam, he used the Talent to pinpoint the sea dragon's location, directing the searing energy along the surface of the sea to wherever the creature moved in its attempts to evade the scalding water.

With no other choice and desperate to get as much of its body clear of the source of its pain as possible, the Bakunawa, still fixated on attacking its prey, lifted even more of itself out of the ocean, less than a third of the sea dragon still submerged.

That's when Bryen saw his chance, firing bolt after bolt of energy at the beast. Focusing first on the many burns on its long body, then shifting to his primary target as the Bakunawa writhed atop the surface.

Distracted, the sea dragon failed to avoid the streak of energy that slammed into its right eye. The extreme heat of the Talent scorched the socket, the once circular orb melting and becoming a bubbling mess that dripped down from the gaping wound.

The Bakunawa shrieked in agony, turning its massive head away. But its suffering continued as Bryen's many other bolts that followed that painful strike blasted through the sea dragon's scales in a half dozen places along its neck, opening bloody, charred gashes several feet in length.

Davin and the gladiators with him were ready, spears and arrows streaking through the air. They targeted the Bakunawa's wounds, the steel biting deeply into the beast's neck.

The agony caused by the gladiators combined with that of the boiling water forced the Bakunawa to lift itself even higher into the air, until only the beast's tail remained in the water.

The sea dragon was desperate to get away from the missiles that inflicted such pain on it, though not a pain that matched what it felt where its missing eye had once been.

Having no other choice, the torment becoming unbearable, the Bakunawa twisted its body away from the ship and dove back into the Burnt Ocean, disappearing from view.

Bryen followed the Bakunawa with the Talent as it swam away from the *Freedom*. He doubted that the hunter would be going very far.

He, Davin, and the other gladiators had caused the animal a great deal of damage, but likely not enough for the Bakunawa to withdraw from the fight entirely. Not with two of its brethren circling in the water below the ship and still seeking to take the ship and its occupants beneath the surface.

Satisfied that the beast would leave them be for a little while, he turned, glad to see that Aislinn and Lycia had been successful on their side of the ship as well. They had beaten off the first attack by these monsters.

Bryen breathed a sigh of relief. They had earned a brief respite.

Even so, the battle wasn't over. He realized then that they needed to take a different approach, because there was no guarantee that he, Aislinn, and Rafia would be able to hold off the beasts again.

The Bakunawa knew what to expect now. They would adjust their strategy.

With that in mind, what were they to do?

One Bakunawa, the one now missing an eye, had swam away to lick its wounds. Despite that major success, Bryen was certain that the sea dragon would return, and two of the massive beasts already were coming back around for another charge. If one of those beasts managed to get its bulk onto the *Freedom*, Bryen had no doubt that the creature would take them all to a watery grave.

He needed to decide on a new strategy. Killing the beasts might not be possible. But what could they do to convince the Bakunawa to find easier prey?

Bryen didn't have time to answer his own question.

Rather than dividing their focus, the Bakunawa beneath the *Freedom* chose to attack from the same direction, targeting Davin's side of the vessel. Two massive wakes appeared just a few hundred yards away from the ship, the sea dragons drawing closer. The turbulence in the ocean resembled a small tidal wave as the creatures increased their speed, their icy blue eyes locked on their prey.

Bryen, Aislinn, and Rafia stepped toward the starboard rail, the Blood Company right behind them, all of them preparing to meet the watery charge of the two beasts. They didn't have long to wait.

Both Bakunawa pushed themselves out of the water simultaneously, their long necks pulling their massive heads back so that they could strike with the speed of a scorpion's tail.

Bryen, Aislinn, and Rafia were ready with the Talent, hoping to persuade the beasts that the *Freedom* wasn't worth their pain and blood. But they didn't want to put too much faith in hope. The knew that doing so could prove fatal, one of Sirius' favorite sayings popping into their heads.

"Hoping doesn't make it real."

Beginning to think that the Blood Company might have finally met their match, Bryen was about to shout out a reminder to his friends to focus on those areas on the sea dragons' long necks that already had suffered grievous harm. He never got the words out, because right at that moment, as the Bakunawa prepared to launch themselves toward the ship, Banshee streaked down out of the sky, wings held tight to her body, claws outstretched.

Soaring between the rearing Bakunawa, she focused her attention on the beast to her right. Dragging her razor-sharp talons through several of the charred wounds, she cut away even more flesh and spilled a torrent of blood, earning a screech of rage from her target as she swept by.

Banshee then tilted a wing before she crashed into the ocean, gliding back into the air, her rear paws kissing the tops of the waves before her strong wings pulled her higher into the sky.

The Griffons had been away from the *Freedom* for most of the day, hunting and exploring. They had chosen an excellent time to return.

Right behind Banshee came each of the other Griffons, claws extended, ripping across the Bakunawa's necks with their talons, tearing off scales and the muscle and meat beneath.

The sea dragons whipped around, their sinuous bodies allowing them a range of motion unavailable to most any other animal but a snake, trying to defend themselves against these swift and fearless attackers.

Despite the frenetic efforts of the Bakunawa, the Griffons were too fast and too smart, never getting close to the sea dragons' jaws, always attacking on an angle that made it almost impossible for the Bakunawa to engage them effectively.

The Griffons succeeded in keeping the Bakunawa in place for several minutes, swooping and swerving, never getting too close to their lethal jaws. Never in one position long enough to get caught in an icy blast.

Banshee and her friends were less interested in attacking and more interested in slowing the beasts down. Their efforts paid off, giving the *Freedom* the time to gain some much-needed distance from the massive sea creatures.

When the Bakunawa, tired of fighting a battle that they couldn't win, finally dove back beneath the waves, the Griffons broke off their attacks and flew toward the *Freedom*.

Bryen and the rest of the Blood Company watched it all from the stern, impressed by the Griffons' bravery and skill. When the Bakunawa disappeared and Banshee and the others turned back toward the ship, Bryen motioned to Aislinn, Davin, and Lycia.

"Come with me. We're not done yet."

The three followed Bryen as he clambered up onto the decks built specifically for the Griffons, arriving at the same time that Banshee landed.

"Glad you could join us," Bryen said to the Griffon before turning toward the Magus. "You know what I have in mind, I take it?"

"I wouldn't miss it," Rafia replied, who had followed the gladiators across the deck. "We've beaten the Bakunawa twice, but the two beasts the Griffons just fended off are coming toward us again. We don't have much choice."

"Let's get to it, then," said Bryen. "We need to take the fight to these sea dragons. The more space we can give the *Freedom*, the better our chances of keeping those monsters off the ship."

"Where are they?" asked Davin, who rode on the back of Fuerza. The male Griffon, who had a habit of taking risks that other Griffons might avoid, had taken a liking to the gladiator, sensing a kindred spirit.

He and the others drifted in lazy circles just a hundred feet above the waves that the howling wind was now whipping up into a frenzy, the oncoming storm no more than a league away and reaching for them with the speed of a Ghoule's claw.

"Just below us," replied Aislinn, who had assumed responsibility for tracking the sea dragons.

"They're still following the *Freedom*?" asked Lycia, both admiring and hating the sea dragons' persistence.

"They are."

"Where's the third Bakunawa, the one Bryen hurt badly?" asked Davin.

"About a mile behind the others. Probably deciding what it wants to do after losing an eye."

"How do we get at the sea dragons if they don't come to the surface?" asked Lycia. "Do they even know that we're here?"

"Watch out!" shouted Aislinn.

The two Bakunawa burst out of the ocean at an incredible speed, snapping at the Griffons and their riders with their massive jaws.

Bryen and his friends scattered, the Griffons all diving in different directions.

Even though the massive sea creatures missed the first time, the dragons kept at it, lunging time after time at the Griffons as they twisted and turned with a remarkable dexterity. Banshee even corkscrewed down toward the ocean before tipping her wing and curling away to escape a very determined attack.

Rafia was lucky to escape, one of the Bakunawa's teeth almost snagging her if not for her Griffon's lightning-fast navigating. Potencia dove toward the ocean and then pulled up at the very last second, relying on the blustery wind to push her beyond the Bakunawa's jaws before they could close around them.

As Potencia pumped her powerful wings to regain some much-needed elevation, the two Bakunawa turned back toward the other Griffons, hissing and screeching, preparing to launch themselves again at their prey, now more interested in killing their tormentors than continuing their pursuit of the *Freedom*.

Wanting to keep the sea dragons focused on them, Bryen infused both Lycia's swords and Davin's spear with the Talent. Now all of them had the capacity to cut through the sea dragons' scales, assuming they could get close enough without becoming a tasty snack for the monsters.

Bryen didn't waste any time. Banshee shot down toward one of the Bakunawa. When they were no more than fifty feet away, she unfurled her wings, the added resistance stopping her abruptly. She then beat her wings rapidly so that she could stay in place, all the while fighting the gusting wind to hover just above the Bakunawa, careful to stay clear of its powerful jaws.

The Bakunawa shrieked in rage, not anticipating the maneuver, thinking that it had a chance of taking its tormentor down its gullet. The sea dragon's ocean blue eyes glittering coldly, eyeing them hungrily, unable to reach them.

Bryen chose that moment to attack, though not in the way the sea dragon thought he would.

Instead of targeting the wounds disfiguring the beast's neck, he sent several bolts of energy toward the Bakunawa's eyes.

The sea creature ducked away just in time, a few of the streaks of energy slicing away the scales along its forehead and charring the flesh beneath, yet doing no more damage than that.

Bryen didn't care that he had missed those menacing orbs, however. His focus was elsewhere, wanting to ensure that the flashes of energy blinded the beast for a few seconds.

Because that's all the time that Lycia needed to take full

advantage of the opening he had given her as she swooped down on Arabella. She sliced across the beast's neck, cutting through scales and into the soft flesh beneath with her blazing twin swords.

The Bakunawa didn't sense her attack until it was too late, twisting away as best as it could, though not before the damage was done. The sea dragon roared in rage as a river of blood flowed down its neck, a gash twenty feet long running across the length of its body.

Aislinn took a similar approach, her Griffon dipping down toward the water and then climbing in a tight circle around the other Bakunawa, the beast spinning easily in the ocean to track their movement.

She sent stream after stream of energy toward the dragon, the Bakunawa avoiding each attack, curling and twisting, ignoring the few times that the Talent struck. Those slight wounds, just a few scales scraped free, were of little concern to the beast.

Her inability to badly injure the beast didn't bother Aislinn. Her objective wasn't to kill the Bakunawa, it was to keep it in place just as Bryen had done. And at that she succeeded.

The sea dragon remained where it was long enough for Davin to dive down from behind, slicing across the back of the Bakunawa's neck with his fiery spearpoint just below its head. His strike was so vicious and so well aimed that it cut through several dozen scales and into the thick muscle beneath, taking off as well several razor-sharp spikes from the beast's spine. The Bakunawa screeched in rage at this debilitating injury, yet found that it could do nothing to thwart its attacker.

Rafia came back around on Potencia to join the fight, making it even more difficult for the Bakunawa to defend themselves. The Griffons swooped and swerved, maintaining their distance, then speeding in tight to the beasts, never doing the same thing twice so that the Bakunawa couldn't discern a pattern and adjust.

The gladiators and the two Magii would have been more than happy to kill the beasts if they could have, but they didn't want to take any unnecessary risks. They needed to be careful, understanding the peril they faced. One mistake could cost them their lives. Because even though the Bakunawa were badly injured, they weren't out of the fight.

Therefore, they remained focused on their primary goal. Delaying the beasts and trying to give the *Freedom* as much of a lead as they could.

Despite their many wounds, the Bakunawa were freakishly fast. Each of the gladiators barely escaped those powerful jaws at least once.

Davin on a more regular basis than the others since he and Fuerza were more willing to take a potentially fatal risk. They often flew in a figure eight around and between the two Bakunawa, the creatures' jaws never too far away from punching through their flesh.

So far, what Bryen and his friends were doing was working. The *Freedom* was already several leagues to the west and not long for entering the approaching storm. The question now was how much longer they could keep this up.

The erratic winds were becoming more of a problem, the ever stronger blasts buffeting them and making it difficult for the Griffons to maneuver. Bryen was beginning to fear that one of them might be taken by a Bakunawa not because of a mistake, but rather because a stray gust of wind placed them right in the path of a dragon's jaws at absolutely the worst possible time.

It was right at that moment that one of those unforgiving and unanticipated blasts caught Banshee, pushing her and Bryen down closer to the surface of the ocean and in between the two Bakunawa.

Banshee did all that she could to keep them out of the waves, flapping her wings furiously, understanding that dropping into the sea was a death sentence. She'd never be able to get back into the air before one of the Bakunawa gobbled them up.

Bryen kept an eye on the two sea dragons, expecting one or both to attack and wanting to make them think twice about embarking on that course of action.

"Bryen, look out!" shouted Aislinn.

He was so focused on what was happening around him, the two Bakunawa turning toward him at the same time, that he almost didn't notice the rush of frothing water just beneath him.

At the worst possible moment, the badly wounded Bakunawa that had lurked for a time just beyond the fight burst out of the waves, jaws opened, seeking to claim the irritant that had taken one of its eyes.

Bryen hadn't been paying attention to what was beneath them, but Banshee was well aware of the danger. The Griffon moved out of the angry dragon's path with one powerful flap of its wings, avoiding the tooth-filled maw by just a few feet.

Bryen recovered from the shock quickly. As the massive beast streaked by, the long body pushing up and out of the waves, Bryen stabbed with his glowing spear as fast as a lightning strike, pulling his weapon back just as swiftly.

The wounded Bakunawa's screech of fury at missing its prey died in its throat as the creature pushed almost its entire length out of the water, the sea dragon hanging there for just a few seconds, before it lost control of its body and flopped back into the ocean with a gigantic splash. Its massive frame of several hundred feet floated atop the surface briefly before sinking below the churning waves.

Although the more immediate threat was gone, Bryen and Banshee were still caught right between the other two Bakunawa. Banshee pumped her wings frantically, gaining more height and then twisting away so that they were well clear of the other sea dragons before the beasts could even think about going after them.

But then, much to Bryen's surprise, the other Bakunawa dropped back into the ocean as well. Bryen and the others waited, assuming that there would be another round to the combat, the Griffons hovering in the air as best as they could as they struggled against the raging winds.

After a few minutes passed, Aislinn confirmed what they all hoped for. "They're gone. For now. They went after the dead Bakunawa instead of continuing the hunt. An easy meal compared to us."

"Excellent strike," said Rafia, who had been in the perfect position to watch as Bryen stabbed his blazing spear through the Bakunawa's empty eye socket and deep into the creature's brain, killing the sea dragon with the well-timed stab.

"Thanks," nodded Bryen, breathing a sigh of relief that the fight had ended for now since the Griffons were struggling more and more to manage the tempestuous wind. "The credit goes to Banshee. She put me exactly where I needed to be."

The Griffon squawked at his statement, apparently agreeing with her friend.

"We're not done with them, are we?"

Bryen shook his head. "They'll be back. Probably when we least want them to be."

~

Captain Gregson waited at the stern just a few feet from the decks installed for the Griffons. He had learned that it was best to leave these magnificent animals alone when they returned, not approaching until they had time to settle themselves.

Seeing how the Griffons' eyes blazed brightly from the skirmish against the Bakunawa, he decided that he would stay right where he was. The Captain of the Blood Company could come to him when he was ready.

As soon as Banshee's paws touched the deck, Bryen jumped off the Griffon's back, running his fingers through the feathers along her chin a few times before stepping down to the main deck. Usually, he would have spent more time with Banshee. He couldn't do that now, however, something that Banshee understood as the sea dragons remained a threat.

The Griffon offered one more squawk of defiance at the Bakunawa they had battled, the other Griffons that were now landing doing the same.

Bryen believed that Banshee was right. They had won that skirmish. Still, it was only a skirmish. There was more to come. The Bakunawa weren't going to let them go so easily.

"Congratulations, lad," said Captain Gregson, slapping Bryen good-naturedly on the back. "I never thought that I would see the day when a man killed one of those monsters, but you did it."

"I had some much-needed assistance," countered Bryen. "Besides, it was more luck than anything else."

"I doubt that, my friend. I'm sure there was some small amount of skill involved as well." Captain Gregson looked beyond the stern railing, grateful to see that there were no unsettling wakes trailing his vessel. Of course, that didn't mean the beasts weren't back there, preparing to come for them again.

"They're still tracking us, aren't they?"

"They are," confirmed Bryen. "About a league back now. Not getting any closer, but not falling behind either."

"They still want us."

"That would be my guess."

Captain Gregson nodded, not surprised. If there weren't any blue whales or other large prey in this part of the ocean, the

Bakunawa would have little reason to let them go. And he wouldn't be surprised if they wanted a little revenge as well.

"Can you kill the other two?"

Bryen sighed, thinking about the question before responding. "I'm not certain. They're hard to kill as you saw. Even with Rafia and Aislinn taking their best shot, we've only eliminated one of these beasts."

"So we need to assume that they're going to try again."

"Yes, they will. I'm certain of it."

"What would you suggest?" asked Captain Gregson.

"As Declan likes to say, it comes down to the environment." Bryen stared out at the grey and blue ocean behind them, the waves already twice as high as they had been when the clash began thanks to the wind that was now more a gale whipping up the already rough water. "In the current environment, the Bakunawa have the advantage."

"How do we change that?" asked Captain Gregson, his eyes going wide when he saw Bryen's broad somewhat worrisome smile. He was beginning to understand what the young man had in mind, and he wasn't sure he liked the idea even though he was the one who had put it there for his consideration.

"Make for the south. Now."

"Are you sure about that? Maybe we can stay in front of the sea dragons and just skirt the edge of the tempest. With your success against the Bakunawa, that's what I was hoping to do."

"You know that both of those are impossibilities, Captain Gregson. The storm is too strong – it'll be over us in a matter of minutes -- and the Bakunawa are too determined."

Captain Gregson shook his head in annoyance, not at what Bryen suggested, but rather because their current circumstances gave them little choice in the matter. "You do understand that this storm is going to be a nasty one. It won't let us go easily. It might not let us go at all."

Bryen nodded. "Better to be consumed by the storm than by a Bakunawa."

It was Captain Gregson's turn to sigh, unable to find fault with Bryen's logic. "I can't argue with you there." With a nod, the Captain of the *Freedom* strode back down the deck toward the helm. "Emelina!" he shouted, "hard to port!"

4

TIME TO TALK

"You don't scare me, lassie," claimed Captain Blackbeard. His jacket and hat were gone. His face and torso displayed the effects of his brief attempt at resistance, a dried cut above his left eye and the bruise closing the right one a match for the many others dotting his ribs. "I'm the most fearsome pirate on the Burnt Ocean! I'm not afraid of anything or anyone. Nothing you do will get me to talk. Nothing!"

Talia Carlomin leaned against the railing of her ship, staring at the pirate captain, though not really seeing him, not really listening to him. Her mind was elsewhere. The man's unending stream of bluster was making it hard to think. His constant boasts about his stamina, his tolerance for pain, and his lack of fear were wearing on her nerves.

She needed information, but was it really worth this level of aggravation?

Talia shook her head, finally turning her gaze back toward her prisoner. The disheveled man stood at the end of the gangplank that Sirena and her soldiers had fixed in place.

She did have a hint as to what was going on along the coast of New Caledonia. Actually more than a hint. Her father's spies, now her eyes and ears, had given her an excellent perspective on the machinations that involved Captain Blackbeard and his conspirators.

But for her to move forward with the plan that she had in mind, to gain the allies who would be critical to her success, she needed confirmation about her suspicions. Hard evidence. Once she got that, she could proceed.

Captain Blackbeard was in the best position to answer her questions. Despite his protestations, he would tell her what she needed to know. Very soon. Whether he wanted to or not. He just didn't know it yet.

"How long have you been working for Hakea Roosarian?"

"You been drinking, lassie? I work for myself. I wouldn't work for a woman."

"Then why were you with her when she visited me after my father's murder?"

"I don't know what you're talking about, lassie," answered Captain Blackbeard, dismissing her comment as a fantasy, though failing to hide his rapidly developing concern as his eyes tightened ever so slightly. "You must have mistaken me with someone else, your grief getting in the way of your sight."

Talia nodded, expecting just such a response. "It would be hard to forget you, Captain Blackbeard, even with my grief. Your beard is a dead giveaway, but it's your stench that really is most memorable. Do you swim in your bilge or is it just your natural odor?"

Talia's comment drew several guffaws and chuckles from the soldiers and sailors standing on the deck. She ignored them, however, her eyes never leaving her prisoner, watching his face instead.

Captain Blackbeard understood the position he was in now. That she knew more about him than he thought possible, the problem being that he didn't know exactly what she knew. So he needed to be very careful.

He was trying to hide his growing discomfort and failing miserably. Talia could see it in his eyes. Every one of his more frequent gulps confirmed for her that he was exactly the right person to speak with about the many topics at the top of her mind.

"You're wasting my time, Captain Blackbeard. We all know that you work with Hakea Roosarian. Why not admit it?"

"Why make it easy for you?" grumbled Blackbeard sullenly, some of his bravado leaving him. "Though I'm not answering your question. I don't work for Hakea Roosarian, so you can stop asking. Never have, never will."

"You've got the last part right at least. Not anymore," Talia murmured quietly, though everyone on deck heard her, a low chuckle working its way through the assembled crew. For the first time, Talia saw Captain Blackbeard's nervousness become something more, his eyes turning slightly wild, his hands shaking despite his best efforts to control them.

"What do you mean by that?" asked the now much more worried Captain Blackbeard.

"I'm sure you'll figure it out when the time is right," replied Talia cryptically. "Sooner than you think, actually."

"Now you listen here, lassie. I've got three more ships coming this way. I suggest that you leave my men and me be and skedaddle while you can. Because when they get here and the roles are reversed and I've got you standing on a length of wood with a watery grave beneath your feet, I won't be very forgiving."

"You mean the three ships that docked under false colors at Rosecrea?" asked Talia, her tone suggesting that she was bored. "The same ships that were supposed to rendezvous with you a little farther down the coast?"

"How did you know about ..." Captain Blackbeard stopped himself before he said too much, grimacing, realizing that he had given her the reaction she had wanted from him.

Talia smiled, knowing exactly how what she just told him would hit the man where it hurt. He was all wind and no gristle.

Why Hakea Roosarian had picked him to lead this small flotilla was beyond her. She could tell that Blackbeard did well when he had all the advantages and could lord it over his captives and his crew.

As soon as she had taken that position of authority from him, he had begun to shrink in on himself. His shoulders squeezing together. His back hunching. His mannerisms uncertain, fearful. The transformation had been interesting to watch, and she was more than happy to make use of it for her own purposes.

"Those three ships are at the bottom of the ocean, as are most of their crews. They made the mistake of trying to fight. Admirable, I guess," said Talia, although her tone insinuated that they had made a foolish mistake. "Still, the wrong decision on their part. We left the dead to the deep. The few survivors were dealt with in another way. You and your men will be joining them if you continue to prove difficult."

Talia didn't offer any more details beyond that, not feeling the need to enlighten her prisoner, allowing his own imagination to do the work for her.

"That's not possible. Those three ships had almost two hundred soldiers among them ..."

Captain Blackbeard stopped himself again. This infuriating young woman kept offering him one surprise on top of another, and because of that he couldn't seem to keep his mouth shut.

"Why protect her?" Talia wondered. "You owe her nothing. She can do nothing to you out here. I, on the other hand, can do whatever I deem necessary to get what I want from you ... and I will."

Captain Blackbeard tried to regain control over the direction of the interrogation by offering what little swagger he had left.

"You're playing at something you don't understand. You won't get anything out of me. I'll always be a better man than you are, lassie."

Talia snorted then smiled at that. "I certainly hope so."

Her comment brought forth another round of laughter from the men and women watching the little drama play out, all of them clearly enjoying the game. They had observed much the same before and knew how it would end. Their Captain had a talent for this that they greatly appreciated.

They all understood what was happening, even though the pirate captain didn't appear to. Captain Blackbeard was already giving them good information, and he would be providing them with even better information.

The fool just didn't know it yet.

But he would, they knew, because they knew Captain Carlomin. And it wouldn't be long now, because she was tiring of the game.

"You're not man enough to be doing this," continued Blackbeard, although he began to stumble on his words, having suddenly picked up a stutter. "You should have one of your soldiers do your dirty work for you, because you're wasting your time and mine. You think you can make me talk, lassie?" The pirate captain tried to offer a deep laugh, but because of his rapidly rising anxiety as he watched how his captor's eyes changed, becoming harder with every word he said, it came out as nothing more than a squeak. "Little girls don't frighten me."

"I'm sure they don't," agreed Talia. "However, I am certain that my friends will frighten you, quite badly in fact."

Before Blackbeard could figure out what his captor meant by that, Talia nodded to the soldier standing with a spear where the gangplank met the ship's deck. He went into action immediately, stabbing with the sharp point. Not to harm, but rather to move.

Captain Blackbeard danced back to avoid the jab, realizing too late that he had very little space with which to maneuver.

At the same time, Sirena motioned toward the squad of soldiers standing with her. The men were holding a rope. As soon as the Captain of the Carlomin Guard gave the signal, they released their hold.

Captain Blackbeard was stunned to find that he was falling through the air. Too stunned, in fact, to even shout when he plummeted beneath the waves, swallowing a small barrel of water as he endeavored to get his head back above the surface with his hands lashed together with a leather strap and his feet tied together by the rope that ran over the yardarm just above the gangplank and now curled limply along the gentle crests.

When he finally pushed his head above the waves, Blackbeard choked and spluttered, gagging as he expelled the water that had found its way into his stomach. Once he had gotten himself back under control, with a panicky, jerky motion he started to spin himself around in the water, struggling frantically to remove with his teeth the leather strap tied around his hands while kicking out as best as he could with his bound legs, hoping that he might loosen the rope and somehow free himself.

"I wouldn't do that if I were you," called Talia, who stared down at him from the deck, still leaning lazily against the railing. The soldiers and sailors crowded around her, an anticipatory, almost hungry look in their eyes. "I doubt that you want to draw too much attention to yourself. Not with my friends in the water with you."

Captain Blackbeard's eyes widened as he began to realize the depth of his predicament, halting his frenetic motions instantly. He was too frightened to even turn his head. Soon he didn't have to, watching out of the corner of his eye as a very large fin cut through the waves no more than thirty feet away from him.

Another fin sliced through the water just ten feet to his left side, and a little farther out near where his two ships lay, just one mast sticking out of the water to mark where they had sunk beneath the waves, he glimpsed several more fins moving lazily through the water before dipping back beneath the surface and then reappearing again a few seconds later.

Judging by the fins, the smallest was probably twenty feet long. He didn't want to think about how big some of the others likely were.

Great whites. They had to be.

A sailor's nightmare.

The rational part of his mind briefly thought about why those beasts were spending so much time over by the entrance to the cove. The answer was quite obvious.

Many of his men didn't make it out of the ships before they went down. Easy pickings.

The less rational part of his mind could barely contain his paralyzing fear. He needed to get out of the water. Now!

"You might not be afraid of me," offered Talia. "But you will be. In the meantime, you can be afraid of them."

Blackbeard barely heard her words, his terror making it more and more difficult for him to think. There had to be a way to get out of this. But how?

For just an instant, he benefited from a much-needed clarity. There was no way to escape this death sentence on his own. She had him over a barrel.

Just then, the first shark that had swum right by his side a minute or so before came back at him from the other direction, the massive animal getting so close that if Blackbeard's hands were untied, he could have reached out and scraped his fingers along the beast's sandpapery skin.

He knew what the great whites were doing, particularly that one.

Testing him.

Waiting to see what he would do.

Wanting to find out if he was a threat or just easy meat.

That realization finally broke through the haze of fear and desperation that had clouded his mind.

"All right! All right! Just get me out! I'll tell you everything you want to know. Just get me out! Now!"

"But you've told me several times already that you don't know anything," challenged Talia, not appearing to be the least bit concerned that another of the great whites had begun to circle the pirate, this one even larger than the last.

It was only a matter of time before one of the creatures made a run at him. She knew that, and so did the pirate.

"Don't play with me, lassie. Not now! You've won, all right. You've won! Just get me out of the water. Please get me out of the water!"

Much to Blackbeard's consternation, the young woman didn't say a thing. She didn't even motion to her soldiers to do anything. She simply stared down at him with those unforgiving eyes of hers.

"Please!" shrieked Captain Blackbeard. "Please! Don't leave me here. Don't let me die like this. Please! I implore you."

Blackbeard continued to scream, beg, and plead, Talia ignoring it all. She turned her gaze away from the pirate, now following the very large fin slicing through the water that had come to investigate from where the two wrecks rested at the bottom of the cove, the other great whites clearing out of the way for the monster.

She smiled then, which worried Blackbeard even more. Seeing that she was looking at whatever was behind him, he twisted around, his face white with fear.

"No, no, no, no, no," he began to say as the shark cut around him tightly before curling back toward him.

The largest of the great whites apparently had decided that it had little to worry about from him. The huge animal, at least thirty five feet long, now swam right toward him at an incredible speed.

"Please!" yelled Blackbeard, tugging on the rope that he had gathered between his hands and realizing that there was no tension in it, the cord still floating on the surface. They were going to leave him here to die. "Please! I'll tell you anything you want to know! Don't leave me here! Please!"

Talia ignored Blackbeard, the man in tears, his expression terror-stricken. Instead, she waited, wanting to time what she had in mind exactly right, the great white now surging toward the helpless pirate.

At the very last second, she nodded.

With a hard yank, the soldiers responsible for the line pulled Blackbeard up and out of the water. The huge great white, jaws opened, sharp teeth glistening, eyes covered with its protective, clear membranes as it anticipated biting into its prey, instead gnashed its teeth together in frustration as it caught nothing but water down its very large gullet.

Blackbeard shuddered with relief even as he hung upside down, dangling in the air, laughing hysterically, not quite believing that he had just escaped such a horrific death.

"You made the right decision …"

Then with a yelp, Blackbeard dropped back down, the soldiers releasing the line until the pirate was headfirst just above the water, his long hair extending down to touch the gentle waves.

"What are you doing?" screamed Blackbeard, no longer able to control his terror after his close encounter with the great white.

Talia looked at Sirena and her soldiers. She had thought

that after the pirate's first encounter with the great white, she could conduct the interrogation on board their ship with little difficulty. It seemed that the Captain of the Carlomin Guard had a different idea in mind, and it was one with which Talia had little cause to argue. So she smiled, then shrugged, liking how her Captain thought.

For almost an hour, Blackbeard hung just above the water, the great whites circling slowly around the cove, not demonstrating much interest in the man, although every once in a while one of the beasts would swim by for a closer look. As a result, the infamous Captain Blackbeard now had no qualms whatsoever about revealing his connection to Hakea Roosarian and providing whatever information he could to the young woman who had yet to demonstrate a single ounce of mercy.

When she had gotten every last piece of intelligence that she thought Blackbeard could give her, Talia stared down at the man for quite some time.

She was pleased. She had gained the knowledge that she wanted. She could use what she had learned in ways both obvious and less so.

Yet even though she obtained what she needed, that didn't reduce the level of difficulty she faced in putting her larger plan into play. Hakea Roosarian was a dangerous foe with a great many resources at her disposal. Many of which, Talia was sure, she still wasn't aware of.

Her greatest fear was that once she challenged the Governor of Fal Carrach directly, she might face some surprises of her own. Talia didn't like surprises, unless she was the one setting them in motion. She would need to do what she could to ensure that didn't happen.

"Into the drink, Captain Carlomin?"

Sirena, who commanded the squad of men holding the line that kept their prisoner just above the gentle waves of the cove, and the predators just beneath the surface, had a hopeful look on her face. She had lost her husband to men like Captain Blackbeard. She had no sympathy for him or the other pirates taken.

In her mind, there was only one solution for men such as these. A slice of steel across the throat or, if circumstances permitted, as they did now, an even more gruesome death.

"You can't," pleaded Captain Blackbeard. "Please, you can't! It was business. Just business!"

Talia thought about Sirena's request for quite some time, seemingly unconcerned when the rope dropped a few feet and her prisoner had to contort his body awkwardly to keep his head out of the water, the sharks cruising slowly through the cove now curling toward this new, interesting stimulus. She ignored Blackbeard's continued begging, the supposedly fearsome pirate now blubbering like a frightened child.

She could agree to Sirena's request. It would give her Captain a great deal of pleasure to gain this small measure of revenge, as it would her as well.

When she finally made her decision, she noticed for the first time that one of the larger great whites, this hungry animal with a fin that rose at least five feet out of the gentle waves, had turned right for Blackbeard.

The great white wasn't being aggressive, at least not yet. It was just curious, so she watched the scene play out.

The massive shark swam right past the dangling man, its rough skin scraping across the terrified pirate's brow. The close call with the shark left the prisoner gibbering in fear as a trickle of blood began to drip into the water, the cut above his eye open again. Because of that, Blackbeard knew that it wouldn't be long before the other sharks circling in the cove took more of an interest in him.

Yes, she could agree to Sirena's request. It would be an easy thing to do. Maybe even enjoyable. And her Captain would appreciate it.

But she couldn't make her decisions based on what she wanted. She had to make her decisions based on what she needed.

"Pull him up and lock him away with the others," Talia said. "We might have a use for the notorious Captain Blackbeard in the future. And if not, we can feed him to the sharks later."

5

SLICING THROUGH THE WAVES

"They're coming back!" shouted Davin.

He had climbed back to his preferred spot in the crow's nest, wanting to get a better view of what was around them. The gladiator didn't appear to be concerned in the least by how drastically the mast he was clinging to swayed in response to the turbulent wind.

Davin had hoped that their and the Griffons' efforts had convinced the Bakunawa to halt their chase, the oncoming storm toward which they raced potentially serving as another deterrent. It wasn't to be, however.

The two Bakunawa demonstrated a tenacity that reminded him of his many encounters with the Ghoules.

Never stopping. Driven to kill. Driven to feed. No matter the cost.

From his perch he could see that this time the two sea dragons weren't coming at them from the rear. Instead, they had adopted a new approach.

Swimming ahead of them, their long, sinuous bodies powered the Bakunawa gracefully through the increasingly choppy waves.

Thanks to their determination, the beasts had reached a point where they could turn back toward the ship and come at it from both sides. As they had done before, they took the perfect angle to split the *Freedom* in two if they hit at the same time.

Davin had to admire their tactics and intelligence, even though it was being applied against him and his friends. These Bakunawa wanted to achieve their kill before they lost the opportunity in the onrushing storm.

A smart move on their part, he had to admit. He just hated the fact that these crafty beasts had chosen the *Freedom* as their target.

Still, that gave them a chance. Get into the storm before the Bakunawa took them below and then they'd only have to go up against a raging sea.

"Seven hundred yards!" Davin called out over the roar of the wind, tracking the sea dragons' approach as best as he could, exerting just as much effort following the beasts as making sure that the wild swaying of the mizzenmast didn't expel him from the crow's nest. "Six hundred!"

The Blood Company moved to both side railings. Several lost their balance over just that short distance as the massive vessel started to buck more ferociously in response to the waves surging toward them, the smallest now cresting at more than forty feet in height.

Despite that difficulty, the fallen gladiators persevered, pushing themselves back to their feet and joining their comrades, preparing for what appeared to be an inevitable and defining clash.

Bryen stood on the helm, listening closely to Davin's updates, keeping his eyes on the onrushing Bakunawa coming toward the port side, knowing from Davin's shouts and the increasing murmurs of Dorlan, Kollea, and his friends at the starboard railing that much the same was happening on that side of the vessel.

The sea dragons had trapped them. Crafty beasts.

He couldn't allow the Bakunawa to crash into the ship. The *Freedom* was a colossal vessel, larger than any two merchant ships combined. Even so, it wasn't strong enough to survive a concentrated hit by two very angry sea dragons.

But what to do?

Very few options came to mind. The ice that he and Aislinn had put in place the first time they had faced this challenge had worked quite well to hinder the Bakunawa, and it might work again. Although he doubted it.

At the speed the beasts were tearing through the waves, he and Aislinn likely would need to form twice as much ice that was twice as thick as they did the last time to have any chance of keeping the beasts from taking the *Freedom* to the bottom of the sea.

With little time to work, the animals only a few hundred yards away and closing frighteningly fast, the Burnt Ocean roiling worse than a boiling kettle, they had to try some other maneuver to have any hope of success.

Maybe that was it, Bryen mused. Maybe his thinking of a boiling kettle gave him the answer that he had been looking for.

"Remember what we did to cross the Boiling Lake and get to the Cauldron?" Bryen asked Rafia and Aislinn, the two Magii standing with him, both gripping tightly to the rails so they didn't lose their feet.

"You mean after you so foolishly jumped onto the Ghoules' skiff?" asked Aislinn, her tone calm, even as her eyes sparked, reminding him that she still wasn't happy that he had taken such a terrible risk.

"Yes, right after I so foolishly jumped onto the Ghoules' skiff," he replied, trying to sound contrite. With the look

Aislinn gave him upon hearing his response, he didn't think his veiled apology had much of an effect on her.

"A good idea," nodded Rafia, choosing to ignore the tension between the two. Now wasn't the time. "Are you ready, Aislinn?"

"We need to turn!" warned Captain Gregson, feet spread, braced on the deck. He and Emelina both held the wheel that rarely wanted to listen to them now as they fought to keep the ship on course.

"Stay on this track! If we turn, we don't avoid the beasts!"

"If we don't turn," argued Captain Gregson, hoping that Bryen could hear him over the shrieking wind, "we're done for!"

"If we turn, we're done for!" countered Bryen. "We'll be steering right into one of the beasts, and then the other Bakunawa will slam into the stern. Stay on course!"

"Are you mad? If we do that …"

"Trust me, Captain! Maintain our course! As steady as you can! We'll take care of the rest!"

Captain Gregson cursed under his breath. Nevertheless, despite his misgivings, he did as the Protector bid him.

Because the lad was right, even though he didn't want to admit it. Only one path to safety lay open to them. Unfortunately, that path was closing much too swiftly.

"Three hundred yards!" roared Davin, both enjoying and dreading the race that they were in.

"Ready, Rafia?" asked Bryen.

"Two hundred yards!"

"I am," the Magus replied calmly. "Aislinn?"

"One hundred yards!" shouted the gladiator from the crow's nest, his voice containing a bit too much excitement for Declan's taste, the Sergeant of the Blood Company struggling across the deck and up onto the helm to join them.

"Yes, ready," replied the Lady of the Southern Marches, as both she and Rafia took hold of the Talent.

"Use just as much as we discussed, otherwise we run the risk of tearing the sails from the masts."

Aislinn nodded in response to Rafia's reminder, understanding exactly what she needed to do.

"Fifty yards!" Davin's hint of excitement now, finally, had been joined by a tinge of fear.

"Rafia," began Declan, his voice revealing his concern as he realized what the Magus was going to do and fearing that she had waited too long.

"Twenty five yards!"

"Now!" cried Rafia.

At the same time she and Aislinn sent a potent burst of energy into the *Freedom's* sails, the huge vessel jumping forward and shooting several hundred yards ahead in just a heartbeat.

They barely escaped the Bakunawa's charge, but escape it they did.

And just in time, the two sea dragons missing the vessel by only a few feet. Unable to slow their progress, they slammed into each other with a bone-crunching force that could be heard over the howl of the oncoming tempest, the beasts' long bodies unavoidably wrapping around the other.

The collision drew cheers from the Blood Company, though they knew that the show wasn't over yet. They lifted their eyes toward the speck in the sky that was steadily growing larger.

As the sinuous sea dragons struggled to untangle themselves, Lycia swooped down on the back of Arabella. The Griffon tried to give her rider as smooth a flight as possible, although it was difficult as Arabella had to fight against the shrieking wind.

The gladiator threw her spear with her left hand, the sharp point glowing brightly, Bryen having infused it with the Talent.

Lycia didn't know if it was luck, skill, or Bryen's use of the Talent. Perhaps it was all three. Honestly, she didn't care. She was just pleased with the result she achieved.

Even with the powerful gusts of the approaching storm threatening to force Lycia's Griffon into the surging sea, her spear flew straight and true through the air, the sizzling steel piercing one of the tangled Bakunawa's eyes.

The monster's terrible screech of torment rose above the roar of the wind, setting many of the gladiators' teeth on edge. They suffered through the discomfort, thrilled that the Crimson Devil had nailed the target.

The wounded sea dragon struggled to dislodge the spear, twisting and turning in a pain-filled rage. Unsuccessful, the Bakunawa unwrapped itself from its brethren and dove back beneath the waves. The beast was done with the chase, thinking only of how to extract the steel that had blinded it in one eye.

Instead of whooping with joy at her success, Lycia almost swallowed her tongue. Arabella swerved wildly from one side to the other, then dove toward the waves before pumping her wings furiously to gain more altitude.

The Griffon almost left it too late, the cold touch of the cresting ocean kissing her paws and giving Arabella an added incentive to get back into the air.

The other Bakunawa, thinking that she might be distracted, had lunged for Lycia, its gaping maw missing her and Arabella by no more than the length of a feather. If not for her Griffon's sudden change in direction, they'd both be sliding down the animal's gullet.

"Let's head for the ship," said Lycia, Arabella turning for the *Freedom* after finally gaining a few hundred more feet in height.

Lycia wanted to get Arabella back down to the relative safety of the deck before the massive front rushing in from the south consumed them. Rather than taking a direct path, Arabella curled widely around, attempting to use the powerful gusts to her advantage.

Lycia breathed a sigh of relief. It looked like they were going to make it, and just in time. Feeling more in control, she finally took a few seconds to congratulate herself and Arabella for their success.

Another Bakunawa forced out of the hunt with what she would readily admit was a lucky throw. But lucky would do.

Even better, she believed that her taking a Bakunawa out of the fight with her throw trumped her brother striking that Echidna that had been about to kill Bryen in the Lost Land. She was looking forward to having that argument with him as soon as she returned to the *Freedom*.

Just then, the gladiator was jolted from her thoughts as Arabella dove to the left, then curled tightly back to the right. Lycia's guts twisted around her stomach as a stream of ice streaked through the air right behind her.

That frigid spray followed them through the air as Arabella cut and curled in the sky. The Griffon allowed the gusty blasts to take her where they wanted, giving her the speed that she needed to pull away from the furious sea dragon that had tried to catch them unawares. Finally, after several very tense seconds, they left behind the Bakunawa, the monster unable to keep up with them.

Lycia rubbed the feathers along Arabella's jaw in gratitude, grateful that the Griffon had been paying attention. Because she hadn't been, instead becoming foolishly enamored with her lucky throw.

She owed the Griffon a debt. Without Arabella's awareness that they weren't yet out of danger, they both would have ended up in the watery deep.

"Thank you, Arabella!" shouted Lycia, trying to be heard over the deafening roar of the wind. "Back to the ship! As fast as you can!"

Arabella screeched in agreement, not bothering to seek any additional height now, the intensifying blasts of air making it too difficult to climb. Instead, the Griffon banked back toward the left, hoping to glide just above the waves and then drop right over the rail before the gusts became too much for her.

Lycia's eyes tearing because of the cutting wind, she looked over her shoulder. The gladiator desperately hoped that they would make it back to the ship. Because she was certain that the last Bakunawa wasn't done with them yet.

She watched as the largest of the sea dragons caused a massive froth on the surface of the ocean, its huge tail flicking from side to side.

The monster was beginning its pursuit once again, uncaring of the howling wind and driving rain that churned the Burnt Ocean into a maelstrom. Caring only for the prey that sought to escape it.

∼

"I CAN'T BELIEVE you convinced me to do this," muttered Captain Gregson. Still standing at the wheel with his wife, he ignored the rain that felt like pinpricks on his skin as well as the bursts of icy sea spray that blasted up over the bow and covered the deck in a slick wash of seawater that at times made him wonder if they were sailing below the surface rather than above.

The *Freedom* was caught within the leading edge of the storm now with no chance of escape, the blasts of wind threatening to tear the sails off the masts. His visibility was governed by the sheets of rain that pounded against the deck like a hammer on an anvil, and the ship creaked dangerously as it rose above and fell over the towering waves that surged toward it in a never-ending rush.

If he had a choice, he wouldn't be here in the first place. But he didn't, thanks to those blasted Bakunawa.

As a result, the Captain's sole focus was on fighting the pull of the sea and keeping the bow of his ship centered on the waves cascading toward him. He understood that if he missed the mark even by just the smallest of margins, one of these thumping waves would catch the vessel amidships and sweep right over them, guaranteeing them all a gruesome death when the ship capsized.

"It was our only choice, Captain," replied Bryen, who stood right next to him, a hand on the helm so that he wouldn't be swept away by the wind, rain, and froth.

Most of the Blood Company had gone belowdecks, wanting to get out of the storm and out of the way of the brave sailors who scrambled across the sails and rigging despite the gale-force winds and blasts of lightning that seemed to crack closer and closer to the ship with every strike.

"I know, lad," grumbled the Captain, "but that doesn't mean I have to like it."

Bryen smiled at that, not feeling the need to respond. In many ways Captain Gregson was just like Declan. The more difficult the situation, the grouchier he got. Yet even in the worst of times, he always remained focused on the task at hand, never shrinking in the face of a threat, instead always rising to the challenge.

"Anything else you or the other Magii can do about this last devil?" asked Captain Gregson.

They had escaped two of the beasts. Only one remained. Much to their regret, this one was the largest of the three and the most determined, and it was gaining on them despite the raging sea.

The Bakunawa kept its head down and swam right through the towering waves, intent on its catch, its colossal wake visible in the seething ocean.

"We'll figure something out, Captain. Have no fear."

However, even as he sought to belay Captain Gregson's concerns, Bryen was worried. With the powerful storm, using ice or heat as he and Aislinn had done before would offer little value, the churning water preventing either application.

And trying to strike the Bakunawa directly with the Talent, what most would think would be an easy task because of its massive size, was just as much of a challenge.

The water surging around the beast helped to shield it, diffusing any attacks with the natural magic before they could do any real damage to their pursuer. Assuming, of course, that they could even hit their target from aboard a ship that was bucking like a wild stallion.

Much to her annoyance, Rafia had experienced that reality firsthand. She had missed more often than not, her streaks of power flying wildly in every direction. And every one of the bolts of energy she threw at the beast that actually was on target fizzled out across the waves before coming into contact with the Bakunawa's hardened scales, which easily dealt with what little energy remained.

For now, they would have to focus on defending themselves and their ship, and while they were doing that hopefully some other idea for either discouraging or killing the beast would come to mind.

Already aggravated because of her failure to hold off the massive sea creature, Rafia took the lead now, doing much as Sirius did when defending Haven from the Ghoule Overlord. She used the Talent to pull up the seawater from along the hull of the ship, creating a liquid shield that solidified in an instant.

Rafia clapped her hands and shouted in pleasure when the Bakunawa slammed right into the barrier. Once, twice, and then a third time.

Despite the strain of using so much of the Talent, the Magus kept the shield right behind the *Freedom* as the vessel raced up and down the waves.

The Bakunawa reluctantly halted its progress after its third attempt to get past the strange wall. Roaring in rage, it dipped its massive head beneath the surface, its sinuous body quickly disappearing from view.

"Where is it?" asked Rafia, who stood right next to Aislinn and Declan at the stern. The three had clambered down from the helm, all of them holding tightly to the railing so that they wouldn't be knocked into the sea by the lather rushing across the deck.

"I can't see it," said Declan, struggling to locate anything in the pounding rain, their world turned a dark grey by the storm that was only illuminated by the much-too-frequent blasts of lightning.

"It's staying with us beneath the waves," said Aislinn, tracking the sea dragon with the Talent. "No, it's catching up. It's coming at us faster." Aislinn pointed to a spot just a hundred yards behind them. "There!"

Just a second later the Bakunawa launched itself out of the water, the gargantuan animal appearing to take flight.

Rafia tried to increase the height of her shield, but she was too slow and the sea dragon was too fast.

The Bakunawa soared over the watery barrier and then splashed down just a few hundred feet behind them. Refusing to give up the chase, the sea dragon cut through the surging waves, its icy blue eyes sparkling with anticipation and hunger as it opened its gaping maw, preparing to pull itself up onto the back of the ship.

Spheres of energy danced across Rafia and Aislinn's palms, the two Magii ready to do whatever they could to stop the beast. All the while they knew that their chances of success were slim at best against the dogged sea dragon.

"Hold!" shouted Declan, who stared in shock at a sight that he had never expected to see during a battle against such a beast. "What is that fool boy doing?"

Distracted, the Bakunawa had turned its massive head to the right for just a second, slowing its attack.

A piece of wood strapped to his feet and a long rope wrapped around his waist that he held tightly in his hand, Davin surfed right next to the sea dragon.

When Davin jumped from the crow's nest and got past the shock of the freezing sea, he stayed beneath the waves, allowing the rushing water to pull him back behind the ship. He didn't try to kick himself above the surface until he felt the rope go taut.

He picked his moment to get above the waves perfectly, leaning back against the rush of water, getting his board in front of him, then nudging the top above the surface.

It was a struggle, though not unanticipated. Somehow, he had actually succeeded in doing it on the first try, which he viewed as a small victory in and of itself because of how rough the surf was.

Gasping for air now that his head was above the waves, on the third try, he found his balance, lifting himself out of the water. He was thankful to have the benefit of being in a fairly calm trough in that moment, although the next wave was coming toward him much too quickly.

He hadn't bothered to congratulate himself on his success. He still had a good deal more to do.

He had trailed behind the ship, careful to keep the front of the board clear of the surface, knowing what would happen if he failed to do so. All the while he fought to keep himself steady because of the strain of the pull and the froth beneath him, taking solace in one aspect of his foolishness that had played out in his favor.

The Bakunawa was completely unaware of his presence, Davin staying in the massive sea creature's blind spot.

Understanding that the gusty wind would probably keep his words from his friends, still, he felt the need to try as he yelled as loud as he could toward the stern deck and pointed with the hand that somehow still grasped his spear.

"The belly!"

Davin could only hope that Bryen and the others heard him. That done, now he needed to focus on the task he had set for himself.

Killing a Bakunawa.

Gripping the haft of his spear tightly, he bent his left knee just enough to tilt the board toward the sea dragon, spear poised at his shoulder, exactly as Declan had taught him.

Davin smiled broadly. Bryen must have seen him, because his spearpoint was glowing brightly. Now all he needed to do was hit his target, which shouldn't be much of a problem since the beast's eye was as large as an archery target.

Nevertheless, he understood that he was only going to get one chance at this and with the next wave about to crash down on him, now was the time to take his shot.

Lining up right behind the sea dragon's eye, he stabbed with his spear, a short sharp punch that the creature wouldn't be able to see until his steel was embedded in its brain.

His luck, which had been with him since he had jumped from the crow's nest, fled at the very last second.

When he turned to the side, he made a critical error. He pushed the front of his board down with his foot, twisting his hips, the carved wood no longer riding cleanly through the water.

About to lose his balance, Davin struggled to stay on his feet while at the same time jabbing at the Bakunawa's eye.

That small jolt of movement was enough to throw off his aim, the glowing steel slicing across the scales around the sea dragon's brow rather than punching through its ice blue orb.

Getting himself back under control, Davin was about to try again when he realized the precariousness of his situation. What he had thought was a good idea, leaping off the crow's nest with the board strapped to his feet so that he could surf behind the ship and potentially have a go at their pursuer, was quickly becoming a bad one.

He had lost the element of surprise with nothing to show for it. The Bakunawa had eyes only for him. And he was about to take a tumble into the sea.

Muttering in disgust, Davin crashed face first into the water, the wave that smashed down on him pushing him more than twenty feet beneath the surface. He held his breath for as long as he could, fearing that he wouldn't be able to get his head back above the waves.

Desperate for air, right before he was about to swallow the sea, he popped back to the surface thanks to the buoyancy of his board.

Davin cursed his bad luck. He couldn't believe he had missed. He had been so close.

The burn of the hemp rope digging into his arm as it pulled him in the wake of the *Freedom* returned his focus to his current predicament, his failure no longer his primary concern. As the cord dug into his flesh, cutting into his skin, Davin did his best to ignore the pain.

He regretted not having the time to put on the leather guard that he had been playing with when he had practiced his new and clearly yet to be mastered skill. But he really didn't have any time for regrets.

Needing to get himself out of the water, he spent the next few seconds pushing himself back up so that he was in the position that he needed to be so that once again he was on his board and he had some control over his movements as the ship dragged him through the Burnt Ocean.

Then he was down again, choking on seawater.

He cursed again. Silently as the froth surged around him.

He had put too much pressure on the front of the board, pushing it into the water and, as a result, flipping himself through the air to land hard on his back, the rope around his wrist almost yanking his arm from his shoulder socket.

The breath knocked from his lungs, he stayed where he was for a few seconds as the ship pulled him through the waves, thinking of how he might be able to get his board back beneath him swiftly. Because if he didn't he was going to drown.

Deciding to try something new before he ran out of time, he twisted on his back and, in the same motion, righted himself, using the rope to pull himself back up so that he was upright on his board.

Davin couldn't believe it. It worked! And just in time.

Then he was down beneath the surface again, though this time of his own choice as a massive wave threatened to crest right over him. He knew that he wouldn't have been able to handle the power of the frothing breaker.

Once more, he gasped for air, having just a heartbeat to take a breath before he dove beneath the monstrous wave.

He tried to get back above the water several times after that. Yet each time either another wave crashed down on him or he misjudged his timing.

Black spots beginning to form around the edges of his vision, having no doubt that if he didn't succeed this time, he was as good as dead, on his fourth attempt he did it.

Twisting around as he had done before and forcing the board beneath him, he lifted himself up, using the rope to aid him. Keeping his legs bent, he gulped down the salty air that tasted so sweet.

Davin was so excited by his success that he lost his concentration for a moment, almost committing the same mistake that had sent him into the ocean twice before.

He caught himself just in time, twisting his hips and bending his knees to move to the left rather than pressing down on the front of the board.

Davin whooped in triumph. He did it! He was still alive.

For how much longer, however, was anyone's guess, because it was then that reality struck him a terrible and demoralizing blow.

He was riding swells that were forty or more feet in height while being dragged behind a massive ship with a storm about to vent its full fury upon him.

To say nothing of the very large and very angry sea dragon that swam right behind him now, nipping at his board.

～

"What is that fool boy doing?" demanded Declan. "He should know better than this."

"He's trying to help," said Bryen.

"By offering himself as a snack to the Bakunawa?" wondered Declan incredulously. "When I drag him out of the ocean, he and I are going to have a very long conversation."

"What did Davin say?" asked Aislinn, having just as hard a time believing what she was seeing as Declan was.

Bryen stared behind them, the *Freedom* struggling a bit more now to cut through the surging waves that were gaining height, the Bakunawa facing less of a challenge as it charged through the breakers and crept steadily closer. Despite the obvious and terribly large threat, he was more worried for his friend.

Unfortunately, the fact that Davin had leapt off the crow's nest and was now riding a wooden board right in front of the snapping teeth of a Bakunawa wasn't too difficult for Bryen to believe. Davin was known for taking risks that no one else would.

For just a flash, Bryen's heart dropped into his stomach. He had lost sight of his friend in the crash of a wave right behind them. Thankfully, Davin reappeared as soon as the crest collapsed.

Bryen breathed a sigh of relief. It looked like Davin was going to stay up on his board at least for a little while longer.

What did Davin scream at them?

That was a good question.

When just a moment later the Bakunawa rose up over a wave and crashed back down with a terrific splash, Bryen had it.

"The belly. He wants us to try for the belly."

"Just like the black dragons," said Declan, his voice incorporating a level of respect for the young man being dragged behind their ship that hadn't been there before.

Now they all understood. An excellent idea on Davin's part. Even so, there were no guarantees that they would get their shot.

Bryen watched intently, worried, waiting, ready for what might be their only chance to stop this monstrous animal, just as much fearing for his friend's life.

He cringed each time Davin tumbled into the water, trying to will his friend to get back up, his heart starting again every time he did.

At the same time, Bryen looked for the opportunity that the Bakunawa might never give him as the beast stayed partially submerged within the water during its chase.

When Davin missed with his spear, Bryen groaned inwardly. And then he grinned devilishly.

Davin had missed his target, but he had angered the sea dragon. That anger might give him the opportunity that he, Rafia, and Aislinn were looking for.

∽

Davin grinned maniacally as he rode his long board through the waves. He was loving every second of this adventure. Even with the sea monster right behind him. Even though he felt as if he had drunk the entire ocean because of his many falls.

The danger only made it more exciting. More worthwhile.

The screech of anger from no more than a few dozen yards behind him that set his teeth on edge forced him to refocus and acknowledge the severity of his current challenge. The Bakunawa was right at his back, having eyes only for him.

He could understand why, having taken a particular pleasure in the fact that he had managed to wound the sea dragon, a long gash above the beast's eye spilling blood down its brow.

But that strike hadn't stopped the beast. It only angered the sea dragon, which was clearly determined to catch its attacker, getting closer and closer to the back of Davin's board with every swish of its massive tail through the water.

It wouldn't be long now before the Bakunawa would be able to rise out of the ocean and take him in one bite. Something that he wanted to avoid at all costs.

Davin thought about that for a moment. Maybe that wasn't such a bad idea after all. It might be their only chance, in fact.

As he had learned on the streets of Tintagel and then in the Pit, such was the way of the world.

Assuming his new role as bait, something with which he had much too much experience, Davin began to swerve through the waves.

Carefully. Very carefully.

He couldn't afford to fall now, so he bent his left knee and then his right, never flexing too much, getting into a comfortable rhythm that allowed him to ride the waves with greater confidence.

The whole time, the Bakunawa stayed right with him, twisting its long body just so, its massive jaws drawing ever closer.

Obviously, the ship was a concern for later. The sea dragon wanted him first.

Davin viewed that development, which would have terrified most anyone else, in a positive light.

About to curl back toward the right, Davin's eyes widened. A wave larger than any he had faced so far was forming directly in front of him.

Not knowing what else to do, he straightened out, riding right up the wave and then flying off the crest.

Davin dropped his spear while he was in the air, grabbing onto the rope with both hands, pulling his knees into his chest, hoping that what he planned to do actually worked. When the board beneath his feet slammed back down onto the water after he had remained in the air for much longer than he ever had before, for just a second, he thought that he was going back into the drink, his left hip drifting too far to the side.

He didn't as he recovered quickly. He kept his balance and his board on top of the sea.

He couldn't stop smiling. Now he was really impressed with himself, having known that if he fell and got dragged behind the ship, he would never have gotten back up, instead becoming a tasty appetizer for the Bakunawa.

When the sea dragon lunged for him as he shot out into the air, the Bakunawa missed him, admittedly by no more than the length of his lost spear.

It would have been a tremendous sight to behold as he looked back over his shoulder, the beast leaping over the crest of the wave and smashing down into the trough with a huge splash, slipping back beneath the water before surfacing right behind him again, if the Bakunawa's dexterity hadn't chilled his heart.

He could only hope that his friends had heard him and that they were ready. Because he sensed that this might be his last and only chance to give them the opening that they needed.

Knowing exactly what he was going to do, Davin began to swerve again, curling away from the beast, the Bakunawa continuing to follow him. Davin's pattern through the waves actually was slowing him down.

But that was part of his plan. He wanted the Bakunawa to stay with him, to be focused solely on him.

When he saw another huge wave rising to his front, Davin knew that this was his opportunity. With a dig of his left hip and knee, he cut right behind the ship, Davin riding to the top of the cresting wave and then launching himself through the air.

He could sense the looming presence behind him. He could feel the Bakunawa's jaws opening wide, its massive teeth that were longer than his legs snapping closed around him.

Then he saw the flashes of bright white light streaking right past him, no more than a few feet to either side, the heat scorching hot.

Davin couldn't look behind him, knowing that if he did he would miss his landing and once again drop back beneath the surface of the Burnt Ocean. Yet he didn't have to in order to comprehend the result of his effort.

The shriek of terrible agony that resonated through his body told him everything that he needed to know.

The Bakunawa was dead.

Bryen or one of the other Magii had done it.

A simple smile of relief graced his features. The threat from the sea dragons was no more.

Still, his worry remained because even with the sea dragon no longer breathing down his neck, he faced another challenge. And in his mind, one just as important as escaping the Bakunawa.

How to get back onto the *Freedom* before they faced the full fury of the tempest in which they were caught.

6

ON THE RUN

Jakob stood in the fog, balancing on his toes, knees bent. He held his sword loosely with both hands.

Not nervous. Calm instead. Collected. Simply waiting.

Understanding that in that moment he exercised little control over the situation.

He couldn't act. He could only react.

Knowing that he needed to be ready.

Knowing what was going to come next.

Just not knowing when.

With that thought guiding him, he searched for any sign that would reveal his opponent.

He couldn't see anything. He couldn't hear anything.

The thick grey haze placed him in a world that was only a few feet around. A world that put him at a distinct disadvantage.

It was frightening. Suffocating. And there was nothing that he could do about it.

He couldn't escape. He could only do what was necessary to survive.

And that meant allowing his instincts to rule rather than his reason.

Jakob pulled his right foot back in a flash, turning his body sideways. The Wraith's three-foot-long dagger, bone-white blades on both ends, cut through the fog right where he had been standing. He continued his motion, ducking, lifting his shoulder and bringing his sword up to catch the dagger on his steel, before stepping a few feet farther away.

This truly was a strange and unsettling world.

Even the sound of metal clashing was muted within the Murk. Just a ping rather than a loud clang.

What was even more disconcerting was how Jakob could still barely pick out his opponent from the billowing fog even though the Wraith stood no more than a few yards from him.

The ghostlike figure, who had been tracking him and his father since their escape from the Sergeant and his slavers, blended into the grey mist as if he were a part of it, the creature's spectral white flesh and light grey leather armor hiding him from view.

Maybe that was the way of it. Maybe the Wraith really was just a creation of the Murk.

Because all that Jakob could make out clearly was the creature's dagger and his hateful black eyes, the only color to be seen in this washed out environment.

Faster than a scorpion's tail, the Wraith darted forward, his steel seeking Jakob's gut.

He wasn't there to receive the fatal wound, spinning away and extending his sword, hoping that his blade might bite into the creature's flesh with a backhanded swing.

Disappointed but not surprised when instead his sword clanged off the Wraith's dagger, Jakob kept moving, dodging to the side, leaping backward, pivoting to his left, then to his right, rolling on a shoulder, then stepping in close before gliding out of the way, feeling more than seeing the Wraith's bone-white steel cut through the space where he had been just a heartbeat before.

Jakob understood that he was in a difficult position. The Wraith was faster than any other adversary he had fought before.

More relentless. More focused.

Perhaps most unnerving was the fact that the Wraith never made a sound. Not a grunt or a grimace or a cry.

Silent, just like the fog.

Jakob wanted to attack, to try to gain some space and regroup, but nothing that he tried worked. The Wraith stayed with him, tracking him through the fog, never more than just a few feet away, refusing to let him go.

The Wraith's first strike that scored him, a cut across his shoulder, brought a gasp of pain. A deep red blood welled up and ran down his arm.

He was numb to the second, third, and fourth slices across his chest and torso as he continued to glide through the Murk. He refused to allow his concentration to waver, knowing that if he permitted that to happen, one of the Wraith's excruciating cuts would be the very last thing he ever felt.

It was with that thought repeating through his mind that he realized he had made a terrible mistake. Jakob had thought that by coming in tight to the Wraith, he might be able to leave a few marks of his own on his adversary as a reminder that he wasn't easy meat.

But he wasn't fast enough. He'd never be fast enough.

Before he could even reach out with his sword, wanting to slice across the creature's ribs, the Wraith slammed into him with his shoulder, knocking Jakob off balance.

When he looked up again after finally finding his feet, he realized that his end had come.

Jakob was about to scream -- not in fear, rather in rage -- as he saw the sharp, double-bladed dagger about to slide across his throat.

"Jakob. Jakob!"

Dougal spoke quietly but insistently into Jakob's ear, not wanting to reveal their location to what might be hunting them. To that end, he shook his son's shoulder gently. That finally did it, bringing Jakob back to the world.

"You all right, lad?" asked Dougal. "Another bad dream, I take it."

Jakob nodded, pushing himself up to a sitting position. Tired, hungry, another headache greeting him, but none of that mattered. All that mattered was that he and his father were still alive.

"The dead?" his father asked in a weary voice, recalling what had plagued his son's slumber since they had escaped the slavers.

Dougal had seen a slaughter before. Too many, in fact. Because of that, he knew how to keep it locked away.

Jakob hadn't mastered that skill yet. Dougal was saddened that his son would be forced to do so.

"Not this time," Jakob replied. He didn't offer any more detail than that.

Actually, he was thankful that he dreamt of the Wraith. It broke the terrifying monotony of the last few nights.

Even so, a touch of worry settled within him. This was the first time the Wraith had come to him while he was sleeping. And it hadn't felt like a dream. It had felt real. Much, much too real.

Probably just a tired mind playing off his past experiences. Or could there be more to it?

Before he had started training with Aloysius, he would have assumed the former. Now, thanks to the Magus, he thought that the dream might have been more than a dream.

Perhaps it had been a warning.

Jakob shook his head in frustration as he pushed himself to his feet, standing next to his father as they both stared toward the east, watching the sun begin to lighten the grey sky, the Sea of Mist glimmering a few leagues in the distance.

The nightmares were worse than what he had just experienced. He would rather come face to face with the Wraith who had tracked him and his father out of the fog than have to deal with the faces of the dead.

Night after night the visions came. A constant reminder of the horror the creatures of the Murk brought with them.

As they hiked slowly through the Highlands, Jakob and his father hadn't seen the fog coming down from the north for almost a week. They were thankful for that respite, though still wary.

They both assumed that it wouldn't be long before the Murk and the dreadful creatures lurking within it returned.

What they had found during their journey toward the northeast had sickened them. Three large groups of slavers and their prisoners. More than one hundred people in all. Or rather what was left of them.

None had survived, the butchery fast, efficient, and stomach-churning. That's what gave Jakob the nightmares that inevitably disturbed the few hours of sleep he got each night.

The Wraiths slaughtered the people they stalked in the fog like animals taken to market. Neat, long slices from the daggers the creatures favored defaced each body. Usually across throats, sometimes the gut. Rarely any puncture wounds.

The Wraiths didn't need to. They came upon their prey silently, killing their quarry before they were even aware that they were being hunted.

There were a few extra cuts on some of the bodies. Forearms for the most part.

That revealed that some of the people had fought back, or

at least tried to defend themselves. It had done them little good other than to buy themselves a few extra seconds of life.

All of it was horrifying. However, the worst part were the slices across the bellies.

Some of those killing slashes had been pulled open by sharp claws, livers, kidneys, intestines, even a few hearts harvested.

Jakob could only imagine why, and he tried not to. His nightmares were bad enough as they were.

Each time they came across the remains of a party of slavers and prisoners, Jakob and Dougal had been quick with their inspection, not needing to spend much time examining what had happened. After the first massacre, there was little to learn from the others since they were so similar.

They needed to keep moving. They couldn't afford to be found in any place where they couldn't defend themselves. They didn't want to experience the same fate as each of the chain gangs, all of which had been caught out in the open.

Usually when they came upon those unfortunate souls, Jakob and his father spent only a few minutes looking for better weapons. They swapped out a few daggers at most.

Dougal had found a sword that he liked. When he realized that he couldn't swing it very well because of his injuries, he picked a scabbard out of the long grass and asked Jakob to carry the weapon across his back with his other blade.

It joined the one that Jakob had taken from the dead Sergeant for which he had yet to find a suitable replacement. It was a simple sword that Jakob had acquired when escaping from the slaver, but it was very well forged and it felt as if it had been made for him.

Dougal liked to think that in a matter of days he would be fit as a fiddle, blade in hand, a help rather than a hindrance to his son.

Jakob wasn't so sure. Still, he took the blade his father

wanted without argument, glad that it filled Dougal with just a little bit of hope. Because, at the moment, hope was in very short supply, as was any help they might require.

They had seen no one during the past week, and they could understand why. Jakob and Dougal had passed by a handful of farmsteads on their way toward the Northern Steppes.

All abandoned.

Two offered no evidence as to why the people had left. When they reached the third and then the others, the cause was quite obvious.

The front door for each one had been pulled from its hinges. That was the only sign of damage.

Walking into the small homes, nothing appeared to be out of place. It was as if the families had left for the day and would be back in time for supper.

Except for the stains of dried blood that splattered the floors and sometimes the walls, although those instances were rare.

Jakob was certain that the Wraiths had done this. It was the only explanation.

The Wraiths were very precise. The creatures that did this had left everything as it was, which in Jakob's opinion was much more frightening than what it would have looked like if the other monster they feared while hiking through the Highlands had murdered those families.

Stalkers.

They had heard a few roars and howls every few nights during their travels. Thankfully always from a good distance off.

Few people in the Highlands had ever seen the beasts. None had any desire to. They knew that just a glimpse likely meant that they were about to die. The monsters were very efficient killers and incredibly elusive.

Jakob had come up against one on that unfortunate night when he and his father were taken by the slavers.

They resembled humans in shape, although they were twice as large. The Stalker's razor-sharp claws and massively muscled torso were frightening, yet it was the blood-red eyes that did the most to chill his blood when he had fought one of the beasts.

He had no desire to come across one of those monsters again. Not with his father still struggling and barely able to defend himself.

Dougal hadn't gotten too much worse. Jakob viewed that as a positive development.

Nevertheless, he wasn't getting any better. The beating at the hands of the slavers had taken more out of his father than either of them was willing to admit.

Dougal still was having a hard time breathing, although it wasn't the gasping breaths that initially made Jakob worry that he wasn't going to last more than another day or two when they had first exited the fog.

He was clearly in pain, even though Dougal tried to hide it. And every so often he caught his father wiping blood onto his sleeve. Whatever was broken within him was still broken and still poking something that it shouldn't.

The most telling sign of Dougal's injuries was their pace. Jakob's father had been a vigorous man. Ten leagues a day had been nothing for him.

Now, he could barely walk four miles in a day. Five was a huge strain on him. He required frequent breaks, needing a great deal of help on the steeper sections of the slopes, of which there were many in the Highlands.

Jakob didn't fault his father for the position they were in. The challenges they needed to overcome.

Rather, he worried about him. He could see what was happening to his father, and his father probably knew as well though he wouldn't admit it. Worse, neither of them knew what to do about it.

The Stalkers never came too close, or if they did neither he nor his father were aware of them. Jakob was grateful for that. Because if those monsters did find them, Jakob feared that his father wouldn't last very long on his own.

That was one of the reasons they hadn't built a fire during the chilly nights. And why they always took their time to find good locations where they could hide and defend themselves while they waited for morning.

"Quite a view," said Dougal in a phlegmy voice, Jakob catching once again the sound of fluid in his father's lungs. They both chose to ignore that fact, because there was nothing that either of them could do about it.

"It is. It's the kind of view I want every day."

Father and son stood on a cliff that allowed them to gaze out over the Highlands toward the east and the Sea of Mist just beyond. Towering heart trees ran along the ridges and up the sides of the mountains, only becoming smaller where the air thinned.

Snow-capped peaks glistened in the early morning light. And, as always, the kestrels so common to the Highlands soared through the air, their broad wings extended, catching the air currents, their orange and white feathers sparkling every time the sunlight touched them.

Those majestic, massive predators entranced Jakob. He had a difficult time taking his eyes away from them as they glided through the sky, waiting to see if they had found any prey.

Several times he had observed when the raptors shot down out of the sky, wings tight to their sides, razor-sharp claws outstretched, disappearing for just a second behind a ridge, before appearing once again, large wings pumping furiously, that day's meal caught within their talons. He was impressed not only by their appearance, their confidence, their audacity and aggressiveness, but also by the freedom that they relished and exercised.

"We need to make for Shadow's Reach," said Dougal, breaking through Jakob's wandering thoughts.

"That's a long way to go," Jakob replied, trying to keep his voice even, calm, not wanting his worry to become apparent. Because he didn't agree with his father, and he had learned from experience that he needed to offer his perspective diplomatically once his father had made up his mind. If he didn't, Dougal would simply ignore him. Of course, he'd probably ignore him anyway. "Maybe we wait on that for a few more days. We can find a place to hole up here. A small village maybe. One of those towers that we've seen off in the distance from time to time. We could make our way into the Northern Territory when you're feeling stronger."

"We can't wait, son. We need to go now. Too much depends on us."

Jakob tried not to shake his head in frustration. What depended on them?

Jakob didn't know. At the moment, they needed to focus on themselves. They needed to depend on each other if they were to have any chance of getting out of their current difficulties.

He was having the same conversation with his father that they had engaged in for the last several nights. Jakob hadn't challenged Dougal when he had decided that they should head toward the northeast, away from any other slavers that might be in the area. It seemed like the sensible move at the time, and it would give his father a chance to heal.

When he realized the real reason that his father had picked that direction, he had taken issue with the choice. Every day they continued to the northeast brought them closer to the Northern Territory, which began where the mountains of the Highlands gave way to the Northern Steppes.

"Why not? Why not wait until you're feeling better? In your

current condition, do you really think we can make it all the way to Shadow's Reach? If we're caught on the plain by either Stalkers or Wraiths, we stand little chance."

"We have no choice, Jakob."

"We always have a choice," replied Jakob, unable to keep the heat from his voice this time.

"It's the right thing to do and that's that," said Dougal, trying to raise his voice to the tone that had served him so well as a Sergeant in the Roo's Nest Guard yet failing to do so because of his debilitating injuries. "Why are you fighting me on this? This is what we need to do and we'll do it. It's as simple as that."

"Because you need time to heal and I feel as if going to Shadow's Reach just takes us into the lion's den. There's nothing simple about any of this."

Dougal ignored his son's concerns about his health, latching onto the last part of what Jakob had said. "Why would you worry about informing the Governor of the Northern Territory about what happened? Kendric Winborne comes from an honorable family. He's in a position to do something about this."

"Or he could be a part of it as well," countered Jakob. "Someone with power and influence is controlling the slavers, and we have no way of knowing who that might be. There's no point in taking the risk that you suggest until you're feeling better."

They both believed that the root of one of the evils in the Highlands lay at the feet of its current Governor, Torstan Sharperson, the slavers working for him. Dougal felt the need to share that information with someone in a position of authority. Thus, the compulsion to meet with Kendric Winborne.

That was just the way his father thought. If there was a problem that needed to be addressed, you moved it up the chain of command. He was a soldier after all, born and bred.

To Jakob's way of thinking, however, if one Governor could be involved in such a scheme, why not another? Why not all of them?

In the Territories, there was little in the way of oversight. The man or woman with the greatest amount of power and wealth could do whatever they wanted to increase both at the expense of anyone who got in their way.

Jakob just didn't understand why, having never met the man, his father seemed to hold Kendric Winborne in such high regard. Yes, informing Winborne as to what was happening in the Highlands could prove useful to their cause. It could also put them right back in the place they had fought so hard to escape.

"Maybe so, but I doubt it," Dougal grumbled. "You have no way of knowing."

"You have no way of knowing either," Jakob challenged again. "That's the whole point. Do you really want to take the risk? Do you really want to put us at the mercy of someone we don't know and have no reason to trust?"

Instead of responding immediately, Dougal held his tongue. His son wasn't a child anymore. He was a young man, and Dougal needed to treat him as such. Even though he was finding it increasingly more difficult to do just that, the pain that was radiating throughout his body not helping.

He shook his head in irritation. They didn't have time for this argument. And it was getting old.

Why couldn't Jakob just trust that Dougal knew what was best?

"We will go to Shadow's Reach, but before we approach Kendric Winborne we will get the lay of the land first."

Dougal believed that he was offering his son a fair compromise, so Jakob's continuing resistance immediately set off his temper.

"I still don't think it's a good idea," replied Jakob. He would much rather find somewhere in the Highlands where he could obtain good care for his father and then try to get a better sense of whether there was any place safe in the mountains where they could hide for a time. He knew that once Dougal had made up his mind, there was little chance of changing it. Still, he felt the need to try. This decision was too important for them to be wrong. "Why don't we …"

"Enough!" shouted Dougal, demonstrating a strength that fled him almost immediately. "We go to Shadow's Reach and that's the end of it. No more discussion. Are we clear?"

Jakob's temper flared, his anger rising. He couldn't let the argument go. In the past, he might have. Not now, however. Not with his father so badly hurt. Not with so many threats circulating around them.

He believed that his father either was being naïve or simply stubborn or both. In consequence, he didn't care if he pushed too hard.

He was about to continue with his argument, even though it would only anger his father all the more, when he felt a faint, unexpected touch in the back of his brain. He looked up. Several kestrels circled in the air about a league to their west.

What was that sensation he just experienced? Was it one of the raptors? Was that even possible?

He didn't know, although the concept certainly intrigued him. He could explore it more later. Because whatever had pulled his attention to the west was trying to warn him.

Jakob didn't see any movement from where they stood on the ledge, but he could sense that something was there that shouldn't be. Having a general idea of where he needed to look, he reached for the Talent and extended his senses.

"What is it?" his father asked, his anger at being challenged dissipating when he saw his son's expression. It was becoming a much more familiar sight now that Jakob could use the Talent more comfortably.

"I think there's something out there. Following us."

"I don't see anything."

"Neither do I. Still, there is something there. I'm certain of it."

"Have you located it with the Talent?" Dougal asked, impatient.

"I'm doing that now," Jakob replied, keeping the hint of annoyance that wanted to seep out to himself.

Jakob searched around them several times each day and always right before he closed his eyes for the night. As he used the natural magic of the world to scan the landscape in every direction, he realized that he was feeling much better, the after-effects of his concussion almost completely gone.

Rather than the pain that made it feel like his head was going to split apart, he was experiencing just a dull headache. So he definitely was making progress. In a few days, he should be as good as new.

"It's not Wraiths," said Jakob. "But we already knew that. The fog is still well to the north, close to Shadow's Reach." He hoped that last statement might catch his father's attention and perhaps make him rethink his decision, though he doubted it. Dougal was incredibly stubborn after all. Instead of pressing his father any further on the topic, Jakob focused on the task at hand. "Not Stalkers either, so that's a good thing. Those monsters are still to our south."

"What could it be then?" Dougal wondered.

Jakob sighed in resignation. No, it wasn't Stalkers or Wraiths. Rather, it was a new threat, or rather an old threat reappearing once again that Jakob had hoped they had escaped for good.

"Slavers."

Dougal couldn't say that he was surprised. "How many?"

"More than a dozen coming this way. They're probably following our trail. They don't have any prisoners with them."

"They've been tracking us," Dougal murmured.

"They probably want to know what happened to the other groups. Ours and the ones we found. Our tracks are the only ones that lead away from all the slaughters."

"Or they just want to kill us," suggested Dougal. "They might blame us for what happened to their friends and want revenge."

"Maybe." The only way to find out was to talk with the slavers, and Jakob had no desire to do that.

"I heard one of the slavers talking before we made our escape," said Dougal, who had spent just as much time listening as he did thinking about how they could elude their captors when he and Jakob were linked to the chain. "They get paid for each slave they bring to the mines. They might not want to show up there empty-handed. They probably think that they can grab a few more settlers along the way once they have us and make their efforts worthwhile."

"That makes the most sense," Jakob agreed.

"Which way?" asked Dougal, trusting in his son's use of the Talent.

"There's a river about a league to the north that turns to the east and the coast," replied Jakob. "We'll head that way. It's our best chance to get away from the bastards."

Jakob was still worried. Just arguing with him had tired his father. Therefore, he had his doubts that even with the aid of the Talent, they could stay ahead of their pursuers.

And if, as he feared, they couldn't, was their fate sealed?

Even with the Talent at his disposal, he wasn't sure he had the strength or the skill to take on a dozen slavers at one time and still protect his badly injured father.

7

THE JAGGED ISLANDS

"Anything left in your stomach, Majdi? I'm guessing not, because I think most of it ran right beneath our bunks last night. It was like a storm of its own in our cabin."

Majdi grinned at Jenus' comment. He wasn't in a position to deny the claim. The gladiator who was built like a small house actually seemed quite proud of his dubious achievement.

"It wasn't all mine, Jenus. I do seem to recall you spewing your guts out multiple times as well while we ran with the storm."

"I'm not a sailor," replied Jenus. "Never have been, never will be. So my spewing my guts out doesn't bother me in the least. I'm just glad we're still on top of the sea instead of below it."

"You've got the right of it there. Although I doubt we would have made it without the Magii."

"What were they doing anyway?" asked Dorlan, who had been curled up on the bunk in his cabin, somehow squeezing himself into the tight space, unable to move, his stomach protesting at even the slightest attempt to do so. "I saw the glow through the porthole, but I was too sick to take a look."

"It was much like the dome the Volkun and the Vedra crafted when the storm came upon us while we were on the Breakwater Plateau and fighting those Slayers," explained Asaia. "The shield covered the ship and then some, maybe a mile in all directions. It helped to reduce the full effect of the storm, just not as much as we would have liked."

"It was quite impressive," said Kollea.

"That it was," agreed Asaia. "I'd have hated to be in that storm without the Magii's protection. As Jenus said, I fear we would have ended up beneath the waves."

"You can thank Magus Rafia for that," said Kollea. "She hasn't slept since we sailed into the storm, keeping that shield in place the entire time that it was necessary. She was able to negate the very worst of the tempest, which I certainly appreciate. I'd hate to think what it would have been like without her."

"While Magus Rafia was doing that, the Volkun and the Vedra powered the *Freedom* against the tempest, filling the sails with gusts stronger than the wind so that we could move against the gale," added Asaia.

"It's frightening to think of what that lad can do now," said Jenus.

"What do you mean?" asked Majdi. "I'm quite pleased by what he can do. And he's not a lad. He never was. He's simply the Volkun."

"I don't take issue with that comment in the least," mumbled Dorlan, still feeling the effect of last night, his balance a bit off, which didn't help with the nausea that reared its head every time the *Freedom* dipped over one of the larger waves that came their way rather than cutting through it.

"I agree with you, Majdi," continued Jenus. "I don't want what I just said to be taken the wrong way."

"Then what did you mean?" asked Dorlan.

"Well, you saw what the Volkun could do on the white sand," said Jenus, doing his best to explain what for him was simple to understand. "His skill in the Talent now makes him even more frightening than he was before, and he was quite frightening to begin with."

"You mean that in a good way," chided Kollea, "don't you."

"Absolutely," Jenus replied immediately. "The more frightening the Volkun, the easier my life becomes. And when I say frightening, I do mean that in a good way. With him around, we have to work really hard to lose a fight. That is something that I truly value."

"I don't disagree with you there," said Majdi. "And I, for one, am quite pleased to be fighting with the Volkun, because I hate to lose."

"You know, I'm actually getting a bit hungry," said Jenus, his comment having very little to do with the current conversation, although that wasn't unusual. He had a difficult time concentrating on only one thing at a time, his attention often flitting about like a butterfly struggling against a strong breeze. "I guess that's a good sign."

"How could you be hungry after the night we just had?" demanded Asaia. "Just thinking about food right now makes me want to spill my guts again."

"I'm still feeling a bit queasy myself, even though I don't have anything in my stomach," offered Majdi.

"None of us have anything in our stomachs," confirmed Kollea.

"Especially Dorlan," said Jenus. "Did you regret finishing the last of the stew before that storm hit, because from what I could tell it got its revenge upon you last night."

"That it did," agreed Dorlan with a soft rumble that sounded like a rockslide. "Although once it came back up the way that it had gone down, I felt a bit better. Thinking about it now, however, I have to admit that I've had it worse."

"I doubt that," said Asaia.

"How could you have been sicker than you were last night?"

questioned Majdi. "I think I saw your stomach the last time you puked when the ship came down off that crest that was taller than one of those sandstone pillars in the Trench. My stomach almost shot out of my mouth right then."

"I know mine did, I don't dispute it," said Dorlan with a laugh. "Wasn't a pretty sight. I think the only person who was immune to that unending heaving -- the ship climbing one watery mountain after another, though I have to admit the climb was never as bad as the fall – was you Kollea."

"I have a steel stomach," she replied. "Always have."

"How is that even possible?" wondered Jenus.

"It just takes practice," offered Kollea, as if that was enough to explain her unique ability.

"How do you practice that?" asked Majdi, clearly intrigued.

"Well, I spent several years in the Colosseum with you lot, didn't I?" Kollea replied with a laugh. "A few ups and downs certainly don't compare to what I had to deal with then."

"What are you talking about?" asked Jenus.

"You mean the wounds?" asked Dorlan, seeking to clarify what his love meant. "Some of those were quite nasty, I must admit."

"No, the wounds were nothing," replied Kollea. "Seeing muscle and bone have little meaning when you see them revealed every day."

"You're right about that," murmured Majdi.

"Then what could we have possibly done that would have prepared you for last night's festival of regurgitation?" asked Jenus.

"Festival of regurgitation," repeated Asaia. "I like that. You can build several good stories with that term."

"Jenus with that abscess on his back that was twice the size of a plate?" offered Kollea.

"That wasn't really bad at all," protested Jenus. "No more than an irritation really."

"That was grotesque," agreed Majdi in his deep rumble. "One of the nastiest things that I've ever seen."

"You're right, Jenus, for me it wasn't until you asked the physick to pop it, and then all that puss spilled out," said Kollea. "That's when it truly became sickening. There must have been enough in there to fill a helmet."

"Two, actually," clarified Jenus. "I did the test myself as to how much fluid was in the boil because I was curious."

"You filled your helmet with pus?" asked Asaia, not wanting to believe what she had just heard, although knowing that with Jenus anything was possible.

"My helmets, no. I used Dorlan's instead."

"You did what?" demanded Dorlan. The large gladiator had the urge to take his flicker of anger out on the even larger Jenus. His still queasy stomach didn't allow for it, nor did his common sense. No one in their right mind challenged Jenus to a combat, not if they wanted to remain whole.

"I cleaned it all up when I was done," said Jenus, "have no fear of that. It's just that your helmets were closer at hand at the time."

Dorlan huffed his indignation, though he seemed to be mollified by Jenus' explanation. They had been good friends ever since both had entered the Pit within a week of each other for the same offense. Killing a superior officer in the Royal Guard who, in their opinions and those of their fellow soldiers, needed killing. Just as with respect to those situations, they were often of the same mind regarding a great many matters.

"That was kind of disgusting, I'll give you that," agreed Dorlan, "though lancing that boil did seem to do the trick."

"You and the physick didn't even know if it was going to work," said Kollea. "You just wanted to do something about it since that growth was making you look like a hunchback."

"True."

"And then Dorlan with the fungus growing between his

toes," Kollea suggested as another example of what she needed to deal with in the training barracks.

"That was disgusting," said Dorlan. "I didn't enjoy that at all, especially when it started getting itchy. I was afraid to scratch it. I thought if I did, and I got that mold on my fingers, it would start growing on any other parts of my body that I touched."

"Since you spend so much time scratching your ass, that was my pick for where it would start growing next," laughed Majdi, the other gladiators laughing with him, even Dorlan.

"Black and grey, maybe with a touch of green though I couldn't tell for certain," recalled Dorlan. "It depended on the light. And I couldn't tell if the fungus looked more like mushrooms or cauliflower."

"Why would you even care about what it looked like?" asked Jenus. "Every time you showed it to us I almost gagged."

"Not wanting to diminish the repulsive nature of the afflictions that my love suffered through, I do believe that Asaia's was the worst," said Kollea.

"I'll give you that," agreed Majdi. "That was truly revolting."

"I disagree," said Dorlan, proud of what he had suffered through and not wanting to belittle its meaning. "How could Asaia's be worse than my fungus? Another life form was growing on me. That's absolutely repellent."

"Growing *on* you, yes, but Asaia had that insect growing *inside* her," clarified Kollea. "That was much more disgusting."

"What was that called again?" wondered Majdi.

"A botfly," said Asaia, who would never forget that horrendous experience.

It had taken weeks to figure out why she had a sore on her knee that only continued to grow. It wasn't until a physick from the south who had grown up around the Mud Flats had poked at it with a scalpel and several larvae had pushed their way through the opening in her flesh that she realized what it was.

"Yes, a botfly," said Jenus. "I remember that. Declan didn't know what to do for you. He must have called in a dozen different physicks trying to find an answer." Jenus nodded his head as he recalled the experience of seeing those terrifying insects emerge, remembering how glad he was that it wasn't him who had been afflicted by that parasite. He could deal with most challenges thrown his way. He had proven that. But not a bug that nested and hatched within you. "Now there's something that's scarier than a Ghoule, and it's barely bigger than the head of a nail."

Murmurs of agreement ran through the group. All of the Blood Company had exited their cabins as soon as the storm abated and had found places on the deck to enjoy the calm seas and the fresh air, glad to be free of their fetid sleeping quarters.

They were all careful to stay out of the way of the sailors, who were working diligently to repair what damage they could that was caused by the storm, helping whenever they were asked. None of the gladiators had eaten since the storm hit, and none had the desire to, except perhaps for Jenus, all of them still not feeling up to it after the challenges of the last night.

When they first entered the storm upon escaping the last Bakunawa, Captain Gregson had tried to sail against the wind, pushing to the west. But even with the help of the Magii, the tempest was too much. Captain Gregson had no choice other than to give up and acknowledge the strength of the gale, following the storm's track to the south.

He hadn't been able to break free until earlier that morning, and that was only because the storm was weakening. When the *Freedom* hit the edge of the tempest, he took advantage of the opportunity presented, more interested in guiding the ship to calmer waters and less so in the fact that they were more than a hundred leagues off course.

The gladiators of the Blood Company didn't care either. They had survived thanks to the strength of the Magii and the know-how of the Captain and his crew. They were more than happy to enjoy the calm of that morning with their friends, knowing that their particular skills would be called upon soon enough.

Because they sensed how the atmosphere aboard the ship had changed during the last hour. A touch of concern, maybe fear, radiated from the sailors, and not because the ship was in need of repair. No, something else was bothering the crew. The gladiators just didn't know what yet.

"Comparing ailments and weak stomachs? That's a conversation I'm glad I missed," said Bryen as he strode past the mizzenmast around which the gladiators had gathered. "The only explanation for that is that you all took one too many knocks to the head."

"And you didn't?" challenged Asaia with a big smile. The other gladiators laughed at her response.

"Good point," Bryen called back over his shoulder as he climbed the ladder that would take him to the helm.

When he reached the top, he stopped for a few seconds to stare out across the bow. A dark smudge at the edge of the horizon was gaining greater clarity with every league the wind blew them to the south.

"The Jagged Islands," murmured Rafia, the Magus standing next to Captain Gregson. "A bold choice."

"The only choice," muttered the Captain, his expression suggesting that he was less than pleased to be heading toward the archipelago that was still quite a few leagues away. "We wouldn't be here otherwise."

"Have you been here before, Captain Gregson?" asked Bryen.

"Unfortunately, yes."

"You don't care for these isles?" asked Rafia, her question more a statement.

"No, I don't. Although they can be useful for a brief period of time."

Bryen nodded, unable to miss the Captain's hesitancy and discomfort. He could tell that Captain Gregson, usually quite open about any topic under the sun, hadn't yet shared everything that he knew about what many sailors often described as the Haunted Isles.

"What will be required for us to do what is necessary to ensure that we can make it to the Territories?"

"Our food supplies are good, and we should have enough to complete our trip to the west, especially if your Blood Company catch another few tarpon or swordfish for us. We do need fresh water. Many of our barrels spilled over during the storm despite the efforts of the Magus to weaken the blow we took. No offense, Magus Rafia. Without you, Lord Keldragan, and Lady Winborne we would all be beneath the waves. My thanks for your efforts on our behalf."

"No offense taken, Captain Gregson. I wish we could have done more. Unfortunately, the power of that storm was quite remarkable."

"It's just Bryen, Captain Gregson. I'm not a Lord of Caledonia."

"If you say so, Lord Keldragan," replied Captain Gregson with a wry smile, turning his attention back to their immediate concerns. "We'll also need to cut some fresh timber. We have some in one of the holds, but it won't be enough for all the repairs that we need to make. Thankfully the masts are intact, the only concern a crack in the jiggermast. Even with that we should be all right. We need to take down several of the sails. Repair those that we can, replace those that we can't. And we'll need to do some work on the hull as we're leaking water in several places. That last is critical. If we leave those cracks in our hull, I can't guarantee we make it the rest of the way across the Burnt Ocean."

"How long will all that take?" asked Bryen.

"Two days at most for the essential repairs."

"That's it?" asked Rafia. "All that work in just two days?"

"My crew know what they're doing," replied Captain Gregson with a nod, confident in his estimate.

"That they do," agreed Rafia. "Because if they didn't, no matter my efforts or those of Bryen and Aislinn, we would be beneath the waves as you said."

"Thank you for your belief in me, Magus Rafia," replied Captain Gregson, nodding to the Magus to demonstrate his respect.

"So then it's fortunate that we're here, isn't it?" continued Rafia, referencing the islands that were growing larger in front of them, the dim shapes giving way to greater detail.

At their current distance, it appeared as if the entire horizon was filled by one massive island. Bryen knew that wasn't the case thanks to his lessons in geography with Declan. The Jagged Islands totaled more than a dozen in all and less than a hundred. No one was really quite sure of the actual number.

The largest were the most visible, many of the smaller ones disappearing then coming back up out of the sea depending on the tides. Because some of the islands were so close together, they wouldn't see the channels separating the land masses until they were closer.

Although Bryen could already make out the gradual shift in colors. Grey and black dominated down near the water's edge before giving way to a brownish scrub that then surrendered to a deeper green the farther up he looked before the grey and black of the peaks, often shrouded in a heavy fog, returned once again.

"That remains to be seen," Captain Gregson answered cryptically.

"Why do you say that?"

Captain Gregson didn't answer the question immediately,

not wanting to give a hasty response. "The Jagged Islands will serve our purposes so long as we are careful and we are smart. We need the time to repair the ship, like I said, and we need a location that gets us off the Burnt Ocean for some of the work. There is a place here where we can do that. We can anchor in Solace Sound. We'll be protected from the weather so that we can complete the repairs that absolutely must be done and we can leave the rest for when we begin again our journey to the Territories. Also, we should be able to find fresh water."

"Captain Gregson, what are you not telling us?" asked Bryen, his sharp gaze bringing a grimace to the increasingly nervous man, which was distinctly out of character for the gruff and usually cheerful shipmaster.

"As I said, I have been here before. Even so, there's something not quite right about the Jagged Islands. There's no good way to explain. After spending just a bit of time here, they begin to feel wrong."

"The Haunted Isles as some of the crew have whispered," said Bryen.

"Exactly so."

Bryen nodded. Based on his own experience with respect to certain places in the world and situations, he could understand that perspective.

"You said no more than two days for the critical repairs. Why only two days? I take it you'd prefer more time if you had it."

"I wasn't going to hide it from you," replied Captain Gregson. "It's just not something that sailors like to talk about. We tend to be a superstitious lot as you know, and many of us have learned that saying something often can bring it down upon you."

"Yes, we had our own superstitions in the Pit," offered Bryen. "If you talked about something that you shouldn't talk about, it inevitably came to pass, and usually with quite dire circumstances."

"Exactly so, Lord Keldragan."

Bryen chose not to correct the Captain this time with respect to the title that he had given him. "So back to my original question. Why no more than two days in Solace Sound? You're worried. You don't want to stay here any longer than that even though you know that several of the necessary repairs will take much longer than two days."

"Most captains don't come this way if they can avoid it," grumbled Captain Gregson, watching as Emelina, the helmswoman and his wife, turned the wheel gently to the starboard side a few degrees so that she could capture the best that the wind had to offer and also to line the ship up with the channel that would allow them to sail between two of the islands and then in among the archipelago. "Those who do, never by choice, always based on necessity, all agree that two days is the limit for anchoring off the coast of any of the Jagged Islands."

"And those who spend more than two days here?" asked Rafia, intensely curious and already guessing at the answer.

"Usually we don't see them again."

"Why not?"

"I don't know. No one knows. All we have are rumors."

∽

"Are those what I think they are?" asked Declan.

Near the top of the mountains on every one of the islands he could make out dark shapes circling around the crags. They were definitely larger than birds. Much larger.

"What do you think they are?"

"Wyverns. We came up against them in the Trench."

"You were in the Trench?" asked Captain Gregson, his

curiosity piqued. All sailors were interested in a good story, and no one had entered the Trench for a thousand years. Not since the Weir was constructed. Or so he had believed.

"Yes, but that's a different story for a different time."

Declan could make out the flying beasts clearly now. Large leathery wings. Long, dragonlike snouts. Sharp claws that could tear through leather or chip off rock with equal ease.

Essentially smaller versions of the black dragons that were such a threat when the Blood Company made its way to the Sanctuary. If wyverns ate well the beasts could grow larger than a draft horse. And these wyverns appeared to be eating quite well indeed.

Declan hadn't liked dealing with these beasts in the Trench. He had no desire to do so here in the Jagged Islands.

Captain Gregson nodded, agreeing with the Sergeant of the Blood Company's assessment. He was certain there was a story worth hearing, but he would wait until the time was right.

"These islands are infested with wyverns," Captain Gregson explained, turning his thoughts back to what they were sailing toward. "They hunt the elephant seals and southern seals that use the beaches on the eastern side of this and the other islands as a breeding ground."

"Why not the western side?"

"Because the eastern side has shallow water usually no more than a few feet deep that extends for several hundred yards off the coast. That bay is a buffet for the seals. It's filled with fish and other sea creatures they like to eat. And they don't need to worry about getting eaten themselves by the predators lurking on the western side, where the sea floor drops off precipitously to an unknown depth just a few dozen yards from shore."

"What kind of predators are we talking about?"

"Great white sharks for the most part. They clear out when the orcas arrive. Although those hunters often come over to the eastern side of the islands as well, hoping that those seals make a mistake from which they can profit. They know that eventually the youngins will need to make a try for the Burnt Ocean. When that time of year comes around, the great whites are always waiting. It's a bloodbath, but there are more seals than sharks, so a great many get away."

"You know quite a bit about these islands even though you clearly don't like it here."

"You've got that right," grinned Captain Gregson. "Although I've never set foot on the Jagged Islands, I've been here several times, and as I said, rarely by choice. I don't like it here. I do like to know as much as I can about wherever it is that I am. I made it a point to sail along the coast of each island a few times, usually while waiting out a storm. I've got a good sense of the entire archipelago and where to steer clear."

"A man after my own heart," said Declan, appreciating Captain Gregson's thoroughness.

"Just so," replied Captain Gregson, having observed the many training sessions Declan had run on the deck of the *Freedom* for the gladiators and sensing a kindred spirit in which preparation in all things was essential not only to success, but also survival. "I've never got so close as to have to worry about what might be haunting these islands. Just close enough to learn a few things that might prove useful from time to time."

"Do we have to worry about the wyverns?" asked Declan, his eyes moving away from the coast and back to the sky, some of the flying beasts curious about the new arrival in their domain and deciding to investigate, although not drifting so low as to give the archers who now manned the crow's nests a chance to test their skill.

"Did you have to worry about them in the Trench?"

"Yes, they were much too curious and much too hungry."

"Then you need to worry about them here. I've heard of unwary sailors being plucked from the deck of a ship by some of the larger wyverns. That's why we always have lookouts on the masts and archers at the ready even when we're anchored here. We don't want to give the beasts an easy meal."

For the next several minutes, Captain Gregson worked with Emelina to navigate the gargantuan *Freedom* in between two of the islands, staying close to the center of the channel, having to tack to the port side and then to the starboard just once, and then from the starboard to the port, knowing from the experience of being here before and how the color of the sea changed in certain locations where he needed to avoid hidden reefs or those smaller stone islands that were a part of the chain that wouldn't reveal themselves until the tide went out.

Once through the gap, Emelina spun the wheel gently to the left, curling around the shore of one of the larger islands and continuing to the south.

All along the way, Declan kept one eye on the much too curious wyverns and the other studying the rocky coasts that they passed.

He couldn't find a beach or any easy way to get ashore. The rough surf, churned into a whitewater because of its passage through the channels, pounded with an angry urgency against the large, sharp rocks that edged each isle. Perhaps seeking to reclaim the islands that dared to rise up from beneath the surface.

Declan assumed that's why the archipelago was named as it was. The thought of trying to land on any of the cays they passed filled him with dread, the threat of being consumed by the raging waves when attempting to do just that all too real.

After another half hour of weaving in between various islands, the frothing water, worked up even more by the strong wind that ran straight through the channels separating the islands, the hidden rocks and reefs beneath the surface creating small whirlpools that Emelina calmly avoided, finally settled.

The *Freedom* sailed into what Captain Gregson named

Solace Sound. For the first time at the far shore of the island to their west, one of four that sheltered this quiet bay, Declan finally caught sight of a sandy beach, what he assumed was the one place where they could safely set foot on land.

Crescent shaped, the beach covered most of the western side of the largest island they had come across. After less than a hundred yards the sand gave way to a dense forest, the peaks that were simply larger versions of the jagged rocks bounding the coast about a mile or so farther in from the shore.

"I can see why these are named the Jagged Islands," said Aislinn as she and Bryen joined Declan and Captain Gregson on the helm. "All I see are shapes that resemble broken glass."

"Even the fins of the great whites," offered Bryen, motioning to the large shark that swam just off the port side of the ship before turning away, uninterested in the vessel that had just invaded its domain.

"I couldn't agree more," said Declan.

"These islands appear to be uninhabited," said Aislinn.

"Appearances can be deceiving, Lady Keldragan," answered Captain Gregson.

"People are living here?"

"Honestly, I don't know." Captain Gregson sighed, then shrugged his shoulders. "There may have been people here before. In fact, I wouldn't be surprised if there were. Some of those who have gone ashore have found evidence to suggest that was the case. But if there ever were people here, it was long ago. I doubt that these blasted isles are still inhabited. I tend not to loiter here if I can avoid it."

"What do you know?" asked Declan, his tone more demanding than he meant it to be. He wasn't one for indecisiveness or incomplete answers, something that Captain Gregson appreciated.

So he ignored the challenge, seeing it for what it was. A hint of nervousness mixed with curiosity, which wasn't a bad thing considering where they were.

"As I told Lord Keldragan, being here for any length of time is a bad idea. The sooner we complete the repairs that are absolutely necessary and we replenish our fresh water, the better. I want to be out on the Burnt Ocean by the day after tomorrow, first thing in the morning at the latest."

That ended the conversation for a few minutes, Bryen and his friends leaning on the railing, looking toward the beach, as Captain Gregson and his crew trimmed the sails, slowed the ship, then dropped the anchor.

The sailors immediately began preparing the longboats to be lowered into the sound, all of them just as desirous as their Captain to be away from this place as quickly as they could.

They knew the stories just as well as he did and had no desire to become caught up in a tale themselves.

Bryen could read all that easily in their edgy movements and the hushed conversations between the men and women, the shouts and laughs so common among the crew, even in the harshest weather, nowhere to be heard.

He could understand why. Even though the surface of the bay was calm and the sun shone down brightly upon them, their presence in Solace Sound didn't feel quite right.

It felt like they were intruding. That they didn't belong there. That they shouldn't be there.

"Much like being in the Lost Land," whispered Aislinn, her comment bringing a small smile to Bryen's grim countenance.

"That it is," he replied, nodding in agreement. "We'll need to be careful. Can you sense anything?"

Aislinn shook her head, not surprised that Bryen knew that she had been searching around them with the Talent. They both did it at regular intervals, neither caring to deal with another surprise such as three Bakunawa intent on taking them beneath the waves.

"No, nothing at all on any of the islands as we passed them. Nothing on the one we'll be landing on. My only concern is those great whites. Some of them are at least thirty feet long."

"No need to worry about those monsters," said Captain Gregson, stepping up to the small group now that everything was proceeding apace to get the work parties ashore. "The longboats are bigger than any of those beasties."

"Not by much," countered Declan.

"True, but you have nothing to worry about so long as you don't fall in."

"That's quite comforting," huffed Declan.

"And if we do?" asked Aislinn.

Captain Gregson scrunched up his face for a few seconds, then grinned broadly, nodding. "Swim as fast as you can."

For just a moment Declan stared at the Captain of the *Freedom* without any expression, and then the Master of the Gladiators broke out into a laugh that jolted many of the sailors working around them as the shocking noise shattered the heavy silence that had draped itself across the vessel. Captain Gregson joined him.

"Good advice. Let's hope I don't have to put it to use."

"You and me both," replied Captain Gregson, clapping Declan on the shoulder before shifting to the reasons they had come to this desolate place. "My crew will begin repairing the rips in the sails and replacing those that can't be mended. We'll also begin working on those cracks in the hull. I'll send a few of my sailors onto the island with you if you feel there's a need, but none have been here before, and the more hands I have on board the *Freedom*, the faster the work will go. Besides, Lord Keldragan, you and your gladiators are much more capable at protecting against any threats you might find ashore than my crew would be."

"I can't disagree with you there."

"Good. Then with that in mind, we'll need to send one crew

for water and the other crew to chop some fresh wood for the repairs."

"I'll take a few squads to get the water. Declan, did you want to take the rest of the Blood Company to get the wood that's needed?"

Declan nodded his agreement.

"Good, that's to the north," said Captain Gregson, pointing farther up the shore, "the only good forest on the island. It's about a mile inland from the beach. It's hard to miss." He then turned his sharp eyes toward Bryen. "There are a handful of springs to the east near the top of the peaks right there." Captain Gregson directed their attention to a spot that was about two-thirds of the way up the slope of the tallest mountain on the island and just below the ring of clouds that haloed the peaks. "Once you find the waterfall, just follow it up to the top. That's where the springs are."

"We can't get the water at the base of the falls?" asked Aislinn.

"No, Lady Winborne. From what we've learned about this island, I wouldn't advise it. Better to stay away from there."

"Why would we need to do that?"

"The waterfall drops right through the ground into a massive sinkhole. There's no way to get to that water without going into the sinkhole, and I wouldn't recommend trying to do that. Not after what I heard from some of the other captains who have been here."

"What have you heard?" asked Bryen. He was beginning to understand why sailors tended to avoid these islands if they could.

"It's just a story that another captain told me when we were sharing a drink in a tavern."

"Stories usually have a nugget of truth," said Declan. "Please feel free to share."

Captain Gregson shrugged again, not willing to testify to

the truth of what he was about to say, but believing in the story enough to offer it to those standing around him. "This other captain spends more time in the bottle than out. You need to keep that in mind. Even so, he told me that he heard from another captain who heard for another captain ..."

"We get the idea," interrupted Declan. "What was the story?"

"That another ship came here in need of fresh water. Some of the crew went to the falls. Instead of climbing to the top to the natural springs as their captain instructed, they decided that it was easier to just try to take the water from the bottom of the falls. They couldn't get across to the falls because the hole was too large, at least fifty feet across, and they couldn't climb along the side of the cliff the waterfall surged down, so they decided to lower their bags into the sinkhole and then pull them back up once they were full."

"That sounds like a fairly good idea," said Declan.

"I thought so as well. From what the captain said, though, supposedly their cleverness didn't work out as they expected."

"What happened?" asked Aislinn.

"One of the sailors fell into the sinkhole when he tried to pull up a water bag. Or rather, as the captain told me, whatever was in the sinkhole pulled him in."

"He was pulled into the sinkhole?" questioned Declan, finding that hard to believe, his tone demonstrating his dubiousness as to the claim.

"I'm just telling you what I heard. No more."

"The sailor died?" asked Bryen.

"Yes, but not from the fall. He fell about fifty feet and splashed into a sizable pool of water."

"If he didn't die from the fall, then what happened to him?" asked Declan, his thoughts already turning down a dark road as he guessed where the story was going. He knew from experience that with stories like this there was only one ending.

"The sailor didn't die from the fall. Rather, he died from whatever lived in the pool of water. Some kind of creature killed him, although the captain I spoke to had no idea what the beast might have looked like, because the one sailor who survived the encounter and made it back to the ship couldn't tell him, the woman dying from her wounds just minutes after she reached the safety of the vessel."

"He was serious?" asked Declan.

"Soberingly serious," nodded Gregson. "The captain said that she was terrified, her eyes as big as dinner plates, her mind gone, numb with fear. Her body was sliced open in a dozen places. Sharp cuts, resembling those made by a blade, but not quite. The edges rougher, he had said, though he really couldn't explain beyond that. The captain said that it was a wonder that she even survived that long, having lost a great deal of blood from her many wounds."

"If no one ever sees the crews of ships who stop here for too long, then how can you give credence to this story?" asked Declan.

"I don't give credence to it," said Captain Gregson. "It's a story, no more. Still, as you said, in every story there's a nugget of truth. I just offer it as a warning. There's a reason most ships avoid the Jagged Islands and those that can't leave as quickly as possible. We need to be careful if we're to steer clear of the same fate that has befallen so many other crews that have ignored the warnings given to them."

"We'll keep that in mind," said Aislinn.

"Good," nodded Captain Gregson. "Keep your eyes open. Keep your ears open. And stay away from any sinkholes, caves, or anything else you might find that doesn't feel right. Whatever it is that haunts these islands, those who have seen it haven't lived to tell the rest of the world what it is. So better that you don't meet it as well."

"A final question, for you, Captain," said Bryen. "The sailor who died aboard the ship. What did she say was it that attacked her and the sailors with her? Did she know?"

"The Kraken," he replied in a hushed tone, as if saying the word too loudly would draw the attention of whatever evil plagued the island.

"Is it a monster or a people?" asked Bryen, who glanced at Declan, the two of them exchanging a look. From his studies with the Master of the Gladiators, the Kraken that he had heard of was a colossal mythical sea creature. That description certainly didn't fit for a creature haunting a sinkhole.

"I don't know," replied Captain Gregson, shrugging his shoulders. "I know the legends quite well, so by the looks of you, you're thinking much the same as I'm thinking. It could be both. It could be neither. All I can say is that you don't want to find out if you can avoid it."

8

THE HAUNTED ISLE

"You all right there, Majdi? You seemed to be dragging a bit during the last part of that climb. All that extra weight you carrying slowing you down?"

Giving Majdi a look, Jenus fought hard to hide the amusement that was threatening to turn his innocent expression into a broad grin. Now that his stomach no longer felt like it was going to turn flips, his natural inclination to prod, irritate, and annoy his comrades, even those few who were larger than he was, had returned.

Getting his feet onto dry land had done the trick for him in that regard. He was feeling so much better, in fact, that he started to give his good friend a ribbing, a pastime that they both enjoyed even under the worst of circumstances.

"Never better," rumbled Majdi. "And all that weight you're talking about is muscle. You might want to think about spending more time in the practice ring. You're getting flabby by the looks of you."

Jenus ignored the barb, not wanting to allow his friend to turn the focus toward him. A tactic that Majdi excelled at, much to Jenus' annoyance. "You almost slipped a few times back there. I was worried. If you fell, I feared that you wouldn't be able to get back up. Might take a tumble all the way to the bottom."

"Worried that I would fall or that I would fall on you?" laughed Majdi, his broad smile brightening what had become a cloudy day the farther up the mountain that they had trekked.

He and all the other gladiators were in a good mood, glad to be off the water for a time. Even Jenus' incessant badgering, which tended to wear on him after a while, was having no effect whatsoever.

"The latter, of course. You're larger than a house. I have no desire to be crushed by one."

"Don't let anyone tell you otherwise, Jenus. But a word to the wise. Size matters."

Majdi and Jenus looked at each other in complete seriousness for as long as they could manage, then broke out laughing.

"You mean in the Pit, don't you children," cut in Asaia, her hard glare suggesting that she was far from amused by their juvenile humor.

"Yes, Asaia," they both replied quickly, nodding, somehow shrinking in upon themselves despite their great size.

Asaia had that effect on people. She never backed down and was never one to refuse a challenge. And when she had to demonstrate her skills, she never lost. That's why they liked and respected her so much, and perhaps even feared her a little bit, although neither of the gladiators would admit that to anyone other than themselves.

"Good, instead of making fools of yourselves, why don't you both take those bags over to the springs so we can get the water we need and go. The sooner we get off this mountain, the better."

"Yes, Asaia," Majdi and Jenus both replied in unison, much like two chastened children. They hustled to pick up several large water skins and then they found a spot along the rim of one of the several springs that clustered on the western side of the peak. From here, the springs flowed into the fast-running stream that just a hundred yards farther along erupted into a cascading waterfall that crashed down several thousand feet into the massive sinkhole.

Bryen watched it all from the edge of the wood, both amused and impressed.

"Remind me never to get on your bad side, Asaia," he said, offering the gladiator, her preferred steel-tipped whip hanging from her belt as always, a nod of respect.

"You have nothing to fear, Volkun," she replied with a pleasant smile. "I have never seen you act the fool or the child."

"The Lady of the Southern Marches might disagree with you."

"As would be the Vedra's right," Asaia replied. She leaned in close to him, as if she were about to reveal a critical secret. "A word of advice, if I might."

"Of course."

"She is much like me. Don't act the fool or the child with her. She has little patience for either and if you do she might decide to stick you with that sword she favors."

"So I've learned."

"Good," replied Asaia, who clapped Bryen companionably on the shoulder, then reached down for a few water bags for herself before walking over toward one of the springs. "Now let's get this done. I prefer being on land compared to the sea. That being said, I do not like it here. We are not alone, even though it seems that we are, and that is not a good thing. It bodes ill."

Bryen smiled as Asaia walked over and forced herself right between Majdi and Jenus, the two sometimes irascible gladiators who were twice her size giving her the space that she demanded without a word of complaint. It brought another smile to his lips. Although that smile faded quickly, Asaia's words playing through his mind.

Maybe that was why walking on this island didn't appeal to him. Maybe it was exactly as Asaia said it was. They were not alone, even though it seemed like they were. And because of that, he couldn't escape the feeling that danger lurked.

As soon as he had walked onto the beach, he had felt uncomfortable. He didn't think that it was just because he had been on board the *Freedom* for several months and that his legs were a bit shaky, this being the first time that he had stepped onto dry land since leaving Battersea.

No, his discomfort, which only increased with every step he took up the mountain, came from another source. One that he had yet to identify.

Maybe his dissonance did indeed result from the sense that they weren't alone. It was quite obvious that the other members of the Blood Company who had come with him on this task were experiencing much the same as he was.

They smiled. They laughed. They were glad to be off the ship if only for a day.

Yet their good humor didn't always reach their eyes. Some of it seemed forced, as if they needed to convince themselves that all was well.

Every so often Dorlan, Kollea, Jenus, Majdi, Asaia, or one of the other gladiators frowned for no apparent reason or glanced behind them or looked to the side with an expression of confusion or twisted his or her neck abruptly as if someone had whispered into their ear or tapped them on the shoulder.

These and a dozen other tells only confirmed for Bryen what he was thinking, because despite the gladiators suspecting that there might be someone else right next to them, there never was.

It was all very disturbing. Disorienting, in fact.

And he didn't like it.

In many ways it felt as it did when he first began fighting in the Pit, that sense of anticipation, of something coming for him dominating his thoughts, even though he didn't know what that something was.

Bryen hated this apprehensiveness with a passion. Nevertheless, he always paid attention to it. This soft voice that warned of danger had never been wrong before.

Needing to find some way to give this nagging irritation substance, he let his mind go to work.

If they weren't alone, what could it be that was watching them? And where could it be hiding?

He and Aislinn had been searching around them regularly with the Talent since they had started to climb the mountain, and they had yet to find anything that would give them any cause for concern other than the wyverns that usually stayed above the clouds when they weren't hunting along the beaches on the eastern side of the island.

Still, remembering his experience with the Echidnae in the Lost Land, that didn't mean a threat couldn't slip by them.

With that memory foremost in his thoughts, he tried again, extending his senses into the caves and sinkholes that dotted the rough terrain.

Nothing.

Not even a whisper of a threat.

Bryen growled in irritation. This enigma really was beginning to bother him.

He didn't like not knowing what he didn't know. One of Duchess Stelekel's favorite sayings that he had adopted for his own certainly seemed to apply to this increasingly frustrating situation.

So how was he supposed to find out what he didn't know if he didn't know what he didn't know?

Bryen cursed softly. Now he was just thinking in circles, which was only working to intensify his annoyance.

"Volkun, are you all right?"

Bryen turned at the call of the name given to him by the crowd in the Colosseum, Kollea having snuck right up on him since he was so distracted.

"Just thinking," he replied with a smile, reminding himself that he needed to keep track of his surroundings even as he tried to work through his nagging vexation.

Several smart replies reached the tip of Kollea's tongue. She chose to keep them there. She could make a witty comment to Dorlan or one of the other gladiators.

Not so with the Volkun. She had gained her freedom because of him. She owed him more than she could ever repay him. So she would not tease him as she would someone else.

"I checked the towers and the steel cables running down to the bottom of the mountain," Kollea said. She motioned to one of the tall structures that was built right next to one of the springs. A narrow pyramidal structure constructed of stone rose up from the ground, a long metal bar fixed across the top. Thick cables on both sides of the bar ran all the way down the slope no more than ten feet off the ground.

As they hiked up the mountain using the path that had been cut out from the forest, they had passed dozens of the same edifices during their climb. The cables weren't fraying and rusting as Bryen had thought they would because of the climate and the long period of disuse. Rather they appeared to be strong and usable.

"Will it work?" Bryen asked, glad to turn his thoughts to something else for a few minutes, even as his subconscious mind continued to gnaw at the larger problem that plagued him.

"I believe it will, Volkun. As you saw on the way up, the forest has not reclaimed these towers. A few vines at most running up the stone, but virtually nothing on the cables themselves. And I checked each one that I passed. The bases are solid. They have not moved an inch since they were first put in place."

"Any idea when that might have been?" Bryen asked, his natural curiosity coming to the forefront.

"Unfortunately not, Volkun. Although I can say that I have never seen work like this before, and by that I mean the metal. It is steel across the top and for the cables, but it is not like the steel that we use."

"Stronger?"

"Yes, and more resistant to rust, which is the death knell to any metal. Some other ore might be mixed in with it, but I can't tell what it might be. I would need a forge."

Bryen certainly was interested in learning how this steel had been made and by whom, but that was a matter for another day. "So we don't have to worry about what will happen when we send our catch down the slope?"

"No, Volkun, I believe it will all work smoothly," Kollea replied. "Before we started our climb, I checked the tower at the very bottom. The buffer seems to be in good shape. Whatever we send down will get there quickly and the system incorporated to slow it down when it gets close to the end of the line should work as it was designed."

Bryen nodded. He trusted what Kollea was telling him.

Before she was thrown into the Pit, Kollea was a blacksmith by trade. Although she had done much more than work with various metals for decades, having earned a reputation throughout Tintagel for her building and engineering skills.

If one of her customers hadn't refused to pay her what she was owed, and then questioned her abilities because she was a woman in an industry usually reserved for men, she'd probably still be there rather than here with him.

"Should we give it a try then, Kollea?"

She smiled. She appreciated how he trusted in her judgment. And she really wanted to see this ancient creation in action. "We should, Volkun. It will work. And it will make it much easier for us to get down to the ship in time."

"Excellent, thank you, Kollea. Could you get everything in place so that we can do just that?"

"At once, Volkun," replied Kollea with a nod, who immediately returned to the tower and, with Dorlan's help since she wasn't very tall, began to attach the long steel rods to the cables.

Bryen, Aislinn, and the four squads of gladiators with them had used most of the day to climb up to the springs. It would have taken longer if not for the path that paralleled the stone towers. Although relatively clear, the undergrowth was biting at the edges, it was quite steep, and several parts of the trail had been washed out over the years.

Those sections of the path created several rough patches, even a few places where gaps ten feet or more in length appeared in the trail. Those obstacles required them to go around and test their climbing skills among the rocks and boulders littering the escarpment, and that only made the climb slower and more difficult.

The thought of having to lug all those water bags back down the same way that they had come didn't appeal to Bryen. Not only because of the required effort, but also because of the additional time it would take them to make it back to the beach.

Captain Gregson had been very specific about when they needed to leave Solace Sound, and every hour they spent on the mountain brought them closer to that deadline. If the stone towers and the cables, what Kollea was calling a conveyor, could ease their burden, then all the better.

Even though he had yet to find any evidence that would support his suspicions, he was beginning to think that Captain Gregson had the right of it. This island appeared to be uninhabited. But it hadn't been at one time.

Some people had lived here. That was undeniable.

Not only because of the stone towers. But also because the forest had yet to reclaim all of their settlement.

Every so often he could make out the stone foundations of a cottage.

There were even a few walls still standing as they hiked farther up the mountain. And they had come across a well with several paths still visible in the scrub leading away from it, likely to other farmsteads.

That, in itself, wasn't all that surprising. Having a few outposts here in the Jagged Islands certainly made sense. As he and the Blood Company were learning, these islands served as useful waypoints between Caledonia and the Territories for those braving the Burnt Ocean.

But appearances could be deceiving.

There were other hints as well that these islands had been visited quite recently. By something else.

What was most disconcerting about that discovery was the fact that these later visitors didn't appear to be human.

He had found the cleanest set of tracks in dried mud that was beneath a rocky overhang that protected the ground from the rain and wind. There were also signs that whatever these creatures were had used or were using the same trail that they were. The marks were very faint, barely even there, but they were unmistakable thanks to his use of the Talent.

What disturbed him was that he didn't know what these other visitors could be.

The scratchings were similar to that of a human based on the size of the imprint, so long as every human was as large as Majdi or Jenus. That's where the faint similarities ended.

The prints that he had found suggested that these feet had sharp claws in the place of toes, punching into the ground several inches. They might even be webbed, though it was difficult to tell because of the age of the markings.

Bryen had thought that discovery strange. Then again, they

were on an island in the middle of the Burnt Ocean. Who knew what really lived in the surrounding waters?

Not knowing what could have made the markings, he decided that he would talk to Rafia, Declan, and Captain Gregson to get their thoughts. His best guess was that Captain Gregson's warning about what might also call these islands home contained more truth than fiction, especially if these creatures were tied in some way to the sea.

And it was thanks to those tracks and some other evidence that he had found that Bryen believed that he knew why the original inhabitants of this island had vanished. He didn't think that they had left of their own free will.

Whatever had come to this island after they had settled here had either forced them from their homes or eradicated them.

Bryen currently leaned toward the latter explanation, because in addition to the crumbling and collapsed stone walls and wells and hearths that still stood, he had found evidence that supported his theory. Not too far below where he was now and just off the path.

A slaughter pit.

Why he had walked into the woods at that particular spot on the mountain, he couldn't say. Maybe it was because there was very little long grass like there was everywhere else along the trail, really nothing more than crushed dirt that led in among the trees.

It was almost as if he were being pulled in that direction. Against his will.

What he had discovered there didn't surprise him, and it likely was one of the reasons the warnings in the back of his head had grown louder and more insistent the farther up he climbed the mountain.

He hadn't realized that he had walked into a burial ground that suggested the murder of dozens of people until he was standing in the very middle of it. He had corrected his count upon taking a closer look at his surroundings. Perhaps a hundred or more. Skulls, only a few still whole. Most cracked or shattered as if they had been broken open much like you would if you wanted to force a walnut from its shell.

The same with the many other bones that had been scattered about in the shallow grave that had never been refilled completely with dirt. Hundreds of bones, in fact, and all of them human. Many chipped, cracked, or broken, confirming a violent death.

A tortured end.

A subdued cheer just off to his left drew his attention from his sanguine thoughts, the gladiators watching with a great deal of pleasure as Kollea affixed two water bags to each end of the metal rod that she and Dorlan had locked onto the steel cables and then gave the bar a gentle shove. The gladiators were impressed.

The very large and heavy water skins began sliding down the cables at a steady pace, picking up speed as they went. Hopefully the gladiators trained by Kollea on how to ensure the buffers were working correctly at the bottom of the mountain would collect them without incident.

Bryen smiled himself, pleased. This small success would allow them to return to the ship that much faster, not having to worry about the extra weight.

Under Kollea's close supervision, they were done in less than an hour. All the water bags they had brought with them had been filled, attached to the conveyor, and sent on their way. Assuming that all was working as it should at the bottom of the mountain, they should now have plenty of fresh water for the final leg of their journey.

"We should have brought more bags," said Aislinn, who came to stand next to Bryen, nodding toward the many steel rods that remained that were neatly stacked next to the tower that Kollea had not seen the need to affix to the steel cables.

"Next time we'll do better," Bryen promised with a grin. "Definitely poor planning on our part."

"You want to come back up here and do this again? Even after what you discovered in the wood?"

While the gladiators had collected the water they needed, she had continued to use the Talent to search around them, her own concerns becoming more insistent even though she had nothing substantial upon which to base them.

She could sense nothing around them that should give them any reason to worry, yet that sense of foreboding only seemed to build up within her with each passing second.

"No, I don't," he replied. "Once we get down from this mountain, it's time to go. For good."

"You feel it too."

"I do. Whatever it is, it's getting closer. Yet I have no idea where it is or where it's coming from. It's masked better than the Echidnae we fought in the Lost Land."

Aislinn perked up at Bryen's comment, who at the same time realized that he had made a mistake. He had been so distracted by the tracks and the remnants of the settlement that he had not tried to search around them in a different way that might prove more effective. In the way that had allowed him to identify the invisible monsters that had been hunting them while they made their way through the Caldera and toward the Cauldron.

He was about to open himself to the Seventh Stone when he felt the first faint touch of fog sliding over the top of the mountain. Looking above him, the descending mist resembled a hand reaching down from the heights, and it was coming for him swiftly.

"I need to show you something," Aislinn said, taking hold of Bryen's arm and directing him toward a location about fifty feet above the tower Kollea had appropriated for their use. They stopped right at the edge of the forest.

She pointed down toward the ground. When Bryen saw what Aislinn had found, a bolt of concern shot through him. More tracks. At the same time that voice of warning began to scream at him, just as the fog began to clot around them.

"They're the same as what we found a little farther down the trail at that uncovered grave," said Bryen.

"Yes, they are," agreed Aislinn. "Although there's one critical difference."

Bryen nodded as he studied the markings in the mud. They were exactly the same as he had found before. A foot that resembled that of an overlarge man, though possibly webbed with sharp claws protruding from the toes.

"These are fresher."

Aislinn nodded in agreement. "No more than three or four hours old. Whatever creatures made these," and clearly they were talking about more than one beast because there were several distinct tracks in the mud, "they were here right before we got here. Almost as if they were watching us as we made our way up the mountain."

Bryen cursed himself for a fool, realizing that he had been ignoring all the hints. Seeing these newer tracks now helped to put in place all the discordant pieces jumbling around in his head.

Just as he had surmised. Webbed feet weren't needed on land. What was watching them wasn't on the island, at least not at the start. Because what was watching them wasn't from the island, although what was watching them clearly had claimed the island.

Captain Gregson's final comment forced its way to the top of Bryen's thoughts.

"The Kraken."

"You think that Captain Gregson is right?" asked Aislinn.

"I think he's not really sure what to believe, but he's more right than he's wrong," Bryen replied.

"So what are they?"

Bryen thought about Aislinn's question for a few seconds. It had to be the Kraken Captain Gregson mentioned.

Watching them. Tracking them. Hunting them.

Based on the tracks, it was as he suspected. These Kraken were a people or a species, not a monster from ancient times.

Moreover, these Kraken were touched by the Curse, because he knew now that was what had been tickling his senses ever since he had walked onto the island.

He really had been a fool, just as Asaia had warned, because he had failed to connect the dots fast enough.

The Curse that emanated from these Kraken had awakened the Seventh Stone within him as soon as he had sailed in among the islands. In fact, it was the artifact that had been offering him the warnings that made the skin on the back of his neck prickle all this time.

Maybe these Kraken were much like the Ghoules, the Curse changing them into what they were now, whatever that might be. Or perhaps they had users of Dark Magic much like the Elders, which would explain why they had hidden so well from his and Aislinn's searches with the Talent.

He didn't know for certain, but he had a feeling that he was about to find out. And very soon.

Opening himself to the Seventh Stone and extending his senses, he finally located the cause for his rapidly intensifying unease.

"They're like the Echidnae," explained Bryen as Aislinn noted how her Protector's expression darkened, his eyes hardening, his muscles tensing.

Aislinn nodded, searching around them once again, though this time taking the approach that she had learned while they were traveling through the Lost Land to the Temple of the

Ghoules. Instead of trying to lock on to a strong scent of evil, she allowed the Talent to drift, finally settling on a cloud of corruption that was advancing toward them down the mountain through the rapidly thickening fog.

"Not too far to the east?" asked Bryen.

"Yes, they're coming right at us," Aislinn confirmed. "No more than a few hundred yards away. With the fog, we won't see them until they're almost upon us."

"What is it?" asked Asaia, coming up right behind Bryen and Aislinn, just two dim shapes in the fog until she got within twenty feet of them.

"I don't know," replied Aislinn. "I've never come across them before. But there are a lot of them."

"Think of them as Ghoules, Asaia," said Bryen.

"That's not something I wanted to hear, Volkun. Nor is it something that I want to think about. How close?"

"Too close," said Bryen, who spun around and trotted back toward the gladiators, Aislinn and Asaia following him. "Blood Company, form shield wall!"

The gladiators responded immediately, all the training they received from Declan and Tarin Tentillin, Captain of the Battersea Guard, demonstrating its value. In just seconds, the four squads were in place, forty gladiators in all, shields locked together, spears right behind, a handful of swords prepared to fill the gaps.

Bryen and Aislinn stood right in the center of the line with the swords, the Talent already racing through them.

"They've stopped," said Aislinn. "One hundred yards away."

"We don't know what they are, but think of them as Ghoules," instructed Asaia, her words traveling down the line, several of the gladiators nodding. They had more experience fighting Ghoules than they would have liked, though they hoped that it would come in handy now.

The silence grew heavier just as the fog did until they couldn't see more than ten or fifteen feet to their front.

"They're not coming around our flanks, are they?" asked a worried Dorlan.

"No, they're still to our front. They're waiting. I think they're trying to figure out why we haven't run yet."

"I'm beginning to wonder the same thing myself," said Jenus, earning a soft chuckle from the gladiators positioned around him.

"How many?" asked Kollea.

"Several hundred," Aislinn responded.

"Then we should have little trouble with these creatures," she said confidently. "It'll be no worse than the odds we faced in Caledonia."

Several of the gladiators around her murmured their agreement.

As the cool, blanketing mist caressed their flesh, setting it tingling with goosebumps, the gladiators began to hear noises traveling down from higher up the mountain. At first it sounded like steel scratching along the slope not too far above them. Then, as it drew closer, it transformed into a scrabbling that reminded many of the gladiators of a crab moving across the rocks of the shore.

"They're here!" called Aislinn, sending a ball of energy into the air above them. Although her torch only expanded their ability to see to about fifty feet in every direction because of the denseness of the billowing mist, her quick thinking did give them slightly better illumination within the fog.

Those strange sounds grew louder, harsh grunts and hisses joining the mix. And then the gladiators had little need to wonder about what was rushing toward them.

The first of these so-called Kraken burst out of the mist.

The beasts resembled a living nightmare.

The creatures stood as tall as Majdi, though not as broad,

their bodies quite slim. They wore what looked to be loincloths, their flesh a bluish white down the chest and the thighs, shifting to a darker blue and grey along their ribs and sides that Bryen could only assume continued on to their backs.

Their coloring reminded him of the great white sharks that prowled these waters. That and the hardened bone that began on their foreheads just above their ears and curled back over their scalps, the protrusion resembling a serrated fin. Their feet were webbed just as he thought they would be, sharp claws several inches in length taking the place of their toes.

Two other features solidified his belief that these monsters came from the sea. First, their flesh, which even with the fog flashed because of the glowing orb above them. Not flesh, Bryen corrected. Scales. And just behind their ears, he could see several slits that he assumed were gills.

There was only one explanation for these beasts, Bryen thought. Just as Captain Gregson had warned, these were the Kraken.

As soon as the bright light revealed their approach, the creatures increased their pace, howling and hissing, swords and daggers that looked to be crafted from bone held in their clawed hands.

"We are the Blood Company!" roared Majdi as he and the other shield bearers took the full brunt of the attack, stopping the beasts cold.

Jenus, Dorlan, Kollea, Asaia, and all the other gladiators finished one of Declan's favorite sayings for the gladiator.

"We stand! We fight! We die!"

9

AT THE WALL

"Behind you!"

Kendric Winborne, Governor of the Northern Territory, spun around at the sharp warning from one of the men standing with him. He held his sword at the ready, looking for the threat that he knew was there but couldn't yet see.

He and his soldiers defended the northern wall of Shadow's Reach. The town was named for the gargantuan mountain under which it sat, the peak putting the now thriving center of business in the Northern Peaks in shadow for almost the entire day except for the single hour at midday when the sun rose to its highest point in the sky.

Kendric wished that he could see that monstrous mountain now, but he couldn't. Not even a glimpse, and it was less than a half mile away.

All he could see was the smothering fog that had drifted down from the north during the early morning hours and blanketed the plateau upon which the town was built along with the surrounding countryside.

It was a strange, unnerving world that he had entered.

Everything around him was muted and washed out.

Sound. Movement. Color.

He could barely pick out anything at all, not even the soldier who had shouted the warning, and the man stood no more than a few feet away. With the fog, the soldier was just a vague shadow who faded in and out of the mist.

Much to his relief, because he was standing right next to the battlements, he could see the long, skeletal hand, what he thought might be a claw though he couldn't tell for certain, grasping the top of the stone wall right in front of him. Without even thinking, he cut down with his sword, hoping to stop the beast before it made it over the parapet.

The Wraith scaling the wall was faster than he was, however. Kendric missed, slashing down with his sword right where the creature's wrist had been. Instead of slicing through flesh and bone the steel sparked upon hitting the wall, gouging out a large piece of stone and plaster.

Anticipating just such an attack, the Wraith launched itself one-handed over the wall with an amazing speed and power, Kendric's stunned mind working diligently to catch up to what he had just witnessed. It did, thankfully, just in time.

The Wraith stood no more than an arm's length away from him.

He studied the creature, just as the creature seemed to be taking that moment to study him.

He couldn't see the Wraith very clearly. The flesh and armor appeared to have a greyish cast, both light and dark, a mesh of sorts that allowed the creature to blend quite easily into the fog.

He could discern that the creature was quite tall, at least a foot and a half taller than he was, and he was well over six feet. The Wraith was also surprisingly thin, almost emaciated.

Kendric couldn't see its face. In fact, he couldn't see much else at all that would offer a hint as to what the creature really looked like.

He could see the glint of the steel the Wraith held in both hands. The bone-white metal that was polished and sharpened so that even in the gloom that had smothered Shadow's Reach, it gleamed brightly. Each curled, double-bladed dagger was about three feet long from tip to tip, a molded steel grip wrapped with leather allowing the creature to grasp it in the middle.

Haladies, if he remembered correctly from his lesson with his father when he was a child. Used with great effect long ago by the soldiers of the Ten Thousand, those men responsible for transforming the now largely forgotten Frisia into the Wyld, and then rarely employed since. How these monsters had come to use these daggers he had no idea.

A nasty weapon in Kendric's opinion. Frightening as well if he had the time to really think about it, which he didn't.

Pushing his curiosity to the side, Kendric tensed, preparing to attack. He wanted to get in a strike before his adversary did.

Again, he was too slow.

The Wraith moved with an almost otherworldly speed, darting in and out of the fog as if he were a part of it.

Maybe the Wraith was, thought Kendric, as he twisted and turned, dodged and sidestepped along the parapet, doing all that he could to avoid the Wraith's uncompromising assault. He demonstrated a speed and skill of his own that he found quite impressive as well, if only someone could see it. Of course, it wouldn't mean a thing if one of those razor-sharp daggers slid across his throat.

Based on the sounds echoing around him in the mist, although he could perceive nothing other than his opponent, the Wraith forcing Kendric along the battlements in whatever direction the creature desired, he could determine that the Wraiths were attacking only along the northern wall.

Kendric viewed that tactical mistake on the part of their attackers as a good thing. That gave Kendric and his Northern

Guard a chance, slim though it might be, to keep the Wraiths from entering the town.

Because he and his soldiers were able to hold their ground, he assumed that the creatures who had scaled the wall with such ease were no more than a scouting party. Five Wraiths most likely. Maybe one or two more.

If it had been a larger force, the Wraiths would be attacking more than one wall. And if that was the case, the monsters of the Murk already would be in Shadow's Reach.

Kendric had learned to fight with his brother, and he had discovered quickly that when he faced a bigger, faster, and stronger opponent, he didn't want to allow his adversary to draw out the combat. He wanted to end it rapidly.

If he didn't, then as the contest played on the advantages would accumulate with his adversary until they became too much for him. His opponent would either get the better of him because of a natural prowess or Kendric would be forced into a mistake.

After doing more escaping rather than fighting against the Wraith for the last few minutes, he realized that he couldn't allow this duel to extend for much longer. With that growing concern fueling him, Kendric attempted to go on the offensive, stepping forward and slashing at his adversary, his next few moves after that already firmly fixed in his mind.

The Wraith refused to go along with Kendric's plan, the creature easily sidestepping his attack and then coming in close, shouldering Kendric backward and toward the battlements.

The Governor of the Northern Territory would have fallen over the parapet and into the courtyard below if not for the crenels that kept him on the balustrade, the hard smack of the stone against his back knocking the wind from him, his eyes flashing with fear as the Wraith advanced toward him.

~

THE BLADEMASTER STOOD in the center of the street, listening to the sounds coming from atop the wall that was only a hundred yards distant.

He knew the cause. He had resided in Shadow's Reach long enough to experience ten Wraith raids.

There was a familiar rhythm to each one. The creatures coming with the fog, appearing atop the wall, fighting the soldiers for a time, never for more than twenty minutes, and then slipping back to the north.

The soldiers had yet to kill a Wraith. They had yet to catch a glimpse of their tormentors other than vague terrifying shapes.

Sadly, the Wraiths had never failed to kill several soldiers during each raid. Probably just to make a point.

Because he was certain that the Wraiths could sweep the wall clean of defenders if they really wanted to.

That's why the Blademaster believed that what was occurring now and had taken place before were nothing more than brief sorties. Not full-scale attacks. Not yet.

The monsters in the mist were testing the city's defenses. They were learning the soldiers' patterns. They would exploit those patterns when they decided that the time was right.

It was quite obvious to him.

The Wraiths clearly were planning a larger attack on Shadow's Reach. There really were no other good reasons for so many of these forays.

Yet he doubted that Governor Winborne had figured that out yet. And if he had, he doubted that the Governor knew what to do about it.

Of course, now that he had retired from the Royal Guard and shifted his loyalty to the Lady of the Southern Marches, that really wasn't his problem anymore, now was it?

Yet if that was the case, then why did that realization still bother him?

He felt the need to take the initiative regarding what he had surmised. But there was nothing that he could do.

He couldn't reveal who he was. If he did, that would defeat his entire purpose for being there.

More worrisome, from what he had seen during his wanderings through the fog during these attacks, although the Northern Guard demonstrated a great deal of confidence, the soldiers gaining a bit more swagger every time they prevented the Wraiths from breaching the city's defenses, they were allowing that confidence to mask the truth of their increasingly more difficult circumstances.

Whether or not they wanted to admit it, they didn't have the training or the competence to ensure that when the larger Wraith attack came, they could hold back the monsters.

The Wraiths were deceiving them. The defenders would pay a steep price for believing what they wanted to believe rather than what they needed to believe.

Admittedly, he had only glimpsed the fights along the battlements from a distance as very little could be seen in the fog. Even so, based on what little he could hear, his experience more than his eyes putting the picture together for him, he had no doubt that the Wraiths could enter the city any time they chose despite the best efforts of the soldiers.

They likely already had, in fact. It only made sense.

Unable to restrain his instincts and his training, he had wanted to get closer to the wall to get a better feel for how the Wraiths fought. During this latest attack, he hadn't scouted very far before he had stopped, standing there in the center of the street, seeking to pierce the gloom even as he knew that it was a wasted effort.

He thought that he caught a faint shifting of the fog just ahead of him. Barely anything at all really, the mist curling strangely. But it was enough to suggest to him that he was no longer alone. That had been more than a minute ago, and he had seen nothing since other than the billowing mist.

The Blademaster was about to continue on his way when a faint prickling along his skin that hinted of danger kept him in place. He remained perfectly still, using more than just his eyes to tell him what might be lurking around him.

Heeding his instincts, he pivoted to his left, raising his sword, knocking away the slash that came toward his throat, only catching the faint shift in the fog at the very last second to warn him of the danger. He then spun to his right, ducking under another slash, cutting with his own blade in a very tight maneuver, aiming for the Wraith's hip, missing, only succeeding in stirring the fog in that direction.

The creature was fast. Faster than he expected, in fact.

That brought a smile to the Blademaster's lips. He always had enjoyed a challenge.

The Blademaster jumped a few feet off the ground, allowing the Wraith's dagger to pass beneath him. He stepped back quickly, parrying the bone-white steel that cut for his throat multiple times before his adversary slipped back into the mist, growling either in annoyance or excitement. The Blademaster couldn't tell which.

He hadn't gotten a good look at the Wraith but he had seen enough to begin crafting an image in his own mind.

Tall. Skull-like features, as if the greyish white skin that blended so well with the gloom was pulled too tightly over his bones. Hands that looked more like claws, probably just as sharp as the two curved, double-bladed daggers the beast used so deftly.

Sensing the movement behind him, the Blademaster had no more time to ponder exactly what he was fighting. Instead, he turned quickly, bringing his blade around in a swift arc from his knees to his head. He caught the Wraith by surprise, the creature obviously believing that he had come upon him unawares. The Blademaster not only knocked away the dagger that once again had come for his throat, but he also succeeded in throwing the beast off balance.

The Blademaster was quick to take advantage of the opportunity that he had just created. Rather than stepping away, he advanced toward the Wraith, not allowing the creature to disengage, cutting and slashing through the fog, more often than not hearing his steel meet one of the Wraith's daggers, that raspy, sharp sound lost in the fight continuing above him on the parapet.

For the next several minutes, he and the Wraith danced around the street. Each one trying through a variety of maneuvers to break the stalemate. Each one failing.

Several times the Blademaster thanked the stars, which he couldn't see because of the fog, for his luck, evading the Wraith's cursed daggers by the skin of his teeth. Once, the sharp steel sliced across his leather armor, thankfully not cutting all the way through and into his flesh. Just the tip. If it had been more of the blade, it would have been a grievous wound.

This Wraith clearly was an excellent fighter, the creature pushing the Blademaster to the very limit of his abilities. Yet even with the fog both complicating and simplifying the Blademaster's efforts -- complicating because one of his key senses had been taken from him, simplifying because the loss of his sight forced him to fight based on instinct rather than thought -- the combat thrilled him in a way that most other fighters could never imagine.

Despite sensing that he barely had avoided his death a handful of times, in a very macabre sort of way the Blademaster was pleased to have this opportunity to test his skills against this Wraith. He hadn't had cause to pick up a blade in anger since the fight in the Highlands while on his way to Shadow's

Reach, and he was gratified to see that he was still just as quick and sharp now as he had been then.

As the sounds of the battle on the wall lessened to a low murmur, the Blademaster sensed that his own combat was coming to an end. His opponent radiated a greater urgency, obviously wanting to leave him in a pool of his own blood on the cobblestones.

Just then, the Wraith slashed for him. Although this time a bit more wildly than any of his previous attacks, the creature showing signs of frustration because of his lack of success.

The Blademaster was quick to make use of the Wraith's impatience, stepping to the side, then returning the favor with an economical stroke. He slashed with his blade not where the Wraith was, but where he believed the Wraith's leading thigh would be. He grinned when he heard the hiss of pain just off to his right side in the fog.

The Blademaster was about to press forward, having a good idea of where the Wraith was now, seeking to end the combat. Instead, he held his ground.

The Wraith was gone.

Kneeling down and studying the cobblestones, he could just make out a thin trail of blood leading toward the wall.

Then he realized why the Wraith chose then to make his escape. The fight on wall was concluding. More squads of the Northern Guard were forcing their way up onto the parapet.

The soldiers of Shadow's Reach would prove victorious again.

He hoped that someone in the Northern Guard knew the truth.

That the Wraiths hadn't come there to conquer. Not yet.

With his opponent having gone back over the wall, it was time for him to take his leave as well. He didn't want to explain to any jumpy soldiers what he was doing out in the street when every other sane resident of Shadow's Reach was staying well clear of the fog.

∼

Kendric fought for his breath as he rolled to his left, narrowly avoiding the dagger that stabbed right into the space where his chest had been, the sharp tip chipping out a piece of rock from the wall. He rolled again, and then one more time before regaining his feet, finally putting some distance between himself and his adversary.

The Wraith appeared to be more amused than concerned when Kendric escaped him.

That sent a surge of angry heat through Kendric's body. He felt as if the creature was playing with him. Testing him. Wanting to see if he had what it took to stand across from him and engage in a real combat.

Kendric's own insecurities, stoked by his rage, told him that the Wraith already knew the answer. Kendric couldn't hold his own against the monster, just as he couldn't hold his own against his brother.

That thought enraged Kendric even further. He tried to attack again, slashing with his sword from his chest to his knee and then back up again in the same motion as he advanced on the Wraith, his anger at the imagined insult driving him forward.

This time, he got in several good cuts and slashes, actually pushing the Wraith back toward the outer wall. Yet he failed to inflict any wounds on the monster.

The Wraith only had to use his long daggers a few times to defend himself. Much too frequently the creature simply twisted and turned out of the way.

Kendric had begun to worry at the start of this combat when he observed how ineffectual he was with his blade. Now that worry was turning into a different emotion entirely, his fury, which had energized him, draining away all too swiftly.

Fear.

His soldiers were still fighting, just as he was, but he wasn't hearing steel hit steel as often as he had before. He was hearing cries of pain, even terror, as well as the sickening sound of steel sliding into flesh.

He knew what that meant.

His soldiers were dying.

He searched desperately for some solution to the problem, the fact that nothing came to mind sending him spiraling down, his fear slowly shifting into despondency. Before he lost himself to that fatal emotion, a bolt of exhilaration shot through him when he heard a sound that he had been hoping for. A sound that he didn't think that he would hear in time.

Before he had climbed to the balustrade, he had ordered Captain Rensom to rouse the garrison, believing that even with several squads of soldiers manning the wall, they wouldn't be strong enough to hold back a Wraith scouting party.

He had been right. On both counts.

Just then the Wraith opposing him hesitated, allowing Kendric to twist to the side to avoid the dagger the monster had been about to drive into his gut. The Wraith jumped away from him, leaning his back against the wall. And just in time.

At that very moment, Captain Argenta Rensom's sword cut right through the space separating Kendric from the Wraith. She missed the creature by no more than a hair.

Then the rest of his soldiers were there, rushing toward the Wraith.

Their attacks were heavy-handed and inelegant, more desperate lunges and wild swings than precise slashes compared to the Wraiths. Kendric didn't care and neither did they.

The soldiers used their overwhelming numbers against the

unwelcome visitor because they knew what would happen if they tried to rely on their skill.

The Wraith had no choice but to give ground as it slid along the wall, though it made a point of parrying every swing and slash with its daggers. The monster wanted the soldiers to understand, and they did.

Even with the dozen or more soldiers trying to get in a strike, the men and women of the Guard realized that they didn't present a threat to the Wraith. Not in any real way.

Then in the blink of an eye the Wraith was gone, the fog hiding him, wrapping itself around him as if the creature were a part of it.

Kendric's soldiers had forced the Wraith against the wall, surrounding it. Rather than trying to continue the fight, the creature had jumped off the wall and vanished. Likely not feeling the need to prove anything else other than the fact that Kendric didn't have what was required to challenge the creature in a fair combat.

Many warriors would be insulted upon reaching that conclusion. They would be angry. They would seek some opportunity to remove that feeling of inadequacy.

He had been just a moment before. Now, Kendric couldn't care less.

He had learned long ago that you couldn't control reality. You could decide whether to accept it or try to fight it.

Fighting against what was had never worked for him, so as he had done since he was a child and having had to compete with his older brother, he accepted the reality that had just hit him square across the jaw.

Good riddance, he thought, acknowledging that on his own he couldn't kill a Wraith in a fair combat. So what. There had to be other ways to kill the creatures, and he would find them.

Besides, fair fights were for fools. If you wanted to fight, and you wanted to win, you stacked the deck in your favor before the fight even began.

Kendric started walking along the battlements as the sounds of the battle slowly ebbed. Every time he came to a body, he hoped that it might be a Wraith.

It never was.

The creatures were deadly adversaries. Since they had begun to harass the town and the Northern Territory, no one had achieved a kill yet.

He always leaned down so that he could see the face of the fallen soldier, wanting to memorize it. The man or woman had fought for him, for Shadow's Reach, and they deserved to be remembered by him and the many who relied on their bravery and protection.

A few times he had to step out of the way, more soldiers rushing past him, steel drawn, charging into the skirmish. They were too late.

The Wraiths had escaped, leaping back over the wall to join the one who had tested Kendric's mettle.

As he continued to walk along the parapet, he realized that this incursion had been a very close thing. Much closer than he had anticipated.

At least twenty of his soldiers, more than two squads – and he had only stationed three on the wall – were dead or wounded. If Captain Rensom and the bulk of the garrison in this section of the town hadn't appeared when they did, these Wraiths could have entered Shadow's Reach at their leisure.

He realized as well that his larger concern was also quite legitimate. One Wraith scouting party had created havoc along the north wall, almost eliminating all of the defenders. In fact, the creatures likely would have if they had been given more time.

What was he to do if a full company of Wraiths attacked? Several companies? A legion?

No matter how brave his soldiers might be, they wouldn't stand a chance against the monsters in this confounding fog.

That was a problem that he needed to address. He just wasn't sure how to do it quite yet.

He needed to talk with Ursina. About what they had discussed before.

Despite his realization that he wasn't much of a match for the Wraith, he felt better than he had in weeks. His thoughts were as clear and sharp as one of the Wraith's curved daggers. There was no haze obscuring his mind. He felt as he did before he couldn't keep anything straight in his head.

Maybe it was because he was back where he was supposed to be. Where life was simpler. Where he didn't need to make as many decisions. Or rather the decisions tended to be simpler to make.

He had always loved working with and spending time with his soldiers, even when his life was at risk. In fact it was then that he felt most alive. He had done it in Caledonia when he and his brother had defended the borders of the Southern Marches, and he did it now here in the Territory that he governed.

"Governor Winborne, are you all right?" asked Captain Rensom.

The tall woman motioned with her still drawn sword toward the long, shallow slice across Kendric's lower ribs, his blood staining the leather armor and shirt beneath.

Kendric looked down, wondering for a moment if that was actually his blood. He had been so focused on the combat, his adrenaline surging through his veins, that he hadn't even noticed when he took the wound.

"I'm fine, Captain. Thank you. No need to worry about me."

"You should have that seen to, Governor Winborne."

"Have no fear, Captain, I will. Before I do, what do you have to report?"

"As you know, we held against the Wraiths," began Captain Rensom. "The wall is clear. No Wraiths got into the city."

"You're sure of that?"

"As sure as I can be. I have ten squads working their way through Shadow's Reach right now just to make sure."

"Good," said Kendric, nodding his head in approval. He would have done the same. "And the fog?" He had noticed that it was beginning to thin out. During the fight, he could barely see his hand right in front of his face. Now, he could see a good ten yards down the wall.

"Beginning to drift back toward the north."

That was the best news he had heard since he had been called to the wall before the crack of dawn. The Wraiths only came with the fog.

"How many soldiers did we lose?"

"Eleven."

"Wounded?"

"Another eleven. Two aren't expected to survive for more than a few hours."

Hearing that, Kendric felt as if a knife had been plunged into his chest. Eleven soldiers killed, more expected to die. The fight couldn't have lasted more than a few minutes. These Wraiths were a monstrous force of nature all on their own.

"That's a very heavy price to pay."

"It is, Duke Winborne. Still, we should consider ourselves lucky."

Kendric couldn't disagree with Captain Rensom. She was correct. The fight could have played out much worse than it did.

"And the Wraiths?"

"No idea," she replied, her anger plain in her voice. "No bodies, just like all the other times that we've faced them."

Captain Rensom surveyed the battlespace which became clearer as the Murk retreated. The Wraiths had attacked Shadow's Reach nineteen times now. The soldiers of the Northern Territory had yet to come across a dead Wraith.

They didn't even know if the creatures took their dead with them, because she doubted that any of her soldiers had gotten in a killing blow yet. She had seen evidence of wounds, blood spilled on the stone walkway that she knew wasn't human, the color wrong, more pinkish white than red.

So she knew that the Wraiths bled. She just didn't know yet if they died.

It was infuriating, but even more so frightening. What would happen when the Wraiths finally attacked in the numbers required to get past the town's walls?

With the fog to protect them, the Northern Guard stood little chance against the Wraiths. Once these monsters breached the wall, it would be open season on the residents of Shadow's Reach.

The Wraiths weren't known for their mercy.

They were known for killing and doing it exceedingly well.

"Once the fog dissipates a bit more, send a company to the north. Have the soldiers follow it. See if they can find any tracks."

"We've tried that before, Governor Winborne. We've yet to find anything. Our best trackers have yet to even locate the hint of a trail."

"I know, Captain Rensom. I understand what I'm asking you to do. Still, humor me. Please."

Captain Rensom nodded. "Yes, Governor Winborne. I'll lead the company myself."

"Thank you, Captain. Now I'm going to get this wound tended to as you suggested." The pain was starting to hit him, a sharp stinging mixed with a throbbing ache that made him want to bend over in agony.

He refused to allow himself to do that. He needed to keep

up appearances in front of his Captain and the soldiers who had fought so gallantly to repel the Wraiths.

"Of course, Governor Winborne. I'll report to you when I return after searching to the north."

Kendric left Captain Rensom there atop the parapet, not reaching for his side until he had walked down the steps and was a good distance away from the wall. It took him twice as long to get to the central square as it normally would, having no choice but to slow his pace, hobbling just as much as he was walking, his hand going to his side and coming away with more blood than he expected.

Captain Rensom was right. This might be a much more serious wound than he had believed initially.

∼

The fog was finally beginning to dissipate, the first faint streaks of the early morning sun breaking through the grey haze. Even so, the Blademaster knew that the streets would remain empty for a little while longer. The residents wouldn't emerge until the bell atop the fortress sounded to announce that the grey mist, and the Wraiths that haunted it, were gone.

As he made his way to where he had been staying since he came to Shadow's Reach, he was thinking of the Lady Winborne and her Protector. They had been right to ask that he scout ahead before they and the Blood Company arrived.

Just as they feared, there was more going on here than met the eye. The Wraiths were an obvious and dangerous concern. That couldn't be denied.

Yet, the Wraiths weren't the Blademaster's only worry. Shadow's Reach held more secrets than it should, and he worried that several of those secrets could prove lethal to Aislinn Winborne.

Reaching the large, two-story house that was built only a

few streets from the southern wall, a small courtyard visible through the gated archway just to his left, the Blademaster tried the door handle. It wouldn't budge.

Locked. Good.

He knocked softly in the pattern that he and the proprietor had agreed.

She had laughed at him when he had taught her, not understanding the necessity. He had been adamant.

Better to be safe than sorry. Especially when there was more to fear in the streets of Shadow's Reach than just the Wraiths.

A few seconds later he heard several locks being undone and then a bar being lifted and placed on the floor. She had been waiting for him again.

He thought the woman who stood in the doorway mesmerizingly pretty with her long white hair curled up and pinned atop her head. Despite her petite size, her head coming up no higher than his chest, and her lithe body, she was wearing a blacksmith's leather apron and holding a heavy iron mallet. Her forearms were corded with muscle that would make a soldier jealous.

He was always struck by that one incongruity about her that was so hard to miss. She seemed better suited to be a dancer, yet she swung a hammer better than any other smith in the town.

"Jurgen, you need to stop making me worry. We've talked about this before."

"I'm sorry, Juliette," the Blademaster replied, placing a large hand gently on her shoulder and giving her a warm squeeze as he walked by her into the house. "But you know how I am. When I can't sleep, I like to wander. It just so happened that tonight the fog came in while I was out."

Juliette nodded, though not in acceptance of his excuse. Her gaze turned shrewd as she studied him. "Strange, don't you think, how you seem to wander every time the fog comes in?"

"Happenstance, no more than that," although the Blademaster knew Juliette heard the lie as he said it. Once again, she was kind enough to allow it to pass.

"Right. Just bad luck. Or perhaps good luck depending on how you look at it."

She stared hard at Jurgen Klines. She didn't realize that the man who had walked into her smithy six weeks before asking for work was the Blademaster and the former Captain of the Royal Guard.

She did know that he could handle himself quite well with his blade, having watched him many a time run through his daily practice regimen in the courtyard, a small crowd of children and even a few adults forming to watch when he did so. When he was done, he always offered the children carved wooden rods for them to use and would run them through several of the exercises that he had just performed so effortlessly.

She had found the entire experience heartwarming. Yet that wasn't why she had allowed him to come work for her. She was a practical woman after all. She had to be. Most essential to her decision, he had proven himself almost a match for her when she gave him the assignment to craft a blade to prove his skill.

That, in itself, was enough for her to hire him. She was already backed up several weeks with orders, and she was certain that he could lessen the strain.

But there was something else about him that had caught her attention, this strange feeling that always tickled the back of her brain. She didn't know what it was specifically.

A sense of loss mixed with a sense of purpose perhaps. Although she wasn't really certain, it tugged at her in a way that nothing had for quite some time.

She did know that she was quite pleased that this itinerant blacksmith had decided to wander into her forge.

"We'll talk about your poorly timed excursion later. Now,

we've got an order for three daggers, a spade, and an axe. What do you want to start on?"

"I'll begin with the daggers."

"Just as I thought you would," smiled Juliette. "Before you do, find a new shirt. We don't want any customers wondering about the blood on that one."

With an impish grin, Juliette walked toward the forge that connected to the back of the house. The Blademaster looked down at his shirt, saw the spots, smiled, then watched her go. She liked to make it known to him, indirectly of course, that there was little that he could get past her.

That was fine with him. That and several other qualities about Juliette had awakened a feeling within him that he thought he had lost long ago.

He pushed those thoughts out of his head when he walked into his small room in the attic.

Before becoming a soldier, the Blademaster had apprenticed as a blacksmith when he was younger. He had enjoyed the work then just as much as he did now. There was a certainty to it that he appreciated.

It was good to get back to it after so long away. Besides, he much preferred focusing on how to create rather than destroy.

Placing his scabbarded sword right next to his bed, he pulled off his shirt. He would wash it later. Then he pulled on a new one. Before he went down to the forge, he pulled the blade from its sheath, took a cloth from his pocket, and wiped the steel clean.

Several streaks of blood marred the weapon. He has glad to see that. It was good to know that the Wraiths could bleed.

∼

URSINA, who had been waiting at the entrance to what Kendric liked to call the Shadow Keep, their unfinished fortress that wouldn't be completed for months at the pace they were going, rushed out into the large square that surrounded the citadel. She placed her husband's arm around her shoulders as she guided him through the main gate, the soldiers standing there seeing the blood and nodding to him in respect.

"What happened, my love?" demanded Ursina, her worry for him plain.

"Nothing, Ursina. Just a Wraith. We got into an argument."

The soldiers stationed in the hallway nodded to their Lord as he passed, all of them standing a little straighter. Kendric nodded back, doing his best to hide the pain that intensified with every step that he took.

He hated that he had lost so many soldiers. The only good thing that came out of the entire endeavor, other than the fact that the Wraiths didn't get beyond the wall, was that he had increased the regard with which his soldiers held him. He could see that in their eyes. That was an important result when faced with the threat presented by the Ghoules.

Because he would need their respect and trust. The real battle for the city had not yet come.

"Your shirt is drenched in blood, Kendric," she said, her voice sharper now, not appreciating his nonchalance. She could see the wound better in the light, and she didn't like the look of it. What at first appeared to be no more than a shallow laceration actually was much deeper than that.

"It's no more than a scratch, Ursina. I promise you that," replied Kendric as they walked farther down the main hallway, Ursina guiding her husband through a doorway to the left and into his private study.

She made him sit down on a couch and then lean back so that she could see his wound clearly, carefully pulling off the leather armor that he was wearing across his chest. The slice had gone clean through. Whatever weapons the monsters in the mist used, the armor of New Caledonia offered little in the way of protection.

"This is much more than a scratch, my love," she countered. "Just a little bit deeper and you'd be bleeding internally. Several important organs would have been cut. You would have died before you reached the Keep."

"But the Wraith didn't do that and I didn't die," Kendric murmured with a smile. He was getting tired, his energy leaving him. "So a good result, in my opinion."

"I don't see how you can treat this with so little concern," chided Ursina as she began to clean the wound with warm water and several clean cloths. Kendric grimaced in pain as she did so. She didn't feel the need to be gentle because of his absurd insouciance.

"It's no more than an irritation," he said, his face twisting into what Ursina took to be a spike of agony as she pressed against the wound, trying to stop the bleeding.

She knew the truth, however, no matter how much he tried to hide it. It was anger.

That was fine with her. Better that he focus on that than on what she was about to do.

Kendric was having a hard time collecting his thoughts once again. He had been doing so well just minutes ago, enjoying a clarity of thought ever since he had ascended the north wall that was rare for him these days.

He shook his head in frustration. His ailment had reared its ugly head once again.

Kendric gasped in pain, almost doubling over, as Ursina dug more deeply into the wound, spreading a paste of herbs that she explained would help prevent an infection. The herbs also would act as an analgesic, numbing the area before she closed the wound.

"Don't worry, my love," said Ursina. "The salve that I'm using, although it stings now, will allow the wound to heal much, much faster. Soon you won't feel any discomfort at all. It will be as if the wound had never been there."

Kendric nodded, hissing one more time through clenched teeth, closing his eyes as he leaned back, trying to lose himself in the couch, not realizing that the muscle that had been sliced open already was beginning to knit itself together again at Ursina's skilled touch.

That was the source of his current pain, not the actual slice across his flesh. But Kendric didn't need to know that. As Ursina had learned quite a long time ago, sometimes it was best if the truth remained a secret.

Once the muscle was back to what it had been before the Wraith's steel had cut through it, she would accelerate the healing process for the skin. She wouldn't close the wound completely. Rather, she would do just enough so that she didn't have to fear for his life. Then, in a matter of days, he would be back on his feet with nothing but a scar to remind him of his foolish decision to challenge the Wraiths in the Murk.

Ursina took her time as she did her work, not wanting to rush, having learned from her mother that going too fast with the Talent was never a good thing, especially when applying it in such a delicate fashion as she was doing now.

Taking her time to aid Kendric also helped to ease the fear that had threatened to be revealed in the form of her explosive temper, something that her husband never responded to well. She needed to figure out some other way to get him to understand that he couldn't just go running off to fight creatures against which they had yet to have any success.

He was the Governor, after all. That's why he had soldiers. The soldiers were supposed to do the fighting for him.

Yet he still hadn't figured that out, or if he did he ignored it. Kendric had a dangerous need to be in the thick of the fighting. To always be with his troops and experience for himself everything that they did.

She needed to find some way to uproot that ridiculous urge and crush it once and for all.

"You must be more careful, my love," said Ursina for what seemed like the thousandth time. "If something happens to you, what of the Northern Territory? What of all the people who depend on you?"

"Nothing will happen to me, Ursina," replied Kendric through gritted teeth, a welcome cool finally spreading out from his wound and beginning to ease his pain. "The Wraith just got lucky."

Ursina chose not to correct her husband, not seeing the point. He would believe what he wanted to believe, and even if he didn't believe what he was saying, he would still tell her what he thought she wanted to hear.

She knew him better than he thought. She knew as well that her husband had been lucky. The Wraith didn't miss killing him by much.

Based on her experience at the Royal Medical School in Murcia, she had seen how this kind of wound across the ribs and the gut could sour quickly. If she wasn't there to minister to him, he likely would have died.

That was something else that Kendric didn't need to know. Not in that moment. Instead, she decided to raise a different topic, one that her husband had balked at before. Perhaps now after feeling the touch of a Wraith's steel across his flesh he would be more amenable to her suggestion.

"My love, it's time. You know that just as well as I do."

"What do you mean?" asked Kendric, enjoying the cool that continued to seep into his body.

"You know exactly what I mean," she replied as she reached for the bandages that she had placed right next to the couch. After her husband had rushed from their bedroom early that morning, she worried that this was where they would find themselves when he returned. If he returned. So she had prepared for this eventuality.

"I really don't."

"Now you're just trying to irritate me," said Ursina sharply, which caught Kendric's attention, her tone breaking through the haze that once again was wrapping itself around his mind.

Kendric looked up at his wife, seeing the tears beginning to form in her eyes.

"I'm not, my love, truly. I'm sorry," Kendric said quickly. "I'm sorry."

Ursina nodded, though a single tear still dropped onto Kendric's hand, the barely perceptible splash making him jump almost as if he'd been stabbed.

"We can't wait any longer, Kendric. We need to do more than we are doing now. We have no choice."

"Yes, but Ursina, if we do what we've been talking about ..."

Ursina cut him off before he could continue. "We have no choice, my love. We can't risk having the Wraiths breach the walls of Shadow's Reach. Once that happens ..."

Ursina left the rest unsaid, one hand now gently rubbing her husband's arm, her sparkling eyes staring up into his. She wanted to allow her husband to take what she was saying to its natural conclusion. Allow him to make his decision.

With just a gentle nudge of course. As she had learned with respect to healing, what she was doing now required a delicate touch as well.

"What if we lose control?" asked Kendric.

His voice wavered. He wanted to offer more protests, but nothing came to mind, the confusion that plagued him so frequently striking him at the worst possible time.

"We won't," said Ursina with an unwavering confidence. "I promise you."

"I trust you, Ursina. You know I do. It's just that ..."

"I understand your concern, my love. I do."

Ursina talked slowly in a very warm, comforting voice, doing her best to hide the irritation that was simmering just below the surface. Not with her husband's concerns. Rather, with the fact that it had taken her this long to get Kendric to this point.

She should have succeeded quite some time ago, yet he had resisted despite everything that she had tried. Finally, her words were slipping past his defenses, her thoughts becoming his, just as she needed them to be.

Reluctantly, she had to give Kendric credit. He had a strong will. She had known that the second she had met him. That was both a good and a bad thing.

In this moment, that strength of will was just another obstacle to be removed from her path. And she was doing that with a careful, meticulous application of a power that few in the Natural World had ever dared to master.

"It's the only way to protect our people," said Ursina, "what we've earned. Otherwise the Wraiths will take it all from us."

Kendric sighed, knowing that his wife was right. There was no point in fighting the inevitable, something else that he had learned while growing up in Kevan's shadow. He nodded in acquiescence.

Ursina nodded as well, smiling, and that filled Kendric with a warmth that only she could bring to him. She removed her hand from his arm, then began to wrap the clean linen around her husband's midsection. She took her time. When she was done, she tied it off tightly, earning a grunt from her husband. Then she patted him on the knee before pushing herself back to her feet.

"I know that you'll want to speak with Captain Rensom about the skirmish and how the wounded are doing. While you're doing that, I'll begin working on what we've discussed."

"Thank you, Ursina," said Kendric with a slight smile,

although that smile didn't reach his eyes. His reservations failed to leave him.

Ursina noticed. "You have done the right thing, my love. As we both know, we have no choice. The sooner that we do this, the better. It will give the Wraiths pause, maybe even keep them away from us for good."

Kendric nodded. She was right. They had no choice. It was a risk that they had to take.

He just hoped that he wouldn't regret what they were about to do. Because once Ursina put their plan into motion, there was no going back.

10

UNEXPECTED CHALLENGE

He had planned the incursion into Shadow's Reach down to the second. It had gone well. Just as he thought it would.

Even the surprise that had come his way had little impact on his timing.

His Scouts had done exactly as was required of them. But that was to be expected.

They were the best of the Horde.

The humans on the wall behaved no differently than they had every other time his Scouts had tested them. They were focused on his Wraiths to their front.

No creativity. No vision. No real grasp of what was really happening.

They never thought that one such as he might sneak by them. They never worried that a single Wraith would scale the wall on his own during the larger attack and enter the city. They never realized that he had slipped through their defenses before the fight on the wall even began. They never considered why he might take the risk.

If he chose, he could clear the balustrade of the soldiers in seconds. All on his own. That's why he led. Because of what only he could do.

The humans wouldn't understand that they were under attack from behind until they were breathing their last.

But there was no need for him to do that. Not yet.

His Scouts could kill the humans just as easily as he could. Yet they had restrained themselves. Just as he had ordered. Because that hadn't been their purpose.

The tall, almost emaciated figure in the mist snorted in disgust.

He stood at the edge of the Murk, the fog that sustained him, that nurtured him, that gave him his strength, slowly retreating to the north.

Toward the Wyld.

Toward his home.

He shook his head in disappointment. There was little challenge here.

The humans were such fools.

So easily tricked. So easily distracted. So overconfident.

He had slipped over the wall between two soldiers, the humans completely unaware that he had passed right by them. The only reason that those fools had learned that his Scouts were there on the wall was because his Scouts had allowed the soldiers to discover them.

It had been necessary if he and his Scouts were to achieve their larger objective, even though they chafed at the deception.

He had scouted Shadow's Reach several times before, testing the city's defenses. Finding them lacking. Confirming time and again that when he brought the Horde, conquering this city and putting its residents to the blade would offer little challenge to his Wraiths.

Today was supposed to have been one of the last tests. He

had wanted to make certain that he hadn't missed anything that could affect his larger plan.

The Wraith Hunter had learned nothing new the last few times his Scouts had scaled the wall, other than the fact that the humans offered a weak and unimaginative defense. He hadn't believed that there was anything more for him to learn.

Not at the wall anyway. He knew how the humans would fight. He had mastered their strategy and their tactics.

As a result, he had sought to explore the city. He had wanted to walk the main boulevards himself and put his eyes on the fortress being built in the center of the town, from where he assumed the bulk of the soldiers defending the city would emerge.

So that when the Wraith Horde came, they would know what to expect once they scaled the wall and entered Shadow's Reach. They would know how to kill the soldiers before they even reached the wall.

When he had gazed through the faint wisps at the towering Northern Peaks to the south, the Wraith Hunter had admitted to himself that all this preparation likely wasn't necessary. In every way the soldiers defending the city were inferior to his Scouts.

The humans would fight bravely. They had demonstrated that, and more credit to them because of the limitations they faced in the Murk. Unfortunately for them, courage could take them only so far in the battle to come.

Slaughter more like.

Even so, the Wraith Hunter had felt the need to do this. To take the risk.

He had tasted failure for the first time not too long ago. And from a quite unexpected source.

He had no desire to taste it again when so much was at stake for himself and the Horde he commanded.

After leaping down from the balustrade to land silently on

the cobblestoned alley, the Wraith Hunter, hidden within the gloom that had blanketed the city, had walked along the bottom of the wall for more than a hundred yards before finding what he was looking for. A larger boulevard, this one broad enough for three wagons at a time.

He had planned to walk down this avenue until he reached the fortress.

He had little to fear from the residents, all of whom had been hiding away within their homes, doors barred, perhaps even some kind of weapon held in their sweaty palms. Believing that they were safe from him.

They wouldn't realize that their belief that they could protect themselves was false until his Wraiths broke down their doors and slit their throats. And that wouldn't take long at all.

The only way to escape his Scouts was to escape the Murk. But these humans wouldn't escape. When the Horde came, the Murk would settle over the human lands forever.

It would be a glorious time for him. Even more so for the Wraith Lord. But not yet. Not until he was certain that the time was right. Thus, his decision to scout the city on his own.

While his Scouts attacked the wall for a specified period of time, the residents would remain off the streets, allowing the soldiers to fight for them.

Yet even if he hadn't been back over the wall before his Scouts returned to the north, the Wraith Hunter wouldn't have been worried.

The fog would have blanketed the city for however long he remained. The Murk wouldn't return to the north until he did. He could explore his strange environs for as long as he deemed necessary.

Because of that, he had been looking forward to the task he had given himself.

Yet he had glided no more than fifty yards down the wide street when he had been forced to stop abruptly.

A lone man had stood in the center of the avenue, blocking his way.

Peculiar, he had thought.

The human hadn't been dressed in the garb of a soldier.

He had stared at the man, trying to determine his purpose. Yet there was little that he could discern about him. The man was no more than a dim shadow in the gloom.

The man stood perfectly still, not making a noise.

Strangely, this lone human had made him uneasy. The man had held a gleaming sword in his hand, obviously well maintained. And by the way he had been standing, the human had appeared to know how to use it.

He hadn't been concerned at first. But appearances could be deceiving, as he well knew from his humiliating experience in the Murk while chasing the boy. The only quarry to ever escape him.

The Wraith Hunter had grinned. Somehow, this human had known that he was there.

Nevertheless, the Murk would hide him, just as it always did.

The Murk would hinder the human. Because the Wraith Hunter was a part of the Murk. Came from the Murk. Lived in the Murk. Drew his energy and spirit from the Murk.

Because of all that and more, he believed that just like all the others, the combat would be short. Still, the Wraith Hunter had looked forward to it.

He hadn't engaged in a real combat since he had faced the boy.

He had pulled his daggers from the sheaths on each hip. He had glided through the fog, barely disturbing the billowing grey.

And then the unthinkable happened. Focusing on it now infuriated the Wraith Hunter, making him reach for his burning thigh.

Despite the Murk, the human had displayed a remarkable skill, fighting based more on instinct than on sight. The human had made the Wraith Hunter work during their brief combat. More troubling, the human had wounded him. A shallow slice, but a slice through his flesh, nonetheless.

For a second time, he had been bested by a human.

Just like the boy had not so long ago, this man had scarred him.

His failure to kill the boy had shamed him, his wounded foot a constant reminder, still not completely healed and always throbbing during the cold nights.

He had thought his hunt for the boy an anomaly. A lesson, in fact, not to become overconfident. To tame his arrogance so that it didn't guide his decisions and his actions.

The man he had fought on the street in Shadow's Reach had reminded him of that lesson.

He had not learned all that he had wanted slipping over the wall. But he had learned enough.

Before he invaded Shadow's Reach, he needed to kill the boy and the man with the blade.

Only then could he regain his honor.

Only then could he ensure the victory of the Wraith Horde.

11

STANDING STRONG

"Blast it, Caellia! Could you at least wait until I'm out of the way! I really don't feel like getting crushed this afternoon because of your manic desire to get the work done as quickly as possible."

Chesin had barely avoided the massive tree, skipping to the side and then sprinting ten yards before it fell right where he had been standing. The string of curses that spouted from the baby-faced gladiator had made many of the soldiers of the Blood Company stop and smile, enjoying the color offered by the youngest member of their troop. A few even chuckled, though softly, knowing Chesin's short fuse.

"My apologies, Chesin," replied Caellia, as if the fact that she had almost crushed one of her peers meant little to her. "I didn't see you there."

That comment earned a few laughs from the gladiators around them.

Chesin was known for his intelligence, for not rushing into a fight, preferring to examine all the possible angles before doing so in order to craft a strategy that ensured that as many advantages as possible favored him.

Always.

Because of that, once he did engage in the fight, his success almost always was guaranteed. That was something that the gladiators who made up his squad certainly appreciated because they benefited directly from his efforts.

He was also slim and slight. That was a strange combination for someone who had survived in the Colosseum for almost three years, and those same gladiators who valued his abilities as a leader never hesitated to poke fun at him for those unique characteristics. Particularly Caellia, who was almost as broad as Dorlan and just as dangerous, although she tended to smile more and for some reason felt protective of Chesin ... when she wasn't trying to hit him with a falling tree.

"Funny, very funny," huffed Chesin. He had risked his life dozens of times in the Pit against man and beast. He had maintained a calm and cool exterior, just as the Volkun and Declan had taught him. However, with his fellow gladiators he struggled to control his temper. He found it difficult ignoring the good-natured barbs thrown his way, too often allowing them to burrow under his skin.

"Not trying to be funny," Caellia replied. "Honestly I couldn't see you. The trunk of this tree is wider around than you are."

Caellia was only speaking the truth, not intentionally trying to antagonize Chesin. Yet her response still earned another round of laughter from the other gladiators. Even Nkia who had lost her tongue when she was a child, cut out by a slaver, smiled at the unintentional barb.

Declan stood just at the edge of the work, unconcerned by the conversation, which was quite a common one among the gladiators. The men and women of the Blood Company spent so much time together and understood each other so well that they knew exactly what to say to get a rise or to calm down one of their friends. Instead Declan kept an eye on Nkia.

He was worried about her. The woman never spoke, so you needed to know how to read her eyes and her hands to get a sense of what she was feeling.

At that moment, her eyes contained a touch of mirth and her hands were well away from her ever-present jambiyas. The traditional curved daggers of her homeland were still in their specially made sheaths, one on each hip.

Declan viewed that as a positive sign. Nkia usually spent her time with Majdi, which was why he found her working there on the beach and Majdi up on the mountain a bit strange. Even a tad worrisome. For her to make that decision, he assumed that they had gotten into an argument.

He'd need to find out what had happened and determine how serious it was, because when Nkia got angry, she usually let her jambiyas do her talking for her. And though Majdi was huge, Nkia was fast.

He'd talk to Tehana. She usually knew everything that was going on and was a good bellwether for the rest of the company. Even more essential, she was good friends with Nkia, the two fighting together many times in the Pit.

He'd need to pick his moment carefully, however, because Tehana could be testy at the best of times, and he had no desire to have to deal with that shortened trident of hers. "The Fork," as some of the other gladiators described her favorite weapon, the spike in the center extending beyond the other two by more than a foot.

Of course, for obvious reasons they were sensible enough never to offer that term within Tehana's hearing. She took a dim view of anyone making fun of her for any reason whatsoever, something that several members of the Blood Company had the scars to prove.

"That was actually Chesin's secret weapon in the Pit," offered Renata. "He won all those combats because his opponents couldn't even see him."

"Really?" protested Chesin, throwing down his ax so that it stuck blade first in the fallen tree that he had already begun chopping the branches off. "You've got nothing better to do than make fun of me? Maybe a little more work and a little less talk and we can get back to the ship that much faster."

Tehana thought about Chesin's comment for a moment, seemingly giving it serious consideration. Then she shook her head. "No. We don't really have anything better to do other than to cut down a few more trees. So we might as well have our fun while we can before we're cooped up again on the *Freedom*."

Chesin shook his head in aggravation, grumbling under his breath. "Why was I such a fool to get stuck with all these grandmothers?"

Unfortunately for him, he didn't grumble his frustration softly enough.

"Who are you calling a grandmother?" demanded Renata, the smile leaving her face quickly, the gladiator assuming the deceptively relaxed posture that had been so much a part of her in the Pit.

She did, in fact, appear to be a kindly grandmother. That was until you took in the hard glint of her eyes, her complete lack of compassion, as well as her skill with the morning stars that she favored, the spiked metal affixed to the end of her two footlong clubs deadly in her quick hands.

"Oh, don't let the young one bother you, Renata," said Caellia, trying to erase the slight bit of tension that she sensed building. "You know how he is. One little nudge and he starts throwing a tantrum."

"Hey, now wait a minute," Chesin tried to protest. "I do not ..."

Tehana cut him off. "Yes, he can be like that, can't he. Don't let it bother you, Renata. Anyone who's just a few years older than him seems like a grandmother. The boy is barely out of the womb."

Another round of laughter echoed through the clearing that the several squads of gladiators were creating all on their own, the other soldiers of the Blood Company listening to the exchange now and enjoying it. Particularly since the anxiety that had been so visible in Renata, who was always quick to anger, seemed to have left her just as fast.

Besides, the conversation and the gentle fun, even at the expense of one of their own, helped to break the monotony of their work. Yet despite its tediousness, the work never slowed.

Many of the gladiators didn't like being on the island, even though at first they were quite pleased to get off the *Freedom* for a time.

Something didn't feel right here. An air of menace hung over them. Like they didn't belong. Like they were intruding.

Declan couldn't disagree with their perception, because he felt it, too. So he understood and appreciated why the gladiators, even with their good-natured joking, went at their work with a will.

They might not have spoken it out loud, but they were all of the same mind. The sooner they were done, the sooner they could get back onto their ship and leave this unsettling place.

Declan smiled himself as the teasing continued. Caellia and Tehana led it now, making sure that it never became more than just a few gentle indignities. Thanks to their efforts, he could tell by the tone that all was well.

Chesin liked to protest the frequent ribbing that he took for being the youngest gladiator in the troop -- only the Volkun was younger than he was when he first stalked the white sand -- even though secretly he enjoyed the attention that he received. He was proud of the distinction that he had earned.

As the young man tried, and usually failed, to give as good as he got, all the while chopping off branches with a vengeance while several more trees came down, thankfully none anywhere near him, Declan walked among the trees toward the edge of the wood where it bordered the beach.

Rafia waited for him there, studying another reason why the gladiators were more than happy to return to the ship even though they were just a few days removed from wanting the vessel to sink because they believed that would be preferable to the rocking and rolling of the storm.

"How did you find this? The Talent?"

Rafia shook her head. "No, the smell."

That certainly made sense to Declan as he and the Magus walked out onto the sand, stopping when the cloud of black flies buzzing through the air became too much for them. The slaughter covered most of the shore.

Neither Declan nor Rafia could identify some of the very large sea creatures that had been butchered on the beach. Judging by the spines, flippers, and fins, most appeared to be whales, although there were a few skeletons, some with strips of flesh still hanging from the rapidly bleaching bones, that looked to be the great whites that swam not too far off the shore.

"What do you think did this?" asked Rafia.

Declan shrugged his shoulders, his critical eye taking in every last detail of what he saw on the beach. Unfortunately, he had viewed much worse, although that never made it any easier when you were surrounded by so much death.

Whatever had done this had been exceedingly thorough. There were still a few ragged lengths of grisly meat on the bones. Not very much, however.

Upon a closer inspection, he confirmed that the cuts were clean. Made by a blade of some type. Sharp, very sharp. A jagged edge would have suggested the use of teeth.

"Can't say for sure, although Captain Gregson's supposed Kraken certainly do come to mind."

"A people or species of some sort?"

"Usually the simplest answer is the right answer."

"That would certainly make sense," replied Rafia, nodding her agreement. "Because this wasn't a slaughter. This was a harvest."

Declan took a few steps closer to the skeletons and rotting carcasses, batting away the black flies that got a bit too curious about him.

"I would agree. Some of these kills are fresher than the others, so whatever did this, the Kraken for now to eliminate any confusion, have used this spot on the beach to do just this very same thing many times before. Take a look over there."

Declan motioned toward a spot just a few feet in front of him.

Rafia took a few steps in that direction, swatting away several of the black flies that were buzzing about her head.

"What kind of tracks are those?"

"I don't know."

"They almost look like the prints of a Ghoule," said Rafia, that thought setting her mind down a road that she didn't want to follow.

"They do, except for that part there along the very edges of the imprint."

"What could cause that?"

"If I had to guess?" asked Declan.

"I'll take a guess."

"Webbing."

Rafia nodded, seeing it now as she peered closer. "Which would only serve to offer another piece of evidence that could confirm Captain Gregson's theory. Especially since those tracks disappear at the water's edge."

"Yes, it would."

"How long since whatever did this was here?"

"I couldn't say for sure," Declan shrugged again, not liking it when he couldn't be precise, yet knowing that in this situation he was offering just as much of a guess, "but based on these newer carcasses here closest to the water, yesterday morning at the latest."

"That doesn't bode well for us," said Rafia.

"It doesn't. Still nothing around that we need to worry about?"

Rafia reached for the Talent once again, just as she had been doing every hour on the hour since they had set foot on the island. "No, nothing ..."

The Magus' voice trailed off. Her use of the Talent pulled her gaze away from the bay and toward the mountain rising above them. Declan turned as well, taking in the thick fog that glided down from the heights with an uncommon speed. Just minutes before those mountains had towered above them framed by a cloudless sky.

"That's coming from where Bryen and the others went," a ball of concern settling in his stomach.

Rafia nodded again. There was something about that fog that didn't seem quite right to her, almost as if it wasn't entirely natural. The thick haze made her think of the one time that she had ventured into the Murk when she was younger and just a novice Magus, Sirius wanting her to get a feel for the strange, unique environment that was home to creatures whose very existence depended on that fog.

With her own worry increasing now that she had started to connect the dots, she extended her senses into the thickening mist. What she discovered after just a few seconds of exploration sent a shiver down her spine.

"We need to go. Now."

"Why?" wondered Declan. "The Kraken?"

"Perhaps," said Rafia, reaching for Declan's arm and pulling him toward the wood. "I can't say for sure. But there is something in that fog, something very similar to a Ghoule yet also quite different. Many somethings."

"That doesn't offer much specificity."

"No, but it does offer a warning. We need to get back to the ship. The sooner, the better. We need to get into a position where we can defend ourselves. We can't do that here, especially if that fog envelops us, as I expect that it will."

"What about Bryen, Aislinn, and the others?"

"Whatever is coming our way, they're already dealing with it."

"I don't like the sound of that," grumbled Declan.

"Neither do I," said Rafia. "But you know those two. Very little stands much of a chance against the Volkun and the Vedra."

Rafia's comment brought a small, very brief smile to Declan's quickly souring expression. True, but he would have much preferred that Bryen and all the other gladiators of the Blood Company were down here with him now. He hated to think what they might be facing in the murk that was quickly consuming every acre of the island.

Locking his concerns away, he strode through the wood. As soon as he got back to the clearing, he issued a quick series of orders.

They would take the timber that they had cut down. Anything that they couldn't carry with them would stay here. Because right now, their primary concern was getting to the ship before the fog did.

～

"Stand strong!" Bryen shouted, the twin blades of the Spear of the Magii glowing brightly. "These beasts are nothing compared to what we fought before!"

The gladiators standing around him roared their agreement. The Volkun was correct. The men and women of the Colosseum likened these Kraken to the Ghoules they had battled so many times in Caledonia.

The Kraken were about the same size and they moved just as fast. Their ear-splitting howls also sounded much like those of the Ghoules, although at a higher pitch that frequently set their teeth on edge.

They had defeated the Ghoules. Every time.

And they would defeat the Kraken. Because they knew that if they didn't they would pay the ultimate price.

Yet despite their confidence, the gladiators of the Blood Company faced a difficult challenge. These new adversaries blended in quite well with the billowing haze that swirled around the mountain crest.

In fact, even with the sphere of energy Aislinn threw up into the sky to give them better illumination within the fists of fog that descended from the mountaintop, the gloom was so thick that the Blood Company couldn't see anything beyond the front rank of monsters surging against them.

The beasts pressed and strained against the shield wall, bone white cutlasses and shortened tridents similar to the one Tehana employed so effectively seeking to cut a path past the barrier of steel. More often than not, the Kraken weapons clanged harmlessly against the scuta. The inscrutable gladiators held their ground, refusing to budge an inch.

The number of attackers meant little to the gladiators. What mattered was meeting the standards of the Blood Company, of performing to a level that would make their comrades proud.

They did that now, demonstrating a combination of finesse, composure, and strength that frustrated the creatures that continued to race out of the fog, screaming for blood.

Even though there were a great many similarities between the Ghoules and the Kraken, there was one key distinction.

And it was one that the Blood Company greatly appreciated and was more than happy to make use of.

A natural, spiky armor covered the Ghoules' shoulders, thighs, and forearms. Not so the Kraken.

They wore no armor other than armguards made of a substance that looked to be similar to leather but wasn't, making Jenus, Majdi, and the others think of hardened seaweed. It certainly made sense since all the gladiators assumed that these beasts came from the Burnt Ocean, the gills they saw just below their ears confirming it for them.

When Dorlan's spear or Nkia's jambiyas struck true, which happened more often than not with a lethal precision, the steel always bit deeply into Kraken flesh, the beasts' armguards only partially blunting the powerful blows.

"Aislinn, in the wood!" Bryen called out. "They're trying to flank us!"

Aislinn didn't bother to respond, immediately addressing the threat that her Protector had identified. She and Bryen had positioned themselves on the edges of the shield wall. Bryen to the north. Aislinn to the south.

Their goal was a simple one. To ensure that any Kraken who got too curious or brave and sought to sneak behind them were made to see the error of their decisions with a finality that would discourage their comrades from employing such a strategy.

The three Kraken who had thought to do just that in Aislinn's area of responsibility, believing that with their brethren pushing against the shield wall, they could steal through the wood and come at the gladiators from the side, could barely be seen in the fog. Their movements were no more than faint disturbances in the mist that if you weren't looking closely could be attributed to the gusts of air coming down off the mountain.

The surprise attack by the three Kraken likely would have

worked. Yet the creatures faced a challenge that they had not anticipated. A challenge that they could never have imagined.

Two Magii who were more than willing and quite happy to introduce them to the Talent.

Aislinn had just as much trouble picking out the creatures seeking to flank her, or rather she would have if not for her use of the natural power of the world. Doing as Bryen had done to locate the beasts creeping toward her, she extended her senses into the fog.

Three incredibly vague shapes, no more than that. But that was enough for her.

For just a moment, her thoughts drifted, remembering her lessons in the Broken Tower with Sirius. In fact, the one lesson right after Bryen had been forced upon her as her Protector.

Her father's decision to do that to her, to enslave another human being and require the gladiator taken from the Pit to serve her, had infuriated her. Yet she had no choice in the matter, and with the Protector's collar already around Bryen's neck, she could do nothing to correct it.

That evening Sirius had wanted to test her precision with the Talent, asking her to craft a sphere of energy. She did that easily. When he asked her to add more of the natural magic to that sphere, she had permitted her anger at what her father had done to affect what she was doing.

She kept adding the Talent to the sphere while also seeking to compress that energy into a very compact ball no larger than the size of a closed fist. She had forgotten that as she did that she also needed a way to release the pressure that was building up within her construction.

The resulting explosion had demolished much of Sirius' chamber and almost brought the Broken Tower down for good.

It had been a useless exercise then, or at least she had thought so. She hadn't been in the right frame of mind for that particular training at that particular time and, clearly, she had failed miserably.

But thinking about it now, she realized that she had learned an important lesson during that session. An unspoken lesson that had stuck with her ever since.

There was a time for precision and there was a time for power. Now, with these three Kraken trying to slip by her, it was time for a demonstration of power.

Three spikes of energy shot from her palm, sizzling through the fog and slamming right into the Krakens' chests. Dead before the beasts hit the ground, she decided that she needed to make more of a statement, seeing that a few more Kraken had been following after those she had struck down, thinking that they could come at her while she was occupied.

A poor and fatal miscalculation on their part.

This time she employed a skill that she had learned from Rafia. Starting on her left side and moving her palm slowly toward the right, bolts of white-hot energy blasted through the fog and ripped into the ground, great geysers of dirt, rock, and broken branches shooting up into the air.

When she was finished, she nodded in satisfaction. She had caught a good number of the Kraken attempting to flank her in what she had just done. Not all, unfortunately. But she could live with that.

Her objective had been to deter any other attempts by the Kraken to come at her from the side, and she had been quite effective in that regard, clearing the space to the south of the shield wall. Still, she'd need to keep a close eye, having no doubt that as more Kraken joined the fight, more of the beasts would try again.

Bryen grinned viciously upon hearing the explosions on the other side of the shield wall. Definitely Aislinn's work, and knowing her, undoubtedly quite thorough.

Several Kraken had thought to do the same on his side of

the line, attempting to slide around the flank. He convinced the beasts that such a tactic was a mistake, a very bad mistake, with a series of well-placed spears crafted from the Talent.

The javelins of energy struck the front rank of Kraken, streaking down on an arc to impale the beasts. The blazing tips drove straight through their chests and into the dirt, keeping the beasts upright as they died.

A macabre display and a warning to any other Kraken seeking to attempt something similar while also providing more light for a time, the javelins burning brightly in the fog as the dead Kraken flaked away because of the intense energy.

In many respects a sickening exhibition, yet also quite powerful. The Kraken avoided the flanks at all costs now, shifting their focus toward trying to batter their way through an immovable and unbreakable shield wall.

"Showing off again?" wondered Asaia. She stood just behind Majdi, the massive gladiator anchoring the slightly curled shield wall with his shoulder against the trees, and right next to Bryen.

Asaia never looked at him, her gaze always to the front, searching for an opportunity to strike over the shoulder of the shield bearer while also trying to keep an eye on him, or rather on any of the Kraken that might try to make a play for Bryen since he was proving to be a major obstacle to their efforts.

"Just doing what's necessary," Bryen replied innocently. Although if he was being completely honest, he was trying to make a statement. A very loud and obvious one, in fact.

"If you say so," she replied skeptically. "Any chance you have a plan for getting us off of this mountain?"

Asaia flicked her wrist, the spiked tip of her whip lashing out right over Majdi's shoulder to take a Kraken in the eye. The beast had jumped up into the air and over one of his fallen brethren, seeking to swing his cutlass down onto the gladiator's head.

The beast died instantly as the steel spike punctured his brain. Becoming a dead weight, he fell back toward the ground, collapsing onto several other unfortunate and now trapped Kraken.

The beasts who tried to pull themselves out from beneath their dead comrade never got back to their clawed feet, Kollea and the other spears near her waiting for just such a chance.

They finished the creatures before they could extricate themselves from their fallen peer. That gift no longer giving, she and the other spears began looking for the next opportunity that might fall right into their laps.

"Working on it," Bryen replied, slashing down with the Spear of the Magii, the blade slicing right through the wrist of a Kraken who had gotten a claw on the top of Majdi's shield and was attempting to force the rim down so that he could expose the gladiator to a swipe of his cutlass made of bone.

The badly wounded beast fell away in the crush of his compatriots, his severed claw still grasping the metal.

"Work faster," Asaia ordered. "We can't stay here for much longer. For every Kraken we kill or force from the battle, two more come out of the fog to take his place."

Bryen nodded. Good advice, he had to admit. They had been tight to the woods to begin with, even more so now as the number of Kraken rushing to join the fight pressed against the shield wall and forced them back.

Asaia was right. They needed to move. Soon. Because if they didn't no matter the skill of arms of the gladiators and the power that both Bryen and Aislinn could bring down upon their attackers, the sheer number of Kraken would overwhelm them.

For the moment, the Kraken continued to focus on trying to break through the shield wall, not yet realizing that they stood little chance of doing so if they couldn't bring more of their number to bear on their adversaries from more than one direction at a time.

No matter how many beasts threw themselves at Majdi, Dorlan, Jenus, and the others, they stood little chance of success, the gladiators standing just as strong as their steel scuta. And so long as he and Aislinn protected the flanks, the stalemate would remain.

Good in one sense. Not so good in another.

There were a lot of Kraken and more joining the fight every minute. He had no doubt that the flow of beasts into the battle only would accelerate.

He could hear the screeches in the fog, muffled though they were, coming down the mountain slope. That, along with his regular searches with the Talent, confirmed the ever-increasing number of Kraken the Blood Company now faced.

The Kraken would learn once they had spent all their frenetic energy and rage on the shield wall.

Eventually, the Kraken would be too many and the tide would turn, and not in the gladiators' favor. One of the creatures would get in a lucky strike or one of the gladiators would slip.

It would be a small event, inconsequential most of the time, though not now. It would change the scope of the battle and shift the momentum to the Kraken, an occurrence that Bryen wanted to avoid at all costs.

Because once the Kraken gained the initiative, he and the Blood Company would never be able to swipe it back.

Just a few more minutes, Bryen believed. That's all they needed. Just a few more minutes.

The gladiators far below them likely knew that there was trouble on the heights. His and Aislinn's use of the Talent were tell-tale signs of the danger even if the gladiators couldn't see through the fog. With all the water bags they sent down, the squad would need just a few more minutes to retrieve the skins and then make their way to the *Freedom*.

Of course, whether they had a few more minutes, Bryen had no good way to judge. Already, he could feel the tempo of the clash changing as more Kraken rushed into the fight. Slowly, true, but still shifting toward the side with more fighters.

The thickening fog didn't help matters. Even with the light provided by Aislinn, it was difficult to track the Kraken. The beasts moved in and out of the mist breathtakingly fast, more accustomed to the environment than he and his gladiators were.

With those realities governing his thoughts, Bryen realized what he had to do next. Focusing on one of the many pieces of advice that Declan had given him while fighting in the Pit, Bryen knew that he needed to change the landscape in which they fought.

Literally.

But they needed to adjust their positioning before he could make that happen.

"More Kraken are coming down from the heights!" yelled Aislinn so that she could be heard over the clash of steel, still making use of the Talent to aid the gladiators on her flank, and now just as often swinging her sword and earning a satisfying crunch and screech as she cut through Kraken flesh to the bone. "This batch is more organized. It's almost as if they're in formation."

"How many?" asked Bryen.

Bryen lifted the Spear of the Magii above Jenus' head, the gladiator standing right next to Majdi, their shields locked together. He caught the Kraken's overhead strike right before it could slam down onto Jenus' scalp.

The Kraken howled in rage. Not only because Bryen

blocked the attack, but also because when the cutlass struck the Spear, the bone-white blade shattered.

"Five hundred."

"Five hundred!" exclaimed Asaia.

"Maybe more," muttered Aislinn. "I can't tell for sure with this blasted fog and the fact that the beasts are so crammed together that I can't get a good count."

"Fair enough," said Asaia. "Still, that's too many for us. What shall we do, Volkun? Our time here has come to an end."

Bryen nodded. He couldn't disagree with her.

For just a few seconds he wondered where the Kraken came from. Likely not from the island, he believed. There was little evidence of them being here other than to wipe out whichever people had settled on the cay however long ago it was.

Judging by the looks of them, especially their gills, the beasts were most likely able to breathe underwater just as they were able to do so on land. He wouldn't be surprised if they came from the sea, marching over the spine of the island from the eastern shore. But did they spend more time on the land or in the ocean?

If he was right that the beasts came from the sea, that begged the question of where in the Burnt Ocean the Kraken originated from, as well as how these creatures adapted over time to two very distinct environments.

Those questions were certainly worthy of consideration, just not now. Bryen pushed his thoughts about the origins of the Kraken to the side. He could worry about all that later. Assuming there was a later.

"More Kraken are coming from the south," reported Aislinn. "They're approaching through the woods behind us. We won't be able to get back to the ship the way we came."

With the Kraken coming from the rear, they needed a more defensible position. They couldn't allow the Kraken to trap them. They didn't have the numbers to take on any more of the beasts than those who pressed them now.

Ever since the Kraken had raced out of the fog, Bryen had been seeking some solution to their dilemma. He had rejected the first few ideas that had come to mind. Until now. His gaze drawn to the stone tower just a few hundred feet to his left.

"Volkun, what do we do?" repeated Asaia, the stress beginning to show in her voice even as her actions remained smooth and precise. Her whip shot out over the shoulders of the shield bearers time after time, seeking to ensure the Kraken never lasted long in front of the shield wall.

Her work and those of the other gladiators positioned behind the shield bearers proved essential to their maintaining a solid defense. Leaving a gruesome pile of dead bodies right in front of the shield wall hindered the beasts seeking to break the line of steel.

"Waterskins," said Bryen, a smile playing across his face even as he lunged with his Spear, the blazing steel slicing right into a Kraken's shoulder near his right arm. With a quick twist of the blade when he pulled it free, Bryen nicked the Kraken's artery, ensuring that the beast would bleed out from his wound.

"What did you say?" asked Asaia, the gladiator sending the tip of her whip back over Majdi's shoulder for what seemed like the hundredth time in just the last few minutes.

She growled in anger. This time she missed the Kraken who was closest to the shield wall. The beast had gotten lucky, unwittingly turning his cheek at the best possible time.

The Kraken howled with pleasure at his success, only to feel the sharp steel rip across the back of his neck a second later as Asaia pulled the whip back toward her. The Kraken's clawed hand went to the wound that spilled blood liberally down his back, Kollea making good use of the beast's distraction to drive her spear right into his ribs.

"Waterskins," Bryen repeated loudly so that Asaia could hear over the clamor of the fight.

"What do waterskins have to do with our escaping this mess?"

"I'll show you."

They were already tight to the woods, the rough bark of the trees just a few feet behind them. Once the Kraken circling around them were in position, they would have no way to defend their rear.

"Blood Company, it's time to show these bastards that you can't attack the gladiators of the Pit and not expect to bleed!" roared Bryen, hoping that his effort to approximate Declan's stentorian voice was appreciated by those around him. "We make for the tower! Form square!"

The soldiers of the Blood Company responded instantly, the command ingrained within them. They shifted their positioning fluidly, never giving the Kraken who still pressed them the opening they sought in the shield wall.

In just a few seconds the gladiators completed the maneuver despite the pressure being applied. It was a very small square, just two rows deep, shields in the front, spears in the back, but it would serve its purpose.

"On my command," shouted Bryen, "slow march!"

The soldiers of the Blood Company moved as one, pushing toward the north, the Kraken slow to respond to the change in tactics.

The beasts were astonished that their enemies had managed to adapt so readily in the face of the pressure they were applying.

"Aislinn, help me clear the path. We need to get there faster."

Bryen didn't have to yell this time, as the Lady of the Southern Marches stood right next to him in the middle of the square. She didn't hesitate at his request. Making use of the

Talent, she crafted spheres of energy that were no larger than a child's ball.

Once again, focusing on the need for power rather than precision, the massing Kraken allowing for nothing else, she threw the blazing orbs just a few feet in front of the moving shield wall.

Bryen mimicked her. The power of each strike, one following right after the other in a deadly rhythm, blasted the Kraken out of the way, leaving torn and broken bodies off to the side as the Blood Company continued its steady, inexorable advance through the mass of creatures.

So it continued for almost a minute, the Kraken struggling futilely against the blazing energy being thrown against them, unable to defend against the Talent, unable to stop their prey from advancing. Until finally, Bryen called a halt, the square now centered on the tower that they had used just a half hour before to send waterskins down the mountain to the beach.

"Kollea, get those bars attached to the cables," said Bryen, pulling the diminutive gladiator aside and motioning to the steel spars leaning against the pole. "Asaia, please help her. One for each gladiator."

Kollea and Asaia went to work immediately. Kollea climbed onto Asaia's shoulders so that she could reach the cables. Asaia handed the bars up to her as soon as she was ready for the next one. It wasn't long before they had exhausted the supply resting against the base of the tower.

"We're going one squad at a time, Kollea."

"That should work," she agreed. Her analytical mind had already done the calculations, judging how much weight the towers and cables could hold without having to worry about the entire structure collapsing.

"Are you sure about this, Volkun?" asked Majdi, the gladiator who was the biggest of them all bracing himself along with Jenus and the other fighters holding the line so that they could block several rushes from the Kraken. "I might be a bit too big to do this. I don't want to take the entire length of cable down with me."

With the Blood Company back in place, the Kraken once again charged at the shield wall with a reckless abandon. They were angry that their adversaries had shifted their location before they could implement their full strategy and had avoided their brethren who were making their way up the mountain from the south.

"It's either you give it a shot and see how it goes or we roll you down the hill," replied Bryen. "Your choice, although I know which one I'd pick."

Majdi only needed to think about his options for a second. "I'll tempt fate on the line. Rolling down the mountainside doesn't appeal to me. I don't feel like being sick again."

"Good decision," agreed Asaia. She shifted her gaze to Bryen. "What are you going to do? I have a feeling that you're not going with us."

"It's my turn to serve as bait," he replied. "Even if we all get away down the cables, the Kraken will be right after us, and they move much too fast. They'll catch us on the beach before we can get back to the longboats."

"So you mean to keep them focused on you." Having known the Volkun ever since she had entered the Pit, she wasn't really surprised by Bryen's decision. He was prone to taking whatever risk might be needed if it helped his friends. Always thinking of others first.

Admirable, in her opinion, though also annoying, as she and the Volkun had discussed several times less than a year before during their journey to the Sanctuary. However, unlike then, this time she had no good way to argue against his decision.

"Kollea," said Bryen. "Your squad first. Get ready."

"This is a bad idea, Volkun. I am not leaving you here to ..."

Aislinn reached out to Asaia, grasping her forearm and nodding her head, letting her know that she understood the gladiator's concerns. "Please, Asaia. We can do this. But we can't do this if we have to worry about you and the Blood Company as well. Do as Bryen requests. We'll give the beasts something else to worry about until you're well away. Then we'll join you."

For the next several seconds, Asaia stared at the Vedra, searching for some other argument that she could offer to stop this foolishness. She growled in annoyance when nothing came to mind.

What Bryen was thinking of doing at first glance seemed a fool's errand. Nevertheless, she could see the logic even though she didn't want to. It was a good plan, just a risky one. So she agreed reluctantly with a sigh of resignation.

"Thank you, Asaia," Bryen said, offering her a nod of respect.

Asaia nodded to him in turn. "If you and the Vedra don't make it off the top of this mountain, Volkun, you and I will have words on the other side."

"I would expect nothing less, Asaia." Bryen turned toward Aislinn, confirming that she was ready for what they were going to do next. "Your squad last, Asaia. Majdi as the tail, just in case. Get the others out of here as fast as you can."

"As you command, Volkun," replied Asaia, all business now that the decision had been made.

"Ready?" asked Bryen.

Aislinn nodded. "We're going to need some space if we don't want the Kraken in here with us."

"Leave that to me. You be ready for the next step."

Bryen opened himself to the power contained within the Seventh Stone, the artifact that had merged with him welcoming his touch. In the blink of an eye, a wall of fire sprang up just a foot in front of the shield wall, the Kraken jumping back, several caught in the flames because of the press of bodies behind them, the gladiators in the front rank turning away from the scalding heat, protected by their shields.

Just as fast as the flames appeared, they vanished, a dome constructed of the Talent slamming into place, preventing the Kraken from getting at the Blood Company.

For just a few breaths, no one moved. Then the Kraken rushed back toward the barrier – enraged, hungry, desperate -- battering helplessly against the dome Aislinn had put in place that rose twenty feet off the ground and was open at the top.

Bryen nodded, pleased. "Well done, Aislinn. Asaia, get everyone going."

Asaia didn't need to be told a second time. At her command, Kollea took the lead, jumping up onto the bar affixed to the cable. With Jenus giving her a gentle push, she began her long glide down the mountain toward the beach, her pace accelerating as the decline steepened. Now it was just a matter of holding on as she sped down the slope, Jenus and all the other gladiators quick to follow her.

"I'll see you on the other side, Volkun," said Asaia. She was the last of the gladiators in the dome except for the Magii and Majdi, all the others well on their way to the beach.

"I'll see you on the other side," replied Bryen, giving her a gentle push as he sent her on her way. Then Majdi right after her.

Just to make certain that his friends could focus their full attention on riding the cables down the mountain, as Asaia and the others left the safety of the barrier that Aislinn had formed around the steel tower, he covered each gladiator with a mist of energy that swiftly solidified.

It protected them from any attempted attacks by the Kraken as they sped right past the beasts, as he didn't want any of them to be knocked from the bars by the lucky thrust of a cutlass. The ephemeral barrier remained in place until the gladiators were well clear of the Kraken, fading away the closer they got to the beach far below.

He was less concerned about their landing at the base of the mountain, even though it might be a bit rough, knowing that they had been through worse. When Asaia was a few hundred yards down the slope, he released his hold on the Talent.

Now it was just him and Aislinn standing within the protective dome and what looked to be more than a thousand Kraken desperate to break through the barrier and rip the flesh from their bones.

12

CLOSING THE GAP

"Just a little farther, father. We're almost there. Once we're at the far edge of the valley, we can stop for the night. You can get some rest."

Dougal, head down, wheezing, concentrating solely on putting one foot in front of the other, could only nod. He saved what little breath he was able to get into his lungs for his next step.

Jakob glanced at him sideways as he walked. The worry that had plagued him since the slavers beat his father, that had intensified every day since they had escaped those bastards, was becoming all consuming. He didn't know what he could do to help Dougal.

It seemed that every mile they traveled his father shriveled just a little bit more within himself, his features becoming gaunter, his skin tightening around his bones, his posture making him think of an old man with a bent spine.

His father had discarded just an hour before the long piece of wood that Jakob had cut for him to serve as a staff.

Jakob had believed that it would help his father maintain his balance and make his trek just a little bit easier. Dougal had thanked him for the gesture, but he didn't want to waste what little energy he had on carrying the stave. He would rely on his son to help him stay on his feet.

He wasn't surprised by his father's fairly rapid transformation during the day. It was a regular occurrence now, what little vigor Dougal was able to acquire during the night lost within the first few hours of the next morning's hike.

When they began their latest slog as soon as it was bright enough to see, Dougal had started in on a familiar topic. He repeated time and again why they needed to make for Shadow's Reach.

Jakob understood that while his father offered this now well memorized diatribe, Dougal was spending just as much time trying to convince himself of the need for the decision he had made as he was Jakob, since he had sought multiple times during the last few days to change his father's mind.

He argued as he had before that better they find a safe place where Dougal could regain his strength before they made for Shadow's Reach. And as had happened so many times before, it didn't matter. Everything that Jakob said fell on deaf ears.

This became their routine. Incredibly frustrating, yet inescapable.

Dougal talking to himself for a few hours to convince himself again that he was right, that they needed to go to Shadow's Reach despite the many perils and uncertainties of that journey. Once done with that, he shifted his focus to giving Jakob a lesson. And then another lesson. And then one more. As many as he could fit in.

And so it went until Dougal didn't have the energy to do anything else other than to put one foot in front of the other and plod along the rough trail that led to the same routine the next day.

It would begin again as soon as the sky began to brighten.

His father always started with a story or two from his time in the army. First as a scout. Then as a raider. Finally as a corporal.

Dougal then would fall back into the last role he had played in the Royal Guard before moving to Roo's Nest as a Sergeant charged with training the new recruits.

Jakob had heard it all before. Many times. Still, he kept his mouth shut even though he knew exactly what his father was going to say and how he was going to say it.

He didn't mind. Because if Dougal was talking, he was walking, and his mind wasn't focused solely on the pain and discomfort that would worsen with each step he took.

The lessons varied each day.

How to track quarry. How to make use of specific types of terrain to remain unseen, whether as a hunter or the hunted. How to work through a thicket without giving yourself away. Where to step in a woodland so as not to leave any tracks. Where to do the same in a marsh, in a jungle, on a beach.

When to walk through streams. Where to walk through streams. Where to emerge after walking through streams. How to walk down streams. When to allow a stream to carry you. Dougal went on for quite a long time on this particular topic, having a great deal to say about streams.

How to judge how far away a noise was when going through the mountains. When walking across a steppe. When walking through a forest.

Where to hide in a wood. Up a tree. In a river. On a plateau. In the long grass. In the snow. In a marshland. Always making sure that no matter where you hid, you always had another avenue of escape.

Jakob listened with half an ear as his father carried on until he began to lose his energy. He stayed quiet, not interrupting, knowing that Dougal's effort to educate helped to distract him.

As his father continued talking in a quiet voice that as the hours passed became more difficult to hear, a clear sign of

Dougal's waning strength, Jakob spent most of his time paying attention to what might be around them, utilizing much of the knowledge that his father already had imparted to him years before.

It was the only tool he could employ that helped to control his increasing worry. About being caught in the open by their pursuers, because if the slavers found them they would stand little chance against so many, but even more so about his father.

Today, just like the last few days, after the first few miles, which had taken several hours to complete, Dougal had stopped talking.

It wasn't that he didn't have anything else that he wanted to tell his son. It was that he couldn't say it. Not if he wanted to stay on his feet, needing to save his breath to keep moving.

Once again, just like the last few days, Dougal had been reduced to a very simple task that was becoming more and more difficult with each step he sought to take.

As another long day came to an end, he and Jakob were making their way through a small valley, towering peaks rising up along both sides. There was a rough trail that meandered through the wood, but they stayed off the path, tracking it as they walked among the trees several dozen yards to the west.

It made their journey quite a bit more difficult. However, neither of them considered surrendering the surreptitious nature of their hike for speed.

Jakob had heard his father's stories and lessons so many times that he could hear them in his head before he went to sleep at night. And still he heeded them.

There were many reasons for staying within the forest. The most obvious was that there was no way to hide his father's shuffle along the trail. Not wanting to make the job of the slavers coming after them any easier than it already was, he opted for a pace even slower than what they would have attained on the path for the relative safety of the trees.

His concern regarding their pursuers never far from the top of his mind, Jakob searched around them every hour, keeping a close eye on the men following them.

A dozen slavers. All of them with the whips he had grown to hate upon being captured soon after their arrival in the Highlands.

The long, bloody streaks along his back had yet to heal completely, reminding Jakob every time he moved the wrong way of the Sergeant's malice and the pleasure the man had taken with every lash. Yet that didn't compare to the pain and suffering that his father was experiencing now because of the beating the Sergeant and his comrades had administered to him that night on the ledge.

Pulling his thoughts back from the dark road they had begun to wander down, Jakob began to think about what he could do to give him and his father a better chance of evading their pursuers.

The slavers were coming steadily closer. The men were only a league or so behind them now. At the pace that he and his father were going, that wasn't unexpected, but that fact didn't make their current situation, which was quickly becoming more dire, any more palatable.

It wouldn't be long before those slavers reached the ridge not too far to their south. They would get a good view of the valley then.

Jakob hoped that by keeping off the trail their hunters wouldn't catch a glimpse of them, because there was no way that he and his father were going to get out of the valley before the slavers arrived.

Just another challenge in what already had been a long, challenging day.

As they approached the far end of the hollow, his father was struggling even more. Dougal's right leg wasn't working as it should, his father finding it hard to lift it off the ground, forcing him to drag his foot through the brush.

His father's difficulty walking was nothing compared to his difficulty breathing. Jakob could hear it. The raspy wheeze accompanied by the sound of fluid in his lungs that made it seem as if his father was drowning with every shallow breath he managed to take.

Jakob wanted to help his father, yet there was little that he could do. He had learned a great deal from Aloysius on the application of herbs for various injuries and ailments, even how to use the Talent to help with various afflictions, including how to mend a broken bone. But Jakob had only limited experience applying the Talent to heal, and he had no idea how to mend what was broken within his father.

He feared that they would soon reach the point where he would need to carry Dougal if they were to have any chance of staying ahead of their pursuers.

For just a second, Jakob closed his eyes at that thought. He could do that if it became necessary, carry his father, though not for long. Dougal had lost a great deal of weight in just the last few days, but he was still taller and broader than Jakob was.

Jakob muttered to himself in frustration.

It was only mid-afternoon. He had hoped that they would escape the valley before the slavers joined them in the dell.

Unfortunately, as was the case with most hopes, it wasn't to be. Not with his father failing as he was.

They needed to stop. Soon.

Reaching out faster than a slaver could snap his whip, Jakob caught his father at his elbow right before he fell to the ground, his dragging foot getting caught in a system of roots that ran across the forest floor. After he helped his father regain his balance, Dougal brushing him off as soon as he could start walking on his own again, Jakob reached for the Talent.

He searched for the slavers and confirmed that they were

about to reach the ridge overlooking the valley. He also examined the ridge on the northern side of the valley toward which they were hiking.

He found what he was looking for just a quarter mile ahead of them. It should serve their purposes well. The relatively even ground of the valley became rougher there, the small hills running all the way to the border of the vale.

It was close to where the winding trail led up and out of the dale, though not too close to the path that continued between the peaks to the plateau above. That was a good thing, because they needed to go in that direction anyway. Just not yet.

Jakob had no intention of going beyond the valley, at least not today. With the chill in the air a harbinger of the coming winter, the sun would begin to fall soon. He hoped that with the darkness and the thick covering of vegetation across the entrance that he had spied thanks to the Talent, he and his father could slip into the cave that he had located and stay there for the night.

If good fortune favored them, the slavers would continue to the north, getting ahead of them rather than pushing them from behind. A good plan, Jakob thought.

Still, only a plan. Good fortune hadn't favored them since they had arrived in Ballinasloe. There was no reason to think that their luck would change now.

"We aren't climbing out of the valley?" Dougal asked, noticing how his son steered him further to the west and away from the trail, leading him deeper among the trees.

"No, not today," explained Jakob, the northern ridge becoming visible through the infrequent breaks in the tree cover, the cave that was beckoning to him only a few hundred yards away. "As I said, we'll hole up for tonight. I'll find us some food. We can get some sleep. We'll start fresh on the morrow."

"Is that wise? Should we not climb to the plateau what with the slavers so close behind us?"

Jakob looked at his father, and not just with a glance this time. He really looked at Dougal, beyond just what he had been focusing on since their escape from the slavers.

Dougal had become more haggard. Worn. Thinner.

That wasn't a surprise.

What was a surprise was that it seemed like he had aged a decade for every day that they had spent free from the slavers. He was bent at the waist, one hand against his battered ribs, his broken wrist badly swollen, the other hand out to the side to provide balance when there was need.

Jakob saw something else there as well, and it worried him more than any of his father's other ailments.

He and his father had already spoken about their plans for the day. Several times, in fact. He and his father had agreed on how far they would go and what they were going to do that night.

Dougal had forgotten. Again. They had spoken about just this not more than an hour past.

Worse, the look he caught in his father's eyes suggested that the man who had raised him wasn't entirely there. The spark in the back of his eyes was barely a glow, his expression more of confusion rather than purpose.

Perhaps it was just that his father was tired. His energy gone.

Jakob had been asking quite a lot of him as they continued toward the north. More than he probably should have asked of him, yet he had been given no choice.

Jakob would need to keep a close eye on his father, even closer than he had been, because he couldn't escape this larger fear now that he had identified it. Dougal's physical ailments were obvious, less so the maladies that now were affecting his mind.

"We'll let those bastards go past us." Jakob didn't bother to add on as he wanted to "just as we discussed before."

He didn't want to agitate his father. He didn't want to start an unnecessary argument. He just wanted his father to get some rest. Hopefully, Dougal's clarity would return with a good night's sleep.

His father nodded, satisfied by Jakob's explanation. "You'll use some of what I taught you earlier today when you look for food?"

Jakob was both heartened and saddened by that comment. Heartened because Dougal remembered having that conversation with him. Saddened because he seemed to think that this was the first time he had spoken with Jakob about surviving in the wild.

"I will. As soon as you get settled in the cave I found, I'll start putting all that into play."

"Good," said Dougal with a short nod of approval. "So you'll be hunting?"

"Yes, and not just for dinner."

Jakob didn't plan on taking any risks. He couldn't. Not when his father depended on him.

But if there was an opportunity to improve the odds they faced, and he could do so without getting caught or putting himself or his father in too much danger, he planned to visit whatever harm on the slavers that he could.

∞

"Can you see anything that would suggest they're still in the valley?" asked Remy.

The large soldier turned slaver stood in the middle of the trail, hands on his hips, his gaze fixed on the steep climb that led to the plateau a quarter mile above them. He could really only see the first hundred yards or so of the steep, rock-strewn path, the falling night blanketing the rest of the way in a deep shadow that darkened as the last rays of sunlight slipped below the horizon to the west.

His dozen men were scattered around him. Most standing, a few sitting on a fallen log that abutted the path. They were tired. They had been up before dawn following a trail through the wilderness that was barely visible to most of them, only Dennis having the skill to keep them on track.

"No, Sergeant," replied Dennis. He was the smallest of the men in this troop, but that was all right. He wasn't with them for his fighting prowess. He was there because his comrades believed that he could find a needle in a haystack. He had served under the Sergeant for several years, and despite his skill, from which the Sergeant had benefited multiple times, he knew that he needed to give a thorough answer in order to avoid Remy's temper, which was never very far from the surface. "But I also can't find anything to suggest that they left the valley."

"No marks on the trail?" asked the Sergeant.

"None that I could see since we came down into the valley. They might have decided to step off the trail and go through the woods, which would mean a slower trek for them and our needing to find their trail again. That would be the smart thing for them to do. It's what I would have done if I were them."

"Be thankful that you're not them, Dennis. They're not going to like what happens when we find them."

"I am thankful, Sergeant. Believe me, I am."

"We don't have time to waste, Dennis. We need to find these two and get back to the mines. We're supposed to receive another shipment in the next few days, and I need to be there for that."

"Of course, Sergeant," replied Dennis, knowing the Sergeant's motivation. If he wasn't there to accept the shipment, he might not get paid all that he was owed. That's something Dennis wanted to avoid, because if the Sergeant didn't get paid what he was owed, none of them got paid what they were owed. "I understand, Sergeant."

"Then if you understand, why would you suggest wasting time backtracking through the woods to find their trail?"

"I'm not, Sergeant."

"Then speak plainly, Dennis, because you're beginning to irritate me."

"What I'm suggesting, Sergeant, is that we know the two slaves came down into this valley. We know that they didn't try to circle around behind us. The valley is too small. We would have noticed. Besides, based on the marks at the top of the southern ridge, we know that one of the two is hurt. He's having a hard time walking with a bad leg."

"Get on with it, Dennis," the Sergeant instructed with a motion of his hand, his aggravation beginning to increase, although he was pleased that his tracker had been able to discern all that from just a few faint marks on the dirt trail that led down into the vale.

"I'm saying the two slaves came down into the valley," said Dennis, rushing out an explanation, not wanting to be the target of his commander's anger. "They either found a place to hide for the night in the valley or they continued on up the trail. However, I can't tell you with any certainty whether they left the valley because the path out of here is more rock than dirt. It's conceivable that they did climb out. I won't be able to tell for sure until morning. So they're either still in the valley or just above us on the plateau. Either way, they can't be very far in front of us now."

"Not even with torches?" asked Jensin, one of Dennis' friends who had signed onto the Sergeant's company at the same time he did.

Like Dennis, Jensin had joined because he had wanted an adventure. They had been in the Territories for more than a year with few prospects, struggling to make ends meet.

Jensin had gotten the adventure he craved during the last two years. That and more. Much more, in fact, than he had ever wanted.

He had done things that he never thought that he would do. He had done things that he never wanted to do. Still, he had done them.

He hadn't had a choice. At least that's what he told himself.

He needed to justify it all to himself somehow. Otherwise he couldn't sleep at night.

Jensin pushed those depressing thoughts out of his mind. It was wasted time, wasted thinking. In for a penny, in for a pound.

He had known what he was getting himself into when he signed the piece of paper that the Sergeant placed in front of him even though he could barely write his name. Just because he didn't like some of what was required of him really didn't matter. What's done was done.

Besides, the work that he performed, particularly the parts that he disliked, paid well. It gave him enough coin to have some fun in Ballinasloe and the Stone when he and his friends traveled there looking for new yardbirds.

"Yes, not even with torches, Dennis?" asked the Sergeant, picking up on Jensin's inquiry.

"Too many shadows with torches, Sergeant," explained Dennis.

Remy gave some thought to what Dennis said, his simmering anger at having missed their quarry for another day slowly dissipating. Dennis was his best tracker. He had no reason not to listen to what he said.

Still, he didn't like the idea of leaving the valley. At least not all of them. Not with the possibility that the two slaves might still be here. Not until he was certain that their quarry had continued up and onto the plateau.

"I'll take the bulk of the squad out of the valley and search the plain before we make camp about a mile from the ridge. You shouldn't have any trouble finding us."

Dennis saw that his Sergeant was directing his comments toward him. It didn't take much for him to figure out what his Sergeant had in mind.

"You want me to stay here. See if I can find anything come morning."

"Exactly," said Remy, knowing that his best tracker would understand his reasoning without needing much instruction. "Not just you, however. Jensin, Ralf, Oogi, and Erick will stay here with you. At first light, take a good look around. If we don't see you by mid-morning, we'll know to come back down because those two slaves are still here. And if you join us by then, we'll know that they're up on the plateau. Maybe just a little farther north than our camp. They wouldn't have gotten far, not if one of them is hurt like you said. So you either take them come morning, or we take them on the plateau shortly after that."

Dennis nodded. He couldn't fault his Sergeant's reasoning. It was sound.

He just didn't like it. He believed that splitting up the squad in this wilderness placed them at an even greater risk than they already faced.

He wasn't worried about the two slaves they were hunting. Taking those two would be easy once he found them.

He was more concerned by the howls that had followed them for the last few nights.

They weren't supposed to have to worry about the Stalkers. His Sergeant had been clear about that. And Dennis really didn't have cause to not trust in the man and what he told him, because the Sergeant's own life was on the line as well.

Still, the Stalkers made him nervous. Just because those monsters weren't supposed to do something didn't mean they wouldn't. Particularly if they were starving.

As Remy used what little light remained in the day to lead the rest of the squad out of the valley and up the steep trail, leaving Dennis and his unlucky friends with him, another howl broke the silence of the falling night.

The sound, just as it always did, sent a shiver of fear through Dennis' entire body.

The Stalker was close. Just outside the valley.

With him and his friends stuck here for the night, Dennis really hoped that monster stayed well clear of them.

Just as it was supposed to.

13

UNWANTED VISITOR

When Jakob stepped out of the cave, leaving his father asleep against the back wall, he made sure that the long vines extending down from the knoll were draped over the entrance to ensure that nothing could be seen of the inside of the crevice.

That task done, Jakob moved stealthily through the forest, careful not to make any noise or leave any tracks, gliding through the wood with the quiet of a Wraith in the Murk.

Just to be certain, he climbed a tree and walked from one to the next on the thick branches that often twisted and twirled around one another above the forest floor. Doing that helped to ensure that there would be no way for any of the slavers to find where his father was hiding if he made a mistake during his scouting and left a discernible mark somewhere.

Whoever was tracking them knew what they were doing. There was no reason to make it easy for them.

When Jakob finally dropped back down to the ground, he stayed several dozen yards away from the trail as he made his way to where the path led up and out of the hollow. Finding a good spot among the brambles where he couldn't be seen but he could see all that was going on around him, he waited there for more than an hour, not moving, barely breathing, allowing the rapidly falling darkness to settle over him.

He had picked this particular location that was close to the trail but not too close after searching the vale with the Talent. Jakob didn't have much longer to wait.

Torches appeared along the meandering path, continuing haltingly until they reached the base of the climb. With those torches came more than a dozen slavers.

He watched intently as the men engaged in an animated conversation, the results of which clearly didn't please some of them. He couldn't hear what the slavers were saying, but he didn't need to. He knew what they were discussing.

The slavers faced a dilemma of Jakob's creation, and in the end they did much as he expected that they would.

After discussing the situation for only a few minutes, most of the slavers started hiking up the steep trail that led out of the valley. Five of the men stayed in the hollow, giving their comrades who were leaving them behind forlorn glances.

Based on the brief glimpses he caught of their faces thanks to the illumination provided by the torches they carried, none of the slavers tasked with staying in the valley appeared to be all that pleased about their fate.

Jakob identified several different emotions, the most common being fear. Clearly, they didn't want to be there, and he could understand why.

Most people avoided being out in the wild at night if they couldn't find a strong defensive position, especially when the clouds blocked the moonlight and the stars. The almost pitch black made it difficult to see more than a few feet around in any direction even with their torches.

The slavers were no exception. That had been made clear when he was a captive.

Not so for Jakob. He welcomed the dark.

Unlike the slavers, he enjoyed a clarity of vision that allowed him to see quite well when night fell. His father told him that his eyes sometimes looked like they were glowing when they used to work out in the fields at night behind their small cottage that was situated a few leagues outside Hardholm.

A gift, his father had said, to be able to see in the dark. Jakob didn't disagree.

And now that he could employ the Talent, his already good night vision had improved dramatically. He put it to use right then.

With the side effects from his concussion now negligible and continuing to fade, his natural prowess and the additional boost gifted to him by the Talent allowed him to see all that was around him just as if he were looking at it in the bright glare of the midday sun.

The howl of a Stalker ripped through the darkness. The cry startled the men who had been left behind, several of them actually jumping a few inches off the ground.

Jakob didn't move, unaffected by the shriek. He remained hidden behind the brambles that grew liberally throughout the wood.

Thanking his father for the skills that he had instilled within him, Jakob judged the beast to be on the other side of the ridge. The chilling cry was not as sharp as it would be if the Stalker was already in the valley.

The monster was a threat. A real one. Just not yet.

Using the Talent, Jakob confirmed the beast's location. It was coming in his direction. Though slowly.

Whether meandering or hunting, Jakob couldn't tell. Definitely a concern, but not an immediate one.

That worry no longer a priority, he could focus on the slavers who remained in the dale.

He had to decide what to do next.

Should he take a more aggressive approach with these men or simply stay in the background and hope that they continued up onto the plateau in the morning following after their friends?

The more he thought about those two options, the more the latter didn't appeal to him. He had been making his decisions based on the actions of the slavers ever since he and his father had escaped the chain and then the Wraiths.

He was tired of doing that. He wanted to be more direct in his approach.

He wanted to take the initiative. Another lesson from his father that had stuck with him.

The tracker with this group of worrywarts was the key.

Several times during their journey from where their group of prisoners had been slaughtered by the Wraiths, Jakob had believed that they had covered their tracks so well that no one would be able to follow them. He had been wrong.

He assumed that the smaller man with the many hulking fellows who clearly had spent time in one of the Caledonian Guards was the reason for that.

If he could eliminate the tracker, that might make it easier for him and his father to escape. Or, it could increase the level of difficulty that he and Dougal faced.

Whomever was leading the slavers likely wasn't a fool. If Jakob killed the tracker, that action would better frame for the leader where he would need to conduct his search for the quarry that had proven so elusive during the last few days.

With his father limited by his injuries, the radius of that search would be small indeed. The conclusion of the chase guaranteed.

That was a result that Jakob wanted to avoid if at all possible.

Those two options played through his mind as Jakob watched the nervous men for a time. The slavers built a very large fire in the center of the trail, the flames licking five or six feet into the air. Once they were done, they all huddled close to the blaze on a few fallen logs that they pulled out from the surrounding wood. Apparently none of them desired to hunt for their dinner, biting into dry rations.

Every so often one of the men glanced over his shoulder into the darkness. Not really wanting to find out what might be lurking right beyond the reach of the dim light, though still worried about it. Still unable to control his nerves.

Just as Jakob thought. These men, who were more than happy to harm and torture innocent people, to force them into the mines and toward a certain death sentence, were afraid.

Good. He could use that.

So what to do next?

He couldn't attack the entire group at once, at least not with steel. He could use the Talent, but the blasts of energy might be visible and heard above the ridge, thereby bringing the rest of the slavers down here. Perhaps even the Stalker as well.

Besides, if he actually succeeded in killing these slavers, the larger challenge still remained. Those above would still come down if these five didn't appear the next day when they were supposed to.

Then he and his father would be trapped in this small valley, because he doubted that he could make it up onto the plateau and remove the leader and the rest of his men before he was discovered. That last part of what Jakob viewed as an overly reckless strategy just wasn't going to work.

Then another thought popped into his brain that made him smile. It might actually work, he told himself, assuming, of course, that everything played out as he wanted it to.

Granted, his father would have scoffed at that notion. Dougal had taught him that as a soldier you couldn't depend on anything during a fight other than the fact that something was going to go wrong.

Still, the strategy that came to mind now seemed like a good move. Its simplicity appealed to him as did what he could gain from it.

As Jakob tried to poke holes in his idea, he realized that his decision was being made for him. The slavers actually were pushing him in the direction that appealed to him the most.

The slaver who Jakob assumed was the tracker had gotten up from where he had been sitting by the fire and talked with the other men briefly. He then headed into the wood, another of the slavers following him.

The tracker probably wanted to scout around them just to confirm that there were no real threats nearby, the Stalker's howl likely making him even more nervous than he already was.

Good. Jakob could work with that.

Even better, these two were looping around him, beginning a long arc that would take them several hundred yards away from the fire and closer to where Jakob had jumped down from the trees.

At present, it seemed like everything was working in Jakob's favor. Just as his father said that it wouldn't. He might as well take advantage of it while he could.

Not one to scoff at his good fortune, Jakob judged where the two slavers would be after a quarter hour of wandering among the trees. Having fixed the location in his mind, he moved. Silently. Allowing his brightly glowing eyes and the Talent to guide him through the pitch-black forest until he reached the spot that he deemed best suited for what he wanted to do next.

He searched around the valley with the natural magic one more time, just to make sure. He nodded to himself, pleased.

The Stalker was still outside the hollow, though it was coming toward the vale on a more direct path now. More important in that instant, the two slavers were right where

Jakob thought they would be and had yet to move from the course that they had selected originally.

With the two men only a few hundred yards away, Jakob climbed the tree he stood next to without making a sound, then perched himself on a limb about fifteen feet above the ground that allowed him to look down on what was a very narrow trail. The muddy ground below suggested that it was a path preferred by the many deer that populated the Highlands.

Jakob didn't have too long to wait. Two torches came into view just a few minutes later as the slavers worked their way along the overgrown path.

Realizing that he had miscalculated by just a few feet, Jakob adjusted his positioning. He moved a little farther out along the thick branch. The wood bent a few inches because of his weight but did no more than that. He had walked along this same branch after he left the cave, so he wasn't worried about it breaking.

He wasn't worried about being discovered either. The soldiers carrying the torches would be able to see about fifteen feet in any direction they looked. They would not be able to see above them, the bright light from the torches blinding them to what hid among the branches.

Jakob just needed to time what he was about to do correctly.

"Do you really think that this is a good idea, Dennis?" the larger slaver asked of the smaller one.

"No, but I don't like not knowing what's out here in the dark, Jensin. There's a Stalker about. I really have no desire to meet that monster in the flesh."

Jakob listened to their conversation with half an ear as the two slavers continued to approach slowly, their torches moving in whatever direction the two men turned their heads at any particular time.

It was as he had thought. The two slavers, or rather the

scout and a friend he had forced to accompany him, were walking a long circuit in the wood around their camp more to assuage their fears rather than to actually look for anything that might be of concern.

A useless exercise for them. Certainly useful for him.

"I know there's a Stalker about," protested the one called Jensin. "That's why I don't understand your need to leave the fire and come out here in the dark."

"It's just an itch that I need to scratch," the one named Dennis explained. "That's all. I don't like to be taken by surprise."

"Do you really think a Stalker is going to attack five soldiers? The beasts are lethal, yes, but they're not stupid. They know what to attack and what not to attack. The Sergeant said that we would be safe from them. That the Stalkers wouldn't bother us. He was very clear about that. Several times, in fact, since some of the men were getting nervous. He said that we were protected."

That last comment caught Jakob's attention. Why would these men believe that they were safe from the Stalkers? What kind of protection did they have?

"Do you believe everything the Sergeant tells us, Jensin? He's only telling us what he's been told, so who knows how many lies are mixed in with the truth? He's only ..."

Dennis never got the last few words out, his tired eyes widening in shock when he turned to argue his point further with his friend. He stared at Jensin, watching in disbelief as a shadow dropped down from just above them, the flame of his torch revealing a glimmer of steel before it disappeared into the back of his friend's neck.

Dennis stood perfectly still, the frightening shadow stepping up close to him when Jensin collapsed to the ground. Before he could do anything more than gulp in fear he felt the bloody steel blade of the dagger at his throat.

Finally, he thought to draw his sword. To scream.

It was too late. He had no options now, all because he had frozen in place, his terror running rampant through him for just a few seconds.

The shadow knocked the torch from his hand, the lantern sputtering out when it fell into the dirt, darkness pressing in on him. He was blind without the moonlight, scarcely able to make out the figure standing just a foot to his front.

All he had before he lost his torch was a brief glimpse of hard green eyes that flashed in the flames before the pitch black smothered him.

"It seems kind of foolish to be out here on your own," said a soft voice that held absolutely no warmth within it.

The coldness almost made Dennis evacuate his bowels then and there. He wasn't a soldier. He was a tracker. This wasn't a situation he had trained for. He wasn't supposed to have to deal with things like this.

"I just ..." Dennis couldn't get the words out, his mouth dry, his throat closing, his body beginning to tremble.

"Who are you looking for?" asked Jakob, stepping one foot to the side when he heard the sound of and then smelled the trickle of urine working its way down the tracker's leg.

Jakob should have felt bad about what he was doing. He didn't.

He didn't like killing anyone. He didn't like putting this man in such a position. Still, what he liked didn't matter. Not now. Not when he viewed any person willing to enslave another as less than human.

Besides, the reality that hit him straight across the jaw was quite simple. If he didn't kill these men and all the others pursuing him, they would capture or kill him and his father. That wasn't a conclusion that he was going to permit without doing everything that he possibly could to prevent it.

Now that the shaking man had relieved himself of all the

liquid in his bladder, Jakob waited a few seconds more for the tracker, the one named Dennis, to respond. The man had become a wreck in less than a minute, the death of his friend and the threat that stood before him affecting him badly.

Needing to help the tracker regain some semblance of clarity, Jakob pressed the dagger harder against the man's throat, drawing a thin rivulet of blood.

That certainly got his attention. Dennis now stared at Jakob with even wider eyes, his blubbering having come to an end, at least for now.

"Who are you looking for?" Jakob asked again.

The sting of the small slice across his throat woke the tracker from his daze. "You, I'm assuming. And one other one. There were two separate prints leading away from the first slaughter. I assumed that we were always following two slaves."

"Slaves?" asked Jakob, the sharp steel cutting a bit more deeply across the tracker's throat. "I am not a slave. I will never be a slave."

"I'm sorry. I'm sorry. I'm sorry." Dennis could barely get his stream of apologies out, his terror all encompassing. "It's just what the Sergeant makes us call those being taken to the mines. I'm sorry. I'm sorry. I'm sorry …"

"Why?"

"What?" asked Dennis, tears streaking from his eyes, snot bubbling out of his nostrils. "Why do we call you slaves?"

"Why are you following us?"

"I don't know," he replied, his breath coming now in hacking sobs. Jakob began to worry that the man was going to pass out.

"What do you mean you don't know?"

"I don't know. I really don't know." Dennis spoke as quickly as he could, hoping that if he answered this phantom's questions he would gain some leniency and avoid the fate that had befallen his friend. Of course, the still rational part of his mind told him that was no more than a dream. "I just do what I'm told. What the Sergeant tells me to do. I thought it was strange as well. Why bother going after two slaves? It didn't make sense, but I didn't have a choice. I didn't have a choice. I have to do what the Sergeant tells me to do."

"Quiet," Jakob commanded in a sharp hiss. "How long have you worked for the Sergeant?"

"Two years."

Jakob pulled back the dagger just enough to remove the steel from the man's flesh.

He was angry. But that emotion wouldn't help him now. And he wouldn't be able to get what he wanted from this tracker if the man became too frightened.

Jakob's small show of charity had an immediate effect, Dennis taking several deep breaths and succeeding in calming himself down, at least a little bit. The man's eyes were still wild, often flicking to the left and right, hinting that he was getting ready to bolt. If the tracker tried, Jakob was ready.

"Why would you take such work?"

For just a second, Dennis considered offering an evasive response. He immediately thought better of it.

What would be the use? If he was caught in a lie he was dead.

Besides, he had little loyalty to his Sergeant or the lord he was working for. It was just a job that paid well. If those two were in the same position as he was in now, they'd be blathering like a baby just as he was.

"There was little work to be found in Fal Carrach or the Highlands."

"There was plenty of work to be found in both Territories," challenged Jakob, the blade of his dagger once again pressing into Dennis' flesh.

"I'm sorry. I'm sorry. You didn't let me finish." The tracker's eyes had gone as big as plates again. This time, however, Jakob kept the steel in place, forcing the tracker to whisper, speaking any louder pushing the dagger back into his flesh. "There was little work that paid well."

"Profiting from the misery of others," murmured Jakob. "Yes, it does pay well I assume, until you're made to pay for your crimes."

"I didn't do anything wrong. I never hurt any of the prisoners like the others did. I was just a scout…"

Dennis stopped whispering as soon as the steel cut more deeply into his throat, the thin trickle of blood expanding. But what frightened Dennis even more than his wound were the shadow's eyes. Bright green. It looked like they were shining in the dark like one of the monsters his father had threatened him with when he was being difficult and didn't want to go to sleep.

"You were complicit in all the crimes committed, tracker. Don't try to escape that. You can't."

Dennis gulped, then nodded, willing to do anything to appease this shadow. Willing to do anything, reveal anything, that would give him any chance at all of surviving this encounter.

"You work for the Sergeant?"

"I do. He's the one who hired me."

"This Sergeant brings prisoners through the Highlands to the mines?"

Dennis began to shake his head no, then quickly stopped himself, realizing that with a blade up against his neck that was a very bad idea.

"No, the Sergeant doesn't. We don't. We're stationed at the mines. If any slaves …" Seeing the green flash of his captor's eyes, Dennis quickly corrected himself. "If any of the men and women forced into servitude escaped, we were always sent after them."

"Did any of the prisoners ever escape?"

"No, never. They were always too weak to go far."

"Why not just leave them? Why go after them?"

"Because the Sergeant feared that even if one prisoner survived in the Highlands, the stories that could be told could prove dangerous to what we were doing there."

Jakob thought about what the tracker had said. It all made sense in a very brutal way.

"Going back to my original question, why bother pursuing us? Just because we might talk if we actually escaped? It seems like quite a bit of effort with very little to gain."

"I don't know." Dennis tensed when he felt the steel slice more deeply into his neck again. "Truly, I don't know. I'm not lying. I really don't know." The tracker's last few sentences came out in a rushed squeak, Jakob pulling his dagger back so that the man could speak more freely. "We came from the mines. We were supposed to find out what had happened to the last few groups of prisoners. None had arrived for several weeks, and we needed the workers. The Sergeant wanted to open more shafts. He had just made a big discovery and sought to profit from it."

"They were dead."

How the phantom said it, his voice somehow carrying heat and cold within it at the same time, made Dennis shiver in fear.

Dennis nodded, having a difficult time controlling his shaking body.

"They were dead," he agreed.

"Then why come after us? I would think that you would have larger issues to worry about than two escapees after finding those many poor souls."

"We didn't want to. Most of us didn't want to. But Remy, our Sergeant, insisted upon it. He wanted to find you. Not so much because he feared that you would talk – he assumed that you and whoever is with you would die with winter coming on – but because he wanted to confirm what happened to you and the other prisoners and soldiers. He feared that there might be renegades in the Highlands helping to free the work parties."

"Your Sergeant couldn't tell by the cuts in their flesh as to what happened to them? Doesn't sound like much of a soldier if that's the case."

"We all could. He knew what happened. It was obvious. But he wouldn't let it go. He thought the two who got away might be able to tell him more."

"All because of curiosity?" asked Jakob. "Sounds like you're stretching the truth."

"I'm not, I swear," whispered the tracker before the steel cut into his flesh again. "This was becoming a larger problem for him. The number of work parties failing to appear at the mine. It was slowing down production, almost bringing it to a halt. He had yet to figure out how to deal effectively with the monsters in the mist."

Monsters in the mists. Jakob allowed the phrase to play through his mind.

That was certainly a good way to describe the Wraiths.

"You and the others should have just gone back to the mines. If you had done so, you wouldn't be here now. Your friend would still be alive."

"I agree," nodded Dennis. "I didn't want to be here. None of us wanted to be here. The Sergeant …"

"Why would you be safe from the Stalkers?" asked Jakob, cutting off Dennis, wanting to follow the path that had been teasing him since he had heard this tracker speaking with the now dead slaver lying at his feet.

"What?"

Clearly this tracker who didn't view himself as a slaver was having a difficult time keeping up with him. So Jakob asked again, his eyes flashing in anger, and that clearly had an effect on his captive.

Dennis tried to lean away from the shadow. Jakob didn't permit it.

"Why would you and your friends be safe from the Stalkers?" Jakob already had a working theory. He wanted to confirm what he believed.

For just a moment, the slaver didn't appear to understand the question. Jakob sensed his hesitation. He decided to provide the tracker with some additional incentive, as if what he had been doing already to the frightened man wasn't enough.

"Your Sergeant isn't here. He won't be coming here to help you. Nor will your friends. They're still sitting by the fire. Even if you scream, and you won't, they won't be coming to help you even if they wanted to. But they don't want to help you. They're too frightened of what they might find if they left the comfort of their fire. You know it just as well as I do."

"How could you know that?" whispered Dennis.

"Because I'm not what I seem, tracker. As I said, I'm not a slave. I never will be. But I know, just as you do, that you are alone. No one is coming to help you. No one is going to know what you tell me. So there really is no point in trying to keep the secret that I know you really want to tell me."

Dennis gulped, thinking about what this shadow had said. Then he nodded. The shadow with the glowing green eyes was right.

"Because the Lord ..."

Sensing a hulking presence at his back, Jakob ducked and rolled to the side. As he spun away, he slashed with his dagger. He was gratified to hear a tight hiss of pain.

By just a hair he avoided the Stalker that had crept up on them through the wood. The beast's wickedly sharp claw, targeting the back of his neck, instead sliced just a very narrow, clean furrow across Jakob's right cheek.

The trickle of blood that resulted was nothing compared to

what happened to the tracker. The Stalker's claw continued right past Jakob and punched first into his flesh and then through his ribs, the sound of breaking bone sickening.

The last thing that Dennis saw before his vision blurred and he collapsed to the ground was the blood-red eyes of the monster that his Sergeant had promised would stay well clear of him and his friends.

Howling with pleasure at its kill, the Stalker spun around, claw covered in blood, seeking the other human. The human it had missed. The human it had been hunting.

With a grunt the Stalker dodged backward, then again. And one more time followed by another, the motion becoming repetitive and irritating. Each time the beast moved, it raised a forearm, the dagger cutting across its flesh rather than sliding into its body.

Snarling with rage, the beast tried to break away, hoping to regain the advantage it had enjoyed when it first came upon its target.

Jakob refused to allow it. He continued to press forward, the Stalker skidding on some wet leaves, that small mistake allowing Jakob to punch his steel between the beast's lower ribs instead.

Enraged by the wound, the Stalker was slow to recover, its shock at being hurt slowing it down.

Jakob took full advantage, ripping his steel free and driving it into the beast's hip.

The Stalker tried to force his attacker back, swiping wildly for its prey's face. That action, again driven by rage, proved to be another mistake. A more critical and more painful mistake.

Jakob pulled his head back just in time and just far enough to escape the Stalker's claws. Then, feinting a stumble to his left, he tilted his shoulder and cut across the beast's belly from left to right in a backhanded slice.

Not wanting to cede the momentum that he had worked so

hard to earn, Jakob continued to press forward, his dagger a blur as he kept the Stalker guessing as to where the next attack would come.

As he did so, Jakob cursed himself for the error that he had made. The error that had almost cost him his life and would have ensured his father's death as well.

He had been so focused on taking the slaver because he was desperate to find out what the man could tell him that he hadn't been keeping track of the Stalker that had been roaming along the edge of the valley. He should have been keeping an eye out and assuming that the beast would come down into the vale, but he had allowed himself to be consumed by another task.

The monster had come right for him. He wouldn't even have known that the Stalker was there if not for that prickle of warning that he felt when the air right behind him shifted ever so slightly when a large presence filled the previously empty space.

And he couldn't allow himself to be diverted now by thoughts that weren't relevant to his staying alive. Watching the Stalker pull back its other claw and anticipating what the creature planned to do – ripping out his heart just as it had done to the slaver – he took a half-step back, pulled his sword from the scabbard across his shoulders, infused the steel with the Talent, and slashed down.

The entire process took less than a heartbeat – all credit to Aloysius for teaching him how to do this -- and even then Jakob was almost too late, the creature's claw less than a knuckle away from cutting into his chest when his blazing steel sliced through the beast's hand just in time.

The Stalker reared back, screaming in agony, all of its clawed fingers except for its thumb dropping down into the dirt of the forest floor.

Before the Stalker completed its cry, Jakob was gone, twenty yards beyond the beast, sprinting through the forest. He sheathed his sword as he fled, just holding on to his dagger, allowing the Talent to guide him as he sought to make his escape.

He dodged around the trees and ducked below drooping branches with ease, even avoiding the slippery patches across the forest floor created by the piles of leaves and mud pits spread randomly throughout the wood.

If not for his use of the Talent, the Stalker would have already caught up to him. But now he had a chance.

A slim chance, true. But still a chance.

The beast howled in rage as it sped after him, shredding branches that got in its way, bouncing off tree trunks, stumbling or slipping across the rough ground, having only one thought in its mind.

Kill the human who had dared to stand against it. Kill the human who had maimed it.

Whatever reason the Stalker once had was gone now, the beast driven into a frenzied rage because of its many wounds. Its badly mangled claw pulsed with a pain that ran up and down its spine, a steady stream of blood splattering onto the ground from where its digits used to be. That was joined by the agony of the long, thin slice across its belly.

With the creature so close behind him, Jakob realized that he couldn't make for the cave. He couldn't risk bringing the beast to his father.

He decided on a different approach instead, hoping that he could put the Stalker's fury to work for him.

Skidding to a stop, Jakob ducked, the Stalker's uninjured claw sweeping through the air where his head had been just a moment before. Rather than finding the flesh the beast so desperately sought, the taloned fingers slammed into the trunk of the tree rising to its front, digging deeply into the wood.

While the beast tugged viciously, trying to pull free its claw,

Jakob sliced down with his dagger, cutting cleanly across the back of the monster's right hamstring. The Stalker wailed in agony as he suffered a second wound to his already injured leg, almost collapsing to the ground when he finally tore loose his claw.

The creature sought to impale his attacker. Instead, the wild swipe pulled the Stalker off balance, the stress of the movement too much for his badly injured leg.

Roaring in rage, the beast collapsed to the dirt. When it finally hobbled upright again, the Stalker realized that once again his prey was gone.

Jakob sprinted toward the east. He considered trying to kill the beast when it fell. He quickly decided against it.

Although the Stalker was injured and vulnerable, he feared that if he made a single mistake, the Stalker would kill him, which would leave his father alone in the cave, a death sentence for Dougal.

Besides, Jakob still had a use for the beast.

Hearing the Stalker's screams catching up to him, though not as rapidly as before, he smiled evilly. This just might work.

The beast was still coming for him despite his many wounds. Hobbled now, however, the Stalker not able to stay with him as the beast had before.

Recognizing that limitation, Jakob slowed to a trot, wanting the beast right behind him for what he had in mind next.

∼

EVEN WITH HIS CUT HAMSTRING, the Stalker forced his way through the forest, dragging his injured limb behind him as best as he could, desperate to catch up to his prey. The rage at his current plight fueled the monster, allowing him to seal away his pain.

How his prey could do as it had done to him, the Stalker

couldn't understand. None of his other quarry had ever even known he was there before they died.

Because of that the beast only thought of the kill now, the desire for revenge. Not even considering the risk of following the prey that so far had outsmarted him.

The beast could see clearly in the dark, not needing the moonlight to find his way.

The Stalker screeched in fury, his large, clawed foot digging up the dirt and the rocks, sending the piles of leaves in all directions, as he pulled his useless leg behind him, eager to repay the human who had harmed him.

His prey was just up ahead, no more than thirty feet in front of him, a large fire visible and putting the human into stark relief.

∼

JAKOB SMILED GRIMLY, hearing his pursuer crash through the forest. He didn't think his plan had more than one chance out of a million of working when it first came to mind.

Now, he grew more confident about the possibility of success. The Stalker was closing on him, less than a dozen yards behind.

The slavers' fire served as a beacon for him, Jakob sprinting again, not wanting to allow the Stalker to draw too near to him. He headed right for the flames, barely even glancing at the three slavers standing there in front of the fire, swords held nervously in their hands.

With just that quick look he could tell that these three slavers, used to meting out a harsh existence to the prisoners brought into the Highlands, were frightened. Visibly so.

Their bodies shook. The constant shrieks of rage and howls of pain erupting within the valley had set them on edge. That and the fact that two of their number had not yet returned.

Jakob wasn't concerned about the slavers seeing him for who he really was. They couldn't. Not in the shadows created by the massive blaze.

The men would assume that he was one of their two missing comrades.

He was sure of it. Or at least as sure of it as he could be.

Jakob ran right for the slavers, hoping for the best, sprinting across the trail and then jumping right through the large fire. The flames singed the skin on his arms, burning off the hair.

The momentary pain was worth it.

Because as soon as Jakob's feet hit the dirt on the other side of the blaze, the enraged Stalker burst out of the wood, racing right toward the three men standing dumbly in front of the fire.

All three hesitated. They didn't understand what was happening. They didn't know what to do.

That indecision didn't bother the Stalker in the least. The beast wanted to kill. And he didn't care what he killed, the strictures placed on him by his master no longer holding because of his pain and bad temper. The Stalker simply needed an outlet for his rage.

The Stalker's screech of fury brought the three slavers out of their daze. All the men had experience as soldiers. They tried to put their training to use as they defended themselves.

After dodging out of the Stalker's way, the beast pulling up short right in front of the fire, almost stumbling into it because of its mangled and bleeding leg, the three men attempted to work together. They surrounded the Stalker, thinking to employ their advantage in numbers.

One of the slavers actually got in a good strike before the Stalker turned around, his sword cutting down and across the angry beast's collarbone. The problem for the slaver was that his sword wasn't made of good steel. The blade barely cut into the beast's flesh, the rusted length shattering against the Stalker's muscled shoulder.

The soldier stared at the hilt of his weapon, speechless, his mind trying to comprehend what had just happened. He didn't feel the swipe of the Stalker's claw as it ripped out his throat.

With one of the slavers crumbling to the ground in front of the fire, the remaining two stood little chance. In less than a minute, the men had joined their friend in the dirt. One was missing his heart, torn out through his back. The other was missing his head.

The Stalker stood over the remains of his kills for a few seconds, blood dripping from the claw that held the heart of the dead slaver. Raising his maw to the moon, now visible through a break in the clouds, the Stalker howled, the sound sending a chill down Jakob's spine.

Then the beast raised his uninjured talon to his mouth, taking a bite from the still beating heart, grinding the tough muscle between his fangs before swallowing. The Stalker took his time, relishing the taste, enjoying his treat.

The Stalker threw what was left of the heart into the fire, then stared across the flames, his blood-red eyes latching onto the green orbs that glowed brightly in the night.

His true prey. The reason that he was there. The reason that he suffered now.

Jakob knew what was coming next.

There was nowhere to run. Nowhere to hide.

He had hoped that the slavers would put up more of a fight before the Stalker killed them, thereby giving him the chance to escape and return to his father. No such luck.

All he could do now was fight for his life. There were no other choices to be made.

Strangely, as Jakob stared into those blood-red eyes that reflected the flames, the beast's gaze became more measured. If Jakob wasn't mistaken, it appeared as if the beast was evaluating him. Perhaps the Stalker saw something in him that was lacking from the men it had just murdered.

"If you come at me again, you die," said Jakob in a hard voice, hoping that the creature understood what he was saying. "You know that. I can see it in your eyes." If he needed to kill the Stalker, he would. But if he didn't have to, if he could redirect the beast's rage, then all the better. "You can find easier prey on the plateau above." Jakob nodded to the trail just behind the Stalker. "Your choice."

Jakob continued to stare at the monster, refusing to blink, not wanting to show any sign of weakness. The Stalker stared right back at him, the fire sending frightening shadows up against the trees that lined the path as it played along the beast's body.

For just a second, Jakob thought the Stalker was going to lunge at him. The creature was bending his good leg, perhaps judging whether he had the strength to leap through the flames at him.

At the same time, Jakob thought as well that he could see an intelligence in the back of the beast's eyes. Jakob believed that the monster could understand what he was saying, because it seemed as if the monster was actually contemplating his words.

In a ragged, stumbling gait, the Stalker disappeared into the gloom. Jakob followed the monster's progress more with his ears than with his eyes as the beast struggled up the steep slope.

His wounded leg slowed the beast down as he sought to reach the plateau a quarter mile above.

Jakob stood there by the fire for several minutes, barely breathing, not moving, sword at the ready. Using the Talent, he tracked the Stalker until the monster was out of the valley and well out onto the steppe.

Still, he held his sword, not sheathing it in the scabbard across his back until he was certain that the Stalker was now the problem of the slavers who made camp above the vale.

The Stalker had taken his advice, moving on to easier prey, the slavers above taken completely by surprise.

Jakob didn't feel a touch of remorse for what he did, though he didn't have the stomach to watch with the Talent what the Stalker was doing to Remy and the rest of his men. Releasing his hold on the natural magic of the world, he closed his eyes and took a deep breath, the first deep breath he had enjoyed since he had ambushed the tracker.

Those men fighting and dying on the plateau had enslaved others. Good riddance to all of them.

∽

"You all right?" whispered Dougal when Jakob stepped between the long vines that hid his refuge.

His father still lay back against the far wall, barely more than a shadow in the moonlight. He looked tired, wan.

A quick scan with the Talent told him that Dougal was more than just tired. He was sweating despite the cool night air.

He had a fever now. His internal injuries were weakening him, his body losing its ability to fight back against the many ailments torturing him.

Jakob took a deep breath to calm himself. His father was only getting worse, and he had no way to give him the care that he required to have any chance of getting better.

As soon as the vegetation fell back into place, the cave became pitch black, hiding his father once again. Dougal hadn't tried to start a fire, which was a good thing with their pursuers so close.

"Yes, fine."

To remedy the darkness, Jakob crafted a tiny ball of energy with the Talent that was no brighter than the dim glow of a small swarm of fireflies. It wasn't much, but it was enough for him to divide the nuts and berries that he had found on his way back.

He gave his father twice what he took for himself, hoping it might give him some much needed strength. He also gave Dougal the last of the bread he had been saving that they had found the day before when they had explored an abandoned farmstead just on the other side of the ridge that led down into the valley.

"What happened to your face?" his father asked.

Jakob's hand went to the trickle of blood that still ran down his cheek. He had forgotten about taking that injury.

"I wasn't watching where I was going. I walked into a tree branch by mistake."

"You should be more careful."

"I should. You're right."

"What was all the racket I heard about an hour ago?"

For just a moment, Jakob ignored his father, focusing on getting a very small fire going with the branches he had brought with him. With his father lying right next to the flames, he hoped that touch of warmth would do him good.

Once the blaze was strong, the flames licking up the sides of the branches, Jakob unwrapped the herbs he had collected on the way back. He placed them on a small, flat rock. Then he retrieved a cup that was in the small pack he had left with his father, pouring in some water from his canteen, then mixing in the herbs.

He set the flat rock over the fire, allowing the stone to heat the cup. Aloysius had shown him what to do with the herbs, having joined the Magus on several of his trips to surrounding villages and farms to provide medical assistance.

The drink should help his father manage his pain better. But he needed to be careful. If he gave Dougal too much, he'd be too groggy to move in the morning.

"A Stalker."

"The beast came at you?"

"It did."

"Did you kill it?"

"No. I led it to easier prey."

"The slavers?"

"Whoever is leading that party that's been harrying us for the last few days left some of his men in the valley to keep an eye out for us. They had built a large fire. They were easy to find. When the Stalker came for me, I was close to their camp. It was easy to distract the beast and turn it on to other prey."

"Clever."

"I was just doing what you taught me."

Dougal smiled at the compliment, the smile turning into a grimace as another bolt of pain shot through him. Once he had gotten the spasm back under control, he turned toward his son, reaching for the cup of tea that Jakob held out to him.

Noticing how his father's hand shook, Jakob held onto the tea for him, dipping it toward his mouth so that Dougal could take a sip.

"Is the Stalker still a threat?" Dougal asked as he leaned back against the cave wall, just moving toward the cup of tea draining him of what little energy he had regained while resting for the last few hours.

"No, it shouldn't be. The beast continued on the trail out of the valley. With any luck it will find the rest of the slavers and introduce itself."

Jakob looked down. He saw that his father had closed his eyes, breathing more deeply, although the sound of a saw scraping through a length of wood accompanied each of his breaths.

He was asleep. Fitful at best, but still much-needed sleep.

Jakob would save the tea and make his father drink some more when he woke up. But he wasn't going to be sleeping tonight.

He needed to keep an eye on that Stalker. He doubted that the rest of the slavers, assuming any survived their encounter, would bother to come back down into the valley. They would simply assume that the Stalker had killed their friends, which would be correct for the most part.

He and his father should be safe for the night. But his worry about the Stalker, which had almost succeeded in killing him, as well as for his father, wouldn't allow Jakob to rest.

Several key questions with no good answers kept playing through his mind.

What should he do in the morning if his father was in the same condition or worse?

What if his father couldn't walk?

What if they couldn't leave the valley?

And why would the tracker think that he had protection from the Stalker?

Granted by a lord, no less.

14

TO THE NORTH

"Can you craft a portal to get us out of here?" asked Aislinn.

She stared out at the seething mass of Kraken, the beasts pressed up against the protective dome that she had crafted with the Talent. Put in place to ensure the Blood Company could escape the beasts and make their way down the cables to the beach.

The thin barrier of energy was their only defense against their rapacious foes. Many of the creatures had given in to their bloodlust, smashing their cutlasses, tridents, and spears made of bone against the shield. A few even tried to gnaw their way through.

"I could," Bryen replied, "although there are some risks involved."

"You don't want to try it?" Aislinn asked, already knowing the answer by the tone of his voice.

"Not yet. I want to keep the Kraken here for as long as possible and give Asaia and the others more time to hit the beach before these monsters pursue them."

"Hit being the operative term."

"Exactly so," replied Bryen, grinning in spite of his trying not to do so. "Most of them should be fine. I'm really just worried about Majdi and Jenus."

If the buffers that were a part of the last steel tower didn't work, the gladiators were in for a very rough landing. But they should work. He trusted Kollea's professional judgment.

Since he could do nothing about that concern from where he was, he shifted his focus to a more immediate matter. The thousand or more Kraken pounding ineffectually against the barrier and screaming for their blood.

"I understand your desire to give Asaia as much time as we can so that they have a chance to get back to the ships safely." Aislinn grimaced. She didn't need to see one of the Kraken open his jaws to an impossibly wide angle and then snap forward. The beast tried to bite down on the barrier, instead only succeeding in shattering several of his sharp teeth, streaks of blood trailing down the shimmering white shell. It made her think of the sharks swimming in Solace Sound. "But we still need an avenue to make our escape, and I'd really like to avoid fighting our way through these monsters if we can."

"Me as well," murmured Bryen. "Although we might not be able to avoid it."

"Why not?"

"Because some of those Kraken on the southern side are already making their way down the slope. They'll catch the Blood Company on the sand. We need to redirect their attention toward us. Give them no choice but to come back here."

"What are we about to do here, Bryen?" asked Aislinn, her eyes widening and her chin lifting.

She knew that look of his. She knew that mischievous grin spreading across Bryen's usually grim countenance. Nothing good ever happened when he smiled like that.

He told her quickly what he had in mind.

Just as she thought. She closed her eyes for a moment,

trying to gather her thoughts and temper what she was about to say. She failed. Miserably. Her rising irritation got in the way.

"Have you taken one too many knocks to the head?" exclaimed Aislinn. "You actually expect that to work? With all those beasts milling about? You'll never get to him."

"Have no fear," Bryen offered, understanding Aislinn's annoyance and trying to tame it with a calm, confident voice and less of a self-satisfied grin. "I'll get to the chief. I can buy us the time that we need."

Bryen had been studying the Kraken as they attempted time and time again to break through the magical barrier Aislinn had constructed. He didn't think the beasts were fools. He had assumed that eventually they would stop when they realized that they had no chance of getting to them.

But they hadn't. The Kraken continued to attack with a wild savagery, only intensifying their efforts with every failure until they resembled nothing more than a pack of rabid dogs. That got him thinking.

When he finally found who he was looking for at the back of the milling mass, he understood what was going on. The Kraken weren't continuing their assault of their own volition. They were being compelled to do as they were by the large Kraken who stood about fifty feet beyond the beasts trying ineffectually to penetrate Aislinn's barrier.

The beast gripped tightly in his claw a massive white spear that looked to be carved from the bone of a whale. Every so often the creature shouted something that Bryen couldn't quite hear from where he was standing. The Kraken around him certainly did, always redoubling their efforts with every one of his commands.

The leader of this band. Ruling through either fear or compulsion or perhaps even both.

The head of the snake. Take the head ...

"How can you be so certain?"

"Because I have you here to help me," he replied with a broad smile and a wink.

Aislinn shook her head in resignation. She had no defense against him when he said such things and looked at her as he was now. But only because in large part she believed that he was right. She would do whatever was necessary to help him.

"When are we going to do this?" she asked, preparing herself for what was to come, understanding that there was no point in trying to argue with him. Bryen had made up his mind and, unfortunately, she didn't have any better ideas to throw his way.

"Soon, I just need to ..."

Bryen allowed his concentration to drift for a moment, using the Talent to search around them as the wisps of fog swirling atop the plateau began to push their way down the slope. With the haze went several dozen more Kraken.

They couldn't wait any longer. He couldn't let those Kraken pursue the Blood Company. Not yet.

Several of the gladiators had slipped from the steel bars. Instead of gliding through the air and making a quick and clean escape, they were scrambling down the rough trail as fast as they could. Which wasn't fast enough. They still had a mile or more to go before they reached the sand.

He'd have to apologize to Majdi. His friend had been correct. He was too big for the conveyor, having fallen off about halfway down the mountainside.

Although he was racing down the trail at a good pace, he wasn't fast enough to stay ahead of the Kraken. The beasts moved on land with an unusual grace and speed for creatures he assumed spent most of their time in the sea.

"We need to do it now," Bryen said, coming back to himself.

Aislinn nodded. "How do you want to do this?"

"I'll make sure that we catch the attention of all the Kraken, even those beginning to go down the slope. Clear the way for me so I can make a run at the Kraken leader."

Aislinn nodded. "Done."

Bryen didn't waste any time once that was decided. The creatures on the southern side had completed their encirclement. That done, the towering Kraken just to his north that he assumed was the leader motioned with his large spear toward those beasts.

Bryen suspected that the creature was ordering them to go after his friends. That was something that he wanted to delay for a few minutes more.

With that goal top of mind, Bryen reached for the Talent, enjoying the welcome warmth of the natural magic as it flowed through him. Next, he opened himself to the Seventh Stone, the artifact offering its own supply of power and magnifying what he already had under his control. For just a heartbeat, he reveled in the almost scalding heat that made it feel as if every part of his body was being scoured clean.

Next, he employed a tactic that Rafia enjoyed using against Ghoule Elders. Raising his arms to the sky, he whipped them down toward the ground.

With the Seventh Stone augmenting his own already formidable strength, two dozen lightning bolts streaked down from the clear sky, exploding right into the ground in the midst of the Kraken seething around them.

Aislinn's barrier protected them from the force and energy Bryen employed. Not so the Kraken.

Those creatures caught in the blasts were ripped apart, their burnt and charred body parts scattered across the plateau. The destructive power was almost unimaginable, the Kraken surging back, seeking to avoid the fate that had been visited upon those too close to the shield, unknowingly giving Bryen the space that he wanted.

But Bryen wasn't done. He added his own twist to this lethal tactic. He had to.

Because he wasn't dealing with just a few Elders but rather hundreds upon hundreds of Kraken.

Raising his arms to the sky and then slashing them down toward the ground multiple times, the lightning bolts continued to blast apart the dirt and rocks and the Kraken who couldn't escape. The beasts behind those caught in the strikes descended into chaos as they struggled to get away. Yet even those creatures in the back weren't spared.

Bryen motioned with his hands, the lightning bolts cascading through the beasts until he had created a circle of devastation a hundred feet in diameter. Those Kraken not destroyed by the storm of power were too stunned to do anything other than roll on the ground, clutching at their heads, the fury and noise of the terrifying attack causing internal injuries or making them feel as if they'd been struck in the skull with a hammer a dozen times or more.

"Cover me," said Bryen as he pushed his way through Aislinn's barrier. He sprinted through the wreckage of his attack, having eyes only for the Kraken leader.

"Why can't you …"

Aislinn didn't have time to finish her question. She had thought that perhaps Bryen's initial success at clearing the space around them would be enough for them to escape, the surviving Kraken struggling and more often than not failing to regain their clawed feet as they experienced the aftereffects of the onslaught.

She realized quickly that her hope was just that. A hope.

It wouldn't work. Not with the several hundred more Kraken streaming down the mountain from the east and the several hundred on the western slope abandoning their pursuit of the fleeing gladiators and coming to the aid of their chief.

At least she and Bryen had achieved their objective of

keeping the Kraken focused on what was happening on the plateau. The Blood Company should make it to the ship now before the Kraken caught up to them.

That conclusion pleasing her, Aislinn turned her attention to Bryen. He ran straight through the disoriented mass of Kraken, many dead, many wounded, just as many still alive although having a difficult time recovering their bearings.

Keeping her barrier in place, she began manipulating the Talent in a different way, watching as the Kraken behind their leader started to emerge from the fog.

The beasts rushed toward Bryen, blades made of bone held in the air, preparing to strike him down.

Her Protector had protected her many times in the past. Now it was her turn to protect him.

She did so with a devastating finality.

Streams of energy shot from both of her palms, the blazing power tracking Bryen on both his left and right so that the Kraken who might think to attempt a lucky strike from the side as he raced past couldn't. Those streams of energy blasted down the crest, streaking past Bryen and circling around the Kraken leader.

Within that space segmented by the walls of flame, there was only Bryen and the Kraken chief. Not one of his creatures could come to his assistance.

When Bryen was only twenty feet away from his target, Aislinn adjusted her application of the Talent. The walls of blazing energy faded away, replaced by a dome similar to the one she still stood within. This second creation was large enough for both Bryen and the Kraken leader.

When Bryen fought in the Pit, he often took his time, allowing his opponent to dictate the beginning few minutes of the combat. Not to incite the crowd as Beluchmel, the former Master of the Colosseum, preferred and thought was the case.

Instead, his approach was based on what Declan had

taught him. He wanted to get a feel for his opponent. For his strengths and weaknesses. Using those few minutes to map out the quickest and most efficient way to kill his adversary.

He thought to do the same now, not only because this habit had been ingrained within him so deeply by Declan, but also because he wanted to learn more about the Kraken and what their fighting tendencies might be. He had a feeling that once he and Aislinn escaped the mountaintop, this particular fight still might not be over.

But at the last second he decided to change his strategy, wanting to test his adversary immediately.

Time was of the essence. He couldn't expect Aislinn to maintain both barriers for very long.

After rushing right up to the Kraken leader and slicing toward the creature's neck with the Spear of the Magii, Bryen pivoted away, coming to stand no more than a few feet away. He avoided easily the swift lunge the Kraken stabbed at his side when he went by.

The Kraken leader, almost a head taller than Bryen, who was tall himself, stared down at him with an evil intent. This beast was a larger version of his soldiers. The only other real distinction, besides the spear he held, was the crest of bone on his scalp.

It began on the Kraken's forehead and trailed down his back much like a horse's mane. Although in this instance the edges were sharper than the barbs of a lionfish and in the swirling fog they appeared to glow a light blue color.

Bryen would have liked a few more seconds to study the beast, to learn his habits, but it wasn't to be. The Kraken wasn't interested in studying him. Rather, the leader of the creatures who had come with the fog simply wanted to kill him, as swiftly as he could.

The Kraken swung the spear that was half a length longer

than the Spear of the Magii with a remarkable speed for such a large weapon, the serrated edge lined up with Bryen's neck.

If the Kraken had connected, Bryen's head would have bounced off the barrier Aislinn had constructed that protected against the Kraken rushing out of the fog behind his opponent. The hundreds of beasts pounded futilely against the shimmering energy, desperate to break through, desperate to kill the one with the temerity to challenge their chief.

The spear didn't connect. Bryen ducked at the last second and rolled out of the way, coming up right behind the Kraken.

The beast didn't even bother to turn, instead demonstrating a remarkable strength and agility, continuing with his motion and swinging with a backward blow for Bryen's shins.

Bryen jumped over the spear and swung with his own, targeting the Kraken's vulnerable hamstring on his front leg.

The Kraken responded impossibly fast, bringing his spear down in the blink of an eye, digging the point into the dirt for added stability, so that when Bryen's steel connected, the blade could go no further.

Growling in anger as he watched his opponent slice off a large piece of bone from his weapon, the Kraken chief spun back around, raising his chipped spear just in time to parry Bryen's slash for his throat.

Having no choice as Bryen continued his attack, the beast stepped back a few feet, and then a few more, avoiding or blocking a series of wickedly fast slashes and cuts.

Seeking to return the favor, the Kraken stabbed at Bryen's gut, then tried to catch Bryen across his ribs with a backward cut.

Bryen was already well clear of the jab, sidestepping the slash and, in the same motion, kicking out with his right leg. His boot smashed into the Kraken's right kneecap, forcing the joint and the entire leg back at an unnatural almost impossible angle.

The Kraken stumbled badly, howling in pain. Bryen had broken the femur with his rapid strike, the tip of the bone sticking out of the creature's thigh, and caused the ligaments in his knee to rupture.

Bryen had spent too long on the white sand to need much time to develop a strategy for defeating an opponent, and such was the case now.

The Kraken chief was strong, striking with a power reminiscent of the Ghoule Overlord. He was fast. He was skilled as well. He knew how to make use of that massive spear of his with great effect.

Still, the Kraken leader had never come up against the Volkun before, who was both faster and smarter and better versed in the ways of single combat. Bryen identified the beast's weaknesses in seconds and immediately attacked them.

That left the Kraken chief in his current state, attempting to figure out how a human, a lander, had gotten the best of him.

Attempting to retreat a few steps more, the Kraken stumbled down to his one good knee, unable to bend the other. It left him in a very awkward and vulnerable position. He saw the human coming toward him, his gaze hard, focused, that double-bladed spear of his spinning slowly from his right hand to his left and then back again.

The chief heard the screams and howls of his people, his Kraken unable to penetrate the barrier that prevented them from joining the combat.

They urged him to continue the fight. To push himself back up. To kill the human who had trespassed on their island and dared to challenge him.

The massive beast sighed, accepting the reality that he faced. It was too late.

He couldn't do it. He couldn't push himself up off the rocky ground.

He could do nothing but wait for his executioner to

approach in those confident strides that made him appear as if he were gliding across the ground.

The Kraken leader closed his eyes, knowing what was coming next. He barely felt the slice of the sharp steel as it cut through his neck, the human completing the difficult maneuver he himself had failed to accomplish at the very beginning of the duel.

Bryen stared down at the remains of the Kraken leader, the head rolling up against the shimmering barrier.

The eyes were sightless. The mouth, filled with razor-sharp teeth, was twisted into a horrid grimace.

Yet there was no fear. Only anger. Not at Bryen, he believed. But rather at himself for his failure.

What Bryen saw didn't affect him, at least not as much as it might someone who had not experienced the daily terrors of the Pit. He had fought too many combats on the white sand for that to happen now.

With respect to the Kraken leader, he had done what was necessary. No more. No less.

Pulling his gaze away from the decapitated body, Bryen looked out beyond the shield.

The Kraken stood motionless, completely silent, shocked by the loss of their leader. They stared right back at him, their eyes locked onto him.

Not saying a word. Not needing to.

Bryen could read their intentions in their bluish grey eyes that strangely reminded him of the Silent Sea.

That silence that had descended at the loss of their leader didn't last long. The Kraken closest to the barrier began pounding on the shimmering energy once again, frantic to get at him. The Kraken just beyond pushed forward, crushing the front rank against the magical shield.

It was time to go. He had achieved his goal, and he had no doubt that the Blood Company was well away from the mountain. Now he and Aislinn needed to make their own escape.

Reaching for the Talent, Bryen called forth a spinning mist that was just a little taller than he was. He stepped through, the gateway closing behind him.

The Kraken stared in awe at what they had just witnessed. The killer of their chief had vanished.

"Could you be any more dramatic?" asked Aislinn drily as Bryen stepped out of a portal of spinning white mist that had formed right next her. Both of them were protected from the Kraken, her original shield still in place.

"Maybe if I tried a little bit harder," he replied.

Aislinn shook her head, a small smile cracking her lips. She didn't know if Bryen was being facetious or serious. It didn't really matter.

Bryen had bought Asaia and the others the time that they needed. Now they needed to get clear of these Kraken.

And he hoped that he could take advantage of the fact that almost all of the beasts had been drawn to the dome that contained their dead chief.

"It's time to go," Aislinn said.

"It is," Bryen agreed.

"I take it that we can't use a portal to get where we need to go." She had searched around them with the Talent, learning where all the soldiers of the Blood Company were, Asaia and her squads almost to the ship.

But they couldn't see Solace Sound or the ship from where they were standing, the fog surging off the mountain and covering a large portion of the bay.

"Not yet," Bryen replied. "Declan and his squads are still making their way back to the *Freedom*. I don't want the Kraken to catch them on the beach."

"So we need to keep the Kraken focused on us for a little while longer."

Bryen nodded. "Perhaps you would like to do the honors?"

"With pleasure," replied Aislinn, already knowing exactly what she was going to do, having thought about it during Bryen's combat.

With all the Kraken that had surrounded her protective dome having followed Bryen toward the one she crafted for the duel, she allowed the one they were standing in now to dissolve. That task done, it was time for the next.

Reaching for a new stream of the Talent, she sent flows of energy into the dome that remained. The shimmering power filled the space rapidly to the point of bursting.

Yet even then she continued with her work, adding more and more energy to the tightly compressed space. She had remembered what had happened when she had done much the same during one of her lessons with Sirius in the Broken Tower. She wanted to repeat now what had then been a failure for her.

Satisfied that she had enough of the Talent in place to complete the maneuver she had in mind, she began manipulating the walls of the dome. She didn't dissolve the barrier. Rather she compressed the circular wall, forcing the massive amount of the Talent into the much more compact space.

The energy became denser. More volatile.

It wasn't long before she gained the result that she had been seeking. The explosion that roared across the crest shook the entire island. Dirt, rocks, roots, and Kraken were blasted up into the air as a crater thirty feet deep appeared where the body of the Kraken chief had been just a moment before.

Aislinn didn't bother to examine her grisly work. Grabbing Bryen's free hand, the Spear of the Magii in his other, she pulled him toward the north. It was the only path open to them. The Kraken hadn't yet moved in that direction, the fog still not having drifted down to that compass point.

"Could you be any more dramatic?" asked Bryen from behind her.

"Probably if I tried a little bit harder," replied Aislinn with a smile, appreciating Bryen's dry humor.

She had been hoping that the explosion would have given them more of a lead. But it wasn't to be.

They had gone less than a quarter of a mile, finding a rough path atop the crest that led toward the north, when they began to hear the sounds of pursuit.

"I can understand now why Davin hated being the bait," said Bryen.

Aislinn could understand now as well. Yet she had no time to think about it.

She could do nothing else but focus on putting one foot in front of the other, sprinting along the narrow ridge.

The Kraken were coming for them, and they wanted blood.

15

PREPARING FOR THE FOG

"Is this the last of it?" asked Captain Gregson.

He watched intently as the two longboats came across the bay with Declan's gladiators in one, dozens of roughly cut pieces of timber stacked in the other. The finer work would be done by the sailors once the wood was brought on board.

"It's as much as we could take with us," said Declan apologetically as his longboat came alongside. "If we got caught in the fog by whatever's in the fog, we wouldn't be here, nor would the timber."

Captain Gregson nodded. "It'll do. Quite nicely, in fact. Thank you." He looked to the beach next. His sailors finally were pushing off the sand with the last load of roughhewn wood. "I've never seen the fog act like this before." The billowing mist was coming right for them, most of the mountain beyond already hidden from sight. "I've seen many strange events during my time at sea. This is one of the strangest."

"I'm with you on that," agreed Declan, pulling himself up to the deck and then following Captain Gregson to the helm.

"Some of your gladiators said we needed to be quick when

they got here," said Captain Gregson, unable to take his eyes from the approaching gloom.

Peculiar.

It felt like the murk was coming for him just like one of the stories his mother used to tell him when he was a child. He had grown up by the sea, so the fog was a common occurrence. Whenever he misbehaved, which he had to admit was quite often, she threatened him with the monsters lurking in the mist.

Seeing this fog now, it was a perfect representation of the image he used to form in his mind whenever his mother told him that. And for the first time, he believed her.

"What's with that fog?" he wondered. "It doesn't look right. Almost as if it's alive."

"It is, Captain Gregson," said Rafia, climbing to the helm after having just come aboard. She wanted to make sure that she was with the last squad of gladiators before stepping into the longboat. Just in case. Thankfully, her fears about what pursued them didn't bear fruit. Yet. "This haze is alive. It's not a natural fog."

"What do you mean it's not natural? How could that even be possible? It looks no different than what I've sailed through hundreds of times on the Burnt Ocean."

"With this fog come the Kraken, Captain Gregson." The Magus said it with such certainty that he couldn't doubt her. "This fog is different. This fog hides them, nourishes them somehow. It carries with it the taint of the Curse."

"The Curse," he murmured. Just the thought of that evil power sent a shiver down his spine. "You've seen the Kraken?"

"Not as such, but I've seen them in the fog through my use of the Talent."

"You can't be serious ..."

He had only heard stories about the mythical Kraken. He had listened with half an ear, thinking, hoping, that much of what his fellow sailors told him was just the result of them drowning in their cups. Nevertheless, his inherent often excessive rationality, no matter how ridiculous much of what his friends told him sounded, refused to allow him to categorize their stories as simply fables.

Learning at that moment that he had been right to keep an open mind filled him with a cold dread. Because those stories of the Kraken were always offered secondhand or thirdhand.

Never from someone who had seen or even gotten close to the Kraken. Because the people who got close to the Kraken usually died. That naturally led his mind down a very unpleasant path if, indeed, the Magus was correct.

"Deadly serious," replied Rafia.

Just then a series of muffled explosions drew their eyes toward the top of the mountain near where the springs would be. The fog swirled violently there, though not dissipating, not giving them a chance to see what was happening.

They were able to discern several flashes of muted light breaking through the gloom. No more than that.

"And there's our additional confirmation," said Declan, his hand going to the hilt of his sword.

He knew what was coming next. It was just a matter of time. What was happening farther up the mountain was just the beginning.

"What was that?" asked Captain Gregson.

"My guess would be the Lord Keldragan and the Lady Winborne," replied Rafia.

"Blasted boy," said Declan, reluctantly taking his gaze away from the fog blanketing the mountain. "He's doing it again."

"What are you …" Rafia began to ask. She didn't need to finish her question. She already knew the answer as several more explosions erupted near the springs, accompanied by more flashes of bright white light that did nothing more than dimly illuminate the murk for a few heartbeats. Fool boy indeed!

"What are they saying?" asked Captain Gregson.

Movement on the shore drew his eyes from the blanketed mountain. Several squads of gladiators were running out of the woods onto the beach and hustling toward the bay, water bags slung over their shoulders. They were shouting all at once and gesturing in the direction from which they had come.

"It's not something that you want to hear, Captain," said the helmswoman. Emelina knew her husband. He handled stress and risk quite well. He didn't handle unknown and unseen threats with the same level of acuity.

"Why would you say that?"

"They're saying the Kraken are coming. That they fought them on top of the mountain and that the Kraken are right behind them."

Captain Gregson clenched his fists tightly. His wife was right. He really didn't want to hear that. He really didn't want to deal with a day like this, when stories and myths were coming to life.

Taking a deep breath, he let some of his tension go. All that didn't matter now.

If the gladiators and the Magus said that the Kraken were coming for them, then so be it. He would deal with the Kraken as he would any other threat to his ship, his crew, and his passengers.

Shifting his thoughts toward what he needed to do if they were to have any chance at all of escaping the Jagged Islands alive, a strategy formed in his mind.

There was no time for worry and fear. Now there was only time for getting everyone back on the ship and out to sea before those blasted monsters came for them.

And he knew for certain that they would. They always did if you spent too much time in Solace Sound.

"Emelina, get Darius and his crew working on the hull repairs. Make sure Marus and Jensen are with him. They're excellent sailors, but their carpentry skills are quite good and can help speed up the work."

"Time frame, Captain?" Emelina never called her husband anything but Captain unless they were in the privacy of their cabin.

"They need to get as many repairs done as they can. No matter what, they don't stop. I don't care if the Kraken board us. They keep working. We need to get out onto the Burnt Ocean as soon as we can, and I don't want to do that fearing that one of those cracks or leaks will burst on us in the deep water."

"I'll take care of it," she said, about to turn away, her husband's voice pulling her back.

"And all hands on deck. If they're not getting us ready to sail, they're getting ready to repel boarders. Clear?"

"Aye, aye, Captain." Emelina slid down the narrow steps that led to the main deck to get the work started, a sparkle in her eye.

She felt a special tingle of pleasure when her husband acted this way. Even when the cause for his commanding presence came about because of a threat that was likely just as dire if not more so than the Bakunawa that they had escaped just days before.

"Fergus, back to shore," Captain Gregson yelled down to the sailor manning the longboat closest to the *Freedom*, three other longboats bobbing in the water alongside the hull. "Get the rest of the Blood Company and the water bags quick as you can. Then stow the boats or leave them if there's no time. We've got a fight coming our way. I want every sailor ready to defend this ship in thirty minutes."

"Aye, Captain," Fergus nodded, turning the longboat toward the beach, the sailors in the other launches following his cue.

Captain Gregson nodded to himself. Good. He spun slowly

atop the helm. Emelina already had relayed his orders, unleashing controlled chaos across the deck as sailors darted about on their various assignments.

They were doing what was necessary. What he thought might help to keep them all alive. Whether it would be enough, he couldn't say at that moment.

Not with the fog and whatever was in it coming for them. And much faster than he would have liked as he watched the murk surge down toward the shore like a massive hand reaching out for him.

Davin and Lycia, who had gone onto the beach and scouted for a few hours, climbed to the helm now, listening to what Declan and Rafia said and then Captain Gregson's orders.

Davin, usually quite relaxed, gripped the haft of his spear tightly. Lycia bounced on her toes, itching to pull the twin blades from the scabbards across her back. But it was still too early to do that.

They had both done this hundreds of times before on the white sand, preparing for a combat, placing themselves in the necessary mindset. Despite the frequency with which they were required to do that, they had never handled the time leading up to the fight well.

Once the duel began they relaxed, not thinking, not worrying, just doing. It was the anticipation preceding the combat that always bothered them the most.

As they stared up into the fog, its first few thin wisps beginning to reach out over the bay, they could only hope that Bryen and Aislinn made it down from the heights before the Kraken did.

"He's doing it again, isn't he?" asked Lycia.

"It certainly looks like it," Davin murmured, nodding his head in a barely perceptible manner, just a habit left over from his time in the Pit.

Lycia offered a few choice curses under her breath. "I

thought that Aislinn would have cured him by now of this urge of his to play the hero."

Their eyes narrowed when they heard another series of muffled explosions toward the top of the hidden peak. They couldn't see what was happening, but they didn't need to in order to envision what was occurring within the haze. They knew their friends much too well.

"I don't know that his tendency to put himself in danger is an urge you could cure. It seems like it's too much a part of him."

For several minutes the twins stood there, just watching the fog, almost mesmerized by the grasping mist as it enveloped the beach and then started to pinch the backs of the sailors rowing the longboats back to the *Freedom*.

It had gone quiet. On the island. On the ship as well, the sailors moving with a hushed efficiency, not wanting to talk, the oppressiveness of the fog already affecting them.

Even voluble Majdi, Jenus, and Dorlan just now coming on board and storing the water bags did so in silence, the gladiators shifting their focus to organizing their squads for the battle that was fast approaching.

"Did you hear that?" asked Lycia.

"Sounds like a fight," said Davin.

"Sounds like a chase," corrected Lycia. "We should have gone with them. They could have used our help."

"It's too late now," murmured Davin, a hint of regret in his voice. He would have much preferred to be up there on the mountain with Bryen and Aislinn then down here on the deck of the *Freedom*, hating the fact that he didn't have a clue as to what was happening above them. "Remember, the Volkun and the Vedra are quite capable on their own."

"How far away?" asked Declan, coming to stand next to the twins and trying to track the sounds emanating from the gloom.

"Less than a half mile away would be my guess," Davin replied.

Declan looked up toward the peak, seeing only a grey gloom, not hearing as much as he would like. There was nothing to do for it now. The fog was reaching for them, the first few faint wisps kissing the hull.

"Where are Bryen and Aislinn?" asked Declan, calling down from the helm to Kollea as she and the last of the gladiators who went to the spring climbed aboard.

"Where do you think?" she replied, throwing her waterbags onto the pile, then moving toward Dorlan to get into position.

"Fool children!" Declan muttered under his breath. "Why those two feel the need to put themselves in danger all the time, I really don't understand."

Shaking his head in frustration, Declan turned away from the rapidly disappearing beach. All he could do was hope that those two got away.

Now, however, he wasn't dealing with hope. He was dealing with reality. He was dealing with an event that he understood all too well.

"Blood Company, the battle comes!" Declan shouted. "Majdi! Dorlan! Jenus! Shield wall on the port side rail!"

16

ATOP THE PLATEAU

"Still behind us?" asked Bryen, pulling himself up a broad rock face, then reaching down with his hand to help Aislinn scale the last few feet of the outcropping.

"Yes, and getting closer." Aislinn had been tracking the Kraken with the Talent ever since they escaped the plateau. For a few miles, she thought that they might have gotten away from the beasts. The Kraken had turned their attention toward the gladiators. But there were so many of the creatures that whoever led the Kraken now had little difficulty dividing his forces. "You really got them angry."

"That was the idea."

"Maybe so, but I don't think that either of us were expecting several hundred Kraken to come after us."

"You're right about that." Bryen shrugged as if to say he was sorry for their unanticipated somewhat unwanted success. "I didn't believe that they'd still want a piece of us after killing their chief."

"That only seemed to strengthen their resolve," said Aislinn, looking back the way they had come.

The fog was drifting toward them now, seeking to cover the

one part of the island that still remained free of its grasp. With it would come the Kraken, just as the Talent had revealed to her.

"Come on. We need to keep moving."

Aislinn trotted after Bryen as he moved farther along the top of the scarp toward the northern tip of the island. The rough, rocky path was no more than two feet wide.

They spent most of their time keeping their heads down, looking at where they placed their feet. One wrong step would send them plummeting down either side of the bluff, guaranteeing them a bloody and broken end when they reached the rocks several hundred feet below.

Still, even with the additional challenge of not falling to their deaths, they held out hope that they could stay ahead of their pursuers. It was a straight shot now to where Bryen was leading them if they could navigate the perils of the rugged trail.

"Do you have any ideas for staying ahead of these creatures?" asked Aislinn. "Because I'm fresh out."

"Kind of."

"Kind of," Aislinn repeated with a touch of heat in her voice. "That's the best that you can do?"

"At the moment, yes," Bryen replied, nonplussed by her reaction. "I want to get to that natural bridge." He nodded in the direction that they were headed. "That looks to be our best chance."

While Aislinn was tracking the Kraken, he had used the Talent to search to the north, the only direction not yet covered by the fog. The very end of the island had caught his eye.

He had spied an exceedingly narrow stone bridge that stretched across the pounding surf for several hundred feet. It connected to a very small island no more than an acre in size that was surrounded by a dozen or more sea stacks.

Bryen couldn't tell for sure since the fog was coming around the coast and beginning to obscure the eastern side of the larger island. Still, he believed that small cay was their best hope for surviving the Kraken.

That brief surge of hope was burned away when he glanced back over his shoulder and saw the first faints wisps of grey sneak over the top of the ridge.

He worried that he had miscalculated now. He had tried to give the Blood Company as much time as possible to escape, but he might have done it at his and Aislinn's expense.

Bryen motioned briefly in the direction that Aislinn had been looking, almost slipping from the slight effort required to do that as his boots slid across a patch of loose shale that gave way beneath him. He caught himself just in time, Aislinn grabbing him around his waist, helping to steady him.

Nodding his thanks, he resumed running down the narrow trail. Aislinn stayed right behind him.

Aislinn understood immediately why Bryen was leading her in this direction. A single defender could hold that bridge for quite a long time. It was so narrow that only one Kraken could attack at a time.

Assuming, of course, that none of the creatures emerged from the sea behind them. That worry began to dominate her thoughts as the small island grew bigger with every step she took.

It would be foolish for the creatures not to employ such a tactic, and though atop the summit they had allowed their anger to drive them at the cost of their reason, she doubted that would continue for much longer. Even now she could sense that the Kraken chasing them were splitting into distinct groups, adopting a more strategic approach for the chase.

One group was trying to get ahead of them by moving below them on the ridge. Another was doing the same on the western side. The third, and the largest of the hunting parties, continued to press them from behind.

"A good plan," she said, though the concern that had taken root in her brain made her wonder if there might be another solution that they should consider. "Are you sure that you can't just create a portal that we could step through that would take us back to the ship?"

"I thought about that as soon as we broke out of the fog," Bryen replied over his shoulder, not bothering to slow down, the sounds of the Kraken racing to catch up to them urging them on.

"But …" Aislinn prompted.

"But with the Kraken swarming the island and the need to give Asaia and the others a head start, it's too late for me to try to craft a portal that would open up on the beach. I worry that we might end up right in the midst of the beasts."

Bryen had created portals several times in the past. He had crafted one to enter the Lost Land in fact. He had learned a great deal about that very useful tool from his uncle.

Viktor Keldragan had been very clear about the dangers of trying to create a portal that took you to a location to which you had never been before or to a location that you had been to before that you couldn't visualize in perfect detail in your mind.

Wanting to ensure that Bryen had understood the risks, Viktor had provided an extensive list of the many ways that you could die if you made a mistake. So extensive, in fact, that Bryen had stopped listening.

He had gotten the gist, however. Making even the slightest error could cost him and whoever might be with him their lives, a very painful death awaiting them. In consequence, he preferred not to take such a risk with Aislinn unless it proved to be absolutely necessary.

"And with the fog covering the bay now," he continued, "I worry that I'll miss the deck and we'll end up in the water with the great white sharks."

"Something that I'd definitely like to avoid."

"As would I. So for now, while the fog holds, I'd suggest we keep moving. We can reevaluate if circumstances become more desperate."

Aislinn nodded, keeping her eyes to the ground as she followed in Bryen's footsteps. The shrieks that drowned out the sound of their breathing jolted them both to an even faster speed, less worried now about the risks of the path.

The Kraken were closing on them, no more than a half mile away at most from what she could tell with the Talent. And just as she assumed, with those creatures came the fog, the first faint, cool touch of the leading edge of the murk caressing the back of her neck.

"We're not going to be on our own for much longer," Aislinn called.

Bryen didn't bother to reply. He could see the fog closing in around them. Aislinn was right. The Kraken would be joining them sooner than he would have liked.

He was beginning to doubt whether he and Aislinn could make it to the bridge before the creatures caught them, especially with the arduous incline to the trail as they ran toward what appeared to be a small plateau bordered on both sides by jagged bluffs, the steep sides of which looked to be shear.

That actually might help them, Bryen thought. Even though he assumed that the Kraken were excellent climbers because of their claws, Bryen also believed that the creatures would struggle on the crags that they were rapidly approaching because of the sharp angle.

The terrain would force the two hunting parties seeking to get in front of them to extend the range of their pursuit. Perhaps he and Aislinn could make it to the bridge if they could stay ahead of the Kraken coming at them from behind.

For just a second he worried that there was no way off the plateau. As he and Aislinn raced farther up the trail, his fears dissipated when he saw that the path ran right between the bluffs and continued down again toward the small island at the far end.

When they reached the top of the plateau, Bryen skidded to a stop. Aislinn almost ran right into him before she caught herself in time.

"I wasn't expecting this," he murmured.

"Nor me."

Aislinn took in the incredible sight. The trail continued straight across the plateau, which was only slightly larger than the square that surrounded the Colosseum in Tintagel.

Bordering right up against the path was a large village, dozens upon dozens of homes made of large stone blocks lining the way. What was most impressive was how those homes were built one on top of the other in a staggered fashion, extending all the way up to the very top of each ridge.

She realized that on each side it was actually a single building carved out of the bluff, each one at least fifteen stories. Aislinn didn't take the time to count to confirm.

Worn paths led along the cliffs between the connected residences all the way to the top. Those paths opened up onto small patches of overgrown ground in front of each home that suggested that at one time they had been gardens. In fact, a variety of different vegetables were still growing there.

Just beyond the residences were several large fields with ramshackle fences along the edge. Probably for whatever livestock these people had once raised.

While an impressive discovery, it was also an unsettling one. It was clear to Bryen that whoever had lived here hadn't been living here all that long ago.

The gardens weren't that overgrown and the homes and fences appeared to be in good shape. Whatever had occurred here that had led the residents to abandon this town had occurred in just the last couple of years.

The shrieks of the Kraken coming behind Bryen and

Aislinn broke the spell that had settled over them. Bryen looked to the northwest, searching for the *Freedom,* Aislinn's suggestion of crafting a portal looking that much more appealing right at that moment.

He cursed in frustration. It wouldn't work.

He couldn't see the ship, nor the Solace Sound.

All he could see was the fog that had smothered the island and the surrounding waters. Only the path that led them toward the smaller island just off the coast that they were desperate to reach before the Kraken reached them remained clear.

That wouldn't prove to be the case for much longer, however. The murk was slowly making its way up both sides of the precipice.

"Why would they settle here?" asked Aislinn as they continued down the trail between the abandoned homes. "Why not closer to the beach?"

"Maybe they thought that they could defend themselves here," Bryen proposed. "Only two ways in and out."

"Maybe," she murmured, finding it hard to disagree with Bryen's reasoning as she studied the village with a more detailed eye.

The residences not only were built one on top of the other, just the garden and a small ledge separating one level from the next, but there were also stone walls running along the ledges that made her think of the parapet that extended along the walls of the Broken Keep. Strengthening her suspicion, every single doorway was a large stone slab that came down from inside each home.

Bryen's theory was gaining traction with her. The homes were built like they were part of a larger fortress.

She was certain now that Bryen was right. This village had been built so that it could be defended.

If the people who had lived here couldn't hold attackers at

the two entrances to the plateau and were forced to retreat into the village, archers on the balustrades of the apartments could turn the trail running through the village into a killing ground.

"Bryen."

Bryen stopped and trotted back a few steps, coming to stand next to Aislinn.

"Just like by the path we took up the mountain."

"Worse," murmured Aislinn, bile rising in her throat.

They stared down a jagged crevice that opened to a large field that tracked the path leading through the village on the western side.

"How many?"

"I don't know," Bryen replied in a soft voice. "I don't want to know."

At the bottom of the steep slope was a burial pit that stretched along the length of the trail for at least a hundred feet and then extended to the west to the very base of the crag, covering most of what they guessed used to be a garden of several acres.

Now the space was covered by a thick layer of cinders that was three feet deep at its lowest point. Throughout the pile flashes of white broke through the ash-colored flakes.

Bones. Hundreds, if not thousands, of bones that hadn't burned. Examining more closely the pile nearest to the trail, Bryen identified the chips and cuts in what he guessed was a femur and what was left of a skull.

All of these people had died violently. He could only hope that they were all dead before they were thrown into the fire.

Bryen shook his head in disgust and disappointment. Whatever safety these people thought they would find here at the top of the mountain was ephemeral at best.

Just as it is for us, Bryen thought. He turned to look at Aislinn. Her eyes were still fixed on the burial pit, and her face revealed the series of emotions that were working their way through her.

Sadness. Anger. Determination. Finally, the desire for revenge.

The last was most important, because he believed that they were about to get the chance to claim what they most wanted.

The fog was thickening around them, speeding along the trail like an arrow streaking through the air. With it came the howls of the Kraken, faint images of the beasts visible at the leading edge of the grey haze.

Bryen turned swiftly, slashing down with the Spear of the Magii, the twin blades glowing with the Talent. The sharp steel sliced right through the arm of the Kraken at the front of the pursuit. The creature stumbled off the path, finding it difficult to acknowledge the terrible wound inflicted upon him, knocked off balance when Bryen checked him with his hip.

The wounded beast was the first to fall into the burial pit, but he wouldn't be the last.

Bryen continued his motion, spinning and bringing his weapon back around, the blade cutting across another Kraken's midsection. The slash was so powerful that Bryen almost cut the beast in two, his anger adding some unnecessary force to the killing blow.

Bryen left the Kraken there. Collapsed on the path. The beast screeching in pain and bleeding out in the dirt served as a useful obstacle for the Kraken coming after him.

Another Kraken jumped over the dying creature, reaching for Bryen with both blade and claw just as he was turning back around.

Before Bryen could square up against this new opponent, Aislinn was there. She slashed with her blazing blade, taking the Kraken's leg off at the knee.

The grievously wounded creature collapsed right on top of

the dying Kraken, several of the beasts following right after him getting tangled in the pile of limbs.

Bryen and Aislinn made quick work of the floundering Kraken, adding to the gruesome wall of bodies that was rising in front of them. As the blitz continued, for the next few minutes, they focused on nothing other than standing their ground and holding back the charging Kraken. Their blazing steel swept through the bloody space the Kraken were so foolish to enter time and time again without even thinking of the consequences of doing so.

"We're fighting a losing combat," said Bryen. "As soon as the Kraken's bloodlust allows them to see the situation for what it is, we lose."

Bryen and Aislinn had been quite successful at bottling up the beasts. The pile of bodies that blocked the path forced the Kraken to climb over an organic barrier that now rose as high as their chests.

Yet despite their early success, Aislinn heard the truth in Bryen's words. This wasn't sustainable for much longer.

The west side of the path dropped down into the burial pit that had captured her attention, and the east side bordered a row of homes. It wouldn't be long before the beasts realized the advantage they had, because she and Bryen couldn't protect their flanks effectively.

Once the creatures recognized that they could skip around them, Bryen and Aislinn ran the risk of being surrounded if they stayed where they were.

That led to one very obvious conclusion.

They needed to move.

But they had no good way of breaking away from the Kraken.

The beasts charged blindly out of the fog in a constant stream. They gave no thought as to what waited for them, not caring how many of their brethren already had lost their lives.

They had one desire and one desire only. To kill the two humans who had cost them their chief and caused so much devastation within their ranks.

Aislinn solved the problem they faced with some quick thinking. While Bryen cut down two more of the Kraken with quick slashes of his steel, she took a page from Rafia's book, throwing several bolts of energy just a few feet beyond the pile of bodies.

The explosions ripped open the ground, blasting away a large section of the trail, the wall of Kraken disappearing as the dead fell into the pit.

"Very impressive," said Bryen.

The hole was thirty feet deep and several dozen feet wide, and it stretched from the edge of the building to their left all the way down to the burial pit on their right. Best of all, Aislinn's application of the Talent created some separation between them and the Kraken.

She had forced the beasts to halt their attack with the newly created obstacle blocking their way. At least until they figured out their next step.

"It's not going to stop them for long," said Aislinn, watching as the Kraken began shouting and shrieking at one another.

Whether because they were angry or they were trying to develop a new plan, she couldn't tell. It was probably a bit of both.

"No, but it will give us a few seconds," replied Bryen with a smile. "Well done."

Not waiting to see what the Kraken were going to do next to clear the obstruction, and knowing that it wouldn't be long before the beasts would be after them again, Aislinn sheathed her sword and sprinted toward the wall of a house just off to her left.

She launched herself at the stone, placing her right foot on the wall, at the same time jumping up and catching the roof with her fingertips. Getting a good grip, she pulled herself to the top.

She didn't want to stay on the path, and she knew instantly that decision had proven to be a good one. She caught out of the corner of her eye the Kraken that already were climbing out of the hole as well as those who were sprinting through the burial pit to catch them on the other side of the trail.

Bryen was right behind her, Spear of the Magii strapped across his back. Aislinn continued to make her way up several floors of the apartment complex, not stopping until she reached the eighth tier. Once she hopped over the ledge, she turned back and offered Bryen a hand, helping him to the roof.

They took the few seconds they had earned to gulp down air, the climb leaving them winded.

"This is definitely an improvement," said Bryen.

"Yes, but it's only temporary. The Kraken are coming."

They both looked back at the way they had come.

The Kraken were coming.

Fast.

Dozens of the beasts had scrambled out of the pit Aislinn had blasted into the path and were already swarming up the building. They were showing a much too adept ability at climbing as their sharp claws allowed them to pull themselves up the staggered floors with a freakish dexterity.

"Ready?" asked Aislinn as she took her place on the edge of the roof.

"Ready," confirmed Bryen, who stood right next to her.

When the first Kraken claw appeared on the stone lip, Aislinn slashed down with her sword. She earned a scream of rage as the beast tumbled back into the Kraken coming after it.

Bryen did her one better. He waited for the Kraken on his side to lift his head above the ledge before separating it from the beast's body. The corpse knocked two more Kraken from the wall right before they could pull themselves onto the roof.

And so it went for several minutes. Aislinn and Bryen fought side by side, demonstrating a deadly efficiency as they prevented the Kraken from gaining a foothold on the roof. Even so, they knew that they couldn't stay there for much longer.

"We're about to run into the same problem as we did on the trail," said Bryen.

He swept his weapon down in a broad arc, slicing across the throat of one Kraken that when he fell took with him tumbling to floor below three more of the beasts. He then cut right across a second beast's brow, blinding the Kraken as blood cascaded down into his eyes.

Bryen kicked out with his right foot, the wounded Kraken crashing down onto the beasts that were attempting to extricate themselves from the Kraken that Bryen had just killed.

Aislinn nodded, not bothering to reply as she stabbed a Kraken through the eye. She then slashed with her steel as she pulled her weapon free to cut across another Kraken's neck.

Both beasts fell away from the ledge, taking several more Kraken with them.

Bryen was right. Their time on that floor had come to an end. Once again, they needed to move.

Quickly.

Because more and more of the Kraken were bunching up beneath them. A massive threat if they couldn't keep the ledge clear. Also an opportunity that Aislinn was more than willing to make use of.

Reaching for the Talent, with barely a thought she sent more than a dozen bolts of energy slamming down into the terrace below them. Pleased by the destruction that she had wrought, she continued her efforts.

She focused now on the terraces on both sides of the one that she had just destroyed. The power blasted apart Kraken and huge chunks of stone, a cloud of dust and dirt joining the thin coating of mist that was following the beasts and slowly working its way over the plateau.

"You seem to have a one-track mind today," said Bryen.

Aislinn shrugged. "It worked before. I figured that it would work again."

"That it did," Bryen agreed.

They didn't wait to see when the Kraken would emerge from the rubble. They knew many of the beasts would. It was just a matter of when.

They used the additional time that Aislinn had gifted them to climb two more floors up the apartment building. They were about to try for a third when Aislinn spun around, spheres of energy shooting from her palms and slamming into two Kraken who had eschewed the howls of their comrades to climb after their prey silently, hoping to catch them off guard.

The beasts almost succeeded. They probably would have, if Aislinn hadn't been searching around them with the Talent.

The Kraken fell backward off the ledge, several angry growls rising from the floor below them as the broken bodies crashed into the beasts who were seeking to follow their now dead brethren.

Before the Kraken could start climbing again, Bryen fixed the Spear of the Magii to the scabbard across his back and sprinted for the next wall, placing a boot against the stone and launching himself up to grab the roof. He reached out with his right hand.

"Come on. We've got to go."

Aislinn didn't need to be told twice. Sheathing her sword, she sprinted for the wall. She got a foot almost halfway up and then reached for Bryen's hand. Her Protector swung her up and over the ledge.

Aislinn continued toward the next wall, doing as she had done before. Reaching the roof, she looked back and saw that Bryen was right behind her.

"Do your thing," Bryen said, in the process of pulling himself up over the ledge, the first Kraken already appearing on the roof Aislinn had just left behind.

Aislinn ignored the Kraken, knowing that Bryen would get himself over the ledge before the beast could reach for him. Instead, just as she had done before with so much success, she sent a blast of energy right into the roof where the beast was standing.

The Kraken disappeared in another cloud of grit and rock as the stone ceiling collapsed. Aislinn earned several more screams of pain and rage for her efforts from the beasts below that were caught in the slide of collapsing stone.

She didn't bother to see if there were any survivors, already catching the movement in the fog just below. Aislinn had taken some of the Kraken out of the fight, but not all. There were just too many of the beasts.

That thought driving her, she turned and sprinted for the next wall. Bryen was already there.

He helped her up just as he did before. And, once again, she destroyed the floor below them before the Kraken could come at them, buying them the time that they needed to climb to the next level.

So it went for the next few minutes, until finally they reached the very top of the staggered homes. The narrow crest of the ridge was only a few feet above them.

Aislinn and Bryen looked back the way they had come. They could see very little, the clouds of dirt and crushed stone deepening the gloom of the fog. But they could hear what was going on below them.

They had succeeded in making the Kraken's climb more difficult. Still, their efforts hadn't stopped the creatures. It had simply slowed them. The screeches of rage were getting closer with every breath they took.

"We're going to need to try something different," said Bryen.

He was looking for some other avenue of escape that wouldn't require them to get into a pitched battle from which they wouldn't be able to make a break for it. That worrisome possibility his primary concern, Bryen jumped up. Catching the edge of the crest, he pulled himself up so that he could peek over the top.

He dropped back down, his expression thoughtful. It just might work.

"I know," replied Aislinn just as she swept her blade, gifted to her by the Blademaster, down toward the edge of the roof. The steel sliced right through a Kraken claw, the beast tumbling back to knock down several more of the beasts right behind it. "I'm up for any good idea you might have because we're running out of time."

"Does it have to be a good idea?" Bryen asked.

He sent several daggers of energy to the far side of the roof they stood on, blasting back a fist of Kraken who were attempting to flank them. He then shot twenty more daggers crafted of light into the fog that was blanketing that side of the mountain.

He had caught the subtle movement hidden within the mist as the creatures tried to get above them. He could only hope that some of his bolts took a few of the Kraken out of the fight.

It definitely was time to go. The beasts would be above them in seconds.

Once that happened, they were done for.

"I'd prefer a good idea," began Aislinn, though upon seeing what the beasts planned to do next, she changed her mind, "but I'll take any idea that gets us out of here."

"Done."

Bryen jumped back up, grasping the top of the crest and pulling himself up. He then reached back down, helping Aislinn climb the ledge to stand next to him.

It wasn't really a trail. It was more like a natural aqueduct that ran all the way down the crest of the bluff. The groove reconnected with the trail where it led away from the plateau toward the small island waiting for them off in the distance.

Yes, this just might work, Bryen thought. And if it didn't, well ... at least they had tried.

Opening himself to the Seventh Stone, Bryen took in as much of the Talent as he could hold comfortably. He then used the natural magic to craft what resembled one of the boards that Davin had used to surf behind the *Freedom* while they crossed the Burnt Ocean.

Jumping on, he extended his hand toward Aislinn.

"Come on," said Bryen.

She looked at him with an expression that suggested that he wasn't thinking clearly because of the increasing stress of their dire situation. "Do you really think this is a good idea? Doing something that Davin did? Here of all places?"

"Probably not," replied Bryen. Then he gave her a roguish grin. "We don't have much choice, though, do we?"

"You've got me there," she admitted.

Aislinn accepted his hand, joining Bryen on the board crafted of the Talent. She then wrapped her arms around her Protector's waist.

"Hope for the best," said Bryen over his shoulder.

"You're not filling me with confidence when ..."

She couldn't get the rest of her words out. Bryen applied a strong stream of the Talent to the board, sending them hurtling down the rut that ran along the top of the crag and leaving the three Kraken who had just reached the roof they had been standing on screaming in frustration.

17

THE HUNTRESS

Talia stood in her office, hands pressed onto the top of her desk. She looked out the long, multipaned window that provided a view of the wharf. The Carlomin docks extended for more than a quarter mile into the harbor and seemed to reach for the horizon when the sun fell in the west.

She smiled as she watched the children walking into the new school that had been built just to the north of the main gate of the compound. More than a hundred students after a quick count.

It wouldn't be long before there were more, because there were more parents interested in having their children attend the school as well. They just needed to hire more teachers.

The Carlomin Trading Company paid the instructors, a free service to the families of their many employees. The school had only been open for a few weeks, and they were already talking to the rector about adding five more classrooms so that they could accommodate the demand.

The tavern at the very edge of the water was doing just as well, better than anticipated actually, based on the crowds that formed in front as the sun began to set. Full every night, the sailors, soldiers, and tradespeople living and working in what many were calling the Carlomin Protectorate, though never loud enough for Governor Roosarian or her soldiers to hear. They liked the fact that they didn't have to leave the guarded compound to gain all that they needed for themselves and their families.

Because of that, more merchants were seeking to become a part of what Talia and her mother were building. Master Hari's sister had built her blacksmith forge with the aid of the Carlomins and already had more work than she could handle for the next six months. One general store was doing a brisk business. So brisk in fact that the proprietor would be adding another location on the other side of the compound next week.

As the day began, Talia watched it all feeling a great deal of satisfaction, the three piers already a bustle of activity. If their plans continued to proceed as they hoped, and there was no reason to believe that they wouldn't, she and her mother would achieve their objective in just a matter of months rather than years.

The land they had acquired around the docks at the behest of her father would become a virtually self-sufficient neighborhood of Ballinasloe. A city within a city.

Perhaps most telling, it would be a constant reminder of the challenge they presented to Governor Roosarian's authority, of their belief that the woman lacked the skills to govern the Territory effectively.

"You've been busy since I've been away."

"It's been easier than I expected," her mother replied, walking into the office to stand next to her daughter, a large portfolio with several pages askew under her arm. "It seems that most of the people we're working with here simply want a fair opportunity. If we give that to them, they do the rest."

Talia nodded in agreement. If there was a truer statement than that, she had yet to hear it.

"And Roosarian's spies?"

"We've identified two," Isana replied. "No others, yet. Although we'll keep looking."

"Who are these spies?"

"One is a sailor we just hired. Supposedly he's crossed the Burnt Ocean a dozen times."

"Really? Quite an accomplishment if that's true. What do you plan to do with him?"

"I've left the problem with Captain Kenworthy. The sailor is on the ship he'll be taking back to Caledonia in a few days' time. He smelled a rat and did some checking. Captain Kenworthy came looking for you to ask what to do about him. I told him to take the man with him."

"What did Captain Kenworthy think of that?"

"He liked the idea."

"So Captain Kenworthy has something in mind?"

"Indeed he does, Talia. He was quite specific with respect to his plan. He didn't think that it would take much to get the man to talk once he had a chance to consider his options when there was little likelihood of rescue by his real employer. From what Captain Kenworthy said, losing sailors in rough seas during the passage is a much too common occurrence."

"So I've heard. And the other spy?"

"A barmaid in the tavern."

Clever, Talia thought. Ply someone with enough ale and you could dredge up quite a lot of useful information without them even knowing, and they likely wouldn't even remember the conversation.

"How was she discovered?"

"The tavern owner, Bridget Kallahan. She thought that something was off about the woman when she started working for her. The barmaid focused a lot of her attention on the men working in the shipyard, asking questions about specific aspects of the ships that were coming into service. Bridget did some digging as well and came to me with what she found. The barmaid's story didn't hold up."

"You told her to leave the woman in place?"

"I did."

"Smart." Better to know the spy in your midst than not. If you handled matters the right way, you could gain more from the spy than her master ever could. "I assume you already have plans for her?"

"I do," replied Isana.

"They're both being watched?"

"They are," her mother nodded. "By people we can trust."

"How can you be so certain about that?"

"Roosarian had their loved ones murdered."

Talia nodded. That would certainly help to guarantee her watchers' loyalty.

For the next several minutes, Isana provided an update on how her meetings were going with the other merchants in Ballinasloe. Two had asked whether they might be able to form a partnership with Carlomin Trading Company. Proposals were expected in the next few days. Isana believed that both were worthy of consideration if the terms were fair.

Several other merchants were seeking a place on the Carlomin docks. Not only because of the thriving business opportunities, but also because of the additional security provided by the wall and the Carlomin Guard.

Talia couldn't fault them. The number of break-ins at merchant offices was increasing to an almost ridiculous level. That and the arson, which was becoming much too frequent an occurrence to be just a coincidence.

Roosarian was either nervous or trying to make a point. Maybe both.

"Are the merchants doing as we proposed?" asked Talia after her mother had run through a few more details on the happenings in town while she was gone.

"Yes, they're taking our suggestion quite seriously. They can't ignore what's going on around them."

After the larceny and the loss of four warehouses in just the last two weeks, it had become quite clear to most as to whom was responsible, though there was little that they could do about it. Therefore, the merchants forming what was essentially a self-defense league only made sense since Governor Roosarian had little cause to protect them against her own predations.

The Council they had named it. At Isana's suggestion.

"So the merchants are coming around to our point of view?"

"They are," said Isana. "It took some very long discussions, but for most the evidence is too strong to be ignored. They don't want to believe, because they understand what that means, but they have no choice. Their survival depends on it."

At first the merchants had not wanted to even consider that the Governor of Fal Carrach was the cause for all the distress they were facing, not only in the town, but also on the water with the pirates terrorizing the coast. Some still didn't want to believe it.

She understood. Although Talia knew that it wouldn't be long before Roosarian's many crimes, including the murder of her father, were brought to light. It was just a matter of presenting all the necessary evidence.

"Will they meet with us?"

"They will, at the day and time prescribed. They actually wanted to meet earlier, but only with you. They've been waiting for you to return."

"Do we need to worry that any of them will try to reach out to Governor Roosarian?"

"A good question, Talia. I don't think so. But ..."

"But just in case you've put safeguards in place."

"Correct. Better to expect the worst and be pleasantly surprised."

"Agreed," said Talia, pleased that her mother was taking such precautions, not feeling the need to ask what they were. "They'll have a difficult time ignoring the proof that you've provided."

"I certainly hope so. Although, I should note that some of the merchants struggling the most with the decision that needs to be made could do with a little extra nudge."

"They'll get more than a nudge, I promise you that."

"And where is the infamous Captain Blackbeard?"

"Stowed away somewhere safe. He won't be found until it's time for him to take the stage."

"Did it take much to convince him?"

Talia smiled at the question. "Not really. He became much more talkative when I noted his very limited options."

"I can imagine," Isana murmured. "Hopefully you did nothing that was permanent?"

"I did no more than what he deserved," Talia replied, earning a concerned stare from her mother. "Don't worry, mother. He remains whole. For now. And he will remain whole so long as he does what is required of him."

Captain Blackbeard had begun to grow a spine again during the voyage north to Ballinasloe. After a few days in the brig, he seemed to have forgotten his encounter with the great white sharks.

To remind him of his precarious position, Sirena, Captain of her Guard, had tied a rope around his arms and then several of the sailors had thrown him overboard. After being dragged behind the ship for less than a quarter hour, Captain Blackbeard's obsequious nature had returned after he had expelled most of the Sea of Mist on the deck.

After that reminder of what lay in store for him if he failed to do as she wished, Talia didn't think that he would prove difficult again. Especially not after he saw the woman thrown into the cell next to his just that morning.

The assassin had tried to kill Talia in her sleep. The soldiers who had deposited her there had been less than gentle, displeased, almost murderous themselves, outraged that someone had attempted to kill Lady Carlomin.

Talia had the chance to kill the woman. The assassin had tried to kill her in her small apartment just down the hallway, but Talia had turned the tables on her.

It would have been so easy to drive her dagger into the back of her neck. It would have been so satisfying.

She chose not to, allowing her reason to reign rather than her emotion.

The assassin served a purpose. Once that purpose was fulfilled, she could decide whether or not to give in to her bloodier urges.

The noise and commotion in her rooms had drawn several of the men and women who also had small apartments on the top floor of the main building, including Sirena. Once the assassin had been taken away, Sirena offered her resignation on the spot, devastated that her employer had almost died because of what she perceived as her failure.

Talia refused to accept it. The assassin had snuck in before they had returned that afternoon from their expedition to the south. She had hidden in the roof just above the ceiling of her chambers, not sliding down through the crawlspace until Talia had gone to bed in the early morning.

There was no cause to blame anyone. Nevertheless, there was a lesson to be learned. Talia charged Sirena with taking a fresh look at their security to ensure that this could never happen again.

It was the unexpected scrape of wood when the assassin first moved the covering that led into the attic that woke Talia from her light slumber. Her first thought was to leap from her bed, the dagger she slept with beneath her pillow in hand.

Instead, she decided to wait, watching as the assassin crept down without making another sound. The woman was good, dangerously so.

And Talia was certain that her attacker was a woman despite the fact that her face was hidden by a cowl. The figure had a rather slight frame to match the diminutive size, and the shape of the assassin's body in her form-fitting leathers was the final clue.

The assassin had taken her time. Apparently she felt no need to rush, having no fear of being discovered, relishing the power she was about to wield. She had crept to the side of Talia's bed and then stared down at her for more than a minute.

That had been the most difficult part of the entire experience for Talia. Pretending to remain asleep even as she watched her attacker through slitted eyes, not wanting to give herself away.

Talia had expected a dagger. It was the easiest weapon to use in close quarters fighting.

She had been mistaken.

The assassin had pulled out a thin needle that was about a foot long, the point razor sharp, the end molded with wrapped leather so that the woman could jab with the weapon and not lose her grip even with a sweaty palm.

Talia was impressed. A punch through the eye or the ear would certainly do the trick with a weapon like that.

It had proven to be an easier fight than Talia had anticipated. When the woman finally lined up the needle with her eye and stabbed down, Talia rolled to the left, pulling free her dagger and coming to her feet on the far side of the bed.

For just a breath, the assassin stood there in shock at having missed her target, not quite believing that she had driven the needle into Talia's pillow rather than through her eye and into her brain.

The assassin quickly recovered. She stepped up onto the

side of the bed and launched herself through the air toward Talia.

That had been the assassin's other mistake besides the soft scrape of wood. Before the assassin's foot left the mattress, Talia kicked the frame, knocking the bed back toward the woman.

Caught in mid-motion and not getting the lift that she needed, the assassin awkwardly fell face first to the floor.

Talia placed a knee to the back of her neck and her dagger against her throat before the woman could understand fully what had happened to her. She picked up the needle the assassin had dropped, pressing it into the soft flesh at the back of the woman's neck.

So tempting, yes, but not the right thing to do.

Even though Talia had told Sirena not to blame herself, she knew that the woman would. It was a part of who she was. And it would be all to the good in the future, because Talia was certain that Sirena would internalize the lessons learned.

Talia hadn't taken any serious wounds during the brief melee except for a slice of the needle across her brow when the assassin's arms were flailing through the air before she hit the floor. She hadn't even noticed because of the adrenaline surging through her veins, not even feeling the blood running down the side of her face, until Sirena pointed the wound out to her.

It had been a bloody mess until her mother had stitched up the wound. Remembering the harrowing start to her day, her hand went to her brow now. She touched the laceration gently, wincing at the pain.

It was a small price to pay to still be alive. If nothing else, she had acquired a new weapon, the long needle placed in a sheath hidden in the outside of her right boot.

She had refused a bandage when her mother tried to wrap the white cloth around her forehead. Talia wanted the stitching to be visible. Why, she didn't know. It just seemed like the right thing to do.

Now, much to her amusement, several of the soldiers and sailors she had seen just that morning had begun to call her the Huntress in a good-natured way. She understood that they meant the term as a compliment, and she took it as such.

She was already a hunter of pirates. Now she was a hunter of assassins as well.

The Huntress had a nice ring to it in her ears.

Best of all, it was a name that she could use for what she planned to do next. Because as she had learned since coming to New Caledonia, perception often was more important than reality.

Her thoughts were brought back to the present, having tuned out her mother for the last few minutes, when they were interrupted by a knock at the open door. Captain Jennison, who had crossed the Burnt Ocean with her father, walked in, his wooden leg announcing him.

"Captain Carlomin, I hope that you are well."

"As well as can be, Captain Jennison, thank you." Not wanting to relive the conversation regarding what had happened that morning for the tenth time, she sought to turn the Captain's focus in a different direction. "You would not be here without cause, Captain Jennison, since you sail on the tide tomorrow morning. What brings you here?"

"A ship, Captain Carlomin. It just came in with the dawn."

"Why is this ship so interesting, Captain Jennison?" asked Isana.

"There is a good bit of damage along its port side. One of our pirate hunters reported just the other day that one of the ships it was pursuing escaped, although not without sustaining a good bit of damage."

"On the port side, I assume?" asked Talia.

"Indeed so," Captain Jennison confirmed.

"So an opportunity?" asked Isana, knowing that her daughter had reached the same conclusion as she did.

"Perhaps so." She turned back to Captain Jennison. "Who's ship?"

"It bore no markings, Captain Carlomin, not even a name. However, it put to at the Roosarian dock."

Both Isana and Talia looked at one another with a shared expression. Just as they suspected.

"Please have a few men watch it, Captain Jennison. Carefully, of course. As soon as it's preparing to leave the port, I want to know."

"Of course, Captain Carlomin. I've already taken the liberty of doing just that."

"Excellent. Thank you, Captain Jennison. And one other thing. Belay my previous orders for you and your squad. Make sure your ships are ready to sail at a moment's notice. If that ship leaves Ballinasloe, I want to be right behind it."

18

MYTH MADE REAL

The fog smothered the bay like a wet blanket. Muting sound and hiding movement.

"Anything?"

Declan and Rafia stood at the port rail facing the beach. They couldn't see anything other than the wispy grey that had enveloped them in just seconds, the fog rushing off the mountain and then reaching out for them across the water like a giant talon. The glowing lanterns lining the rails and placed at various spots around the deck gave off no more than a dim radiance at best, fighting a losing battle against the murk.

Declan hoped that battle between light and dark wasn't an omen for the larger clash to come.

The Blood Company lined the rails on both sides of the ship, shields in front of the spears, prepared as best as they could for the creatures that had yet to attack. Majdi, Jenus, and the other gladiators who had gone to the spring were more than happy to tell them all about what they had faced and how they had escaped.

Barely escaped, Majdi had confirmed. Although the gladiator viewed the conveyor as more dangerous than the Kraken after his tumble and then race down the mountainside.

Rather than being rattled by the stories, the Blood Company had enjoyed a good laugh, all the while taking in what their comrades told them so that they knew what to expect from the Kraken.

Now they stood as silent as the heart trees of the Dark Forest. Straining to hear any sound that might give away their approaching enemy. Ready to test their skills against another opponent.

They were certain that the Kraken would be coming for them. Majdi believed that the beasts who failed to defeat them on the mountain wanted another crack at them.

Majdi usually was right about such things. Yet that didn't bother them in the least.

Man or monster, it was all the same to them. Just another combat to be fought.

Kill or be killed.

They had lived that way for so long that they couldn't live any other way now.

They saw the world for what it was. Not as they wanted it to be.

They understood the danger of making that mistake.

As they sought to pierce the gloom, they heard nothing but the water lapping gently against the hull of the ship. The gladiators sensed that the Kraken were close and coming closer with each passing second. They could feel the beasts, but their inability to identify their attackers was beginning to make them edgy.

They hated waiting. If a fight was inevitable, as this one was, they wanted to get to it.

"They're coming," said Rafia in a voice that traveled the length of the ship, wanting to make sure that all the gladiators heard her. She had been searching around them with the Talent ever since the fog drifted in over Solace Sound.

Nothing had caught her attention. Until now.

"How close?"

"A hundred yards."

"Where?" asked Declan. "Even with this fog, I should be able to see boats coming across the water, but nothing."

"They're not using boats," said Rafia.

"They're not using boats," pondered Davin. "This forced trip to the Jagged Islands is just getting better and better."

"Stand ready!" shouted Rafia.

"Where are they?" asked Davin.

"They're coming out of the water."

"Of course they are," grumbled Declan. "Shields to the front!"

The gladiators standing right next to the rails raised their scuta, ready for what was going to come their way. That didn't stop Dorlan's natural curiosity from almost getting the better of him.

He lowered his shield just a hair so that he could peek over the side of the *Freedom*. He jumped back in a flash, sensing rather than seeing the movement. A claw swept through the grey, digging into the wood rather than taking his eyes.

Dorlan didn't hesitate despite his initial shock, punching forward with his shield, many of the gladiators standing with him doing the same.

Because of the fog, they didn't get a good first look at their attackers. They saw little more than a claw, a bone-white blade, or an angry maw filled with sharp teeth.

Nevertheless, the Blood Company stood strong. They refused to yield the railing, knocking many of the beasts who scuttled up the hull like crabs back into the water.

For several minutes, nothing changed. The Kraken rushed out of the bay much like a swarm of ants, scrambling up the sides of the massive ship, seeking to gain the deck by using their greater numbers to overwhelm the defenders.

The gladiators allowed the beasts no purchase, shields blocking their way, spears shooting forward, wounded and dying Kraken falling back into the bay. The water turned into a bloody froth as the great whites picked at the many offerings given to them by the Blood Company.

"Jenus, take your squad to the stern!" ordered Declan. "We have a breach!"

The massive gladiator responded immediately, pulling out of the shield wall along with several other fighters. Majdi and Dorlan covered the resulting gap as Jenus and his gladiators rushed to the rear of the *Freedom*.

The decks built for the Griffons had been empty since they had reached the Jagged Islands, the animals yet to return from their hunt.

Empty except for the several fists of Kraken who had already made it to the deck, dozens more swarming up behind them.

Believing that this would be the most difficult section of the vessel to attack, Captain Gregson had placed a squad of sailors there, the Blood Company too few in number to defend the ship's entire breadth.

The Kraken had proven his assumption wrong right from the start, the creatures from the deep having little trouble scaling the additional height.

After slaughtering most of the sailors, several of the beasts, dripping water, blades of bone in clawed hands, and shrieking at the top of their lungs, leapt down to the main deck.

Those few sailors who were still alive were about to join their dead mates, their painful end only delayed when Jenus, Asaia, Chesin, and several other gladiators arrived with the simple though challenging, perhaps even hopeless, task of stemming the tide.

Jenus used his shield as a weapon, knocking two of the beasts back into one of the shelters used by the Griffons. One beast landed hard on his back, the force of the blow taking the breath from him. The other attacker hit the wood headfirst at an awkward angle, the snap of his broken neck audible even over the din of the fight.

Asaia flicked out her whip, the sharp steel tip catching a Kraken in the mouth, knocking out several of his sharp teeth and lodging itself in the back of the beast's throat. A hard tug pulled the steel free along with a good part of the Kraken's jaw.

Chesin followed right after Jenus. Leaping up onto the Griffons' deck, his blade was a blur of steel as he charged in among the beasts. The baby-faced gladiator's bravery halted the Kraken's progress long enough for his comrades to join him.

Because of their courage and skill, for several minutes Jenus and his squad earned a stalemate with the Kraken seeking to swarm the ship from the stern.

But it didn't last.

It couldn't last.

A half dozen fighters from the Pit, no matter how competent, no matter how determined, no matter how brave, couldn't hold for long against several dozen Kraken being bolstered by the seemingly unending stream of creatures coming up behind them.

All that they could do was try to delay the inevitable and give Declan the time that he needed to shift the Blood Company's formation.

Because if Declan didn't, in a matter of minutes the Kraken would cover every inch of the vessel.

19

THE KING KRAKEN

"Watch it!" Aislinn shouted into his ear.

Bryen dipped his left knee down toward the curved board. Aislinn mimicked his movement just as she had done since they had begun their rapid descent down the crest, the magical construction they were riding lifting up on the right side just enough so that they skimmed across the top of a large rock that protruded from the rough sluice rather than slamming into it.

Bryen was certain that they were riding down an aqueduct. It was uneven, a bit craggy, but he could tell that the people who had lived here before their unfortunate encounter with the Kraken had carved out a path across the top of the peak so that they could catch the rain. The water ran down the conduit to flow into several drains cut into the path that led to large stone basins far below.

Very clever and a complete waste of time to be thinking about as he struggled to maintain control over the board. He had to give Davin credit for his success against the Bakunawa. This was not an easy thing to do.

Using the Talent to speed up and just as often slow them

down, Bryen's primary concern was making sure that they didn't leap over the curled edge of the channel and sail off into the chasing fog to meet their end somewhere on the side of the mountain.

Having cleared their latest obstacle, Bryen quickly shifted his weight to the right. Aislinn followed suit. He did his best to ensure that they ran down the middle of the rough track whenever they could.

With that goal in mind, every so often he trailed the tip of the Spear of the Magii behind him, digging the glowing steel into the stone so that he could make minor adjustments in their route, pushing to the left or the right as required much as he would if he were managing a tiller on a boat.

"How many?" Bryen yelled. "And how far away?"

They had made excellent time since they had begun skidding down the empty waterway. The northern entrance to the plateau and the trail that was just beyond that would take them to the very tip of the island was coming upon them fast.

Yet even with the rush of the air in his ears, he could still hear the Kraken scrabbling behind them. He assumed that just as many of the creatures that were climbing down the rubble of the apartment complex to continue their pursuit were racing toward them along the trail that split apart the abandoned hamlet.

"They're just beginning to stream out of the village now," Aislinn replied, using the Talent to check on their hunters, the dense fog caressing their backs and hiding them from view for the moment. Holding onto his waist, she avoided looking behind them or to the left, not wanting to throw Bryen off balance by turning or twisting in an awkward way. "We've gained a few hundred yards on them."

"I take it that's the good news!" Bryen needed to shout so that he could be heard above the rush of the wind and the clatter of their board across the rough rock beneath them. "What's the bad news?"

"Just as many of the Kraken as we escaped by the tower are coming after us, and right behind them several hundred more are trying to catch up."

"Wonderful," Bryen muttered.

He had wanted to pull as many of the beasts after them as he could, hoping to give Asaia and the others the time they needed to make it back to the ship. It appeared that he and Aislinn had proven to be more successful than they ever could have hoped to be.

Much too successful, in fact. He worried now about the number of beasts still hunting them.

If he and Aislinn could get to that natural bridge leading to the smaller island just off the coast, they could hold off the Kraken for a time, although admittedly probably not for very long. Even with their skill with a blade and their use of the Talent, there were too many creatures chasing after them.

They would be consumed by the swarm of monsters.

It made him think of the jumble of crabs that he had spied on occasion on the beach along the coast of the Silent Sea, scavenging the remains of whatever sea creature had washed up onto the shore. A gruesome end, and one that he hoped that he and Aislinn could avoid.

If the Kraken sought to come at them from behind and they were slow to swim the channel separating the smaller island from the larger, then perhaps the fog would clear enough for him to attempt to make it to the ship through a portal. Of course, as soon as Bryen thought of that, he realized that his desire for clear skies was no more than a foolish hope.

He knew the truth.

So long as the Kraken were after them, the fog would stay with them as well.

A simple strategy then. Reach a more defensible position.

Hold off this swarm of bloodthirsty beasts. Buy some more time. Then find some solution to a likely unsolvable dilemma. Easy.

"We need a new plan!" shouted Aislinn, having just reached the same conclusion as he did.

"We need a new plan," Bryen agreed. But what?

Bryen glanced down quickly at the bay as they sped along the top of the crest. Solace Sound was shrouded in a thick mist that billowed as if it had a life of its own.

He couldn't see the *Freedom*. He couldn't see the water.

He did catch the first flash of the Talent and then another. Declan, Rafia, and the others were engaged in their own clash.

Bryen was concerned for his friends, but there was nothing that he could do for them now. He needed to shift his focus back toward the aqueduct and their escape, so he pulled his eyes away from the fight that was just beginning far below them.

Whatever time he had bought for the Blood Company had run out. The Kraken had taken their hunt to the water.

He would worry about that later if he could. Now, he and Aislinn were almost to the bottom of the ridge. He needed to worry about how they were going to evade the beasts that were demonstrating such an irritating persistence.

They couldn't expect any help from their friends. The Blood Company would have a hard enough time keeping the Kraken from taking the vessel, if only because of sheer numbers.

They were on their own.

He and Aislinn would need to get themselves out of this mess somehow. And quickly if they wanted to have any chance at all of returning to the ship and helping their comrades before the Kraken overran them.

"Bryen, to the left!" warned Aislinn.

They were about to return to the trail, just a hundred more

feet to go, but a pack of very motivated Kraken had beaten them to the junction.

Bryen shook his head in frustration. These particular creatures, instead of pursuing them when he and Aislinn had started to climb the building, had planned ahead.

They had allowed their brethren to maintain the chase, instead continuing to the north and paralleling the trail through the burial pit to the very end of the plateau. Because of their forethought, these Kraken were perfectly positioned now to catch their prey.

"This day just keeps getting better and better," grumbled Bryen, now at least twenty of the beasts on the trail, impeding their way, with even more still scrambling up over the side of the path to join their comrades.

"What do we do?" asked Aislinn.

For just a few breaths, because that's all the time that he had, Bryen studied the Kraken. The beasts had formed a loose formation that in some ways resembled the shield wall the Blood Company had employed so effectively when they first encountered these creatures.

A smart move. Yet even though the beasts were demonstrating a coordination and discipline that had been lacking up until now, Bryen saw that the Kraken still couldn't contain some of their more instinctual urges.

The monsters howled as they watched their prey come to them. Some of the beasts used their claws to urge Bryen and Aislinn on as they hurtled down toward them, certain that their hunt was over.

An imposing sight. Yet not an unbeatable one.

Bryen noticed that although the Kraken had formed a ragged line, it was really no more than that. The creatures did not have scuta like the gladiators did that could be locked together to form a movable, almost impenetrable defense.

Bryen smiled upon recognizing that. Declan always liked to

say that the best plans were the simplest plans. And his plan now couldn't be simpler.

"We keep going!" Bryen called over his shoulder. "Hold on tight!"

He might have heard a groan escape from Aislinn. Maybe even the words, "I can't believe we're doing this."

Bryen couldn't tell for sure as he guided the board down the slope. He did feel Aislinn tighten her grip around his waist.

What he was about to do would either be a spectacular success or a catastrophic failure. He hoped for the former, and to strengthen that likelihood, he opened himself to the Seventh Stone.

Flicking his wrist as the curved board shot off the crest and curled back onto the trail, Bryen dug the Spear of the Magii into the ground, directing them right toward the center of the Kraken line. Bryen added more natural magic right at that instant, giving their conveyance a needed burst of energy to increase their speed.

At the same time, using the energy given to him by the Seventh Stone, he formed a wedged shield right to their front, much like a plow used to till a field, though in this case it was much larger and stronger than steel.

Bryen watched with a calm and cold expression as the raging Kraken realized the challenge that they now faced. Many of the beasts who were screaming with pleasure at the approach of their prey now let out strangled gasps, fear and concern marring their frightening countenances.

The creatures had good cause to be afraid as Bryen and Aislinn slammed right into the Kraken line. The Talent strengthened by the Seventh Stone blasted right through them, sending the beasts flying through the air, Bryen and Aislinn continuing down the trail as if they had hit no more than a minor bump.

To add insult to injury, Aislinn used the natural magic to

send a handful of javelins arcing back over her shoulder to fall among the dead, injured, and disorganized beasts. The ground rocked with the power of each strike, the dirt and stone exploding into the air and clouding her view when she looked back briefly to survey the destruction she had wrought.

She couldn't tell how effective her attack had been as the fog swiftly draped itself back over the scene. Even so, she believed that Bryen's quick thinking and her additional gift to the Kraken had bought them at least a few more minutes. It wasn't much, but it certainly was something they could work with.

Pleased with the lead they had just gained, Bryen slowed the board, though only just a touch, wanting to make sure that he maintained control. Still using the Talent he continued to speed down the trail, not wanting to make a mistake that could lead to an accident and give back to the Kraken the precious time they had earned.

They covered the last half mile in less than a minute, Bryen finally bringing them to a stop right where the narrow bridge led out to the small island.

"You enjoyed that, didn't you?" accused Aislinn as she released her grip from around Bryen's waist.

Her Protector stepped off the board after she did. With a twist of his hand, the board spun around, the curved front now facing the direction from which they had come.

For just a few seconds, Bryen pointed toward the board, streams of energy surging from his fingers, infusing his creation with even more of the Talent until it pulsed a blinding white.

"Why would you think that?" asked Bryen, finishing the task that he had set for himself.

"Because you can't seem to stop smiling."

Bryen grinned even more broadly at that, then shrugged his shoulders. "You've got to have fun when you can. Davin taught me that."

Aislinn shook her head in concern. "You really need to stop spending so much time with Davin. He's a bad influence on you. It took me quite a while to get used to having a stoic, usually uncommunicative Protector. I don't know what I would do if I had a fun Protector."

"You're probably right," Bryen admitted. "That would be unsettling for both of us."

"What are you doing to the board?"

"Just my last bit of fun," Bryen replied with a wink.

"Seriously?"

"Trust me. You'll enjoy it." Then his focus returned to their current predicament. "Come on. They're not too far behind us."

Aislinn heard the angry screams coming down the trail toward them although they couldn't see the Kraken yet because of the encroaching fog that slowly reached for them.

She and Bryen had bought themselves some time. Just not enough. The beasts would be on them again much too quickly.

That concern guiding him, Bryen had taken only a few steps out onto the bridge when he stopped abruptly. This time Aislinn did run into his broad back.

"What's the matter?"

Bryen pointed.

Aislinn offered up a few choice curses. From where they had been atop the plateau, the narrow bridge had appeared to be whole. Upon closer inspection, however, it wasn't. Far from it. A large gap very close to where it connected to the small island was visible. It had to be at least fifty feet in length.

"Do you think it's a natural break?" asked Aislinn. She cringed. From where she was standing she could see the large fins cutting through the water frothing beneath them as the waves struck the ragged shore. "The sea wearing it down over time?"

"I don't think so," said Bryen.

He had noticed several notches in the side of the bridge. He looked down over the edge from where he was standing, nodding.

Yes, he was right. The notches ran along the length of the bridge every ten feet or so. The residents of the island had brought the bridge down on their own.

Presumably, those who survived the attack on the village had the same idea as he and Aislinn did. To get to the smaller island and carry on the fight from there.

A losing strategy for the islanders. Hopefully not for them as well.

Aislinn, looking over Bryen's shoulder and seeing the pins sticking out of the rock that ran down the length of the bridge, grimaced as the realization struck her. Worse, that knowledge did little to help them.

They couldn't jump the gap and they didn't dare try to swim across. Her next thought was to use the Talent to construct a bridge across the break just as the Ghoule Overlord had done when attacking Haven. But then a better idea came to mind that wouldn't require their use of natural magic and potentially leave a path for the Kraken to follow in their footsteps.

"Come on," Aislinn said, grabbing Bryen by the arm and pulling him toward the coast a little farther to the west.

After Bryen had brought their magical conveyance to a stop, she had glimpsed the large stone tower built like a ship's lanyard that resembled the ones running up the mountain, although this one was at least ten times larger. Two steel cables ran from the top of the tower all the way across the channel to the smaller island where they connected to another tower, this one not as tall. With the cable on their end extending down on an angle, it certainly would meet their purposes.

"Fight or go?" Aislinn asked.

It didn't take Bryen long to make up his mind, watching as hundreds of Kraken sprinted over the rise, the beasts screaming for their blood, the thick fog following along in their wake.

"I'd prefer to go," Bryen replied in a tone that suggested that her question was completely unnecessary.

"Me as well. Here." Just as at the other tower built near the springs atop the mountain, several long steel rods with wheels attached on each end lay against the base of the structure.

She handed one to Bryen, grabbed one for herself, and then began climbing up the tower using the steel bars that protruded along its length every few feet. Bryen didn't need to be told twice, following right behind her.

"Quite a view from here," Bryen said as they climbed the steel rungs.

Aislinn didn't bother to reply, not wanting to give him the satisfaction of knowing that he'd offered a clever quip. She also didn't look at him. A good thing, too, because a small smile curled her lips, a reaction her Protector didn't need to see.

"You ready?" asked Aislinn. As soon as she reached the top, she placed her bar on the two steel cables, locking the wheels in place.

The cables and the towers appeared to be in good working order. Even so, that didn't guarantee success.

Assuming she made it across to the island without falling into the channel, she had to assume as well that the buffers on the far tower still worked. If they didn't, she was in for a very hard, potentially fatal landing.

She didn't like making decisions based on assumptions, but she didn't have a choice.

"Just a moment," said Bryen, giving her another grin. "Just a little bit more fun to be had."

He turned back around, watching as the Kraken raced down the decline, the gleaming board that remained on the path functioning as a beacon to the monsters. Just like a moth was drawn to the light, the Kraken were pulled toward that board.

Aislinn offered Bryen a grin of her own, realizing what he was about to do.

With a flick of his hand, the board shot forward at an incredible speed, hurtling up the path in a streak of white and smashing into the Kraken, who were now no more than a few hundred yards away.

In addition to knocking dozens of the creatures into the air and clearing a path much as Bryen and Aislinn had done to break through the Kraken line upon coming down from the crest, Bryen's creation offered one more surprise as it clattered through the beasts.

Once Bryen judged the board to have reached a point where it could do the most damage, he closed his fist. The response was instantaneous.

A massive explosion erupted among the Kraken, all the Talent Bryen had infused within the board blasting out in all directions, the compressed energy so powerful that the tower he and Aislinn stood on shook violently.

Thankfully, it did no more than that, and the cables connecting their tower to the smaller tower remained in place.

"All right, now I'm ready to go," said Bryen, turning back toward Aislinn with a broad grin on his face.

He didn't bother to examine the devastation he had caused, instead taking the momentary silence that fell upon their pursuers as confirmation that his strategy had worked. He had wanted a big explosion. He just hadn't realized how big it would be based on the amount of the Talent he had forced into the board.

"You really are having too much fun," said Aislinn.

"Just doing what's necessary."

Aislinn grunted at that. "Then let's get to it. You'll be right behind me?"

"There's no place that I'd rather be than right behind you," Bryen replied with a wink. "Don't worry."

Aislinn gave him a hard look, then shook her head in resignation. "Humor like that at a time like this. I'm really beginning to wonder about you. Am I going to have to limit how much time you spend with Davin?"

Then without another word, she grabbed onto the bar with both hands and pushed off the tower with her feet.

Bryen watched her speed across the channel, thankful that the cables were, indeed, still in good shape.

When Aislinn reached the tower on the island after only a few seconds of soaring through the air, he placed his bar on the cables and locked the wheels in place. Abruptly, Bryen lifted up both feet, sensing the movement from below him just in time. Some of the Kraken who had avoided the blast had made for the tower, this one almost digging his claw into his foot.

Hanging from the bar, Bryen kicked down with his left foot. He caught the Kraken, which was lifting itself up the final rung with the intention of stabbing him in the back with his bone knife, right in the face, crushing his nose and the cartilage beneath.

The Kraken's natural reaction was to drop the knife and lift his claws to his face. When the beast did, Bryen's right foot whipped down, hitting the Kraken in the ribs and knocking him from the tower.

Not wanting to have to deal with the many Kraken who were following after the one he had just dispatched, Bryen lifted his boots to the stone and pushed off. His escape was met by howls of anger, several of the Kraken no more than a few feet behind him when he evaded their claws.

Bryen didn't feel a touch of sadness at the Kraken's disappointment. He flew across the channel knowing that his latest victory would be short-lived.

The fog was following the trail. It wouldn't be long before the grey haze blanketed the entire island.

And after that, the smaller cay he was rushing toward would be next. Their hoped-for haven likely wouldn't be a haven for very long.

As he approached the smaller tower, he was glad to see that Aislinn had made it across safely. For some reason, however, her face, growing bigger by the second, appeared to be more worried than usual, and she was gesturing behind him even though he was in no position to look back to see why.

He understood just a heartbeat later, the steel cables he was riding down drooping dangerously. Bryen almost lost his grip on the bar because of the jolt, a shriek of rage and hunger sounding not too far behind him.

One of the Kraken had found a bar and put it to use.

Yet there was nothing that Bryen could do in that moment to defend himself. He needed to focus on where he was going.

He was almost to the other side. Once he got there, he could deal with the Kraken.

Assuming he made it to the cay.

Because of the additional weight, the steel cables were sagging dangerously. Bryen lifted his legs, bringing them up to his chest and just in time.

With that adjustment, he barely cleared the rocks that made up the border of the island. He almost lost his grip right before he reached the smaller tower, fighting the urge to dodge out of the way as a streak of the Talent shot over his shoulder.

"That was close," Bryen protested as he dropped down from the bar, the buffers built into the tower doing their job, the cables snapping back into place right after his boots touched the dirt of the cay.

"Just doing what's necessary," Aislinn replied with a straight face.

Bryen shook his head, trying not to smile but failing

miserably as Aislinn sent his own words back at him. The smile that the Lady of the Southern Marches gifted him then suggested that she was much too pleased with herself.

Turning around to get a better sense of where they stood with the Kraken, he saw that the cable behind him was clear. Just as he expected, Aislinn's aim had been true, the bolt of energy striking the pursuing Kraken and sending him tumbling into the water.

Although the Kraken was a creature of the ocean, from what he could see the sharks were more than happy to feed on this unexpected visitor to their domain.

Nevertheless, the larger problem remained. There were still bars on the other side. Several of the Kraken already were attaching them to the cables, preparing to follow their dead comrade despite his grisly death.

Aislinn provided the solution to that dilemma, sending a bolt of the Talent streaking back across the channel. The white-hot energy tore right through the broad base of the larger tower. The stone and metal lanyard, almost seventy five feet in height, remained erect for a few seconds more before it crashed down onto the rocks, both cables snapping from the force of the blow.

The Kraken that had been on top of the structure either fell to the rocks below them, breaking bones and backs, or splashed into the rough water separating the larger island from the smaller.

The great whites swimming through the channel, having already gotten a taste of the first Kraken, turned immediately to investigate this latest disturbance.

"Well done," said Bryen. "Very final, as usual."

Aislinn smiled at her Protector's comment. "I do have my uses."

"That you do," he replied with a wink.

She held back her retort. She could deal with him later. They still weren't clear of the Kraken.

The beasts, having recovered from Bryen's exploding magical board, now were massing on the narrow bridge, studying the gap, clearly intent on finding a way across.

"Now what? They won't stop coming."

"We keep fighting," he replied.

Aislinn nodded. They really had no other choice.

The fog was closing in, just as the Kraken were, the beasts at the end of the collapsed bridge now scrambling down the side. They were preparing to dive into the water despite the presence of the great whites, more interested in killing them than worrying about what was waiting for them beneath the waves.

"It won't take them long to get across," warned Aislinn. "There are far too many for the sharks."

"Then we need to move."

Understanding that it wouldn't be long before the Kraken reached them, Bryen pushed his way through the dense undergrowth, going faster once they reached the small forest that ringed the island.

He and Aislinn hiked up the steep hill that rose almost in the very center of the cay. It didn't take them long to gain the top despite the difficulty of the climb caused by the rocky terrain and loose shale that formed the sides of the knoll.

Aislinn agreed with Bryen's decision. If they had no chance of escaping the Kraken, better to pick the most defensible spot on the island and make their stand there.

It wasn't much of a hill, really. More just an outcropping. Even so, it gave them the ability to see all around them and it would force the Kraken to attack up the ragged slope.

At least they would have those advantages to work with while they defended themselves.

Standing atop the knoll, they pulled their weapons from the

scabbards across their backs, getting an excellent view of the Kraken emerging out of the water, the sea creatures using their sharp claws to climb with little difficulty the sheer sides of the island.

There seemed to be a lot of activity going on beneath the gap in the bridge, the water churning more violently, several large pools of blood visible. Yet even with the great whites harassing the beasts, the Kraken were too many, a few lost to allow the rest to reach the island a fair trade apparently. And Bryen assumed that some of the sharks were among the dead, the Kraken likely not going to their deaths without a fight.

It wasn't long before the Kraken smothered the island, the beasts circling around the base of the hill upon which Bryen and Aislinn were prepared to make their stand. Strangely, none of the beasts rushed up the slope, seeking the kills they so desperately desired.

They simply stood there.

Waiting.

Growling.

Hissing.

Staring at them.

Hate and hunger mixing behind their greyish blue eyes.

"What are they doing?" asked Aislinn.

"I don't know." Bryen reached for the Talent once again, infusing the steel blades of the Spear of the Magii, Aislinn having already done the same to her sword. "I can make something up if you feel a need for greater certainty."

"Now is not the time to be smart," chastised Aislinn, sweeping her gaze over the beasts. The rabidness that she had associated with the Kraken ever since they had first appeared on the mountain had disappeared, replaced by a strange slightly unnerving calm. The creatures made no move toward them, apparently satisfied to have them trapped on the knoll.

"Sorry, couldn't help it."

"You really are spending too much time with Davin. His humor, or lack thereof, is rubbing off on you in the worst possible way."

"I'll keep that in mind if we get out of this."

"Please do. And what do you mean by *if*?"

"Just looking at what we face with a dose of realism."

"A habit ingrained in you by Declan."

"Just so. It looks like we're about to find out why the Kraken are acting as they are."

Bryen nodded toward the rim of the skerry, a quiet commotion occurring as the Kraken, packed together much like fish in a barrel, found it difficult to move out of the way as a tall figure partially lost in the blanket of fog passed silently between them.

Aislinn followed Bryen's gaze. The path through the Kraken opened and closed rapidly, whoever was making their way toward them already coming up through the trees.

A quiet murmuring among the Kraken began when the new arrival stepped out into the open. Bryen realized that the words, though he couldn't make them out from where he was standing, weren't a discussion among the beasts. Rather, it was a greeting of respect.

His assumption was confirmed when the sea creatures to his front knelt in deference before stepping out of the way so that the towering Kraken could take up a position just below where the knoll began to slope upwards.

Bryen really shouldn't have been surprised. Initially, he thought that he had killed the Kraken chief on top of the mountain, that action inciting the beasts' fervor and desire to pursue them. Yet that combat had proven less challenging than he had anticipated, making Bryen think that the loser of that combat was just a subordinate.

Clearly, he had been correct, because he was absolutely certain that the true leader of the Kraken stood below him.

The creature was several heads taller than the Kraken around him. In addition to the loincloth that all the beasts wore, an armor that appeared to be carved from the hardened shell of a huge lobster graced his shoulders. In one massive claw he held a spear just like the other Bryen had come up against atop the mountain, likely carved from the bone of a whale as well, although this one was at least twenty feet in length.

He guessed that it was more ceremonial than anything else. A weapon that large was best used as a lance in battle and would be of little use in close quarters. Still, it was an impressive and frightening sight. Likely just how the Kraken chief wanted it.

"I'd really hate to see that spear in action," whispered Aislinn. "It would be like defending against a small tree."

"Agreed," said Bryen, although his eyes never left those of the beast who stood before him, taking in everything that he could about the creature.

He felt like he had been in this position before, and then he realized why. It was much like it had been when he faced off against the Ghoule Overlord.

The same look in the Kraken's eyes. The same posture. The same confidence radiating off the beast.

And something else as well. An essence that he really wasn't surprised to discover, not after spending so much time in the fog that now encircled the cay.

A tainted power that he had been battling since he had been taken from the Pit. A power with which he was all too familiar.

Although he and Aislinn were surrounded by the creatures, it felt as if they were alone with this towering beast that stood even taller than the Ghoule Overlord. Most of the Kraken below him disappeared in the mist, only the knoll and the first rank of the monsters remaining free of the murk.

The strange quiet lingered for several minutes, the wispy fog swirling around the large beast as if it answered to his commands. The only sound came from the powerful waves pounding against the rocks.

Bryen and Aislinn felt little need to break the silence, using the time provided to them to consider how they might escape what had become an almost inescapable situation.

Unfortunately, nothing came to mind. Both of them realized that there would be no chance to evade this many Kraken unscathed.

"You and your people trespass, boy." The massive Kraken gestured to the larger island behind him. "Among our kind, there is only one penalty for that transgression."

Bryen nodded, not needing to guess what the penalty was. He had a fairly good idea after studying the burial pit in the village.

"I'm sorry, who are you?" Bryen asked in as condescending a tone as he could.

He and Aislinn had little chance of getting out of this situation. But if he could make this creature angry, he might be able to push him toward making a mistake. A tactic that had proven useful in the Pit. A very slim chance of that happening here, admittedly, but in that moment he'd take anything that he could get.

"I am the King of the Kraken," bellowed the massive creature that had been studying them just as they had been examining him, the hint of anger in his voice confirming that Bryen's insolent barb had struck home. "You have come to a land where you do not belong. You have come to our land."

"You speak our language," said Bryen, somewhat surprised.

"No, you speak ours, boy," replied the massive beast. "How that is possible, I do not know."

Bryen's suspicions were gaining greater substance. He was

certain now what that other presence he had sensed upon the King Kraken's approach was. He hadn't been mistaken.

Just like the Ghoules, these Kraken had been touched by the Curse. He didn't know how. But he was sure.

Because of that, the Seventh Stone, a repository for both the Talent and the Curse, just as it had done when he engaged with the Ghoules, allowed Bryen to speak the Kraken tongue.

"What are you saying?" asked Aislinn, clearly not understanding what Bryen and this monster were talking about.

"I'll fill you in later," Bryen replied in a whisper, if indeed there was a later.

"We didn't come here by choice," Bryen said, returning his focus to the gigantic figure standing just below him. "A storm forced us here."

"That doesn't matter," answered the King Kraken. "You have encroached on our territory. Why you are here doesn't matter. The fact that you are here, desecrating our land with your presence, does matter."

"So that's the excuse you used to slaughter the people living on this island," challenged Bryen. "They were here before you, were they not?"

For several seconds, the leader of the Kraken simply stared at Bryen, clearly reevaluating him. Not only because of his ability to speak their tongue, but also because of the power that he could sense within the boy. A power that felt all too familiar yet also one that he had not come into contact with for centuries.

"They knew the cost for coming here," the King Kraken finally said. "All know the cost. These islands belong to us. Besides, it never matters who got where first. The only thing that matters is who is standing at the end."

"Why kill them? Why not just let them leave?"

"Where's the fun in that, boy?" asked the King Kraken. "Often an example must be made."

"The words of a coward. I would have thought better of the King Kraken."

Bryen's insult earned hisses from the many Kraken standing around the knoll, only their leader barking a command gaining silence once again.

The King Kraken studied Bryen a little while longer, almost as if he was trying to read his thoughts with a look.

Bryen stared back at him with an implacable glare that finally earned a nod and what he took to be a smile from the large beast, although he wasn't quite sure. It was hard to tell with the creature's teeth-filled maw.

"You have a hardness about you, boy, that was lacking in those that we slaughtered. You probably understand better than most. As I said, sometimes an example must be made. Though with you, seeing the coldness in your eyes, I assume that any example we make now would be lost on you."

"So you plan to slaughter me and my friends. Not very original on your part."

"I do, and you're right," confirmed the King Kraken. "Not very original. But still quite effective. We will kill you and the girl here. My Kraken who assault your ship even as we speak will kill the rest of your friends. When we are done with you, there will be nothing left for anyone to remember you by. Just another pile of bones."

"You make a dangerous assumption."

"What would that be, boy?"

"That you can kill me. That you can kill my friends."

The King Kraken laughed at that. Strangely, he was enjoying this conversation.

This boy had a fire that was rare. Even so, he would die just like all the other humans would. It had to be that way.

The Kraken were on the rise. Their kingdom was expanding.

The only way to ensure that they conquered the seas was to

remove all those who might get in their way.

"I appreciate your confidence, boy, misplaced though it is."

"Without confidence, you have nothing."

"The words of a warrior," the King Kraken nodded in appreciation. "Well said, but still not enough. Not enough for you to survive when I unleash my Kraken upon you."

"Come at us if you want," said Bryen, his voice cold, matching his eyes now. "You do so at your own peril."

"Brave words from a condemned man."

"Maybe," Bryen replied. "Maybe not."

"Think of yourself as lucky, boy," offered the King Kraken. "When you die here, I promise that it will be quick. Not so when I take my people to the mainland. When the Kraken come, examples will need to be made again. You do not want to be there when that happens. Better for you to die now."

Bryen nodded. "This is just the start for you, then? These Jagged Islands first, then what? Caledonia? The Territories?"

"Quite so, boy. All those lands and more, because the seas belong to us. We can go wherever we want. We can take whatever we want. You cannot stop us."

"You speak from pride, not truth."

"Every word I say is the truth," roared the King Kraken. "Pride has nothing to do with it."

Bryen smiled at the monster's outburst, pleased that he could irritate him so easily.

"Say what you want, that doesn't mean what you say is the truth. Your Kraken believe you, they take anything you say as the truth, because they have no choice. They must. The rest of us? No. Your words aren't the truth. They are only a dream. And few dreams ever come to fruition."

"A fool for being here, though not quite a fool after all," murmured the King Kraken. This boy certainly was full of surprises.

"Why seek to conquer the seas?" asked Bryen, curious,

though also trying to buy some additional time. "Be ready," he whispered to Aislinn out of the side of his mouth.

She looked at him with an expression of confusion, not understanding what he was going to do next. An expression little different from the one she had worn during Bryen's entire conversation with this monster.

Of all the choices he could make based on their current situation, and there were very few, she assumed that he was going to attack the monster.

Kill the chief, and maybe they would gain the time they needed to escape.

More hope than reality, but when you had nothing but hope, you had to cling to it fiercely. So she bent her knees, putting one foot in front of the other, standing on her toes, getting ready for the combat that she expected was only seconds away from beginning.

"Why not?" replied the King Kraken. "My Kraken grow. Our world shrinks as a result. We need to expand our world so that we can expand our reach. Expand our power. We live below the sea much of the time, but not all of the time. We will take what we need, whether below the sea or above. We will take what belongs to us." The King Kraken pounded his chest then to make his point. "And I say that all the world belongs to us."

"You know, I heard much the same from another beast much like you."

"And what happened to this other beast?" asked the King Kraken, curious.

"I killed him."

Before the King Kraken could say anything else, Bryen pounded the glowing Spear of the Magii down onto the top of the hill. A blast of energy erupted from the blades, the blinding white light requiring the King Kraken to turn away and raise a claw to shield his eyes as he did so, his vision momentarily taken from him.

The brilliance was so strong that for just a second, it revealed the thousands of Kraken waiting in the fog before the grey returned once again, those many beasts forced to turn away as well.

Then just as soon as Bryen stood straight again, he was gone, plucked off the ground by two strong paws, a screech of victory blasting out across the channel.

Aislinn smiled, realizing what Bryen had been doing. Keeping the monster talking so that Banshee could get there in time.

With a gentle jolt Aislinn was pulled up into the air as well, strong paws gripping her by the shoulders though not piercing her flesh. Astuta. The Griffon who had befriended her.

The two Griffons pumped their wings, rising into the air, ignoring the shrieks of anger that came from the beasts below.

The Kraken had lost their prey once again. Clearly, they were none too pleased about that, the loudest roar coming from the King Kraken himself.

Pushing the commotion below her out of her mind, Aislinn watched as Bryen climbed up Banshee's paw to her shoulder before swinging a leg over so that he could sit on her back. Aislinn did the same, dropping down onto Astuta's back.

"Were you going to tell me that the Griffons had returned?" asked Aislinn.

"I would have if I could have," Bryen replied, Astuta now flying right next to Banshee. "I needed to keep the King Kraken talking. The longer he talked, the better our chances that our friends would arrive before he sent his beasts up the knoll."

"King Kraken?"

"That's what that monster called himself."

"What else did he say?"

"None of it was good, though I'll tell you later," Bryen replied. "After we get to the *Freedom*. Hopefully it's not too late."

20

BATTLE FOR THE FREEDOM

"Can we sail?" asked Declan. The Sergeant of the Blood Company stood at the helm. He issued a constant stream of orders, shifting gladiators from one position to the next, the situation on the deck fluid and tenuous as the Kraken sought to seize the ship.

The fight was made all the more difficult because of the fog that blanketed the *Freedom*. Declan could see nothing more than vague shapes at a distance of fifty feet. Beyond that, he needed to trust in the skills and intelligence of his gladiators to ensure that the Kraken were kept at the rails.

Those factors didn't really bother him. He and the Blood Company had faced circumstances like these before, such as when they defended against the Ghoules on the spiral ramp that circled the stone spire upon which the Sanctuary was located.

What worried him were the numbers. The Kraken never stopped coming, more of the creatures emerging out of the water by the second.

A ravenous unending swarm.

The Blood Company demonstrated a skill and courage that

couldn't be matched. Nevertheless, there were only so many gladiators to stand against these seemingly innumerable Kraken.

Majdi and the others in the shield wall continued to hold the rails on both sides of the ship. The gladiators fought with a precise fury that served them well in keeping the beasts from the main deck.

The Kraken coming up over the bow and stern were the primary problem at the moment. The beasts had gained footholds on those key sections of the ship, the gladiators there now battling desperately to ensure that the beasts couldn't expand their footing and get down into the hatches.

If that happened, the battle was lost. The Kraken could work their way through the ship from below and come at the defenders from multiple directions at once.

"Yes, we can," replied Captain Gregson, who stood next to his wife, both he and Emelina demonstrating that they were both quite good archers. The two fired shaft after shaft into the melee, rarely missing their targets, sending a dozen or more beasts back into the drink each on their own. "The most necessary repairs have been made. All the others we can manage out at sea."

"That's good to hear," said Declan. "So we have a chance. Davin, Lycia, take your squads to the stern! Help Jenus! We can't allow the Kraken to break through there!"

Neither Davin nor Lycia bothered to reply, instead stalking off with their gladiators, more than ready to aid Jenus in his fight. The twins and their squads were functioning as a roving reserve, jumping into the battle wherever and whenever they were needed. The blood streaking their weapons testified to the success that they had enjoyed so far.

Yet the assignment that Declan had just given them was the most difficult by far. The beasts swarmed over the Griffons' decks, and though they had not yet been able to force their way beyond the thin shield wall holding them back, Jenus keeping the Kraken in check even with just a ragged line of scuta and only a few gladiators with spears to prevent the beasts from flooding over his shield bearers, it wouldn't be long before the beasts achieved a breach.

Declan was concerned that the break was going to happen sooner rather than later. From the helm, even with the fog, he could see the beasts climbing over one another to gain the deck.

If the Blood Company didn't do something swiftly to change the dynamics of this clash, then the math would do it for them. The Kraken's greater numbers would prove to be too much.

"And you expect us to sail out of this?" asked Captain Gregson, unable to keep his disbelief from his voice.

He sent another steel-tipped arrow streaking through the mist, the quarrel slamming into a Kraken right between the eyes, the beast foolishly standing on the railing and serving as an excellent target. Instead of urging his brethren on as he had been doing, the beast fell back into the bay, becoming nothing more than food for the great whites.

"I do, indeed," Declan replied with complete confidence. "It's just a matter of when."

Captain Gregson shook his head, not quite believing the Sergeant of the Blood Company. Even so, a small smile cracked his grim visage as he nocked another arrow. "You're either a fool or you know something that I don't."

"Definitely not a fool," said Rafia, who stood right next to Declan.

Bolts of energy shot from her hands in every direction as she slowly spun in a circle, seeking to help those gladiators in the direst of circumstances, her power slamming into the Kraken with a precision that Declan admired and relished.

When there was need, she crafted a shield of energy right

where a breach was about to occur in the shield wall. Her quick action time after time gave the gladiators the chance they needed to reform their line before the Kraken could break through.

And when she wasn't doing that, she was using the Talent to sweep the Kraken from the rails, spheres of light punching the beasts back into the water. Unfortunately those successes were much too brief, those creatures from the deep replaced seconds later by more of their brethren. A battle that resembled the waves rolling through Solace Sound, she mused.

There was no elegance to this clash, though admittedly there rarely was in a battle. Rather, the fight reminded Rafia of a combat she had watched in a tavern centuries before between two bare-knuckle brawlers.

The two huge men had held their ground, refusing to budge an inch. Hitting one another time after time. Not stopping until one of them couldn't hit the other. Only then did the combat come to an end.

She believed a similar conclusion would occur in this current engagement.

"Rafia, Renata could use your assistance."

The Magus nodded in response to Declan's comment, turning her focus toward the bow.

Renata was leading the push to reclaim that section of the ship. She and her squad were doing well, having eliminated a good number of the beasts and constricted the space under their control. The gladiator lashed out with her morning stars in what appeared to be a chaotic approach but was actually a rhythm that only she could hear.

The Kraken clearly didn't. Therefore, they had no choice but to retreat in the face of her onslaught.

To assist Renata in her efforts, Rafia threw several strategically placed javelins that burned through the fog. The spears impaled one beast after another, slamming the creatures into the side of the ship or the foremast.

The spears ensured a painful death for the skewered Kraken. They served another purpose as well, continuing to burn brightly, providing the gladiators with a light to help them see more clearly in the billowing fog.

For several more minutes, the fight raged around the periphery of the ship, little changing but for Renata and the gladiators with her retaking the bow thanks to Rafia's assistance.

Majdi and the shield bearers held the railings.

Declan redistributed the gladiators as he deemed necessary to keep the Kraken in check.

Davin and Lycia bolstered Jenus and his fighters, strengthening the ragged shield wall that stretched across the rear deck.

Yet despite their best efforts, it wasn't to be. Their defense was weakening.

A bulge appeared on the stern, the number of Kraken climbing up onto the deck and pushing against the shield wall becoming more and more untenable with each passing second.

The line hadn't broken. Not yet. But it was bending back toward the helm.

The breach was inevitable, even with Davin and Lycia doing all that they could to assist Jenus, Asaia, and the other gladiators with them.

"Declan, the Kraken are about to break through!" shouted Jenus, trying to give his comrades some warning.

Hearing Jenus' call, Rafia turned quickly in that direction. She prepared to unleash a torrent of power upon the Kraken seeking to drive through the gap that was slowly developing right in the center of the shield wall.

Instead, she hesitated for just a breath. Then she smiled, her expression reminding Captain Gregson of a cat about to pounce on an unsuspecting mouse.

"I suggest you and your sailors get the ship ready to sail," she said.

"Now?" he exclaimed, not quite believing what he was hearing. "We're about to be overrun!"

"What we see now isn't what will be," Rafia replied cryptically.

"What are you talking about, Magus?"

"Rather than the victory they expect, Captain, the Kraken are about to meet their match. Get the ship ready to sail. Trust me."

Just a heartbeat later a powerful blast of light much like the beacon of a lighthouse pierced the gloom. Yet this stream of brilliance did more than just illuminate the haze. It burned away the fog, revealing the *Freedom* and the fight playing out across its deck.

That stream of light then began to expand steadily, reaching out to the railings of the ship and then beyond, blazing through the gloom. The thick wisps of grey pulled back, seeking to escape. Unable to move fast enough, the energy from above burned through the mist, slowly, inevitably clearing a larger space around the ship.

Many of the Kraken, shocked by what they were witnessing, stopped fighting. The gladiators didn't.

They knew where the light came from, and they were quick to make use of their opponents' mistake. Battling with a controlled viciousness, they pushed even more of the beasts back toward the rails, Jenus, Davin, and Lycia working to close the gap in the center of their line as the Kraken attack at the stern faltered.

"What the ..." wondered Captain Gregson, looking up at the clear sky that had been hidden from him since the fog first swept over the bay. "Lord Keldragan certainly does know how to make an entrance."

"That he does, Captain," agreed Rafia. "Now do whatever is

necessary to ensure that we can sail for deeper water. We need to be away from here as fast as we can."

"Right away," he said before he slid down the ladder, pulling sailors from the slackening fight and ordering them to the rigging.

Right through the gap in the fog, Bryen soared down on Banshee's back, the Griffon diving toward the ship, extending her wings to slow her descent at the last possible second. Right behind her came Aislinn on Astuta and then the three other Griffons who had flown away from the *Freedom* in search of a meal.

The Griffons wasted little time in joining the fight. Fuerza, Potencia, and Arabella streaked across the deck, deftly avoiding the masts and rigging, reaching for the Kraken with their sharp talons.

Ripping through Kraken flesh with an unstoppable power, they swept the deck clean, knocking the beasts back into the water and helping to lessen the strain on the gladiators.

Astuta hovered near the mainmast, allowing Aislinn to wreak havoc from above as she sent streams of energy blasting into the Kraken.

Many of the creatures from the deep had no choice other than to dive off the side or risk an immediate and painful death. They were more fearful of the Magus on the Griffon than the churning water below that was caused by the feeding frenzy of the twenty or more great whites gorging on their brethren already killed in the fight.

Rafia threw her efforts behind Aislinn's, though she focused her attention on the stern. She could do little about the beasts who were engaged directly with Jenus and the other gladiators, not wanting to strike the Blood Company with an errant blast of power.

She could, however, reduce the number of beasts charging toward the shield wall, and she did that with a cool resolve, sending blazing javelins shooting across the deck to clear the stern rail of attackers. From there, she worked her way back across the Griffons' decks, targeting any Kraken foolish enough to remain on board.

Leaving the battle on the *Freedom* to Aislinn and Rafia, Bryen guided Banshee around the ship in ever-expanding circles. Using the Spear of the Magii, the twin blades blazing brilliantly, steady streams of power shot from the tips, incinerating the fog that just moments before had smothered the vessel.

Bryen understood that the Kraken attacking the ship and the thousands on the beach seeking to join their ilk were too many to fight, even with the power of the Seventh Stone at his command. Instead, he chose to test a theory that he had been working through during his and Aislinn's escape from the mountain.

The Kraken came with the fog.

They only came with the fog.

If he could remove the fog, did that mean he could then remove the Kraken from the fight without the need for blade or Talent?

He believed the answer was yes, but there was only one way to find out.

As he flew more and more concentric circles around the ship, expanding his reach with every loop, he was pleased to see that he was right. As he destroyed the fog with the Talent and the almost limitless power of the Seventh Stone, the Kraken reluctantly pulled back, unwilling to stay beyond the edge of the murk for very long.

Those beasts caught out on the deck sought to escape the light. They scrambled toward the rails, clearly not wanting to continue the fight in the bright of the day.

However, their efforts to return to the gloom proved to be a challenge. They scrambled across one another to get over the rails and gain the relative safety of the water, yet the gladiators refused to allow the Kraken to escape unscathed.

It was at that exact moment, when the beasts began to jostle one another, desperate to evade the blazing light, that Davin and Lycia led the counterattack. They and their gladiators employed the flying wedge that had worked so effectively against the Ghoules, eliminating the Kraken as if they were no more than stalks of wheat as they cleared the main deck, the invaders more concerned with making good their escape and less so with defending themselves.

The gladiators' efforts were aided by Potencia, Fuerza, and Arabella. The Griffons, having cleared the rails, landed deftly on the deck and launched themselves at the Kraken, sharp beaks puncturing flesh with just as much finality as their potent claws.

Pleased that he had proven his hypothesis, Bryen called on even more of the Talent, harnessing the Seventh Stone to expand the blaze of brilliance that tore through the murk.

The power was so great and so intense that in less than a minute the light reached as far as the shore and revealed the thousands of angry Kraken waiting on the beach who could not comprehend how swiftly the clash had turned against them.

Bryen decided to push a bit farther, seeking additional confirmation of what he believed, by extending the range of his efforts. As soon as the fog at the waterline burned away, those beasts standing there stepped back a few feet, forcing the Kraken behind them to move back as well.

Bryen grinned. He was quite pleased that his theory was indeed correct.

His confidence growing, Bryen applied even more of the power contained within the Seventh Stone to his task, the ring of light reaching farther up the beach.

Once again the Kraken shifted back a few feet, avoiding the touch of the sun. And then a few feet more as Bryen sped up his efforts, the fog vanishing at a much more rapid pace thanks to the scorching light, revealing even more of the sandy beach.

Feeling comfortable and confident with the power he controlled, Bryen pushed the brightness all the way up to the trees, forcing the Kraken back in among the woods.

The battle was done. Although not yet won.

Bryen's swift attack turned what had been an orderly retreat by the beasts into a mad dash for cover. Yet still the Kraken remained. Waiting. Expectant.

Satisfied that they now had the time they needed to get out of Solace Sound, Bryen asked Banshee to return to the ship.

The Griffon turned on her wing and glided back over to the vessel. Landing on her deck with a gentle touch, she revealed her distaste for the dead Kraken littering her space with a low rumble. Then with her big paws she swatted the bodies over the side before Bryen even had a chance to hop off her back.

"I'm sorry, my friend," Bryen said. "We'll clean this up as soon as we get the chance."

Banshee's rumble turned into a soft purr, her anger mollified by Bryen's promise.

"Good timing," said Declan, approaching Bryen and Banshee as he stepped around the Kraken dead, stopping every few feet just to make sure that a beast had breathed his last by punching the tip of his blade through a throat before continuing on his way.

With the ship clear of the Kraken, the wounded gladiators were already being seen to, Aislinn and Rafia taking on that task.

The Kraken faced a different fate, Majdi and those not needing immediate medical attention unceremoniously throwing the bodies over the sides and into the bay.

"We're lucky we're here at all," Bryen replied as he jumped down to the main deck.

He clapped Declan on the back, glad to see that his friend

and mentor made it through the clash unhurt. Bryen had no doubt that all the blood on Declan's blade and his leather armor belonged to the Kraken.

"You can tell me about it later," said Declan, "and we can talk about why you felt the need to put yourself at greater risk atop the mountain as well."

Bryen sighed in resignation. He should have expected as much, and he couldn't say that he was looking forward to that discussion. Because with Declan it would be less of a dialogue and more of a berating. "Later then. Are we ready to sail?"

"We are," Declan confirmed.

"Good." Bryen strode down the deck, Declan right at his side, both nodding in respect to the gladiators who had fought so bravely and well to prevent the Kraken from taking the ship. "We need to go."

"How bad was it on the mountain?"

Bryen shrugged. "I expect just as bad as it was here."

Declan smiled at that. Bryen was always one to understate the difficulty of a challenge. He would need to talk with Aislinn to get a better sense of what really went on. Judging by Bryen's lack of desire to provide more detail, he assumed that it had been a truly harrowing experience.

"How long will the light last?"

Bryen still grasped the Spear of the Magii, the blades glowing brightly, as he climbed up to the helm. The energy that Bryen used to burn away the murk was still in play, keeping the fog at bay. At least for now.

"So long as I maintain control over the Talent, we will remain in the eye of the storm," he said, referencing the hole that he had created in the fog. "Still, we need to leave quickly or we'll be in for another fight. The eye will only shrink with time. I can only hold back the murk for so long."

"What do you mean?"

"The fog isn't natural. It serves as a shield for the Kraken.

With the fog, the Kraken can go wherever they want. Without the fog, walking in the light causes them pain. It burns their flesh." Bryen looked up as he passed the mizzenmast, glad to see the sailors working their way across the lanyards, the repaired sails already in place. "I can feel him even now pushing against the barrier that I've created. He wants to send his legions at us again. He won't be able to do that until he destroys the eye."

To make his point, Bryen nodded toward the shore. The trees that rose a few hundred yards from the water and at the very back of the beach, which had been visible just a few minutes before, were once again hidden by the murk.

At that very moment, faint wisps of grey reached out into the light, seeking to reclaim what Bryen had taken.

He had suspected as much.

His new enemy was anxious to recover the space that Bryen had stolen from him, sending out threads of gloom to test his strength. The light Bryen had created with the Talent incinerated much of the wispy gray, but not all of it.

The light emanating from the Spear of the Magii didn't stop the fog from pushing against the power Bryen was employing. It only slowed the advancing haze.

The trees were once more under the control of the Kraken King. The white sand of the beach would be next.

"Feel who?" asked Declan, not yet understanding.

"The King Kraken."

"Who?" Declan's confusion was plain, although it didn't take him long to start putting the pieces of the puzzle together, Bryen helping him.

"Think Ghoule Overlord, the only difference being this monster lives beneath the waves."

"I don't want to think about that. I've had enough of the Ghoule Overlord and all the other monsters of his sort."

"The King Kraken?" asked Emelina, the helmswoman

standing at the wheel, anxious to be gone from Solace Sound. "The story is true?"

"I don't know the story," said Bryen, "but the King Kraken is real. We had a nice talk before Banshee and Astuta came by to rescue Aislinn and me."

"The King Kraken is real?" asked Captain Gregson, climbing the ladder and rejoining his wife on the helm, having spent the last few minutes working with his crew to ensure that all was as it should be so that the *Freedom* could get underway. His face turned white at the thought of a nightmare coming to life.

"All too real," Bryen replied, "and he's coming this way. Very quickly."

"What did you do, Bryen?" asked Declan with a raised eyebrow.

"Nothing that you wouldn't have done in my situation," he replied.

"That would explain the need for haste."

"It would," Bryen agreed. "If you don't want to meet him, I suggest we get underway. Now. Because he was not in a good mood when Aislinn and I left him."

Captain Gregson didn't say a word for several heartbeats, only nodding his head. Then the fear that had appeared in the back of his eyes evaporated. Nightmare or no, this was his ship. He refused to gift it to the Kraken King.

"Fergus!" he yelled all the way down to the bow. "Raise the anchor!"

Fergus and his crew got to work immediately, turning the winch to haul up the iron. They completed the first few rotations without a hitch. It was the fourth time around that proved to be the problem, the winch locking in place, the handful of very large sailors unable to budge the mechanism any further.

"Fergus, what's going on?" demanded Captain Gregson, his

voice strong, even as he worked hard to control the fear that threatened to give him the shakes.

He could see that the fog along the edge of the eye was no longer so clearcut. The gloom twisted and turned as if it was preparing to move back into the space from which it had been banished, a large segment of the beach covered in grey once more.

"We're stuck on something, Captain! We'll try to work it loose."

Fergus and his crew released some of the tension on the rope, preparing to turn the winch again.

"Captain Gregson," said Bryen, motioning toward the island. "We need to go. Now."

Captain Gregson looked toward the shore again, astounded by how rapidly the fog had consumed the beach. It was almost to the water's edge. Hidden within the fog would be the Kraken as well as the nightmare that sailors liked to talk about with their friends when they were swimming in ale.

He had seen enough of the Kraken and he had no desire to see their King with his own eyes. Lord Keldragan was right. They needed to leave while they still could.

"Fergus, cut the line!"

"But Captain, we almost …"

"Cut the line!" repeated Captain Gregson. "We have another anchor in the hold. Cut the line now!"

Fergus obeyed in an instant, picking up the large axe kept there for just that purpose and severing the thick rope in a single swing.

The ship now free of its mooring, the sailors scrambled across the rigging, working the sails, searching for the wind.

"Emelina, take us out."

"Aye, aye, Captain," the helmswoman replied, spinning the wheel several times hard to port, the breeze skimming across the bay and filling the sails, pushing the ship away from the island.

As the *Freedom* began to glide through the waters of Solace Sound, the break in the gloom that Bryen created stayed with them, the fog burning away as soon as it came into contact with the Talent.

The Spear of the Magii blazing so brightly that no one could look at it directly, Bryen continued to harness the power of the Seventh Stone to prevent the fog from retaking the space he had claimed as his own. The space that the King Kraken required if he was to achieve his objective of killing Bryen and everyone with him.

Yet though he was still exercising a good amount of control over the haven he had created, it was becoming more of a challenge for him. Bryen needed to call on even more power to keep the sphere around the ship free of the murk, the gloom pressing with greater vigor against the edges of the boundary.

As Bryen engaged in an unseen fight against the Kraken King, the Talent battling the murk, he could feel it now. Increasing in intensity as it became a larger player in the combat.

The Curse.

Pushing back against him now.

Surging through the fog.

Feeding the gloom.

Forcing the murk to reclaim the area that Bryen had stolen from it.

With the Curse came the Kraken King.

Bryen could sense the monster just as he had been able to locate the Ghoule Overlord.

Just as in the Lost Land with the Ghoule Overlord, the Kraken King was the source of the Curse in this part of the world.

Bryen was sure of it.

The Kraken King was the host for that tainted power. The monster might believe that he controlled the corrupted energy, but that was a lie.

Once the Curse touched you, who you were no longer mattered. You became whatever the Curse wanted you to be, needed you to be. You served the Curse even as you believed falsely that the Curse was serving you.

A different part of the world, yet he had stumbled upon the same challenge as he faced in Caledonia. A challenge that right then he knew that he could not overcome.

Blast it all!

"Declan, please find Aislinn and Rafia. I need them here now."

Declan nodded, then slid down the steps, striding down the deck and calling for the two Magii in the stentorian voice that reminded all the gladiators of their time in the Colosseum.

"Emelina, can we go any faster?"

The helmswoman shook her head in frustration. "I'm sorry, Lord Keldragan. We're at the mercy of the wind. What we're catching now is barely enough to keep us from getting pushed back against the beach. If you can believe it, it's almost as if some unseen force is being used against us. We should already be a quarter mile from shore."

Bryen nodded thoughtfully. Again, something else that he had come up against before. "I can believe it."

That last comment caught the attention of Emelina and Captain Gregson, husband and wife looking at one another, first with an expression of surprise, and then one of dread.

Was that even possible?

The fact that the *Freedom* was now moving closer to the shore despite the slight breeze teasing their sails and attempting to push them away from the island suggested that it was.

Wanting to confirm his belief, Bryen searched around them with the Talent. Not above the water this time. Rather below.

It was as he expected.

The Kraken were coming for them. Thousands of the creatures still waited at the edge of the fog, hidden from view. Thousands more swam beneath the surface from the north, protected from the light, at a speed that matched that of a dolphin. And with them came the Kraken King, now less than a half mile away.

Bryen was certain that as soon as that monster arrived, he would send his Kraken for them again.

The Kraken King wouldn't care about the light that Bryen had crafted that burned the flesh of his creatures.

He wouldn't care how hard Bryen fought with the Talent against the Curse contained within the fog.

He would still send his Kraken forward, caring little for how many fell. Caring only that he gained the victory that he sought.

The monster had demonstrated his ruthlessness during his and Aislinn's escape. And why wouldn't he? The Kraken King always had more creatures at his disposal, no matter how many he might lose.

He also had the power to battle the Talent. Even the Seventh Stone.

Inevitably, the fog would consume them once again.

And, eventually, Bryen would face the Kraken King a second time.

That thought didn't frighten him. It likely would be no different than coming up against the Ghoule Overlord.

Still, he really would prefer to avoid that encounter while the lives of all aboard the *Freedom* hung in the balance.

"Don't let it worry you, Emelina," said Bryen, sensing in her voice her anger at herself for some imagined failing. "We have no control over the wind, but we can still make our escape. Be ready."

Just then Aislinn and Rafia climbed up onto the helm.

"You need me?" asked Aislinn.

"I do. Badly."

"Be careful how you talk, Protector," said Rafia with a wink. "You're not alone with Aislinn here. We wouldn't want to give anyone the wrong impression."

For just a moment Bryen appeared confused, then he chuckled. He hadn't given much thought to what he had said, his focus on the Kraken King who was now only a few thousand yards beyond the edge of the eye.

"The King Kraken is coming for us," said Bryen, "and we need more speed."

"We just need speed," mumbled Emelina, getting more nervous as the *Freedom* failed to move at the touch of the wind, continuing to drift backward toward the beach that was now only a few hundred yards to their rear and barely visible with the fog pushing at the boundaries of the space Bryen had created with the Seventh Stone.

"The King Kraken?" asked Rafia.

"I'll fill you in later," said Aislinn. "The wind?"

Bryen nodded. "The wind."

"We'll take care of it," Aislinn said. "You ready?"

"As ever," Rafia replied.

The two Magii reached for the Talent, both preparing to do as they did during their flight from the Bakunawa.

Any hope that the King Kraken might have had for catching up to the Magus who had escaped him from atop the knoll, who had spoken the Kraken language and demonstrated little fear in his presence, was shattered in an instant.

Rafia and Aislinn sent first a gentle gust of energy into the sails. The *Freedom* jumped forward a few thousand yards like a bucking bronco, Emelina managing the wheel, though it was something of a struggle until she got used to the force being put into play.

"Are you ready, Emelina?" asked Aislinn.

"Don't worry about me," she replied with a confident grin. "I can handle whatever you want to give me."

"Not to be rude, ladies," interrupted Bryen. "But we need to be gone. Now."

The eye he had created within the fog remained, though he was finding it more difficult keeping it in place as the Kraken King drew closer, the hint of the Curse growing stronger and more pervasive.

More strands of the gloom pushed into the space Bryen had cleared, seeking to compress the barrier he had crafted and then eliminate it altogether.

Bryen fought back viciously with the Talent, seeking to maintain the stalemate. Yet he found the struggle becoming more of a weight upon his shoulders that he knew eventually would crush him against the deck if it continued for much longer.

Once the monster arrived, Bryen would need to turn his full attention toward the Kraken King. That would force him to let go of the eye, placing the ship and its passengers right back in the same deadly situation they had escaped just moments before.

"As you wish," said Rafia.

Nodding to Aislinn, they increased the energy they were applying to the sails, providing a steady and constant stream that they strengthened every few seconds once they were certain that Emelina could steer the massive ship around the islands and shoals without fear of a wreck.

"Better?" asked Aislinn.

"Much," Bryen replied. "Thank you."

As the two Magii took the place of the wind, Emelina deftly guiding them to the north through the various channels back toward the Burnt Ocean, Bryen sensed the Kraken King falling farther and farther behind them. At this pace they would be free of the threat presented by that monster in just a few minutes more.

"While we sail for the Burnt Ocean, Protector," said Rafia, "tell us of this conversation you had with the Kraken King."

21

SACRIFICE

"Just a few more steps, father, and then we'll be clear of the valley."

"You said that ten minutes ago, and then ten minutes before that," Dougal huffed, struggling to get any air into his lungs. "You're just trying to distract me like I did to you when you were a child and you got tired during one of our hikes."

"I'm just trying to keep you focused," Jakob replied, smiling. His father was exactly right. The roles had been reversed between them. "How many steps it takes to get to the top doesn't matter. All that matters is that we get there."

Dougal couldn't help but grin at his son's response. Like father like son. It seemed that some of his personality had rubbed off on Jakob. Dougal had always wondered about that. About what kind of influence he would have on him.

Jakob walked right next to his father. They had gotten through the roughest spots on the trail that led out of the vale where it wasn't a path so much as a slide of larger boulders that required climbing.

Now it was just a few hundred yards farther up the relatively flat stretch. Jakob kept an arm around his father's waist as he helped him climb the incline, ready in case Dougal slipped again.

His father's walk had become more of a ragged stumble. Still, it was getting them where they needed to go.

It wasn't too much longer before they reached the top, the large plateau that ran toward the north and split the towering peaks spreading out before them.

They had gone no more than a hundred yards up the slope before his father had begun to flag. It had been a hard climb for him. So much so that Jakob spent just as much time carrying his father up the trail as he did assisting him as Dougal tried and failed to manage on his own.

Recognizing that Dougal needed a chance to catch his breath, he helped his father sit down on a large rock that marked the beginning of the path back down into the vale.

They had left their cave before the sun rose in the sky, neither of them sleeping well, both of them wanting to put as much distance between themselves and the slavers as they could.

When he examined his father that morning, the poor condition that he was in, Jakob thought at first that perhaps they should stay in their hiding place. He discarded the idea reluctantly though quickly.

Remaining in the valley knowing that the slavers would come back this way was too much of a risk to take. Once the slavers came down into the valley, he doubted that he and his father would ever escape the vale. So better at least to take a chance and try to craft a reality that didn't necessarily guarantee their deaths.

Jakob made that decision in large part because his hopes of what would happen after his success during the night before weren't following along the path that he wanted. Rather than being upset, he accepted that disappointing truth and moved on to what he needed to do next. As his father liked to say, better to focus on what needed to be done, not on what you can't control.

Besides, such was the way of it if you dared to place so much in the hands of a fickle fate. He hoped that the slavers would stop their pursuit once the Stalker found them on the plateau. That they would realize that it was better for them to return to the mines.

No such luck, unfortunately.

The Stalker that Jakob had directed toward the slavers killed one of the men before the remainder succeeded in driving the monster away. Because of the attack, the slavers had left their camp on the plain and moved a league to the west and closer to a ridge. Spending the night there, the cliff at their backs, they battled the Stalker as it launched several attacks out of the darkness, attempting to catch them off guard.

Jakob had watched it all with the Talent. He had been rooting for the Stalker.

Unfortunately, the leader of the slavers, the one the tracker had named Remy, was too savvy for the beast. Unsuccessful, in the early morning the Stalker left the slavers where they were, moving deeper into the Highlands, toward the west, likely looking for easier prey.

Jakob searched around them again with the Talent to see what had changed during their climb. He grumbled to himself. Just as he feared.

"The slavers coming back this way?" asked Dougal, his voice tight from the pain in his ribs that shot up into his chest with every breath he took.

"Yes, unfortunately so."

Dougal nodded. "It was a good try. Devious. Sometimes, though, the best plans don't work out the way you want."

"Don't I know it," grumped Jakob.

"Come on," said Dougal, trying to push himself up from the rock though not getting very far, needing Jakob to help him.

"We should keep moving. For as long as we can. No reason to make it easy for them."

Jakob heard the finality in his father's words, which worried him. Still, he couldn't disagree with him. He reached down and lifted his father gently to his feet and once again began the shuffle and walk that had gotten them out of the valley.

A valiant effort on the part of his father, but a doomed one. After just the first hundred feet, Jakob knew that they weren't moving fast enough to escape the slavers.

They would never be fast enough. Not with his father's steadily worsening condition.

Dougal likely sensed it as well when he tried to pick up his pace. All that did was lead to a stumble that took them both down, delaying them several more crucial minutes.

When Jakob got his father back to his feet and they were on their way again, he caught the look in the back of his father's eyes.

Jakob understood that his father's resulting curses, mumbled under his breath, weren't directed toward him. Rather, they were directed toward himself. He knew from that one glance what was playing through Dougal's mind. An acknowledgment that their race had been run.

They were still leagues away from where the Highlands met the Northern Steppes. There was no way that they were going to make it to Shadow's Reach.

They were never even going to make it out of the Highlands. They probably wouldn't make it more than a mile before the slavers finally caught up to them.

One more time, Jakob thought about going back down into the valley. Maybe they could try for the cave that had served them so well the night before.

He realized as soon as that idea popped into his head that it would be foolish to even try. Based on where the slavers were now, at their current pace, those bastards probably would come upon them while they were climbing down the trail, catching them on the slope and sealing their fate.

"Do you need to rest, father?"

"Not yet," Dougal gasped, sweat pouring from his brow, his color worsening. "We need to keep going." Dougal coughed harshly, the force of it bending him at the waist, though somehow he was able to keep his feet moving beneath him. Jakob didn't miss the specks of blood that shot from his father's mouth. "A little farther."

This wasn't working. Jakob knew it, he just hadn't wanted to admit it to himself. His father had given all that had been asked of him. More, in fact, than should have been asked of him.

Dougal had very little left to give. Trying to get his father to go faster would only make them go slower.

That realization breaking his heart, Jakob did all that he could to help his father through the long grass. Using the Talent, he had found a more defensible spot just a quarter mile to the east, closer to the coast and well away from the trail. At this pace, they should gain a few minutes before the slavers made their appearance, the men likely having no trouble following them despite the loss of their tracker.

Thankfully, they didn't have any more spills along the way. Jakob helped his father, who now wheezed shallowly rather than breathed, sit on a boulder that had rolled to a stop in front of the knoll that Jakob had selected.

The small hill rose on the edge of a cliff that extended out over the plain. Mountains shot up out of the earth to the north and south while to the east there was a drop of a thousand feet or more to another plateau, the glimmering Sea of Mist visible just a few leagues away.

Jakob offered Dougal his canteen, his father accepting it gratefully. He struggled to hold onto it, his hands shaky. Jakob grasped the canteen and helped to raise it to his mouth so that he could take a sip.

That's all that Dougal could manage, struggling through several short breaths after choking on the water. He tried to fill his lungs with the air he so desperately wanted and needed but found it incredibly difficult to do because of the blinding pain that radiated from his sternum.

"I meant to ask, and I never had the chance," said Dougal, once he regained some semblance of control over his body. "I forgot about it when we needed to make for the harbor so quickly in Roo's Nest."

"Ask what?" Jakob replied, not really paying attention.

Jakob shook his head in annoyance. He was right. The slavers found their trail through the long grass without any difficulty. Now, their pursuers were just deciding what to do. He was certain of what was going to happen next, his luck having been poor ever since they left the cave.

"What did Aloysius give you? I assumed it was a necklace."

"How did you know?"

"You touch what's hanging around your neck when you're thinking."

Jakob smiled. Just like his father. He never missed much. Even when he was in such bad shape.

Jakob pulled out the gem that blazed a bright red in the early morning light, the sun now peeking above the eastern horizon.

"Is that what I think it is?" gasped Dougal, though whether out of shock or his continuing difficulty breathing, Jakob wasn't certain.

"What do you think it is?"

"The Blood Ruby."

Jakob nodded, impressed by his father's knowledge. Then again, Dougal had always been a fount of information, almost all of it useful, some of it obscure, some of it just annoying.

"Aloysius said it was, yes."

"Why did he give it to you?" Dougal's eyes had taken on a

pained, faraway look, as if he was remembering something that he didn't want to remember.

"He said that I would need it." Jakob chuckled as soon as he said it. "I still don't know what he meant by that. He didn't have time to tell me. He hustled me out of his cottage as quickly as he could as soon as he placed the gem in my hand, telling me that I needed to go. That I would find the answers that I was seeking on my own. At the time, I didn't know that I was seeking any answers at all."

"Why was he like that?" wondered Dougal. "I really should have asked you more about what happened that night, but you didn't seem to want to talk about it."

"I didn't," Jakob confirmed.

"Of course, I was also distracted, wanting to make sure that we got the ship that we needed. And then once we were on board, my thoughts turned to what to do once we reached the Territories."

"He was agitated," said Jakob, answering his father's earlier question. "I had never seen him like that before. He was usually very calm, very composed. Nothing could rush him. He always made his way through the world at his own pace."

"A right earned by most Magii," offered Dougal.

"I guess so."

"What was Aloysius agitated about?"

"Because of the Skath that I helped him fight off."

That piece of information left Dougal speechless for a moment. "You fought a Skath!"

"I fought what was attacking Aloysius. I didn't know it was a Skath until after Aloysius told me."

"Why would you keep this from me?" demanded Dougal. "One touch from a Skath and you die."

"The Skath didn't touch me as you can see."

"Don't be smart with me, Jakob," scowled Dougal, breaking out into another coughing fit as soon as he said it.

"I'm not being smart," Jakob replied softly, wanting to calm his father, not wanting Dougal's increasing agitation to make things worse for him. "You said it yourself. When we left Roo's Nest you were distracted, focused on other issues. I didn't want to bother you with it, and I assumed that since we were on the ship and where we were going we were safe. I was going to talk to you about it once we got settled, but it slipped my mind what with the slavers and all."

"Learning that you destroyed the Draugr was bad enough," murmured Dougal, accepting his son's explanation. "I had hoped that would be the end of it. But a Skath of all that could possibly come for you? Now, at the worst possible time, it's happening."

"What's happening?"

Dougal ignored Jakob's question. "You told me about the Draugr. You didn't tell me about the Skath."

"You didn't ask."

"Jakob!"

"Sorry, force of habit," Jakob replied with a small smile, chagrined.

"After you drove off the Skath, what did Aloysius say?"

Jakob wanted to pursue what his father had just left unanswered, but realized that now wasn't the time. His father was afraid, an emotion that he had never seen in him before, and it wasn't because the slavers were now coming their way.

"He said that the Skath would return. That he didn't have the power to destroy that monster. That it was worse than a Draugr. He didn't want me to be there when that happened. He said I needed to get away."

"Did he tell you what a Skath was?"

"He did, though quickly. He was more interested in making sure that I got away with the Blood Ruby. He wanted me gone as quick as I could."

Dougal stayed quiet for several seconds, thinking. His face

twisted into an expression that Jakob couldn't interpret, whether the result of what he had just concluded or a spasm of pain, he didn't know.

"What is it?" asked Jakob, knowing what it meant when his father was like this. Dougal was deciding whether to tell him something that he really didn't want to tell him.

"A Skath is a servant of the Ancient One."

"Aloysius said as much," confirmed Jakob. "Still, the Ancient One? The Ancient One is just a myth."

"Just like Draugr? Just like those Wraiths in the mist are a myth?" challenged Dougal. "Just like those Stalkers?"

"Good point," Jakob murmured softly.

"The Ancient One has not been seen or heard from since he was imprisoned in the Spirit World more than two thousand years ago. That Skath walking on this earth means that the separation between the Natural World and the Spirit World is weakening. The Ancient One is trying to touch the world of man again."

"The Skath was there for Aloysius?" Jakob asked.

"No, the Skath was there for what Aloysius was hiding," corrected Dougal in a rasping whisper, talking becoming even more of a challenge for him. "How far away?"

Jakob didn't ask to what his father was referring. They both understood the reality they faced.

"We have a few minutes."

Dougal nodded, looking down into the valley that spread out far below them. He needed to help Jakob get away, but he couldn't do that before Jakob learned more about what he was truly up against. Otherwise Jakob was a dead man. Better to use the last few minutes they had together with that objective in mind.

"You saw what the Draugr was?" asked Dougal.

"How could I not," replied Jakob, shivering at the memory.

"As you saw, the Draugr are undead. In case Aloysius didn't

tell you, Draugr are brought back to life to serve the Ancient One and those who serve him. Draugr are the soldiers of the Ancient One. They obey the Skath. All the creatures of the Ancient One obey the Skath."

"That's why the Draugr were there? They were hunting for Aloysius?"

"No, the Skath was using the Draugr to hunt for the Blood Ruby. It just so happened that it was in Aloysius' possession."

"How do you know all this?" wondered Jakob in amazement. "It's all almost too much to believe if not for the fact that I lived through it."

Dougal nodded, knowing how hard this was for his son. Although looking into Jakob's eyes he saw that he did believe what he was telling him. That was important, because though a sea separated them from the Skath that was searching for the Blood Ruby, the Burnt Ocean wasn't a barrier that would prevent that monster or any other servants of the Ancient One from coming after the artifact.

"Because once, long ago, your uncle and I were in possession of the Blood Ruby."

"What are you talking about?" demanded Jakob, shocked by his father's words. "Why would that even be the case?"

"Because the Blood Ruby and the Blood Dagger are connected to our family."

"I don't even know our family," Jakob said with some heat. "I thought it was just you and me."

"I'm sorry. I should have told you. I thought ... I hoped ... that if you didn't know your past, your past wouldn't catch up to you. But I was wrong."

Jakob let it go, feeling the press of time, wanting to focus on what he felt was most important in that moment. "We only have a few minutes more. You can't hide this from me any longer."

Dougal nodded, acknowledging the truth in Jakob's words.

"Aloysius may have told you, but I need you to understand this. The Blood Ruby fits into the Blood Dagger. Two artifacts, powerful on their own, even more so when brought together."

Dougal coughed, spitting up a thick, dark blood. He motioned to the canteen. Jakob helped him take a drink. Dougal didn't even try to hold onto it. He allowed Jakob to hold it for him.

Then he started again in a weaker voice. Jakob could see that what little strength his father had left was fading dangerously fast.

"The Blood Ruby is an artifact from a time most have forgotten. A time that only a few still guard against. From the time of the Ancient One himself, a creature who terrorized all the lands of man. A creature said to be the very source of the Curse."

"Why is this still important if the Ancient One, assuming he even really existed, is still imprisoned in the Spirit World?"

"The Ancient One existed." Dougal said it with what little fire he still had left. "The Ancient One still exists. I promise you that."

Jakob stared at his father. It was almost as if he was seeing him for the first time. "You knew." The look of guilt that passed across Dougal's face confirmed it. "You knew that the Draugr could come. This Skath as well. That's why we kept moving when I was a child. That's why we are where we are now. And yet you never told me."

"I suspected," Dougal whispered. "I feared. I didn't know. I hoped that what happened would never come to pass. But …"

"If the Ancient One is still imprisoned in the Spirit World, why did the Skath come for the Blood Ruby?"

There were so many more questions that Jakob wanted to ask. Yet with his father's flagging strength, with the slavers approaching, this was the one question that was most important to him since Aloysius had made him the bearer of the Blood Ruby.

"Because combined with the Blood Dagger our histories say that the Blood Ruby gives its wielder the ability to destroy the Ancient One or, in the alternative, if the Ancient One gains control of the weapon, rip the Veil between the Natural World and the Spirit World entirely. Doing that would allow the Ancient One to come back into our world once again and to bring his Skath, Draugr, and all the other monsters serving him. The Ancient One would seek dominion over the Natural World and the Spirit World. He would seek to make both worlds one."

"How does the Blood Ruby work with the Blood Dagger?"

An interesting story, Jakob thought, and some of it corroborated with what Aloysius had told him. Even more than that, frightening. But before he took it for fact, he needed more information.

"I don't know."

"Where is the Blood Dagger? Aloysius didn't have it."

"He wouldn't have had it," replied Dougal, "and I don't know. Although from what my father said, and his father before him, and his father before him -- you get my meaning -- someone attuned to the Blood Ruby can find the Blood Dagger. The two artifacts were made as a set by the Giants of the Rime. They're linked. The Blood Ruby bonds with the bearer. Find one and you can find the other."

"That's why the Blood Dagger is somewhere else, isn't it? To make the Ancient One's task of finding the two more difficult."

"Yes, our family feared that if the two artifacts were together, it increased the chances that the Ancient One would find the blade and the jewel and seek to free himself from his prison. It was that fear that brought me and your uncle to Caledonia." Dougal reached out for Jakob's left palm, turning his hand over so that he could examine the skin. He could see it. Faintly. The mark of the Blood Ruby. "Aloysius blooded you."

"He did," Jakob admitted, remembering when the Magus placed the Blood Ruby in his hand for the first time and the feeling of warmth that had surged through him when the sharp point at the end pricked his flesh. The tiny cut had healed instantly, although not as he had expected. There was a faint design in the flesh of his palm now that mimicked the jewel.

"You should have told me. The slavers after us and the Wraiths in the mist are nothing compared to the danger presented by the Ancient One."

"Why us?" asked Jakob, not really hearing his father as he searched around them with the Talent. It wouldn't be long now. "Why our family?"

"Think about our last name," said Dougal, who was shaking his head, more angry at himself than his son for waiting to pursue this topic at a time such as this. If he had known what Aloysius had done, he might have made different decisions when they landed in the Territories.

Blackgard? thought Jakob. But that doesn't ...

It was beginning to make sense as he recalled his lessons with his father when he was a child. The last part of his name certainly was appropriate if Dougal spoke true, as did the first now.

Well before the Curse had become known as the Curse -- the term most frequently used now when describing the tainted evil of the world, the Curse had been called other things. At one time the Magii had described it as Dark Magic, most commonly the Dark Arts or the Black Arts.

He had never reached this conclusion before because he had never had the need. Until now.

His family name explained what his family had done. Still did apparently. Guard against the Black Arts, and, from what his father was pointing him toward, guard against the return of the Ancient One.

"Why haven't you ever told me any of this?"

"Because like I said, I never thought that it would be necessary. I hoped that it wouldn't be. But now, after seeing the Blood Ruby, and you telling me that Aloysius faced off against a Skath, I can't keep it from you. You need to acknowledge the seriousness of the threat."

"What do you mean *me*?" asked Jakob.

"Because Aloysius blooded you, Jakob," replied Dougal, his voice filled with resignation. He reached out and grabbed his son's hand, making him look at the mark in his flesh. "He did that for a reason. And that's why he gave you the Blood Ruby. He knew what was coming for him. If not that night then another. He knew that he wasn't strong enough to defeat a Skath on his own. Few of us are."

Jakob pushed himself up from the rock he had been sitting on with his father, his body tensing. His eyes focused on the west and the small gap between the rising hillocks that led back toward the trail they had left.

"They're close, aren't they?"

"They are. They'll be here in a minute. Maybe less."

"You need to go."

"I'm not going anywhere. I'm not leaving you here on your own."

"You need to do just that. You need to go," Dougal repeated. "You must. You have no choice now."

"I'm not going." His words were clipped, as hard as the stone his father was sitting on. "I'm not leaving you."

"You can't help me, Jakob. I'm just a liability to you now. Let me help you."

"I'm not leaving you, father. It's as simple as that."

"You don't understand," said Dougal, his voice tinged with an unexpected misery. "Haven't you been listening?"

"What don't I understand? Tell me. Please."

"I just told you. You're a Blackgard." Dougal suffered through another coughing fit, spitting out a huge glob of thick blood, and perhaps some other parts of his insides that he didn't really want to think about. "Aloysius gave you the Blood Ruby. He had the jewel because he's a Blackgard just like you are."

"He's a Blackgard?"

"Yes, he's a Blackgard. He's your great grandfather, several times removed. That's why he gave you the jewel. He wants you to carry on the responsibility that our family accepted two thousand years ago, just as I want you to. He gave you the Blood Ruby so that you can find the Blood Dagger. If the Ancient One is seeking to escape the Spirit World, then you need to find that weapon. It's the only way to defeat that monster. You need to find the Blood Dagger before the Skath finds you."

"But father, I can't ..."

"No buts," said Dougal with more force than he had been able to muster since he had been beaten on the ledge by the Sergeant and his slavers. "You are a Blackgard. Your primary responsibility is to your family, to the Blackgard name, not to me."

"You want me to do what, then? Leave you here so that the slavers can kill you?"

"I want you to leave me here so that I can fulfill my responsibility. Helping you escape so that you can carry on the traditions of our family. You're a Blackgard, blast it! If the Skath are in our world again, then the Ancient One is seeking to return. You must find the Blood Dagger and then do all that you can to prevent that evil creature from destroying the Natural World. You need to go ..."

Dougal's words died in his throat. He realized that it was too late. The slavers were there.

Jakob turned away from his father, watching as the tall

figure walked toward them. The slaver who had been giving orders down in the valley the evening before pushed his way through the long grass, coming to a stop when he was no more than twenty feet away from Jakob and his father.

The slaver didn't say a word. He simply stared at them.

A sad, almost inevitable, look draped his face. The rest of his men were only a few steps behind him, spreading out in a ragged semicircle so that Jakob and his father had no easy path for escape.

"You two are more trouble than you're worth," said the leader, hooking his thumbs in his belt.

"Your friend Dennis likely thought the same," offered Jakob, who remained where he was by his father, radiating an almost unnatural calm, not yet having drawn his sword.

The tall slaver processed Jakob's comment, his bemused expression twisting into a frown. The boy appeared to be more curious than scared, not what he had expected with the number of men at his back.

"You killed him?"

"No, I killed his friend. Jensin. The Stalker killed Dennis. And then it killed the other men you left in the valley."

The tall slaver's frown shifted to one of surprise, knocked off balance by that statement. Although he realized that he really shouldn't be. Not after having to fight off the Stalker that came for them last night.

"Is that even possible?" asked one of the men behind him.

The slaver motioned with his hand for his men to stay quiet. He needed to think.

He didn't believe that the young man standing in front of him was lying. He doubted that this boy would have survived if he had attacked his veterans. He probably just got lucky, catching Jensin when he wasn't paying attention.

Yet even if what the boy said was true, why had the Stalker gone after Dennis and the men with him?

It certainly was possible that the beast had done the rest of the killing down in the valley. The screams that he and his men had endured before that monster had appeared at their campfire certainly testified to that possibility.

And that Stalker had been wounded. The injury probably was inflicted by one of his men before he died by the claws of the Stalker. It also was likely the only reason that he had lost just one man in the melee that had forced them to retreat to the ridge. The ghastly gash across the beast's leg and its damaged knee had slowed the beast, giving him and his men the chance that they wouldn't have had otherwise.

Still, it didn't make sense. This all wasn't supposed to be possible.

The Stalkers were supposed to be under control at all times. They were not supposed to think on their own. They were only supposed to do what they were instructed to do. They were not supposed to be able to break the compulsion.

"Before I kill you, we're going to need to have a talk, boy. I need some information from you."

"Life is filled with disappointment, Remy," Jakob replied with a hard glare. "We're not going to have a conversation, because before that happens, I'm going to kill you."

"Brave words," Remy laughed.

The men behind him joined in, in large part because this slave who had freed himself made them nervous. There was a confidence there, a lack of fear, a belief in himself and what he could do, that made them distinctly uncomfortable. The fact that the boy also knew Remy's name suggested that he was speaking the truth about what had happened to Dennis and the other slavers.

"True words," Jakob replied, cutting off the laughter, understanding and relishing the effect that he was having on these men who spent so much of their time terrorizing those who could no longer protect themselves.

"We'll see, boy."

Remy nodded to the men behind him. The two closest to him stepped forward, swords in hand.

Jakob watched them approach, the slavers coming right at him, not bothering to give Dougal even a glance. It was clear that they didn't think his father posed much of a threat.

He couldn't fault them for that, what with Dougal sitting on the rock, bent over like an old man with a bad back, his broken wrist pressed against his aching ribs.

Taking one of his father's many lessons to heart, Jakob chose not to wait for the slavers to make the first move. Better always to strike first, especially when you were taking on more than one opponent at a time.

He did just that with the speed of a scorpion, lunging forward and pulling his sword free from the scabbard across his back in a fluid motion, catching the first slaver by surprise.

It was actually that surprise that saved the man's life, his disbelief at the speed of Jakob's attack causing him to slip in the grass and then lose his balance. Because of that stumble, Jakob's blade sliced across the slaver's thigh rather than cutting into his belly.

While his comrade rolled in the long grass, struggling to push himself back to his feet as blood gushed from the wound, the other slaver threw himself at Jakob. The man swung his blade for Jakob's shoulder, hoping to cut into his neck and end this fight with a single stroke.

It wasn't to be. Jakob spun away and then ducked, punching backward with his sword, the tip of the blade digging into the exposed slaver's side.

Not able to pull his blade free easily with it caught between the man's ribs, Jakob raised his left arm above his head. The first slaver to attack him had gotten back on his feet, slowly hobbling toward Jakob from behind on his bad leg, sword screaming down toward the back of his head.

Rather than splitting his skull, the blade clanged uselessly against the thick steel manacle encircling Jakob's wrist. In that moment, Jakob realized the value of the gift the slavers had given him, and he congratulated himself for not seeking to remove the metal as soon as he gained his freedom. The manacle that was a symbol of his brief slavery had saved his life.

Giving his sword a twist so that he could pull the blade free from the slaver's side, he could tell by the look in the wounded man's eyes that the slaver already knew his fate, blood spurting out onto the ground when the steel came free.

Jakob left the dying man there when he fell onto his back, turning his full attention to the slaver who kept one hand pressed to the wound on his thigh as he limped toward him again, spitting out a series of very colorful curses to which Jakob paid little attention.

The limping slaver's other mistake, the first being that he believed that he could kill Jakob quickly, was to walk by Dougal without paying him any mind.

Despite the fact that he could barely move and that his breaths were now no better than shallow gasps, Dougal still had the strength to push himself up for just long enough to pull the dagger from his belt and drive it right into the man's kidney.

The slaver sagged to his knees, then collapsed face first into the long grass, a stream of blood leaking from his side.

For several heartbeats, there was silence. Remy and his men had a difficult time coming to grips with the loss of two of their friends in less than a minute.

Then Remy's face darkened into a mask of rage. He'd had enough of these two slaves. He had no desire to take them to the mines now. He wanted revenge.

"Kill them both!

The slavers at Remy's back rushed toward Jakob, who had retaken his place in front of his father.

Jakob spent the next few minutes caught in the midst of a desperate fight, not only trying to defend himself, but also needing to do all that he could to keep the slavers from coming at his father. Dougal sagged even more heavily on the rock now, his attack on the slaver demanding the last of his rapidly fading strength.

Taking on so many experienced fighters at once was a difficult enough task without having to worry about his father. It was made all the more difficult because the slavers all were soldiers.

They were smart. They had seen how good he was with a blade. They spent just as much time attacking him as trying to divide his attention.

They had no desire to join their dying comrades, so they weren't in a rush. They would take advantage of the right opportunity when it was presented to them. And they were certain that would happen. It was only a matter of time.

Dougal watched his son in action, a surge of pride running through him. Jakob was putting up an excellent defense, but it didn't take him long to see what the slavers were trying to do. Dougal couldn't allow that to happen.

Even though he had taken one of the slavers from the fight, the rest judged him to be a spent resource. They planned to deal with him after they killed his son.

Jakob was doing the best that he could to hold off the slavers, weaving a web of steel around them. And despite the caution of his opponents, he had gained a few slices across their forearms, and with one a deep slash across his chest because the man hadn't expected Jakob to pivot toward him so quickly.

As a result, the slavers remained wary, though angrier than

they had been at the start of the clash, never expecting the boy to make what should be a simple kill so much of a challenge.

When Dougal felt the first faint touches of the mist drifting between the mountains, he turned with some difficulty toward the northeast. Then he saw the billowing Murk working its way toward him.

Dougal knew what was coming with the fog. It could be a death sentence for his son. Or, since they already had survived the monsters in the mist, it could be Jakob's one opportunity to escape.

Either way, he needed to at least give his son that chance.

"You need to go, Jakob. Now!" Dougal's attempted shout came out in a choking gasp.

"I'm not going without you."

Dougal knew that was going to be his son's response. He loved him for it.

Dougal also knew that he was dying. There was nothing that Jakob could do for him in that regard. And there was no way that he was going to take his son to the grave with him.

Launching himself up from the rock with the last of his strength, Dougal rushed forward, or at least he tried to. It was more of a disjointed stagger as he pushed through the long grass. Still, it was enough for him to do what he wanted to do.

Jakob and the slavers, taken by complete surprise, watched as Dougal slammed into one of the men who had been trying to angle around Jakob and come at him from the side.

Dougal more fell on than wrestled the slaver to the ground, but that didn't bother him in the least. He was just glad that he had hit his target.

As he did so, Dougal felt the man's blade slide into his chest. The pain was excruciating.

Even so, Dougal was pleased with himself.

Because as he smothered the slaver he brought his dagger

up, using his momentum to punch the steel into the man's throat.

Closing his eyes, a chill working its way from the wound in his chest into the rest of his body, he sagged atop the dying slaver, what little energy that he had left draining away for good.

At least he was dying the way he wanted. He was taking one of these evil bastards with him. And he had done all that he could to protect his son.

"Father!" Jakob saw what happened out of the corner of his eye, not able to help him.

He had been facing off against two of the slavers with Remy striding toward them when Dougal's wild attack stopped them all for just a second. He saw the blossom of red on his father's chest and how his eyes were glazing over.

"Go, now," Dougal said in a bloody gasp, wheezing out the last words he would ever say. "Into the mist. Please. For me."

Jakob slashed to his right with his blade, forcing one of the slaver's back. Then he spun on his heel to block a strike from Remy who thought to take advantage of the distraction.

Jakob couldn't believe what his father had done. The sacrifice he had made for him.

Then again, actually he could. Dougal was his father. He would have done anything for him, just as he did now.

Kicking out to the side, his boot crunched into the knee of another slaver, the joint bending in a way that it wasn't supposed to and earning Jakob a scream of pain that sounded as if he had thrust his sword right into the man's chest. When he did just that a heartbeat later, the slaver couldn't make a sound, his lungs sliced open by the length of steel.

Jakob glanced to his right and saw the very edge of the fog coming down from the north, already covering the mountain and working its way across the plateau. His father wanted to give him this one chance.

He couldn't allow his father's sacrifice to be in vain. Although he felt like a coward, Jakob did as his father instructed.

Jakob lunged toward Remy, driving the leader of the slavers back a few feet. Before the other slavers could come at him, he pivoted and ducked, pulling his dagger and driving it into Remy's knee. Then he sprinted toward the east.

Hearing the scream of pain behind him, Jakob jumped off the ridge, disappearing into the fog that was rapidly blanketing the Highlands.

22

FAIR GAME

"You were right, Captain Carlomin. They're moving in the direction you said they would."

"All is ready?" she asked.

Talia had never doubted herself when she made her prediction. She stood at the helm of the *Venture*. The newest ship to join the Carlomin Trading Company's fleet had just completed her sea trial.

Captain Jennison nodded. "We signaled the other ships when we left port. They waited a few hours before coming after us just to be certain. The vessel doesn't seem concerned that we're trailing behind it, likely because the traffic here at this time of year tends to be heavy. They might even be thinking of turning on us once we're farther out."

"We can always hope," replied Talia, never taking her eyes from the large vessel about a mile to their front. "That would certainly make things easier for us."

It had only made sense, the vessel turning to the south. If the Roosarian ship wanted easy pickings, and it likely did, it would need to head down toward Rosecrea and Newry where the Sea of Mist met the Endless Ocean. Her belief in that conclusion was buoyed based not only on her own experiences, but also the information that she had gained from her eyes and ears in the harbor.

As soon as the Roosarian ship sailed from Ballinasloe, the left side of the hull a patchwork of repairs, the captain did exactly as she anticipated, his goal fairly obvious. The ship was going back out to hunt for any vessels unlucky enough to sail into its path.

"Let's fall back another mile or so. We don't want to get too close. Make them nervous. Catching up to them when the time comes won't be a problem."

"Of course, Captain Carlomin." Captain Jennison nodded toward their stern. "I don't think we'll need to worry too much about this fog. Looks like clear skies all the way down the coast for now."

Talia glanced to the rear, gazing at the bank of fog that was drifting in over Ballinasloe, the city already a league behind them. Faint touches at first that would quickly cover the town and countryside in a thick, grey blanket.

Captain Jennison was correct. Still, she would need to keep an eye on that fog if it continued to follow them to the south. She didn't want to lose the vessel. Not with all that was at stake.

"Agreed," she replied, her eyes still on the mist forming behind them. "The weather seems to be behaving for us."

This fog wasn't coming in off the Sea of Mist, a body of water notorious for its consistent inconsistency. The weather conditions along the coast guaranteed at least a day or two a week of a dense fog that would shut down shipping but for those foolish enough to risk their lives and their cargo on the hidden rocks that often extended out more than a mile from the shore. That fog came in off the ocean so quickly that there was little time to prepare for it.

The fog that she was staring at was coming down from the north. This was a new development. It had been happening more frequently lately, and with this fog came stories of monsters hunting in the mist.

She had yet to see one of these monsters herself. So before she gave any credence to these tales, she preferred to have real evidence other than the imaginings of the sailors and farmers so deep in their cups in the local tavern that they barely remembered their own names.

Nevertheless, she found it hard to discount these stories. She was certain that there was some truth to them.

She had to believe given how her father was murdered. Captain Jennison had told her that he had died in a fog much like the one she was watching drift down from the Highlands.

"Where do you want to take our prize, Captain Carlomin?"

Captain Jennison's question pulled Talia from her dark thoughts, bringing her back to the present. They had not begun their pursuit until the ship had sailed out of Ballinasloe and was past any point where it could turn back to safety without running into the *Venture* and her other two ships.

The *Furious* and the *Frenzy,* exact copies of the *Venture,* were almost upon them. They would catch up along the starboard and port sides in just a few minutes.

The three vessels were all new additions to her small but growing flotilla. All of the ships benefited from the many advances incorporated by Hari Hoohannen, her Master Shipbuilder.

Talia would be the first to admit that much of her success resulted from his ingenuity and his remarkable inventions, thanking the stars every day that he had deemed her worthy enough for him to put up his shingle on the Carlomin dock. Of course, she had done all that she could to convince him. The Master Shipbuilder relished the freedom she gave him to innovate.

Some of what Hari dreamed up didn't work. That didn't bother her in the least. Better to try and fail than not try at all.

Because much of what he imagined and then tested did work, all to the advantage of her ships and her crews.

Of course, Hari's decision to work with her wasn't based entirely on that, even though it was a large part of it. No, the fact that Governor Roosarian had put his sister out of business certainly didn't hurt. Because Hari not only believed that he was doing good work for the Carlomins, but also that much of what he did was like poking Hakea Roosarian in the eye, and that was something that he wanted to do as frequently as he could.

"Right before they reach the eastern side of the Isle of Mist."

Captain Jennison nodded with appreciation, a predatory smile appearing on his usually stern expression. "Exactly what I was thinking."

∽

"She's struggling, Captain Carlomin."

"A pity," Talia replied. She and Captain Jennison stood on the *Venture's* helm, having kept their position through most of the night and into the early morning, neither wanting to lose sight of their prey. "Although we really shouldn't be surprised."

"No, we shouldn't. All credit to you and Master Hari. There's nothing faster in these waters than our ships."

"The only competitor that comes to mind is a Bakunawa," offered Talia, her gaze fixed on the ship running just a few hundred yards to their front now.

"Let's not talk about those devils, Captain Carlomin. My father used to say that to speak of those sea dragons was to bring them down upon you."

"An old wives' tale, Captain Jennison. Right now, we are the Bakunawa."

"I stand corrected," he replied with a laugh.

He liked Talia Carlomin for many reasons, one of the most prominent being her unwavering focus and confidence. Another being the fact that she reminded him of her father, Abram being one of his best friends before he passed.

When they neared the northeastern coast of the Isle of Mist, Talia put her plan into motion, releasing her hunters and surging toward the ship that displayed no markings other than the large black flag that had been raised on the stern.

She assumed that the captain of the ship thought that announcing that they were pirates would deter her from continuing her pursuit. The captain was badly mistaken. His action only confirmed her suspicions and hardened her resolve.

The *Venture* came up fast on the ship, its unique design allowing the cutter to slice through the waves, the vessel more often than not riding above the water rather than on it thanks to the ingenious design of its hull. The *Furious* and *Frenzy* remained a hundred yards to each side, each adding some sail to catch the wind and speed up along the starboard and port sides of the fleeing frigate so that it couldn't turn away from its present course.

Talia smiled devilishly when she saw the frantic activity occurring on the deck of the larger ship. Their efforts would do the pirates little good. They already had been caught. They just hadn't realized it yet.

Just then the pirate ship banked hard to the starboard side, making for the coast. The captain likely hoped to cut free from the rapidly closing noose by using his vessel's much larger size to force the *Frenzy* away from her.

A smart play under most circumstances. Not now, however. Because the captain of the *Frenzy* had anticipated that the pirate would try to do exactly that.

As soon as the ship turned toward the *Frenzy*, a long metal rod curled out from the side of the Carlomin ship and dropped down to the waterline, three-foot-long steel spikes sticking out toward the pirate vessel. The pirate captain recognized the danger immediately, turning his ship back to the starboard side just as quickly as he had come to port, only to find that he had made his situation much worse.

The *Furious* had drawn closer while the pirate sought to break free, the same mechanism that could rip easily through another ship's hull now extending from its side.

The pirate captain's attempted escape had only served to box in the larger ship more effectively.

Talia smiled, pleased that all was going as she thought it would. Even better, one of Master Hari's creations was proving its utility. The Master Shipbuilder was going to be quite pleased when she told him. Now the only chance the pirates had to escape was to outpace the *Venture*, and that wasn't going to happen.

Although she would need to be careful. They were coming up quickly on the Isle of Mist, the rugged coast a constant danger because of its hidden shoals and rocks and the unexpected currents that swirled just off the shore. Better to end this chase now while they were still out on the open water.

"Are you ready, Captain?"

"We are, Captain Carlomin."

Captain Jennison issued several short commands, the sailors on the bow moving to their task with a brisk efficiency, pulling free the tarp that covered Master Hari's latest contrivance. At the same time, sailors on the helm used flags to signal the *Furious* and the *Frenzy*, the same device soon revealed on their bows as well.

"When you have a good shot, Captain Jennison."

The *Venture's* Captain didn't bother to reply, jumping down from the helm and stomping toward the bow, his wooden leg thumping across the deck. To Talia's discerning eye, he appeared to be a young boy finally getting the chance to play with a new toy.

Captain Jennison focused on the pirate ship's rising and falling stern. He didn't want to waste the shot, not with Talia Carlomin on board, so he needed to do this right.

"Aim for the stern cabin, lads," he ordered the sailors working the large bow.

It had taken four men to pull the very large bowstring back and lock it into place, one other sailor carefully nocking the harpoon.

"Yes, Captain," replied the sailor leading the crew. "On your command."

Captain Jennison waited for almost a full minute, wanting to get just a little closer, timing the strike for when the stern of the pirate vessel dipped down toward the waves, knowing that as soon as it did it would be coming right back up.

"Fire!"

The sailor standing at the very rear of the large ballista pulled on a lever at the back of the device. The harpoon, ten feet long and made of a thick steel with a barbed head, shot off the bow and smashed right through the windows in the pirate captain's cabin, burying itself in the wood at the far end of the chamber.

"Well done!" roared Captain Jennison.

The sailors working the ballista weren't paying attention, already moving on to the next step in their assignment, using a winch to pull taut the thick rope that now connected the *Venture* to the pirate vessel.

At first glance, the successful attack appeared to be a poor idea. The pirate vessel was too heavy to be slowed very much by the sleeker and smaller *Venture*. In fact, several of the men standing at the stern of the pirate ship actually laughed and made crude gestures at their attackers despite the damage to their vessel.

That only made Talia's smile even broader. Those pirates were in for a rather rude awakening.

Focused on what was happening at the stern, the pirates didn't realize the true nature of the danger they faced until two more harpoons slammed into their ship. One dug deeply into the pirate vessel's port side. The other sliced through the mainmast and embedded itself into the far railing. With the last shot, pirates ran in all directions to avoid the collapsing mast and flurry of sails that came down with it.

The pirate ship was, truly, too heavy to be slowed a great deal by one of Talia's cutters. Three, on the other hand, could more than manage the job.

"Well done, Captain Jennison," she called as she jumped down from the helm and made for the bow. "Soldiers of the Carlomin Guard, prepare to board!"

~

THE PIRATE SHIP was dead in the water, held in place by the *Venture*, *Furious*, and *Frenzy*, moving only at the whim of the current. The sailors manning the winches had tightened their grip on the captured prize, trying to keep a distance of between five and ten feet.

Not too close to have to worry about the sides of the ships slamming together, not too far away for the squads of soldiers lining the deck to make it across the gap.

Still, the boarders needed to be careful going across. No one had any desire to risk falling into the sea and becoming caught between the ships, either getting crushed between the hulls because of an errant wave or drawing the interest of the great whites known to haunt these waters.

With all that running through her mind, Talia didn't rush as she balanced on the bowsprit. She needed to time her jump just right because of the waves rocking the hull.

When the *Venture* rose a few feet in the water, she made use of the extra elevation, leaping across the six feet separating her ship from the pirate vessel, rolling forward on her shoulder, coming right back to her feet with her sword in hand.

Her soldiers were right behind her, jumping from the bow, landing on the deck, rolling, and then immediately heading off to their assigned locations. Several more squads of soldiers were already well beyond the stern of the pirate ship, swinging across from the ropes tied to the foremast that had been placed there for just that purpose.

Only the soldiers from the *Venture* were going across for now. The soldiers on the other two ships stood grimly by the rails, reluctantly waiting in reserve, many of the men and women anxious to get into the scrum as well.

Talia doubted that their services would be needed this time. Evaluating in a single glance the clashes that were erupting to her front, she strode for the helm.

Even though these pirates fought more like soldiers, she wasn't worried. Rather, she was confident that the fight would be ending soon.

She had more fighters. They were better trained. They also were far better motivated. Many of them had lost family members to the pirates marauding up and down the New Caledonian coast.

Talia never doubted what the result of this clash would be. It was just a matter of how much blood needed to be spilled to bring it to a close.

Her soldiers were doing exactly as her captain and sergeants had taught them. They avoided individual combats when the pirates challenged them.

Instead, they always worked in squads of five, making their way across the deck with a lethal precision. The first two soldiers used spears against any pirates who failed to surrender immediately. The soldiers following behind with short swords, maces, and battle axes were more than happy to convince those who decided to put up a fight the error of their ways.

By applying such precision and discipline, the pirates stood little chance. Particularly since so little coordination was employed in the defense of the ship. With most of the main deck cleared, her troops were already moving down into the hatches.

Climbing up the ladder, Talia stepped onto the helm, her hard expression becoming granite when she caught sight of the man facing the bow of the ship. He was screaming orders to a rapidly dwindling crew, most of the pirates either dead or captured.

Those brigands still not among those two groups but soon to be probably couldn't hear what he was shouting. And even if they did, there was no way they could implement the man's instructions, not with the soldiers of the Carlomin Guard working their way down the deck with such a cold and often brutal efficiency.

"Surrender the ship, Captain. This fight was over before it even began."

The man bristled upon hearing the voice behind him, slowly turning around. He carried a cutlass in his hand, though clearly it had yet to be used in this fight. It was too clean. Too shiny. It seemed that the Captain preferred to have his men do his fighting for him.

"The Huntress," he said, motioning to the stitches still visible just above her right eyebrow. "I should have assumed that it would be you who would come for my ship."

"Surrender, Captain," repeated Talia. "This farce of a resistance is wasting my time."

"How did you find me?" Then the pirate's eyes brightened. "You saw me in the Ballinasloe harbor and decided to take a chance. Well done, Huntress. Well done indeed."

"Actually, I just followed your stench. It was hard to miss. Carries on the sea breeze for leagues."

"Competent and funny," chuckled the pirate. "A dangerous combination."

"Like I said, you're wasting my time, Captain. Surrender the ship. Tell what few men you have left to lay down their arms. Who knows? Some of them may even live."

"You want me to go down without a fight? Against you?" The Captain nodded, as if he was actually considering the option she had presented to him. "Then again, this might be my chance." An evil grin curled his too full lips. He took a step toward her and then one more, closing the distance between them. "Kill the Huntress and all the problems we've been facing along the coast will go away. We could go back to the fun we'd been enjoying until you decided to make our lives so difficult."

"Don't do it, Captain," said Talia, watching as the man sidestepped around the wheel, then took another step toward her. She had yet to move, still holding her sword against her leg. She appeared to be unconcerned by his approach.

"Don't do what?" he asked, taking another step toward her. "Challenge a girl playing with steel who barely comes up to my chest? If I take you I might have a way out of this mess. Your soldiers won't want to risk you to get to me."

"You're just wasting your breath and ensuring a good deal of embarrassment and pain for yourself, Captain." Talia shook her head to demonstrate her disappointment. "I took your ship. Don't think for a second that I will hesitate to take your life. You're no more than scum. You don't deserve a clean death."

The hulking pirate stopped his slow advance, just a few feet between them now. He took a long moment to study her.

Talia understood what he was doing. The man was preparing himself, needing these last few seconds to bolster his courage and confirm in his own mind the plan he had worked out as soon as she had come upon him.

The pirate captain was going to act the fool just like every other man with a sword readily at hand. He was choosing to ignore the many signs that suggested that she, although a petite woman, was more than capable of defending herself against someone almost twice her size and carrying ten more stone than she was.

When she identified the spark in the back of the man's eyes, Talia knew that the Captain was ready. He had made his decision. He was going to ignore the evidence that stood before him that told him that this was a very bad idea. He was going to make his move.

Still, she waited. She would allow him to do what he wanted to do. He needed to be taught a lesson. A hard lesson. Because she had plans for him once he stopped acting the fool.

The Captain smiled then, opening his mouth as if he was going to say something. Instead, he lunged for her, sword coming up, the steel tip aimed for her thigh.

A disabling wound, thought Talia, seeing her opponent move as if she were watching him in slow motion. A predictable move if his goal was to take her as his hostage. Also a mistake, which the pirate was about to discover much to his regret.

Talia pivoted to the side, not even bothering to parry the stab, allowing the steel to slide by her. The pirate grunted in surprise, never having come up against an adversary who could move so swiftly.

Of course, that didn't stop him from trying again. Thrusting with his cutlass, he growled in anger. Talia simply pivoted once more, keeping her blade against her thigh as she evaded the lunge, barely having to move.

The pirate tried again, and then one more time. With each failed attempt his lack of success only increased his aggravation, particularly since his target glided out of the way with such ease.

It was as if the Huntress was playing with him, and that realization set the pirate's temper boiling. That was something he simply could not abide.

"You seek to make a fool of me, girl," the Captain growled. "That is going to cost you."

"I'm not seeking to do any such thing," Talia replied in a mocking tone and a quirk of her eyebrows to emphasize her contempt for him. "You're making a fool of yourself all on your own."

Roaring in rage at the insult, the pirate lifted his cutlass above his shoulder and swung for her neck. He forgot because of his fury that he wanted to take her prisoner, now just desiring to separate her head from her body.

Talia effortlessly ducked beneath the attempted slash and spun away, slicing her blade along the back of his left leg as she did so.

The pirate roared again, this time in pain. Sensing Talia behind him, he lashed out wildly with his sword.

Talia was already gone, having moved to his other side. This time she stabbed him in his right knee in between the bones, cutting right into the joint and slicing the tendons and ligaments.

No longer able to stand, with a cry of shock and anguish the pirate collapsed to the deck, dropping his sword, his hands trying to stop the blood from pulsing out of the gash.

"You're going to pay for this, you bi ..."

His angry words got stuck in his throat when he felt the tip of her sword pressed into his throat.

"We could have done this in a much easier and less painful fashion, and one that doesn't leave you a cripple for life," said Talia. "Too late now. Although that might be the least of your concerns at present."

"So confident," gasped the pirate, a surge of pain wracking his entire body. "So stupid. You can do nothing to me. I'm protected. When this is all over, I'm going to take my sword and …"

Once again the pirate was forced to cut off his own words abruptly, having a lot more to say but realizing that now wasn't the time. Not when several of the Carlomin Guard climbed onto the helm and stood around him.

One of the larger soldiers looked down at him with dead eyes. Maybe even with hunger, which he found quite odd and slightly terrifying. For some reason, the man looked familiar.

"Remember me?" the soldier asked, the man crouching down so the pirate could have a better look at him. "You killed my brother when we were working a cargo ship out of Rosecrea."

"I did no such thing …" began the pirate. Just as fast as he offered his denial, he stopped, his eyes and slackening features revealing the truth.

He did remember this soldier. And he recalled doing exactly what he was being accused of.

This soldier's brother had refused to kneel. He had refused to obey. The pirate couldn't have that, not when he had to lead so many bloodthirsty cutthroats. So he had sliced the boy's throat without a second thought to make a point.

The pirate couldn't admit to the truth, knowing that doing so was a death sentence. Rather he tried to mask his growing fear, turning his gaze away from the soldier when the man stood back up, finding the woman with his eyes instead when she removed the steel from his throat.

He hoped that he might be able to find some way for them to reach an agreement that would allow him to live through this experience.

Yet the pirate never had the chance to begin to make his

argument. He couldn't say anything at all. He couldn't even breathe.

The large soldier with the dead brother and the even deader eyes stepped down on his mangled knee with his boot, sending a fiery wave of pain through his entire body that intensified as the man applied more pressure to the savaged joint.

With a nod from the Huntress, the soldier finally removed his foot.

"How dare you ..."

Talia crouched down, nodding to the large soldier, the man more than happy to press down again with his boot. Those waves of sizzling fire threatened to crush what little reason the pirate had left.

"Are you done?"

The pirate couldn't respond, even though he desperately wanted to. The agony that he was experiencing was so great that the best that he could manage was a soft, sad hiss and then squeak that turned into a whimper.

"That's what I thought," said Talia. She directed her next comments toward the soldier. "Keep him here, Zakary. Don't let him bleed out." She then turned to climb down to the main deck, the sounds of the fight having receded. The ship was hers. Only a few more pirates were still free, those either brave or foolish or terrified men attempting to escape the slaughter on the deck by climbing the rigging. It was a useless effort. Archers were already stepping forward to cut them down from their perches. "At least not yet."

"Yes, Captain Carlomin," Sergeant Zakary replied, his hard eyes fixed on the man who murdered his brother.

He would have liked nothing more than to return the favor. But he wouldn't. Not until Captain Carlomin ordered the man's death.

Because he was certain that the pirate was going to die. It

was just a matter of when. He would just have to wait a little while longer for the vengeance he craved.

Talia left the pirate to his increasing misery and strode past her soldiers, who were already throwing the dead bodies over the side. Those pirates who had surrendered before they could be killed had been herded to the bow where they could be watched more easily.

If any of the men decided to jump over the side and try their luck in the water, the soldiers were inclined to let them. They knew just as well as the pirates what lurked beneath the surface.

Walking down into the hatch, Talia returned the nods of respect and offered a few kind words of thanks to each of the soldiers in the corridor who had helped her take the ship.

Nevertheless, her thoughts were elsewhere. She knew this ship. It had looked familiar during the chase, and now she knew why. She had been on this vessel before.

This ship belonged to the Dinnegans. They had come over from Caledonia around the same time that her father had.

She had heard that the ship had been lost at sea. Whether to pirates or a storm, no one could confirm. Now she knew the answer.

She would be able to give the widow some clarity on how her husband had died. Perhaps she could even give her some satisfaction knowing that the people responsible for her husband's death were brought to justice. And although she could not return her deceased husband, she could return the ship to the widow.

Not a fair trade, in her opinion. But it was the best that Talia could do.

"Captain Carlomin," said Sirena. The Captain of her Guard waited for her at the entrance to the main hold.

"What did you find, Sirena?"

"More than we expected, Captain Carlomin. Although I guess we shouldn't be surprised. See for yourself."

Sirena stepped out of the way, allowing Talia to walk into the hold. The soldiers charged with inspecting the cargo had placed lanterns along the wall, giving her a good view of what the pirates had taken.

Talia couldn't stop herself from smiling as she swept her gaze from one side of the massive hold to the other. She could understand now why the ship hadn't stayed in Ballinasloe, remaining at the Roosarian dock only long enough for the necessary repairs that would allow her to get back out onto the water and where she needed to be. Away from the city where rumors of what she was carrying could cause quite a stir.

The hold was full of stolen cargo. Some had probably been taken by the pirates on board. Some was probably placed here for the journey south, because none of this could be sold in the capital of Fal Carrach. The merchants from which it had been stolen would recognize the goods.

She remembered several recent conversations with her peers about the ships they had lost. Just from where she was standing, she believed that she could identify at least two of the cargos that had been referenced.

Her decision to go after this ship had been a good one for a variety of reasons. Removing the seas of the vermin that plagued it certainly was cause enough. Even more so, what she had discovered here would help to bring any wavering merchants to her side.

Definitely a good haul all the way around.

But all that would have to wait. She wanted to find out more about how the pirates worked and where this ship was headed.

Best of all, she had a ready-made source waiting for her on the helm above.

It was time to talk to the captain, whether the captain wanted to talk to her or not.

"You picked this spot on purpose, didn't you?" hissed the badly wounded Captain. "No one really comes to this side of the Isle of Mist, what with the hidden rocks and what lurks just beneath the surface."

Talia didn't bother to reply, just staring at the man with a flinty gaze. He was right, of course. There really was no other reason for being where they were.

She crossed her arms as she waited for Zakary to tie the rope around the man's wrists. The Sergeant had wrapped clean cloth around the wounds on each of his legs.

He had followed her instructions not to let the pirate bleed out, although he had not gone much farther than that. The large and spreading bloodstains on the bandages and the slow drip coming from her stab to his knee confirmed that fact.

That was fine with her. She just didn't want the man to die from blood loss. Not until after she was done with him.

Talia glanced down over the side of the ship. She didn't see any of the telltale fins, although she knew that the great whites were there. This was prime hunting ground for the animals what with the sea lions and elephant seals that frequented these waters spending a good bit of time sunning themselves on the beaches that were just a mile distant to their southwest.

"You're a hard one, Captain Carlomin," continued the pirate, hoping that getting his captor to talk would help him avoid what he feared was coming his way. "I get it. You don't need to prove anything to me."

"We did much the same to Captain Blackbeard as we're doing to you," Talia offered. "It didn't take him long to talk. Let's see how long you can last."

"That's because Captain Blackbeard is a coward at heart," challenged the pirate.

"All pirates are cowards at heart. It's just a matter of how long it will take to break you."

"I'm telling you that you don't need to do this," replied the pirate, a jumpy worry seeping into his voice. The man was sweating profusely. Whether because of his wounds or his fear, Talia wasn't sure. It didn't really matter. Either reason worked to her advantage. "You don't need to prove to me what you'll do. Your reputation is already well known. It's growing by the day. I know the lengths you'll go to get what you want."

"And what do I want?" asked Talia.

"You want the person who's responsible for all this."

Talia stared down at the pirate, her eyes blazing with fire. "I want so much more than that."

"I can give you what you want," pleaded the pirate. "You don't need to do this. You don't ..."

"You will give me what I want," cut in Talia in a voice as cold as ice. "That's guaranteed. But you misunderstand what's happening."

"I don't. I don't. I swear!" The pirate's hisses were filled with fear now. He was beginning to comprehend that the Huntress wasn't someone he could negotiate with. She wasn't someone who could be swayed from the path she had selected already. "I can give you what you want. I can give you ..."

"I'm not doing this to prove anything to you, Captain," said Talia, getting tired of the man's pleading. "I'm doing this because it's necessary. You ordered the murder of Zakary's brother. He deserves blood for that."

Just then, Zakary finished binding the pirate's hands with rope. Giving the thick length of twine a final tug just to be certain, he then threw the twisted cord to the sailor waiting atop the lanyard so that he could loop it over the wood and send it back to the Sergeant.

"Please, you don't need to do this," begged the pirate, not

knowing what else he could say, what else he could do, to get himself out of this situation that was of his very own making.

"I was quite clear, wasn't I? I do need to do this."

"Please, Captain Carlomin. Don't do this. Don't do this. I can help you. I can help you. I swear."

Talia ignored the pirate, who was visibly shaking now, the reality of his fate sinking in. She nodded to Zakary, who with the soldiers in his squad gave the rope a hard tug.

That was enough to pull the pirate up so that he was hanging just a few inches above the deck, his hands reaching up toward the sky. That one jolt sent a few more trickles of blood running down both his legs.

"I can help you," the pirate repeated, his words becoming more frantic. He was desperate to put a stop to what was happening, only he didn't know how. "Stop! Just stop! If you stop I can prove useful to you. You'll gain the revenge that you want. I can help you with that."

None of the soldiers and sailors standing around the pirate paid him any mind. With another nod from Talia, Zakary and his squad prepared to push the pirate out over the side of the ship.

Zakary stopped when he heard Talia's voice. She had told him to be ready, that this was how the interrogation was going to play out. He was impressed that so far it was progressing exactly as she said it would.

"Tell me."

Her voice was hard, cold, almost disinterested. Still, it was the lifeline that the pirate was seeking. At least that's what he believed. So he grasped hold of it tightly.

"I might have some information that you want."

Talia grunted with displeasure. "I don't deal in what might be. I deal in what is." She nodded to Zakary, who with the help of his squad swung the pirate out over the side of the ship and began lowering him toward the water.

"Please, please!" shouted the pirate, his desperation threatening to consume him. "I do have information that will be of use to you. I do. I swear it!"

The pirate looked down as the waves of the Sea of Mist crested closer and closer to his feet. He watched as drops of his blood spilled into the water.

He knew what was coming next. It was only a matter of time, although his mind, already stressed, tried not to acknowledge that fact.

"Tell me," repeated Talia in a very soft voice.

The pirate shuddered, taking a deep breath, thankful for the reprieve. "I got word from some of the other captains. We're supposed to meet in a fortnight just to the south of Ballinasloe."

"Where and when specifically?"

The pirate hesitated, his natural need and inclination for secrecy getting in the way again, as well as his very strong desire to live. "I'll tell you when you bring me back on deck."

Zakary didn't need Captain Carlomin to tell him what to do next. He and his squad allowed the rope to slip through their fingers, dropping the pirate even closer to the water. The terrified marauder now hung only a few feet above the waves.

"No, no, no!" the pirate yelled.

His words died in his throat when he saw the first fin of a great white shark break the surface, the large animal circling around him, no more than fifteen feet away, drawn by his blood. Then another fin just a little farther beyond the first shark to take an interest in him appeared, cutting through the sea, coming straight toward him. The first shark disappeared in a flash, this massive newcomer scaring it away.

"Smuggler's Cove," the pirate said quickly. "Two nights after the full moon."

He hoped that the soldiers holding on to the rope would pull him up after he provided the Huntress with that information. Much to his disappointment, he remained exactly where he was.

"Which one?" Talia asked calmly.

"What do you mean which one?"

Talia nodded to Zakary, who prepared to drop the pirate even closer to the waves. She knew that there was more than one Smuggler's Cove. Their locations depended on the week.

"All right, all right!" the pirate screamed. "The one farthest to the south just past the Trident."

"Who will be there?" Talia asked. She knew exactly where the pirate meant.

"All the captains."

"You're certain?"

The pirate squealed when the rope dropped another foot, the soldiers easing him down closer to the water and the very large fin now circling beneath him.

"Yes, all the captains. Except maybe the few nearer the western Territories. But all the others. I swear. That's what I was told. I can only tell you what I was told."

"Why there?"

Talia knew that at this time of the year it was common for the icebergs that broke off from the ice sheets to the south to drift to the north on the current that ran up the coast. It was a dangerous place to be if you didn't know the shoals and you didn't keep a sharp eye.

"I don't know why there. That's all I know," the pirate replied in a panicky voice. "Now I've told you what I know. Pull me up as you promised."

"I promised no such thing," corrected Talia, "and I doubt that you've told me all that you could tell me."

With another nod, Zakary and the soldiers with him let the pirate drop even further, not stopping his progress until he was just a few inches above the waves. More blood leaked out from his wounds because of the sudden jostling.

"All right, all right," the pirate shrieked. "You're a hard woman." Before he could say anything else that very large fin that slowly had been circling closer passed by the pirate on his right side, no more than a foot away from him.

His terror knowing no bounds now, he talked as fast as he could. "The Lady picked the place. She wanted to keep the meeting quiet and she thought that was the best place to do that. Few would make for that cove during this time of the year."

"Which lady?" asked Talia. Finally, this conversation was getting interesting.

"You know. I can see it in your eyes."

"Tell me," Talia said. "I need to hear it from you."

"Governor Roosarian," cried the pirate so that all aboard his former ship could hear. "Governor Roosarian set the meeting. She picked the place. The pirates answer to her."

Talia smiled again, this time with a rapacious grin. It had taken longer than she had expected, but in the end she had gotten what she wanted.

The pirate was right. She knew who he was going to reveal.

Still, she needed to hear it from him. She needed everyone with her to hear it as well.

This was the last piece that she needed. None of the merchants could dispute her claims now. None of them would. They would do as she proposed.

Right then, there was a massive surge in the water beneath the pirate. With a macabre fascination, she watched as the jaws of the massive great white emerged vertically from the ocean, biting through the pirate's midsection, then pulling him down beneath the waves.

The soldiers let the rope go, unwilling to challenge the power of the animal. The pirate was so shocked by his fate that he didn't even have time to scream.

Talia stared at the churning water for several seconds after the pirate disappeared, nothing to suggest that he had ever been there but for the pool of blood that appeared on the surface.

"That was unlucky," said Talia.

"Yes," said Zakary, who continued to stare at the water, his eyes watering, Talia knowing that he was thinking of his murdered brother. "But justified."

23

INTO THE MURK

Jakob ran deeper into the fog, strangely grateful for the heavy mist that at that very second was swamping the Highlands, the mountains, the heart trees, the valley that he was racing through disappearing with a frightening though welcome speed.

Movement and noise ensured a quick death in the grey haze. That knowledge had been forced upon him, and though reluctant to acquire that learning, still he valued it.

Applying his previous experience in the fog, despite knowing how quickly he could get lost in the Murk even if he believed that he was moving in a straight line, to escape the slavers he adopted an uneven pattern to his movement.

Sprinting forward and then stopping abruptly.

Staying still for a few seconds.

Allowing the mist to settle around him, then stepping to the left or right a few dozen feet before stopping again.

Waiting.

Checking to make sure that he didn't hear anything or see the fog move in such a way that gave him pause.

Then sprinting again.

Varying his movements.

Never doing the same thing twice, even doubling back a few times.

The haze hadn't thickened yet to its usually impenetrable grey, the edge of the fogbank moving steadily toward the south. A straight run through would be obvious to the men chasing him.

He hoped that the approach he had adopted would give him a better chance of fading into the mist as it swirled around him while also allowing him to avoid what lurked within.

Fading into the mist?

Now that was an interesting concept. For just a second, he wondered if it was possible.

Before he could ponder that idea further, he stopped abruptly. He crouched down to one knee and tried to make himself as small as possible. He hoped that in the fog he would look like the many small boulders strewn about this hidden plateau.

He heard the slavers coming toward him. They had spread out, approaching in a broad semicircle.

Obviously, they had a general sense of where he might be. The question was, could his pursuers narrow their search despite the encroaching fog?

Jakob crouched down even closer to the ground, willing the fog to condense around him. He reached for the dagger at his belt, fingers clasping the hilt, when he realized that the slavers were going to be upon him faster than he had anticipated.

He had hoped that his killing several of the men and wounding Remy would keep all the slavers up on the plateau. But it wasn't to be.

He could still hear Remy's shrill voice when he had escaped the clash. The man had spouted a stream of curses, several of which Jakob had never heard before, and that was saying quite a lot since his father used to be a soldier.

Even with the fog coming in, the leader of the slavers had ordered a fist of his men to go after him as he tended to his wound. Remy clearly was less interested in bringing him to the mines now and more interested in exacting his revenge.

"Did you see him?" asked a soft voice about twenty yards to Jakob's left. "I thought he came this way."

"No, did you?" rasped another slaver only a few yards away from the first.

"Yeah, I think he's over there," whispered another of the slavers, the man not realizing how far his voice could travel in the silence of the gloom. "I saw movement there before this blasted fog closed in around us."

"Then go after him," urged the first slaver.

"I'm not going after him by myself," protested the slaver who had yet to quiet his voice. "You saw what happened to Jonny and Ensi and then the Sergeant. If I can't see him clearly, then I can't fight him. I'm not taking a chance that the boy gets in a lucky stab."

"You're a coward!" hissed one of the other slavers, this one only about a dozen yards to Jakob's right. The man had moved up on his side as the slaver wandered a bit deeper into the fog than the others, right hand extended as if he was trying to keep himself from walking into something, the other holding a loaded crossbow against his leg.

"Damn right. That's why I'm still alive, and I plan on staying that way."

"I think I just saw something move," whispered the slaver closest to Jakob.

Hearing the twang of crossbow bolts being released, Jakob slumped to the ground, lying prone in the dewy grass. He breathed a brief sigh of relief.

The slavers hadn't seen him. They were just shooting blindly. Mostly out of fear.

Still, he didn't want to take the chance that one of them might actually hit him by mistake.

Just a second later, Jakob's eyes widened. His breath caught, and he needed to remind his lungs to start working again.

He was thankful that the fog around him was getting denser and giving him more protection. Because his primary concern now wasn't just the slavers.

No, they were no longer alone in the Murk.

In addition to the sharp snap of the string as another of the slavers let fly into the gloom, he had heard, just for a heartbeat, the soft sigh of movement off to his left.

Maybe fifteen yards at the most. No more than that.

It sounded like a snake moving through the grass.

Barely there. More question than fact.

But he knew the truth, having heard that noise before.

He would have welcomed the snake.

Because what had made the sound was a creature that had proven much more lethal than the bloodsnakes that haunted the caves in the Shattered Peaks or the slavers themselves.

Jakob willed himself to remain perfectly still when he heard the first scream, although it took a great deal of effort, his body shivering ever so slightly. Inevitably the shouts followed.

The stumbles and falls within the fog.

The whoosh of a few more crossbow bolts being released.

The kiss of the gloom on a creature that moved with a precise, almost invisible, deadly gait.

Finally the sickening squelch of steel being thrust into flesh.

All of that occurring in just a few seconds, silence reigning once again.

It was just as it had been the last time Jakob had been in the fog.

The same sounds. The same patterns. The same terror.

The same silence.

That didn't last for much longer.

"Wraiths!" shouted one of the slavers.

Jakob heard several more bolts streaking through the mist, and then the screams started again. One slaver shrieked in terror, the teeth-rattling sound cut off abruptly. Another scream erupted from Jakob's other side, no more than ten yards away. The sound of steel being swiped across a throat was all too recognizable.

Jakob forced his burgeoning fear back down, knowing that to give in would ensure his death. Instead, he allowed what was happening around him, hidden by the fog, to work through his mind.

Based on his calculations, at least three of the slavers were dead. He had yet to see the Wraiths, which was to be expected. Although he had heard them glide through the fog for the briefest of moments.

There were no Wraiths without the Murk. It was as if they were a vengeful physical manifestation of the gloom.

He kept his head to the ground, only turning his neck slightly so that he could look at his hazy world from the side. That allowed him to catch a few incredibly fast movements that jostled the grey no more than a dozen yards away from him.

Always where he assumed a slaver had been standing. Now most likely where a slaver lay dying.

A chill ran down Jakob's spine, and not because of the wet grass that was soaking his clothes. He had been in this same position before. He knew what was coming next.

The Wraiths had a preternatural ability to find their prey in the Murk. They had killed the slavers. Still, they wouldn't be satisfied with that. Not with them knowing that he was close by as well.

And he was certain that the Wraiths knew that. They always knew who was in the mist with them.

Jakob cursed himself for being too slow and too distracted. If only he had been smarter about his escape.

He had jumped off the ridge in a very specific spot, a location that he had identified with the Talent while he waited for the slavers to come upon him and his father.

There was a small cleft in the ridge that allowed him to drop down about thirty feet into a runnel, dry at the moment because of the lack of rain. He then slid and scrambled down the rill for several hundred more feet to another, smaller plateau hidden beneath the ridge that extended out from the steppe above.

The entire time he had skidded down the run he had feared the worst. To guard against tumbling head over heels, he had angled himself toward the ridge. He had been less concerned by the scrapes, bruises, and cuts he was earning than the increasing possibility of a gruesome death if he lost his balance and flipped head over heels and tumbled all the way to the bottom.

Once he had reached the lower plateau, he had moved to the east, making for the grove of heart trees that rose soaring into the sky a quarter mile away. At the same time, he had kept an eye on the fast-approaching fog descending from the north that was smothering the Highlands.

He had done his best to stay out of sight, but he understood how difficult a challenge that was. Until either he reached the forest or the fog reached him, the slavers would have no trouble locating him on the open steppe.

Much to his relief, the fog had won the race.

Jakob had come to a stop when he was still a good distance away from the wood. Not only because he didn't want to appear predictable to the slavers, but also because his emotions had threatened to overwhelm him.

His thoughts of his father almost had caused him to make a fatal mistake.

Jakob had been so distracted and overwhelmed by Dougal sacrificing himself that he hadn't thought to use the Talent to search around him.

Because of his error, as the haze began to cover his section of the steppe, he had walked right into the slavers who had found another way down from the larger plateau and had worked their way around his flank.

He associated the gloom with death, but in this instance the fog had saved him.

The slavers had become disoriented in the mist, losing track of where he was when the wisps of grey began to swirl more violently and cover the valley. So they had been just as surprised to see him as he had been to see them.

Before any of the slavers could react, Bryen had whipped out his dagger, driven it into the belly of the slaver closest to him, and then sprinted deeper into the fog. He had hoped to reach the heart trees before his quick strike jolted the shocked slavers into action.

No such luck, however.

The slavers had come after him immediately, recognizing that their comrade was a dead man, their desire for vengeance giving them a burst of speed.

That's why Jakob had adopted what resembled a drunken stagger through the fog, hoping that the slavers wouldn't catch on to the deception. That they would pass him and continue on to the forest that had been his goal.

He could then go back in the direction from which he had come, leaving the slavers to the fog.

And it was working. Even though the slavers had been close, they had no idea where he was in the Murk.

Or it had been.

Until the monsters in the mist had appeared.

He could sense the Wraiths coming toward him. The easier prey taken, now they sought the fox hiding in the undergrowth.

His fear burning away his sorrow, Jakob did as he should have as soon as he entered the Murk. He reached for the Talent, the thought that had slipped through his mind just minutes before returning.

Fading into the mist.

Unwilling to risk moving with the Wraiths so close, and having nothing to lose if he failed -- other than his life, of course -- he concentrated on the fog. How it looked. How it felt. How it moved. Even how it smelled and tasted.

Taking all that into account, he applied the Talent, seeking to ingrain all the attributes of the fog within himself, to blend himself into the mist, to become a part of the Murk.

Right when he hoped that he had succeeded he sensed a menacing presence right behind him, no more than a few feet away. He didn't bother to look. He understood that the simplest of movements would reveal him to the hunter.

All the creature needed to do to find him was to take one or two steps forward. In fact, the Wraith was so close that he should have been able to see Jakob.

Thankfully the Wraith didn't. If the monster had, Jakob would have felt the creature's steel slide into his back.

Jakob realized with a small burst of satisfaction that the Wraith couldn't see him. What he had done with the Talent had worked.

He prevented a proud grin from curling his lips. He needed to maintain his control of the Talent and concentrate on staying still.

Staying silent.

Barely breathing.

Being nothing more than a part of the Murk.

After several minutes passed, the presence behind him moved away. Not making a sound.

Jakob didn't hear the Wraith slip to another position in the gloom. Rather he felt the weight of the creature's hate lifted from the back of his shoulders.

Before he could congratulate himself on surviving that encounter, a bolt of fear shot through him.

It was justified.

The risk he faced had just increased exponentially.

Jakob kept his gaze focused on the ground. He willed himself not to look up.

Out of the corner of his right eye he spied the telltale grey leather boots that flickered in the mist, blending in then being revealed with every swirl of the fog.

The Wraith was no more than a few feet away. The creature would only need to stab down with the blade in his left claw and Jakob's escape would be over before it really even began.

Seconds passed. Then minutes. The boots didn't move.

Neither did Jakob.

He slowed his breathing. He worried that if he exhaled too frequently or too loudly the Wraith would discover him.

The Wraith didn't move a muscle, standing stock still, blending into the mist. Clearly not in a rush.

The Wraith knew that Jakob was close, but he didn't know where he was specifically. That didn't faze the hunter. The creature was more than willing to wait him out.

Several more minutes passed.

Jakob judged that it must have been at least a quarter hour since the Wraith had taken up his position.

Still the monster in the mist didn't move.

Another fifteen minutes slowly dragged by.

The Wraith remained right next to him. Seemingly content to stay where he was.

It wasn't until Jakob guessed that an hour had passed that the Wraith finally glided away into the fog in search of his prey.

In search of him.

Even though those grey boots were no longer standing right

next to him, Jakob stayed where he was. He remained in the same position for another thirty minutes, continuing to hide himself with the Talent.

He had no doubt that if he wasn't using magic to make himself a part of the fog, the Wraiths would have gutted him by now.

Yet even though the Wraith that had been stalking him had moved away, he didn't believe that the Wraith had gone very far.

This was a tactic that Jakob was quite familiar with. The hunters in the mist moved away from their target, making him or her believe that it was now safe to move. Then they struck with the speed of a cobra as soon as their prey revealed itself.

He had assumed that's what the Wraiths were doing the last time he was in the Murk, having put that knowledge to good use then. Now, he was certain of the ploy, able to track the Wraiths with the Talent even as he hid himself.

After just a few more heartbeats, the boots appeared again. Just as close as they were before, though now on Jakob's other side.

It was a wonder that the Wraith hadn't stepped on him.

Jakob kept his head down, staring at the dirt and grass, watching the grey leather boots out of the corner of his left eye now.

The Wraith was content to wait him out. So be it. Jakob accepted the challenge.

He almost lost the contest he had set for himself a few seconds later, the raspy voice that played through the fog, emanating from the figure standing just to his side, sending another chill down his spine.

"You are nothing more than meat, human. Enjoy what life you have left. It will be coming to an end very soon."

He had never heard a Wraith talk before, not realizing that

they spoke the same language. And he really had no desire to hear the hunter speak again.

Still, it gave him a small bit of pleasure to know that he was frustrating these monsters in the mist so much that they had broken the silence they relished.

Jakob stayed where he was for another half hour. Not moving. Afraid to take more than a shallow breath. Thankful that he had learned how to hide with the Talent. Knowing that if he hadn't he would be dead.

Finally, as the silence of the fog almost became unbearable, the Wraith slipped away again. Barely making a sound. Jakob only knowing that the creature had moved because the boots were gone.

Jakob didn't feel any safer. He knew that the game of cat and mouse wasn't over yet.

Not trusting that the Wraith actually had left, Jakob used the Talent to search around him.

The first time Jakob had looked for the Wraiths, it had been a challenge. He had found it difficult to distinguish the creatures from the fog itself, as both contained the Curse.

But with practice he had refined his approach. Now he had little difficulty confirming what waited for him in the fog.

Five Wraiths, all within one hundred yards of him. The one that had been most keen on killing him had only moved away from him by about five yards.

More than enough distance for the creature to disappear completely within the fog. Yet at the same time close enough to drive one of his daggers into his flesh in a single leap if Jakob revealed himself.

Clearly, although Jakob's use of the Talent was protecting him, he had not fooled this Wraith entirely.

True, the creature couldn't see him, but for whatever reason the Wraith had a good sense as to where Jakob was.

As the minutes slowly passed, Jakob not moving, the

Wraiths remaining where they were, the hunt continuing, the fog began to darken.

Night was falling. He had been playing this stressful game of hide and seek for almost the entire afternoon.

Jakob also realized that he couldn't wait here forever.

He needed to move.

To find someplace safe.

Or at least safer than where he was now.

Because eventually he would make a mistake or the Wraith so intent on killing him would get lucky.

For the last several hours he had been mulling a new tactic. He figured that now was as good a time as any to try it.

Jakob didn't succeed on the first try. Or the second. Or the third for that matter.

On the tenth, he did, and he was thrilled at the reaction that he got from the Wraiths.

Using the Talent, he threw a sound thirty yards to his left. To his ears it sounded like he was pushing himself up off the ground. It likely sounded the same to the Wraith stalking him.

He knew that the Wraiths hadn't moved despite the faint noise, but he could feel the tension building around him. As if the creatures were preparing to dash off in pursuit.

Jakob sought to give the creatures the final incentive to do just that, sending another noise rustling through the fog a little farther away from the first.

To his ears it sounded like he was running away, making for the heart trees that were only a few hundred yards distant.

The Wraith who was closest to him launched himself into motion, speeding through the fog in a grey blur, tracking the noise that Jakob was making. The other Wraiths joined the chase.

It was working!

Even so, he needed to be smart about what he was doing.

With that stricture constantly playing through the back of

his mind, for the next half hour he led the Wraiths toward and then into the grove of heart trees.

He used the Talent to throw the noise of his sprinting through the fog and then stopping. Waiting. Just as he had done before.

Sending that noise farther and farther away from him. Taking the Wraiths farther and farther away from him.

The Wraiths fell for his ruse. Moving when he did. Stopping when he did. Then racing forward again, only having to come to a stop and wait for their quarry to make himself known again.

Although Jakob was desperate to escape these creatures, he had learned that patience was the key.

That was the only way to escape the Wraiths.

He had to beat them at their own game.

Finally, after another hour had passed, he confirmed the positioning of the Wraiths. All of the hunters were deep within the forest, the closest more than a quarter mile away.

His ploy had worked.

Still, even though he knew exactly where the Wraiths were, he remained wary.

Pushing himself up off the ground slowly, stretching his stiff and aching muscles, he stood still for several minutes.

He scanned around him with the Talent the entire time, fearful that the Wraiths would figure out the deception and come back in his direction at a ferocious pace.

The monsters didn't. They stayed among the trees, waiting for the next noise to draw them closer to their prey, even though they had yet to gain any ground on him.

Certain now that he could make his escape, Jakob began to move back the way that he had come. He didn't seek to climb back up to the plateau from which he had slid down to this lower steppe. Rather he angled toward the smaller wood on the southern edge of this hidden valley.

He took his time.

He walked no more than a dozen feet before he stopped and searched around him with the Talent. He confirmed time and time again that the Wraiths remained within the forest of heart trees.

Finally, after two more hours had passed and darkness had blanketed the land, Jakob only knowing that the fog remained because of its cool touch on his skin, he reached the small wood he had been seeking.

Identifying the tree that he thought would serve his purposes best, he pulled himself up the branches and rough bark of the heart tree, not stopping until he was several hundred feet off the ground.

If the Wraiths found him here, he had a good chance of defending himself. The branches were so thick and intertwined that they would only be able to come at him from the front.

Although he hoped that it didn't come to that.

Searching around him with the Talent one more time, he realized that he had succeeded.

He was free of the slavers.

He was free of the Wraiths.

For now.

The Wraiths were on the other side of the valley. Still in the forest. Still waiting for him to make a mistake.

He was safe.

Exhausted, he lay his head back against the trunk of the tree. He wanted to sleep. He knew that he needed to sleep. He hadn't the night before.

But he couldn't now. Not after all that had happened.

Every time he closed his eyes, images of his father's death played through his mind.

Torturing him.

Reminding him of all that he had lost.

As the night slowly passed, knowing that sleep wasn't going

to come, he took a lesson from his father. Dougal had taught him at a very young age that you were never done with the work that needed to be done.

As soon as you completed one task, there would be another that required your attention. And another after that.

So he focused now on what he needed to do next, not on what had gone before, because he assumed that the danger he had evaded would remain so long as the fog covered the Highlands.

Escape the Wraiths.

Stay clear of the slavers.

Gain his revenge on the men responsible for his father's murder.

24

SAD NEWS

"You're certain? No mistake?"

"Completely certain, my love," said Ursina, thrilled by her husband's reaction. She hadn't known how he was going to take the news.

"No doubt whatsoever?"

"None whatsoever," laughed Ursina softly. "Simply enjoy what is happening now. We won't have long before our entire world changes."

Kendric nodded, his broad grin wavering for just a heartbeat. He wondered, if only for a moment, whether his wife's remark was a premonition that went beyond what they were discussing. And if so, whether it was one to be savored or feared.

"I will try, my love."

"I have other news, Kendric."

"What would that be?" he replied, his joy knowing no bounds. "Nothing can compare to what you have just told me."

"I reached out to Governor Roosarian as you requested since we have not received word of the ship your niece was traveling on across the Burnt Ocean."

"What did you learn?" he asked, a tinge of concern in his voice. "She should have been here by now based on what my brother said in his letter. And if not here, at least in Ballinasloe."

"Governor Roosarian looked into it personally, my love. The ship your brother said she was on, the *Freedom*, has not arrived."

"That does not bode well," said Kendric, his smile slipping from his face.

He knew that the journey across the Burnt Ocean was a dangerous one at the best of times. It was not unheard of for a ship to be lost along the way. Whether because of weather or the sea dragons that hunted in those cold waters or some other cause ... who was to say.

"You fear for her?" asked Ursina.

"I do," he replied softly.

He loved his niece. He remembered the games they used to play together in the Broken Palace when she was a child.

Aislinn loved playing hide and seek, and when she grew bored of that she would force him into the training circle, even at that young age. They used wooden sticks, the Lady of the Southern Marches demonstrating a remarkable prowess in the martial arts even then.

"We must be prepared for the worst, my love," said Ursina softly. "I'm sorry, Kendric, but Governor Roosarian said that a delay such as this suggests that the worst has befallen them."

"Governor Roosarian would know, wouldn't she?" Kendric bowed his head, fearing for his niece. Hoping that she still might be alive. But having no reason to disagree with Hakea's conclusion.

Ships arrived late to Ballinasloe all the time when crossing from Caledonia. Never this late, however.

"Your love for her does you credit," said Ursina. She kneeled down next to her husband, her warm hand gripping his forearm, then rubbing gently. "She has been delayed more than a month. Nevertheless, we can still hope that she arrives. But ..."

"But our hope might be wasted," finished Kendric, his eyes, which had been so clear just seconds before, losing some of their clarity, the fog that plagued him so frequently clouding his mind once again.

He cursed his bad luck, shaking his head in frustration. Why was this happening to him? And now of all times? What was the cause of his ailment?

Ursina, even with her skill in healing, had been able to do very little for him. The other healers that his wife had brought to the Shadow Keep also had met with little success.

No one had been able to identify the source of his illness. No one knew what to do about it. How to cure him. How to prevent his mind from wasting away.

Yet even those questions, concerns, and emotions drifted into the wispy grey blanket that fogged his mind.

With it went his anger at his fate. A calm settled over him. A feeling of contentment. As if all his worries, all his fears, were fading away.

"Yes, it likely is," agreed Ursina. "Ships are usually not so delayed in making the passage across the Burnt Ocean unless there is good cause. Unless something terrible has befallen them."

"Yes, terrible, isn't it, the fate that has befallen Aislinn. And who was the one with her?"

Ursina smiled gently, continuing to rub her husband's arm. She was pleased that his focus had shifted so swiftly.

As soon as they had received the missive from Kendric's brother, she had viewed his niece as a potential threat. Simply another obstacle that would need to be overcome in order for them to realize their goals.

Now, however, based on this latest information, assuming

that it was accurate, perhaps that problem no longer required her intervention.

She wouldn't shed a tear if, indeed, Aislinn Winborne had died during the passage. Sad, yes, in some respects. Her husband had been looking forward to seeing her again. Fortuitous as well.

"Her Protector, my love."

"Yes, her Protector," he murmured. "I would have liked to have met him."

"As would I," she replied, although there was little truth in her words. "It is terrible, the loss we have suffered."

"Yes, terrible," Kendric agreed again, though it seemed that he was really just mimicking his wife's words rather than thinking about what he was saying. Thinking about much of anything at all.

Ursina pushed herself up, walking over to the window that allowed her to look out onto Shadow's Reach and the massive mountain that rose above the town, the reason for the growing city's name.

"Of course, we must find the good even in the most terrible of events."

"How so?" asked Kendric, his voice stronger now, the confusion that had bedeviled him just a moment before dissipating somewhat.

"We both wanted Aislinn to join us here."

"We did."

"But we were worried as well."

"We were," replied Kendric, beginning to understand what his wife was hinting at, the grey fog that had smothered him so swiftly pulling back just as fast. Allowing him to regain his reasoning.

"A terrible loss, if indeed your niece's ship has been lost. But that terrible loss removes a possible threat that we were seeking to avoid."

"I still don't think that my brother was sending his daughter here to spy on us, Ursina. It's not his way. If he was worried about what is happening here, he would have come himself. He's never hesitated to push his nose into something if he saw the need."

"As you say," murmured Ursina, frowning at Kendric's return to clarity. "Still, think on what you have just said. Do you think your brother suspects the challenges that we have overcome? That we face now?"

"Suspects?" Kendric wondered for a moment. Then he shrugged, feeling much better. Thankfully the haze that affected him much too frequently had faded away. For now. For how much longer, he didn't know. "Who can say? The only information that he's likely getting is from us."

"You're certain of that?"

"I have no reason not to be."

"You don't think that he suspects what we've done? What we're doing?"

"How could he?" pondered Kendric. Many lost their lives during the crossing from Caledonia. He worried for his niece, yes, but his wife was right. He also needed to worry for himself and his wife and the future that they were trying to build together. "Why would he?"

"You still don't believe that your niece was coming here at his request?"

"No, I don't. Aislinn was always strong willed and adventurous as a child. I doubt that has changed as she's grown older. She's likely coming here, or was coming here, for that reason. The desire to have an adventure. She loved adventures."

"I'm glad that you're confident about this, but don't be naive, Kendric. We talked about this before. There has to be more to it than that. More to it than just a young woman's desire to have some fun or get away from her responsibilities for a while. To cross the Burnt Ocean just for those reasons would be beyond foolish."

Kendric chuckled at that. His wife was never satisfied with the simplest of answers. It always had to be more complex than it really was.

"You need to stop looking for conspiracies around every corner, my love. Not everyone is out to get us."

"But some people are," she whispered so softly that her husband couldn't hear her. She knew that firsthand, having experienced it to an almost lethal degree. It was for that reason, in fact, that she left Caledonia for the Territories. And as fast as she could.

"Besides, we won't give her cause to suspect anything when she arrives."

"If she arrives," Ursina corrected.

"Quite so," agreed Kendric, a touch of sadness returning to his voice. "If she arrives. You know, I do hope Aislinn makes it to Shadow's Reach."

"Why would that be, my love? It seems that fate may have removed her as a problem for us."

"Because then we can talk with her ourselves and quell these fears that seem to be plaguing you."

"Of course, Kendric," replied Ursina, needing a few seconds to mask her true feelings, offering her husband a bright smile when she turned away from the window. "My worries are just getting the better of me. Probably just a consequence of my new condition. I'm sure all will be well, and I look forward to meeting my niece. If she arrives."

Yet as her husband returned her smile with one of his own, walking to her and taking her in his arms, she still couldn't escape the sense of doom that weighed down her spirits. She believed her fears were justified, understanding full well what could happen if Aislinn Winborne made it to Shadow's Reach.

Though the news from Ballinasloe certainly played in her favor, still she needed to be ready. Just in case.

She couldn't trust what she had learned. She needed to ensure that if the Lady of the Southern Marches and her Protector somehow made it across the Burnt Ocean and did appear in the Northern Territory, they couldn't get in the way of what they were building here.

The journey across the Burnt Ocean was perilous. That was well known. But the Territories could be just as, if not more, menacing.

That thought gave Ursina Winborne the peace of mind that she had been seeking.

25

THE HUNT CONTINUES

The Wraith stood among the heart trees, double-bladed daggers gripped loosely in his claws.

He savored the touch of the Murk against his flesh.

Its smell. Its taste. Its vitality.

The Murk was his home. The Murk gave the Wraith his strength. His power.

Yet strangely, on this day, for the first time, the Murk had deceived him.

Or rather the human he and his comrades had been hunting had deceived him.

Killing the slavers, that had been an easy task.

Too easy.

There was no challenge to that hunt. Almost a waste of his time and effort.

The men had been foolish. Not understanding the danger of the Murk. Not perceiving the mortal threat until it was too late.

But this other human.

The Wraith shook his head from side to side, so slowly that the movement didn't disturb the fog that settled around him.

This other human was a challenge. He was worthy of being hunted.

Yet even so, the Wraith Scout should have killed the human by now.

He hadn't.

The Wraith was having a difficult time coming to grips with that fact.

He had never failed in a hunt until now.

The Wraith knew that it should feel anger at that. He didn't. No, instead he was curious.

He remembered his conversation with the Wraith Hunter. At first, he was surprised that the Hunter had shared his own failure with him.

He thought that the Hunter would want to keep that story to himself. To shield himself from embarrassment, worried that the warriors of the Horde would view him as weak and incompetent.

But now, having experienced his own failure, the Wraith Scout understood why the Hunter had shared his encounter with the human who had evaded him.

The boy.

The Wraith Hunter was teaching him a lesson. The Scout just hadn't known it at the time.

He wished he had picked up on the meaning of the lesson prior to now. It might have served him well during this hunt.

Because this human who had escaped him sounded much like the boy who had evaded the Wraith Hunter.

The Wraith Hunter had said that the boy had moved within the Murk as if he were a part of it. As if he belonged in it.

The Wraith Scout had laughed at that conclusion, finding it quite hard to believe. Yet now ...

Now he had no reason to disbelieve.

The Wraith Scout slowly twisted his head to the left, then grumbled softly.

Not his prey.

One of his hunters shifting through the mist to a different position. Thinking to spook their prey.

He doubted that the ploy would work.

Their prey was smart. Cunning. Not easily frightened.

They would wait a while longer.

Night had fallen.

He knew the human was still in the Murk. He probably had gone to ground and would emerge in the morning.

When his prey did, the Wraith Scout promised himself that he would be there.

He wouldn't just kill the human. He would take his head and he would bring it to the Wraith Hunter.

He wanted to know if the human he hunted now, the human who had escaped him, also had escaped the Wraith Hunter.

If so, then this human truly was a worthy kill.

But the human was no more than that.

Just prey.

Just vermin to be killed.

The End of Book 2.

I hope you enjoyed Book 2 of *The Tales of the Territories*. Keep reading for scenes from Book 3, *The Dance of the Daggers*.

BONUS MATERIAL

If you really enjoyed this story, I need you to do me a HUGE favor – please follow me on Amazon and BookBub. And if you have a few minutes, consider writing a review.

Keep reading for two chapters of *The Dance of the Daggers,* Book 3 of my series *The Tales of the Territories.* Order Book 3 on Amazon or from my author website at PeterWachtBooks.com.

PETER WACHT

THE DANCE OF THE DAGGERS

TALES OF THE TERRITORIES 3

The Dance of the Daggers
By Peter Wacht

Kestrel
Media Group, LLC

Book 3 of The Tales of the Territories

This book is a work of fiction. Names, characters, places, and incidents are the product of the author's imagination or are used fictitiously. Any resemblance to actual events, locales, or persons, living or dead, is coincidental.

Copyright 2023 © by Peter Wacht

Cover design by Ebooklaunch.com

All rights reserved. In accordance with the U.S. Copyright Act of 1976, the scanning, uploading, and electronic sharing of any part of this book without the permission of the publisher constitute unlawful piracy and theft of the author's intellectual property.

Published in the United States by Kestrel Media Group LLC.

ISBN: 978-1-950236-36-7

eBook ISBN: 978-1-950236-37-4

Library of Congress Control Number: 2023904674

❦ Created with Vellum

1. COMBAT IN THE MURK

Jakob spent a long, restless night in the heart tree, the rough bark digging into his back. The cold helped as well, the damp fog caressing him, the plummeting temperature making the moisture feel like ice.

He didn't bother trying to sleep. He didn't want to sleep.

Not tonight.

Not after what happened to his father.

Not with the Wraiths still searching for him.

He dozed on occasion, not by choice, his exhaustion getting the better of him, although never for more than a few minutes at a time.

During his waking moments he searched around him with the Talent. Fearful that the creatures hunting him would find him before he found his way off the plateau and out of the Murk.

Time and again he pinpointed the exact location of the fist of Wraiths who were seeking him. Thankfully, they remained more than a mile away in among the heart trees to the north.

He had fooled the monsters in the mist, sending them to one side of the plateau while he went to the other. He doubted, however, that his deception would continue to meet with its current success for much longer.

He assumed that the Wraiths believed that he was still on the plain. They just didn't know where he was.

He wanted to keep it that way until he found a path that would lead away from his predicament. Either to a place where he could hole up or out of the Murk entirely.

Because he had no doubt that if he stayed on this hidden steppe, the creatures would find him.

With the pitch black of the fog shifting to a dark grey, Jakob judged it to be the right time to continue on his way.

He was still several leagues from safety. He needed to be careful. Smart. Patient.

That's what had allowed him to escape the Wraiths yesterday. He hoped that it would be enough for him to do the same today.

As Jakob made his way slowly down the trunk of the tree, the challenges facing him dominated his thoughts. Yet he couldn't rush despite the urge to increase his pace growing more and more insistent within him. If he fell and twisted an ankle or broke a leg, he was done for.

When he reached the forest floor, he stood there for several minutes.

There was nothing but the wispy dull grey of the haze.

He couldn't hear anything. The squirrels, birds, and other animals of the Highlands had gone to ground with the coming of the Wraiths.

He wanted to get a feel for what was around him. He needed to know when the Wraiths would come for him.

A bolt of fear wiped away the remnants of his exhaustion upon searching through the haze for the hundredth or more time in just the last few hours.

The Wraiths were leaving the forest to the north and making their way back across the small plateau. The monsters

1. Combat in the Murk

were taking their time, moving methodically, seemingly confident that he couldn't leave the plain before they found him. They just might be right.

He needed to move. Now.

Jakob used the Talent as his guide so that he could navigate the thick fog. He moved toward the south, going in the opposite direction from the hunting Wraiths, to where he believed the edge of the fog to be.

The entire time, two critical questions continued to run through his mind.

How far must he go before he escaped the fog?

And would the Wraiths catch him first?

The monsters in the mist continued to make their way toward him at a steady pace. Apparently they had decided that since they failed to find him among the heart trees to the north that this was the only direction that he could have gone.

It was sound logic.

Logic that very likely would lead to Jakob's death if he didn't get out of the Murk in time.

Still, that knowledge didn't faze him. Jakob had grown accustomed to playing this game of cat and mouse with the Wraiths.

He just needed to stay patient. Focused. And, most important, quiet.

As he did the day before when the fog first drifted in from the north to cover the Highlands, he moved in an erratic manner, never taking a straight path, always shifting this way and that, more concerned with stealth than speed.

Never rushing.

Never doing anything that would give himself away too easily.

Without making a sound, he glided through the Murk as if he was a part of it. Being able to see everything that was around him with the Talent gave him a boost of much-needed confidence, the grey haze no longer a hindrance.

But he didn't allow it to go to his head, understanding the consequences if he did.

His objective remained the same.

He headed toward the south in a pattern that couldn't be discerned. To have any chance of finding him, the Wraiths needed to detect some sign of his passage across the plateau, which based on how he was moving could lead them in multiple directions if they weren't paying close enough attention.

Consequently, the monsters gained nothing by trying to get ahead of him. They would be taking a shot in the dark. That meant that they would have to move slowly. They would need to take their time and check every one of his false trails. They would question their decisions.

That increased his chances of getting out of the fog before the Wraiths slit his throat.

Even so, despite his best efforts, he felt as if the Wraiths were slipping a noose around his neck. That they were giving him just enough rope so that he could hang himself.

The monsters were working their way across the plateau in a pattern that slowly but effectively narrowed the space in which he could be hiding.

Jakob had to admit that because of his much-too-frequent experiences in the Murk and his use of the Talent, he was learning quite a bit about Wraith tactics. Whether he'd ever be able to make use of that information and the other knowledge that he was acquiring during his attempted escape ...

He feared that he knew the answer.

He just didn't want to admit it to himself.

He forced that debilitating thought out of his mind.

There was nothing to do but keep trying.

His father had fought for him. Died for him.

1. Combat in the Murk

Jakob wasn't about to let Dougal's sacrifice go to waste.

∼

The Wraith Scout worked his way slowly, diligently, across the plateau. His comrades were spread out around him in a broad arc that resembled a crescent moon.

He had just missed his prey the afternoon before. The Wraith Scout had been so close, in fact, that at one point he believed the boy had been no more than a few yards away from him.

But the boy had kept silent. Kept himself under control. Demonstrated a skill that made him think the boy was more Wraith than human.

That had irritated the Wraith Scout. He should have completed this hunt by now.

But it also impressed the Wraith Scout. It took a spine of steel to maintain your composure when faced with certain death.

In all the time that he had hunted south of the Wyld, he had yet to find in any of the other humans he had killed the iron will and calm self-possession this boy had when faced with the inevitable fate of a slit throat.

Nevertheless, that held little meaning to the Wraith Scout. He would still kill the boy. It was only a question of when.

Unfortunately for the boy, his luck was going to run out this morning.

The Wraith Scout would not miss him again. He would bring this chase to an end, running the steel of his dagger across the boy's throat.

The Wraith had been right to wait in the forest during the night. There was no easy way off this plateau, so he was certain that his prey remained close.

Closer than he had thought, in fact.

As soon as the fog began to brighten to a dull grey, the Wraith Scout assumed that the boy would slip out from wherever he was hiding.

If he was to evade his hunters and break free of the Murk, there was only one direction for him to go.

The Wraith Scout had ordered his hunters back toward the south, working their way in a very precise manner through the Murk. They broke their search into quadrants, hunting across every foot of ground in each one before moving on to the next, ensuring that their prey had no opportunity to try to double back on them.

Every so often he and his hunters stopped.

Waiting.

Watching.

Listening.

Searching for any sign of movement up ahead.

Hoping for any sound that might betray their quarry.

Whenever they did, however, there was nothing but silence and the slowly drifting grey mist.

Frustrating.

Fun as well.

Each time they waited, the Wraith Scout smiled menacingly when they had no choice but to continue toward the south, seeking to flush the boy from his hiding place.

This boy truly was a worthy target. Finally, he and his hunters faced a real challenge, a true test of their skills, beyond the borders of their homeland.

He and his comrades had a good idea as to where the boy might be now. They had made thorough though swift progress across the steppe.

The only question that bothered the Wraith Scout was whether they would catch him before he escaped the fog.

He pushed that concern to the side. They still had time.

Based on where they were now on the plain, they could be

1. Combat in the Murk

no more than a few hundred yards behind him, and the outer edge of the Murk was still several leagues distant.

Plenty of time and space to conclude the hunt.

Besides, the boy was about to reach a harsh conclusion. There was no way to get off this plateau without coming back toward the Wraiths.

Therefore, there was no need to rush their search. Better to be precise in their work.

The Wraiths continued to adhere to a strict pattern with their hunt. They searched for any hint of their prey's passage through the long grass, understanding that if they could find his trail, it would lead them directly to him.

The Wraith Scout stopped again, his hunters doing so as well. They waited for several minutes, seeking any sign as to where the boy could be.

No sounds.

No movement.

Nothing to reveal their quarry.

The Wraith Scout's eyes widened in delight. The boy truly was a worthy opponent. But as he had learned time and time again, everyone made mistakes.

Rather than beginning the search of the next grid, the Wraith Scout knelt, his clawed fingers reaching down to brush the crushed grass. He grinned, running his tongue across his sharp teeth.

The boy had been here. Lying on the ground. Based on how flat the grass was and how little dew had collected on the stalks compared to the grass around this flattened space, it hadn't been very long ago.

Less than an hour.

The Scout stood carefully, then walked to his left for a dozen yards.

He saw it in the dirt. The faint trace of a boot.

He followed the tracks, needing to go slowly because the

impressions were barely there. The trail led him thirty yards to the south.

The Wraith Scout stopped again, kneeling, wanting to make sure.

The boy stopped here as well. He was certain of it. His razor-sharp fingers traced the faint marks in the dirt and grass.

The Wraith moved to the left again, this time for ten yards, then he strode toward the south again for another thirty yards.

He stopped abruptly, fearing that he had lost the trail.

No, he hadn't lost the trail. His prey was simply trying to make it more difficult for him.

Looking behind him, the Wraith Scout saw how the boy had backtracked, stepping back to the north for a dozen yards before walking to the right for twenty yards and then continuing toward the south.

The boy was smart. He knew what he was doing. He didn't seem to mind being in the Murk.

Maybe the Wraith Scout's first assumption had been correct when he lost the boy last night.

No human ever had escaped him in the Murk.

Until now.

Maybe this human truly was the same one who had shamed the Wraith Hunter.

The Wraith Hunter had said that the boy had moved within the Murk as if he belonged in it.

As if he was a part of it.

As if he was a Wraith himself.

This boy certainly met those criteria. He moved almost as well as his hunters, flowing in and out of the grey as if he were born to the Murk.

Still, his unique abilities when it came to the fog would not save the boy.

The Wraith Scout had yet to fail on a hunt, and he wasn't about to start now.

1. Combat in the Murk

He called to one of his hunters with a sharp, shrill whistle. The Wraith appeared right next to him, coalescing out of the fog as if he were a part of it.

After the Scout issued a few brief instructions, the Wraith sped off, moving toward the southwest.

The Wraith Hunter now knew where their prey was. If the hunter just sent ahead didn't kill him, he would keep the boy in place so that the Wraith Scout could do the honors himself when he arrived.

The hunt had almost come to an end. Soon the Wraith Scout would slide the bone-white steel of his blade across the boy's throat.

Soon he would taste his prey's blood.

2. DON'T PICK THE WRONG FIGHT

"Is it as we thought?" asked Bryen.

The three ships were almost upon them. They still didn't fly any colors to show who they were, although their black sails confirmed for the crew that they had become the next prize for the pirates haunting these waters. Assuming the brigands caught them, of course.

The captains of the vessels clearly were quite skilled. Throughout the chase, the three ships remained in a tight, triangular formation, tacking easily in response to whatever direction Emelina turned the wheel as she sought any additional speed that she could find as the gusty wind blew them closer to the New Caledonian coast. Even so, despite her obvious competence, slowly but steadily, the distance between the ships shrank.

Just as Captain Gregson suggested they would, at the outset of the hunt, the ships attempted to curl in toward them. They tried to time their approach so that they could pull up along both sides of the *Freedom*, wanting to box them in.

Emelina refused to allow that to happen, demonstrating a rare skill as she milked even more speed from the wind, seeming to have a preternatural ability to keep their vessel on course while finding an even stronger blast that kept them just ahead of their pursuers.

The vessels behind them had no other option but to adjust their approach because of Emelina's unique ability to frustrate their efforts. Missing by just a few minutes the spot where their paths would have brought them right up against the *Freedom*, the hunters shifted their focus to tracking the *Freedom* from the rear, knowing that with time, the speed of their lighter, smaller ships would play to their advantage.

Even with Emelina's masterful efforts to stay clear of the sea dogs barking at their stern, eventually the race would come to an end, and not in their favor.

Bryen watched all this from the Griffons' deck, smiling every now and then, appreciating Emelina's skill and experience. The helmswoman usually took them no more than a degree or two to port or starboard as she followed the wind, each time she did so thwarting another attempt by their pursuers to draw alongside.

His smile slipped, his usually grim visage returning, when he saw the two ships flanking the lead vessel break away, curling farther to the east and west respectively. He didn't understand why they would do that, seemingly giving up the chase, until he glimpsed two more dark specks emerge from a fog bank to the southwest that Emelina had been heading toward.

He was about to call out a warning, but there was no need. Emelina saw these two new arrivals to the hunt the same time Bryen did, Davin's cry from his place in the crow's nest offering an additional warning for all aboard.

With the two new ships, both with black sails, only a few hundred yards off their bow, Emelina turned the wheel sharply, making more for the northwest.

A smart move, Bryen thought. The two ships that sailed out

of the fog cut across their wake, missing them by only a few hundred feet. He watched as the pirates scrambled across the rigging of their ships, adjusting the sails so that these two frigates could join the chase.

And because they were so close, he also heard the curses from the captains standing at their helms fly across the space separating them. The raiders had not expected such a bold move from such a large ship.

The only move really, Bryen knew, but it came with a cost. Because now they were hemmed in on both the port and starboard sides by the ships pursuing them from the start.

Emelina's only choice now was to run with the wind for as long as she could, all the while knowing that the frigates on both sides of her would slowly but surely cut in toward her until the boarding ropes were flung across.

"Does it look as bad from up there as it does from here?" asked Bryen, turning his gaze toward the low-lying clouds above them, a consequence of the fog bank that they had been skirting. He couldn't see who he was looking for, but he didn't have to. He knew where she was.

"It doesn't look good," Lycia replied in Bryen's mind, the Protector connecting to the gladiator with the Talent.

Lycia often spent much of the day flying above the *Freedom* on the back of Arabella, she and the Griffon having become fast friends. Hidden in the clouds, she offered Bryen a birds-eye view and perhaps a few useful options as well.

"How long before they're on us?"

"A quarter hour at most," Lycia replied. *"Those two ships that sailed out of the fog are coming back around. They're less of a concern at the moment. But those two ships blocking you in, there's little that Emelina can do about them with that third vessel closing in on the stern."*

"Positive as always," murmured Bryen.

"Just telling you how it is."

"I would expect nothing less. What are we facing?"

"Give me a moment to get a better count."

"What do you see, Lord Keldragan?" asked Captain Gregson. He stood next to his wife at the wheel, though he was careful not to get too close so that he didn't interfere with her as she searched for better wind and some way to break free from the frigates pinching at both sides.

"You were right to be wary," said Bryen, not bothering to remind the shipmaster that he didn't care for titles. "It almost seems like they knew we would be here."

"It does, doesn't it. I had never imagined that pirates could coordinate their efforts so effectively."

Captain Gregson wanted to think more on what Bryen had just said, but he didn't have the time to consider how these raiders might have known of their passage, especially after the delay caused by the storm. "Any information our eyes in the sky would be willing to provide would prove helpful."

Just then, Lycia spoke again in Bryen's mind. *"On the two ships to the port and starboard, more than fifty men are preparing to board. So more than hundred in all."*

"And on the ship at our stern?"

"More than the others. A hundred. Maybe a dozen more than that, but I can't get a good count. There are too many of them running around the deck like their breeches are on fire."

Bryen gave Captain Gregson a quick update on what they were facing. He believed that the Blood Company could handle those numbers. What were several hundred pirates compared to the Kraken or Ghoules?

Even so, he preferred not to take the risk if he could avoid it. As Declan liked to say, the best battle was the one you didn't have to fight.

"You can deal with that many?" asked Captain Gregson.

"If necessary," Bryen replied, "but you know from experience that you never know what could happen in a fight. Once the blades are out, all bets are off."

"Right you are," agreed the Captain. He took a few seconds to think. "Maybe there's something we can do to improve our odds. If we can't dissuade these pirates from following us perhaps we can reduce their numbers so that when they do try to board us, it will be a more certain clash." He turned toward his wife. "Emelina, please take us into the Floe."

Captain Gregson said it as if he were making a simple request, but Emelina clearly didn't take it that way. Her look of concern mixed with excitement when she looked at her husband made Bryen think of Davin's constant need for a new adventure, usually the riskiest and most dangerous one possible.

"Are you certain?" she asked, her eyes sparkling with anticipation. "You're not teasing me?"

"Well, if you don't think you can manage it, I can always take the wheel."

"Not even when I'm dead," growled Emelina, a broad smile breaking out on her face.

Turning back to her task, with a harsh turn of the wheel, the *Freedom* heeled hard to port, cutting right in front of the pirate ship on that side. Emelina avoided a collision by no more than fifty feet.

In fact, they were so close that the pirates actually shot flaming arrows in their direction. None struck home, however, all of them falling into the sea. Emelina's surprising maneuver had caught them off guard.

Bryen turned his gaze to where they were headed, less concerned by the pirates shifting course to pursue them than the challenge they now faced. The hazy line of white that was still a league distant gained greater clarity as the *Freedom* sliced through the waves.

Captain Gregson had told him of the Floe. A field of

icebergs that drifted from the south to the north, melting as they floated into warmer water, pushed there by the current created by the Sea of Mist meeting the Burnt Ocean.

Bryen had been curious about what Captain Gregson had described. However, that didn't mean that he had any desire to sail in among the mammoth icecaps at speed.

THE END OF CHAPTER.

To keep reading *The Dance of the Daggers*, visit my author website at PeterWachtBooks or Amazon to get your copy.

LOOKING FOR MORE ...

This short story is a prelude to the events in my new series *The Tales of the Territories* and is FREE to readers who receive my newsletter.

Learn more at PeterWachtBooks.com.

Printed in Great Britain
by Amazon